In praise of

MASK OF DREAMS:

"Congratulations, again, on your manuscript MASK of DREAMS taking home the Chatelaine Grand Prize, a division of the CIBAs!"
- *Kathryn Brown, president, Chanticleer Reviews, LLC*

"As a scholar specializing in Venetian Renaissance art who has some expertise in Balkan history and culture, I have been struck by Ms. Grant's in-depth knowledge of the social and political history of both these regions, and the effortless way in which she integrates that knowledge with her lively plot and memorable characters. Venice of the 1490s and the first years of the 1500s is a rich but largely untapped setting for the modern historical novel, and Ms. Grant's work makes the period come alive."
- *Paul H. D. Kaplan, Professor of Art History, Purchase College, SUNY*

"Wow! What an achievement--in the writing, the research, the narrative, the dialogue, EVERYTHING!! I am so impressed with "MASK OF DREAMS."
- *Patricia Brooks, author, N. Y. Times columnist*

"One of the best novels I have read in many years. Ms. Grant is so articulate and thoughtful while simultaneously weaving an exciting page-turner. She has the rare ability to combine a comprehensive knowledge of historical fact with an exciting plot and characters who come alive."
- *Robert Kruger, Ph. D.*

MASK OF DREAMS

Leigh Grant

*Watch a man in times of adversity to discover what kind of
man he is;
for then at last words of truth are drawn from the depths of his
heart,
and the mask is torn off.*

— *Titus Lucretius Carus*, De Rerum Natura

CARTELLINO PUBLICATIONS LLC
99 COMSTOCK HILL AVE.
NORWALK, CT 06850

ISBN: 979-8-9869362-0-8 (pbk)

This is a work of fiction. Names, characters, places, and incidents either are the product of the author's imagination or are used fictitiously. Any resemblance to actual persons, living or dead, events or locales is entirely coincidental.

For My Beloved Tony
and
My Family

HUNGARY

N
W   E
S

○ Zagreb
SLAVONIA

● Belgrade

Venice ○

VENICE

○ Senj

○ Ravenna

○ Florence

CROATIA

Zara ○

PAPAL
STATES

Adriatic Sea

OTTOMAN EMPIRE

ZETA

Ragusa ○
Cattaro ○

● Rome

KINGDOM OF
TWO SICILIES

Durazzo ○

Naples ○

Tyrrhenian Sea

Butrint ○
Párga ○

Návpaktos

○ Palermo

Ionian
Sea

Methoni ○
Monemvasía ○

Venetian Empire and Zeta c. 1490

– – – International Boundaries

//// Venice Territories

▨ Zeta Territories

Mediterranean Sea

0   50   100   150   200 Miles

House of Vinciguerra in Venice

Caterina – a Venetian maiden, half noble/half citizen, only
   daughter of a successful merchant
Ludovico – Caterina's father, a very wealthy citizen merchant
   of Venice
Nonna – Caterina's nurse and substitute for the mother she
   never knew
Sofia – a maid
Cook – known only by the name of her profession
Giovanni – an older man, retainer, the family's gondolier
Cristofolo – Giovanni's replacement for the summer, a black
   African
Tommaso – tutor for letters
Bartolomeo – tutor for mathematics
Orseolo – a Maltese dog

The Dorsoduro house in Venice

Alberico – manservant, former bowman, guard
Battista – manservant, guard, a mountain of a man with
   superior fighting skills
Antonio – manservant, guard, more a leader than the other two

Caterina's friends

Simonetta – Caterina's friend, also from a wealthy citizen's (as
   opposed to patrician's) family
Umberto – Simonetta's brother, interested in astrology
Ginevra – Caterina's other friend, also from a wealthy citizen's
   (as opposed to patrician's) family

Also living or working in Venice

Alessandro Boldu` – a nobleman's son
Gerolamo Boldu` – Alessandro's father, a merchant and
   nobleman, Ludovico's friend
Ragazzo – the water seller's deaf six-year-old son.
Rosa – a prostitute

Associated with Ludovico

Ariosto – a nobleman, Caterina's aging suitor
Mario – a factor working for Ludovico in Milan
Pasquale – second officer on board the *Brenta* (galley)

Winter Quarters on the Bay of Cattaro below Zeta

Rade – a Slav, brigand, pretender, driven by fate
Vuk – a Slav, an old man, soothsayer, mentor to Rade
Miloš – a Slav, second-in-command on the *bergantin*

Associated with Rade

Mordecai – moneylender, go-between, Jew, friend to Rade
Conti – professional maker of masks and artifices for festivals

CALENDAR

The Venetian year began on March first rather than January
first.

MAPS

The map centering on the Doge's Palace and surrounding area,
is a portion of the famous woodcut featuring a panoramic view
of Venice. It was executed just before 1500 by Jacopo Barbari
(when privilege was granted him) and had taken him three
years.

The other map was redesigned by creativeforce.com from a
historical map of the late 15th century.

GEOGRAPHICAL PLACE NAMES

In general, the place names used in this book are those
employed by the Venetian Empire at the time in which this
book is situated. Venice has been substituted for Venezia.

Bojana River – flows through both Montenegro and Albania on its way to the Adriatic Sea

Bornu – (today) Nigeria

Candia – (today) Crete

Cattaro - (today) Kotor, Montenegro

Fano – (today) Fano, province of Pesaro and Urbino, Italy

Coronati – (today) Kornati, an extensive archipelago stretching along the Adriatic coast near Zadar and Šibenik, meaning "crowned ones"

Parenzo – (today) Poreč, on the Istrian peninsula, in Croatia

Valona – (today) Vlorë, Albania

Scutari – (today) Shkodra or Shkodër, Albania

Zara – (today) Zadar, Croatia

Zeta – once known as Raskia, the last remnant of the Serbian Empire, (today) Montenegro

GLOSSARY

Follows the Afterward.

Prologue

If the first button of one's coat is wrongly buttoned, all the rest
will be crooked.
— *Giordano Bruno*

Venice, October, Venetian Year 1492 – Caterina

In the half-light, Caterina sat up on the rumpled sheets, her pale hair in a long braid, the linen of her nightdress as tired as she was. Her nurse Nonna, both defender and betrayer, and as yet oblivious, snored softly on the other side of the bed. There was no undoing this dual role. It was already set in stone. Even in sleep, her face as full and benign as a harvest moon, framed by iron gray hair that linen imprisoned in daylight, Nonna was a fortress. Had Mama survived even a portion of Caterina's fourteen years, surely she would have stopped this whole wretched undertaking. For Caterina knew that as the October days grew shorter and the light failed, and that November saint's day approached, dread would flourish in the darkness.

She stood up and undid her plait of hair, combing it out between her fingers. The terrazzo was cool under her feet, and as she began her habitual crisscross of the room, the usual unwelcome thoughts came crowding in. To progress from a life of laughter to this. *To this.* Where was that gondola spy, pursuer of light reflections, sugared almond thief? Where was that child she'd been only five years before? If only she hadn't thought it, said it, shouted it, because now that what she'd said was public, she could never take it back. And it didn't seem to matter that she'd spent all those hours on her knees. That she'd flung out every prayer, entreaty and promise that she could imagine. Even the Holy Mother had chosen to look the other way.

Those last childish days came to her mind in the way that some things are tacked to one's soul. Driven in with self-inflicted nails. Gone over more times than could be counted. Nail head by nail head. What had happened to her had been so utterly, patently unfair.

Chapter One

*There is nothing in our civil life that is more difficult than
properly marrying off one's daughters. —Francesco
Guicciardini*

Venice, Venetian Year 1487 – Caterina

She was, as Nonna referred to it, "almost ten." Surely ten
must be some high water mark or crossroads along the way to
marriage that she could never quite figure out. All she knew
was that the Venetian Council of Ten, the grim defenders of the
state, were to be avoided at all costs. One might want to be
elected to it but no one wanted to be judged by it. So it might
have been that ten was some sort of Judgment Day.

Whether it was rolling the bronze incense ball down the
stairs in the dead of night so that the household daggers could
be seen and counted or drawing a beard on the small painting
of Prudence or putting a cicada in Nonna's soup, Caterina
found opportunities for adventure, some said mischief, despite
the confines of the house. Household gossip, which she
discounted as exaggerated, labeled her as an unfettered rascal,
along with some other less repeatable epithets.

"*You*," scolded Nonna, stamping her foot after a
particularly trying episode, "are a *vixen*."

Turning eyes on her nurse—eyes which were sometimes
green, sometimes brown, depending on how the light chose to
interpret them—she stopped trying to reassemble the shards of

what was now beyond hope. "It was a lizard."

"Now you've passed from vixen to scoundrel. *Truly?* Something that weighs less than a sleeve tie knocked over a pottery flask? It must have been a veritable *dragon*!"

"He was lovely, Nonna. And so quick."

"Sofia *just* cleaned it. Put it up to dry in the sun. Your father's *favorite*."

"I only needed to get a little higher to make a grab."

"After climbing on the credenza to reach the window sill! What sort of behavior is that! *What do you think would have happened if you'd fallen out?*"

It was a long way down to the courtyard from that particular sill.

"The flask wouldn't have broken?" She went to lay her head in Nonna's lap to apologize, despite the danger of decapitation, but for Nonna, it was too late.

As the darling of the noble house, the cherished object of her father's eye, the only child, Caterina knew she'd be forgiven—even if today was lost to shouting. It was the useful side of being almost ten.

*   *   *   *   *

Despite what others saw as pushing boundaries, hers was an orderly, encapsulated, interior world. A world whose edges, as she grew older, grew larger on paper than in actuality. The narrow streets and canals outside the noble house formed a network on which she journeyed to church or out into the *bacino* for some great celebratory event, always in the company of familiars, always protected, and more recently, always veiled. The one great freedom was the villa on Terraferma where they went in high summer. There she could ride and leave the veil at home.

It was her lot to know the newest doge by a coin tipped into her palm by her father and a few comments overheard through a door: "Barbarigo; self-willed, irascible; succeeded that indecisive brother." To feel the beard, long nose and *cornu* under her thumb, the closest she will ever come to the man himself. To hear an unseen Venetian is queen of Cyprus through kitchen gossip gathered in the marketplace. To discover that Cyprus is practically in the Levant where, on Papa's map, there are fearsome oddities in the sea—and worse, Ottomans.

For as long as she could remember, she had observed the true sustenance of commercial life, her merchant father's livelihood, bales of goods, boxes and barrels, come and go at their house, the noble house on the canal. The bulk of it progressed into the storeroom where the rat lived so she was careful to stamp her pattens, recite incantations, and speak loudly if she had to fetch something for the larder.

Although the house was a monumental tribute to her mother's family, she felt no grief for the mother she had never known. Of whom personal memories had never been constructed. And whose absence had been amply filled by the square, opinionated haven that was Nonna. It was Nonna she fled to when Papa was angry or a scrape needed tending. It was Nonna who held her in her arms at night when a nightmare frightened her or she was simply cold. And it was Nonna who tended her when she was sick, filched the occasional extra treat for her, or whispered endearments into her ear. But within hearing of the household, perhaps to preserve her station, Nonna liked to pretend otherwise.

In Dorsoduro, at the western edge of Venice, there was another house, plain and sea-worn, where her father's three menservants lived. But she had only been there once when the noble house was being refurbished. When she'd met *him*: the future that her father, Ludovico, planned for her. That house, ser Ariosto, their first and only meeting, the resulting, still unseen contract drawn up by her father, blessed by an auspicious positioning of the planets, and signed by her betrothed, had by now become a far distant event. Like the war in Ferrara that had coincided with it. She hadn't seen that

either, but the evidence that it did exist—the sight of the
monster guns, bundled onto long galleys, propelled across the
bacino in a forest of sails and pennants—had remained in her
mind.

*   *   *   *   *

Had her lady mother lived, she would have instructed
Caterina in the stewardship of a house: the economics of
management, the minutiae of items to be counted or polished
or fixed, the understanding and concoction of simple remedies,
the properties of foodstuffs, the governance of servants.

"It will be your duty to provide increase," declared Nonna,
who had inherited the job.

"Then we should buy four rabbits instead of two."

"That's not what I meant."

"When I count things, like plates, there are either the same
number or less. Plates don't beget plates. We might have more
luck with rabbits."

"We'll start with handkerchiefs. You've lost two in the
canal. The material is over there. You'll make four more. With
embroidery. Consider *that* increase."

However, she knew for her father, "increase" was not
enough. Wanting more for his only child and drawing on the
humanist direction of his library, he decided to educate her
further. There were two choices, as the academies were limited
to boys: the convent, where he would have had to give her up
for two to three years, or private tutors. To her relief, he'd
chosen the latter. Two men had been engaged, both carefully
vetted: one, Bartolomeo, for casting a reckoning, and the
younger one, Tommaso, for letters. They slept in the attic.

"I maintain a library," he told the younger one. "Use it."

Filled with zeal, Tommaso interpreted his mission as a
foray into popular literature—of which of course there was
none to be had in that library. Thus, despite Nonna's evident
disapproval, Tommaso brought the lais of Brittany and the

Round Table into the classroom—and, over time, into Caterina's dreams.

*   *   *   *   *

They were doing their needlework, to Caterina, a necessary evil of household life. She had once told Nonna what she'd thought—in retrospect, clearly a mistake—as almost immediately, there'd been more needlework than ever.

"Of them all, I'd marry Eliduc," she said, pulling at the embroidery she'd managed to sew by error to the part hanging from the frame. "Or Tristan. Or Lancelot."

Nonna stared at her. "Couldn't you pick one who wasn't an adulterer?"

"They were faithful to the women they loved. And besides, they were heroes."

"Whatever happened to Aeneas? Or Achilles?"

"They weren't knights," said Caterina, finally separating the two pieces of cloth. "I'm only interested in knights."

"Romances," her nurse said in a disapproving tone. "And foreign as well. Certainly *not* epic literature. Sometimes I think Tommaso ought to go back to Padua and stay there. I don't know why universities think it's necessary to disseminate all these useless new ideas. Besides, if Tommaso didn't have such a lilt to his voice, I don't think you'd listen to him."

"I'd still watch his Adam's apple. He has a big one."

"People who are built like storks often do. I don't think the poor soul ever gets enough to eat." Nonna looked at the snarl of threads that had arisen from Caterina's needlework and sighed. "Your betrothed, ser Ariosto, is not a knight."

"Then I shall instruct him to become one. I only want to marry a knight."

"There aren't enough to go around. And they have a tendency, when war comes along, to get their necks broken. And if you don't pay more attention to what you're doing, the next demise may be your own."

*   *   *   *   *

A few weeks later, Caterina was sent to chop vegetables at the trestle table in the kitchen, the same one the menservants ate at when they stayed for supper. Even now she could still see where Battista had started to carve his name into the wood—and been stopped. Probably because Cook had hit him with something large and made of iron. Cook was not averse to such actions. She always said she knew how to handle men and besides, in her domain, it was her table. Papa often remarked that if the noble house was attacked, he expected Cook to be first in the line of defense. She'd liked that.

"Ser Ariosto will be here tonight," Cook announced, arms bloodied by the preparation of the meat. She cocked her murderer's knuckles on her waist. "First time in five years. Your betrothed has come to have a second look."

Caterina went on chopping onions. "It is *I* who shall have the second look."

"It is *he,* however, who shall have a say in the matter."

Caterina lifted her chin. "He'll see the Empress of Tarot, wearing a crown of stars and hung with pomegranates."

"*Is that so?* Well then, Empress, you'll need to clean the onion out of your hair. Or the pomegranates will be wasted on him." And Cook delivered a great blow that shot blood, fat and meat onto the front of her apron. "And what, pray, are you doing playing tarot at your age?"

At that point, still unscathed, Caterina thought it the better part of valor to escape.

*   *   *   *   *

As her father directed, Caterina seated herself on the daybed against the wall in the elegant setting of the great chamber. The prospect of sitting silently for two turns of the hourglass, encased in a heavily ornamented dress, at a gathering of indifferent men—indifferent to her—had taken on the aspect of an adventure gone bad. To be seen, not heard, was the order of the day. Having drawn herself up into the straight, prim posture of the well-behaved gentlewoman, she tried not to fixate on the suffocating weight of the dress. Nonna filled up the spot beside her, and then some.

So it was that Caterina found herself, perched like a limpet on a rock, peering waist-high through the sea of male guests at her future spouse. However, she had to ask which one he was—for she could not remember what he looked like.

Ariosto stood, canted sideways against a chair back, not twelve feet away. Below capped hair streaked with gray, a bony brow shadowed deep-set eyes and drew itself down into the lengthy blade of a nose. By comparison with others, it was a high-bridged Roman nose, overshadowing his other features. A nose as noteworthy as Tommaso's bulging throat. And although Nonna whispered uplifting observations about greatness of features reflecting greatness of character, to a child in thrall to heroes, there was nothing to admire. Caterina saw only the overburdened profile, the odd set of spidery limbs, the magpie colors of a month-old beard—and her stoutheartedness shriveled. The man was not only ill-favored to gaze upon, God knew, bearded, he looked older than her father. It wasn't until the day had ended, bristling with the unpleasantness it had spawned, that she'd realized, in an otherwise clean-shaven crowd, Ariosto must have been in mourning.

Weighed down by this unwanted task, she watched the bowl of wine go steadily round the guests. She watched them drink. Converse. Grow louder. As the crowd eddied about him, Ariosto paid Caterina no heed, neither addressing her nor acknowledging her presence. He was seated now, arguing frequently, leaning forward, crouching in doing so, as if ready to spring.

After a time, to Caterina, this recurrent show of contentiousness began to prove entertaining. Picking up the imagined gauntlet, she devised a mental exercise for conversing with this man. This sparring partner. What he might demand. What she might respond. Which remark would spawn an argument. Whether she would argue back. Time passed agreeably enough until, immersed in the fantasy, she leaned over, lowered her head, and pushed out her elbows just as a guest, deep in the dispute, glanced away from his adversary—and noticed her stance. He stared back at Ariosto, and guffawed with delight.

Before she was able to straighten up, Ariosto saw her, too.

"You devil!" His gaze traveled over those close to him and back to her person. "Ribboned, frilled and tacked up in *sarcenet*," his voice cut through the babble, "and all this time, quiet as oil."

Attention focused on her presence. Mortified, she shrank back against the daybed.

"Drink up, my lords. We are to be diverted."

"By what?" drawled a curly-haired man by Ariosto's side. "A chit of a girl?"

"A girl who behaves like a dancing bear clearly intends to perform."

The wine bowl went around again and the group surrounding him looked expectantly at this child shadowed by the heft of the daybed. The placement of candles had purposefully shed clarity on the finery of *pourpoints*, the silks of togas and the jeweled insignias of the guests. Hers was an unknown quality. A gem, or a rock, in a box.

"Would you deny a dog its bone? A popinjay its grape? Come now," Ariosto gestured toward her, "offer us an artifice."

Caterina began to wish for some great calamity: a strong wind rushing through the house, a fierce brawl in the street, an invasion of bats.

"Come out, miscreant," boomed a nobleman with a red face. "Give us an act for penance." He sounded almost kindly. "Perform well..." he glanced at Ariosto, "and ah, well, at least *I* will forgive you."

"Give us a dance," commanded another.

A young man, sparkling with emblems, piped up. "I once saw a street urchin juggle mice."

Not mice, she thought and shuddered.

"No, no. More mime, gentlemen!" cried the man who'd laughed. "She had you, Ariosto, to the set of your beard."

Her betrothed reddened but his reply was smooth and unhesitating. "Speak to us, *cardoon,*" purred Ariosto. "The mime was passably amusing... to those embalmed in malmsey." The bowl was passed. He drank more. "*Do it now.* We've waited long enough."

She shook her head, digging her fingers into the cushion, and wished fervently to be even more like a *cardoon,* a spiny-leafed plant.

"I've had more enjoyment from a dressed dummy," growled a tall, elegant man in black velvet.

"And what exactly did you do to it?" And they all laughed uproariously.

Ariosto suddenly clapped his hands. She flinched. *"Get on with it!"*

"Christ's blood, Ariosto, look at her. The only act she's capable of playing is *you!*" cried the man who'd laughed.

If only it would stop. Holy Mother, make it stop! If only Papa wasn't at the far end of the room—with so many people in between.

Ariosto flushed and looked about him. "I've seen many a tiresome troupe of tricked-out animals at festivals. They don't speak but at least they perform. But a fancied-up urchin who doesn't speak?"

They all began peering at her. Deafness might be unattainable but now it seemed muteness might be too.

"Why doesn't the brat speak? Does it not have a tongue? Have they cut it out?" came the staccato beat of voices, one right after the other.

She wondered if they were going to converge on her and pry open her mouth. Probe inside for her tongue. Her throat filled up with fear.

To her horror, Ariosto said, "Show us your tongue, or I for one, won't give you a single coin for your performance."

"Show us your tongue," chanted some drunkards.

A prickle of panic ran down Caterina's spine. She squeezed her eyelids shut and clamped her hands over her mouth. *Where is Papa? Where is he?* She felt Nonna's padded, comforting arm enfold her and pull her closer.

There was a growing rumble of disgust from the onlookers.

"*Enough!*" cried Ariosto unexpectedly. "How divinely clever!" And in a wondering voice, "Truly, it doesn't speak."

"Why not?" asked a voice rough with drink.

"*I* have never known one to speak," he replied.

"Known *what* to speak?" asked the red-faced nobleman.

"An ape. It is *an ape*, you fools! A Barbary ape. Dressed like a child. Masked. Coiffed. Costumed." Ariosto levered himself up, spread his arms, and turned full circle. "That is the trick! We are undone!" And he slumped back into his chair.

His companions rolled about, crying and hooting with laughter.

Their senseless hilarity turned the fear that had dried up Caterina's throat into growing resentment. And that, in turn, fueled a volcanic response. She felt it rising inside her, hot and unstoppable. Molten, she shrugged off Nonna's embrace. Springing to her feet with a defiant glance at her tormentors, she addressed them in the sharp, carrying voice of a child. "It is *you* who are *apes*!"

The group roared.

"It not only speaks, it bellows like a watchman!" cried the curly-haired man.

"And as for *you,* ser Ariosto," her voice shrilled through the laughter, "clearly *you* were born under an *unlucky* star, during an *ill-favored* hour, on an *unfortunate* day! *And...*" she drew a sharp breath to continue, but Nonna was already moving to stifle the rest.

Those close to her swiftly drew back

Once out, the unladylike pronouncement scythed through the din like a curse hurtling down from the sky. No one was above the bane of superstition. The catcalls and jocularity dribbled away into silence. Nonna's nails worked their way into the flesh of her arm. The hairy spider turned purple and she was hastily removed from his presence.

*   *   *   *   *

A fortnight later, after drawn-out apologies, after numerous attempts at conciliation, she had to stand in that room, her father's *studiolo*, where he kept his books and worked at his desk, like a felon. They all blamed *her*, even Nonna, her personal bulwark of strength. *She* was in the wrong. The verbal attack on her had been unfortunate, but considering the inebriated state of the guests, all men of privilege, ultimately excusable. But what she had said was *not*. It was not only unseemly, ill-considered, and insulting, but it had put in jeopardy the family's reputation and ability to move up in the world. It had seriously endangered the betrothal. Considering that silence was a known attribute of chastity, her outspokenness might even have removed her from the marriage market altogether. And to crown it all, that latter fact might have the impetus to bring her father's line both to an end, and worse, to everlasting ignominy. Because of her. Because of what she'd said.

She felt the icy shaft of betrayal penetrate her heart.

Obedience, virtue, and modest restraint were the accepted trinity of female behavior. Of the three, only virtue remained intact. The latest letter from her betrothed was quite specific.

She barely noticed the glumness of the tutors. Full bed and board were notoriously hard to find. Tommaso's prominent Adam's apple made its sporadic journey up and down his throat, and on old, fat Bartolomeo, the mathematician, a multiple set of chins quivered in geometric harmony.

"She's not quite ten," Nonna reminded them—as if

Caterina was not standing there beside her.

"And educated," growled her father. "She ought to know better." He fixed his gaze on her.

Blinded by tears, Caterina was unable to return it.

He turned to the tutors. "What have I paid you for? To teach her to *insult* a nobleman? To encourage disobedience in a *child*? Worse still, a *female* child!"

The two men waited, fearing the worst, while the tempest that was her father raged on until it ran out of wind.

"Have her study that Barbaro essay," Ludovico ended abruptly. "The one on marriage." He looked sternly at the downcast tutors, her nurse, and his gilt-crowned daughter, and said between his teeth, "I shall attend the result."

That week, at the height of his disapproval, her father commissioned a plate from the pottery. Completed, it was displayed in Caterina's room as a reminder of duty. On the ceramic ribbon curling about a gaily painted lady, it said: *Nem sua sorte chontentus* / No one is content with their destiny. It was notable that amongst the blaze of color, the message was in black—and that the plate was set above her reach.

*   *   *   *   *

Nonna was appointed interim tutor. For three blissful days, Tommaso, with the speed of a boar, escaped to Padua. When a foray to the booksellers turned up the work on marriage, Caterina was assigned her task. In halting Latin, for hours, she waded through a litany of embellished phrases and Classical examples, including some on subjects she thought she ought not to know. At last, she turned the page, her voice cracking from the long recitation, and hesitated.

"Don't stop there," said that familiar voice, muffled. "You haven't finished." Nonna backed out from under the huge domed cover of the linen chest, stood up, shook out a large cloth, and examined it critically for moths.

Caterina went back a page and silently reread. She leafed

back a third time. A vestige of hope rose in her chest. She stabbed at the print with her finger. "Nonna! I *found* something! *Listen!* It says: *'only permit their daughters to marry those with whom they had exchanged, as virgins, mutual signs of love.'* Nonna? *Nonna?* Did you hear what ser Barbaro said?"

"Mmmm," replied Nonna. "There's one. Aggh! A veritable city!" And she plucked the veiled offenders from the cloth.

"And here again! *'Love that is mutual, therefore, and voluntary, should be zealously sought, increased, and preserved.'*" Caterina shut the book. "I don't love him."

Nonna's voice rose from the depths of the chest, "Ser Barbaro has been dead for years. I doubt he'll care."

"I don't love my *betrothed*. What's more, he doesn't love me."

The domed cover fell shut. Nonna's gaze rested on her face. "How would you know?"

"I *feel* it."

"At your age, one doesn't feel anything. Puberty doesn't come at almost ten."

She so wanted it to be settled. She glanced up at Nonna for some sort of confirmation that it was. That it would be. That it could be soon. But the look on Nonna's face said something very different.

How could you have been such a fool! By God, Caterina, you cursed him! And in public.

*   *   *   *   *

A dove brought deliverance to Noah's Ark. A falcon bore a fatal choice to Prince Lazar. The Mameluke sultan of Egypt still received shipping news by pigeon. Humanists exchanged quick-witted philosophies in letters. Swift couriers brought important papers. Ships, winged with sails, delivered vouchers, bills, and missives to distant ports. Even that thorn in her side, ser Ariosto, sent constant messengers to her father.

There was no letter then. No thought of a letter. No inkling of what it might bring. Time was already encapsulated, spoken for, calendared. Because the child, for whom an unlikely chain of events would soon be set in motion, was still a little girl of almost ten.

Chapter Two

*Every man waits his destined hour; even the cities are doomed
to their fate.*
—Poggio Bracciolini

Late February, Twelfth Month, Venetian Year 1492 in the
Balkans – Rade

He took the mare on impulse. An impulse that could easily
serve up an early death. A fleeting thought for a man of
twenty-eight—or was it twenty-nine?—and quickly discarded,
for death was unimaginable, outside the dictates of fate, while
danger, in any form, brought pleasure.

Unguarded, standing in the line of horses, the mare stood
out, as distinctive and as elegant as a white tree against a
shadowed wood: her bridle hung with colored tassels, the
morning light playing on the outlines of her fine legs and pale
hide, her breath rising in a soft gray cloud. The other mounts
stood winded, heads down, sides heaving, drying sweat
stiffening their shaggy coats. Around them, the quagmire of
snow and mud threw off a trail of running footprints. Despite
the sound of voices in the low peasant structure nearby, no one
had come outside. The act was effortless. He simply made the
exchange and slipped away—but he took care to leave the
ornamented bridle behind.

What began as a quiet, orderly retreat gathered momentum
as the day progressed, evolving in late afternoon into a full-

blown gallop. Rade tested the mare's speed crossing the high mountain pasture and felt the shock as her hooves met the frozen ground and the surge as her body uncoiled for the stride to follow. And caution be damned, he gloried in it! In the frigid upland air, the north wind tore at his cloak, the gray wool one, straining the flapping cloth caught at his throat and driving it against the horse's pale hide. Beads of ice encrusted his hair and eyebrows, and where there was warmth, the beads melted and ran down between the cloth and his skin, augmenting the razor's edge between pain and pleasure. At his back, the saddle bags and bundles beat a muted tattoo, urging her onward. He bent his body over the flying mane and muscled neck and as the mare bunched and flexed and flung herself forward over the open ground, he felt no fear of pursuit—only the high exhilaration that recklessness brought. And speed. And the light layer of snow on the windswept ridge blew like billowing smoke behind them.

Rade rode the mare hell-bent into the trees before the folly of it rose up in his mind. With that, he pulled her up to walk off the effects of the long gallop. The wind had dropped and the dusky forest reached out to embrace them. In that sylvan stillness, the horse's heavy breathing overlaid all other sound and was rivaled only by the blood pounding in his head. *The hero, Marko, resoundingly evident on his winded steed.* He stifled an urge to laugh. Vuk would have argued that the Marko of song on the stallion Šarac would have done far more than trick some fief-holder out of his horse. He could hear the old fox badgering him now:

"Had you been Marko Kraljević, you'd have barged into that hut, crowded the *pasha* to the wall, and been paid for taking that horse."

"There were eight of them."

"Enough ornament for a fortress gate."

"But not our fortress."

"Not yet, but with Marko along…"

"He's been dead a hundred years, Vuk. Since Rovine. And

on the wrong side."

"Legend or not," the old man would have said, "Marko lives. Is he not forever on our countrymen's lips? On every singer's *gusla*? Even Ivan the Black found himself in Marko's boots."

"If, like Marko, I were a Turkish vassal, I'd have a hard time explaining why I killed their men."

"Rade, you black-haired bastard, you're Orthodox. Slav. Killing them is in your blood. As killing you is in theirs. If you'd played your cards right, you'd be weighted down with gold. A hero. And we wouldn't have to spend the winter in a stinking hut."

"So that's what this is truly about—winter quarters."

"No," Vuk would have insisted, "it's about what Marko would have done and what you *should* have done."

Conversing with Vuk was like trimming a sail in a contrary wind. The wind always swung around to some quarter you didn't expect. The old man had saved him, served him, dressed his wounds, watched his back, told his fortune, and on occasion, questioned his orders. On the long journey home, Rade found he missed him.

He relinquished the darkening path for a cluster of boulders when, with a feeling of foreboding, he discovered the leather satchel that held his victuals was gone. He swore under his breath and then out loud. Dark had fallen and in the morning, the snow, tell-tale to the end, would inform another of his loss.

He took a second look around his campsite. And a third. The small fire glowed, the mare had been fed, and he had just started melting snow for water. He thought longingly of the dried meat. Reaching up to take the sack of grain from the limb he'd hung it on, he drew out a handful of oats and chewed slowly knowing these would be all he dared eat. The sack was heavy but there was little left inside. The mare would need her strength more that he did his. The *pasha* would come hunting—and he wouldn't come alone. Yet the border was a scant four, five days ride and the horse had food, even if he hadn't. And she was swift. And valuable.

*   *   *   *   *

For the next three days, Rade became the quiet burden that the mare bore steadily over heights that fell away into the trough of the mountains or down inclines where the streams wound darkly and the rocks glistened with ice. Along the way, he chewed beech twigs, put pebbles under his tongue, drank melted snow, even wrapped a strip of leather tight around his waist—as the mountain people did when they were hungry. He dared not stop to hunt. And as the mare's pace ate up the miles, he reveled in the distance.

From time to time, the wind groaned as if laden with a language it could not express. It made him think of the new words slipping across the border into the chatter of the Mediterranean. Words like *reaya*, *timur*, *spahi*, and *balkan*—the last being the Turkic for the mountainous lands the invader had crossed and conquered. They sat rudely on the tongue, pushing aside names and terms that had been in use for centuries, an audible reminder that the only constant was the land itself.

*   *   *   *   *

By the fourth morning, his body was stiff with cold and hunger had driven away sleep. In the pale dawn light, Rade shrugged off his discomfort, fed the mare the last of the oats, and blearily resumed his journey. One day more. He even began to think in hours.

He was half asleep in the saddle when the horse shied and a panicked stream of pack animals poured from the turn by the towering outcrop on the high trail. He jerked the mare around in time to catch an accompanying blur of movement as five men, turbaned, hatted, and padded in sheepskins, burst from the rocks. His sword and dagger were already in his hands and he drove his heels into the horse and shouted her forward, slashing out on either side.

"Bastard!" screamed the big man he'd sliced with his dagger. "Get the horse! *Get the horse!*" And then the shouting changed to a cacophony Rade had no time to comprehend.

And he would have made it save for the thickset man who grasped the reins, and when he cut them, her bridle. And the other, who, clutching an armful of cloak, jerked him backward so that he missed his aim. He twisted free of the cloak, unbalancing his attacker, but the hard thwack of a cudgel landed on his upper arm, numbing it to the bone. He found the blade was loose in his hand and even though he tried, he wasn't able to fully grasp it. But he managed to ward off another blow with his left and hold the steel until it slid off his dagger's crossguard and the man fell behind him. The downward slash of another sword caught his blade and was deflected as he leaned sideways, throwing his weight behind the almost useless arm. But the force of the blow wrenched the weapon from his hand.

He saw the fur-hatted man crowding in for a second cut but Rade also saw he was avoiding injuring the horse. He jammed his heels into the mare's flanks, and reins gone, yanked back on the headpiece of the bridle with his left hand, forcing the bit hard against her mouth so that the mare reared, flailing with her forefeet. For a moment, his attackers fell back but quickly grabbed at her again as she came down. The cudgel blows rained down and Rade ducked or parried as best he could with the dagger.

He had gone beyond pain, even beyond conscious thought. Instead, he burned with a rage that consumed everything in its path. Screaming, he urged the mare into the train, the two men hanging from her bridle, shoving them against their own beasts of burden, trying to shake them off. The jumble of packs jostled them and one man, shouting and swearing, was dislodged but the other held fast. But through it all, the blows

continued and though he'd done what he could to ward them
off, he saw he couldn't win.

When they dragged him reeling off the horse, he had only
the dagger and it too was wrenched from his hand. While
they'd held him down so that he couldn't protect himself and
pummeled and beat him, between blows, he waited for the
blade—but it didn't come. Instead, there was a shout from the
cliff and then something hard smashed into his head. And after
that, there was nothing.

*   *   *   *   *

"Neck's broken," said the unseen voice. "Half the load is
scattered where I can't get at it. *That fucking bastard!*"

Rade's first thought was surprise that the Turk spoke his
language. His second that if the two horses hadn't slipped and
fallen during the melee, he would no longer be alive. The
mountain gelding had been coaxed and beaten from his icy
ledge back to the trail but the second horse, unevenly loaded
with booty, supplies, and arms, had fallen onto the boulders
below. Rade had been unconscious when the booty was
brought up the cliff but not when his captors argued about the
meat. In their world, horse meat would normally be *yasak*,
forbidden, but the accident seemed to sanction its use. Had it
been evening, they would have eaten their fill and amused
themselves with his death. However, as fate would have it, the
day's journey lay ahead and they now had a reason to keep him
alive. So they unbound their captive and loaded him up with as
much dead horse as they were able. Even wrapped in its skin,
the heavy, butchered load leaked blood and as he staggered
down the trail, the pack animals shied away from him—
including the one to whose harness he was tied.

Rade made it to evening on willpower alone. He had
known not to fight them, not to hinder their march or incur
their displeasure. Instead to narrow his mind down to what
would keep him alive: the next step and the one after; not to

foul the tether; to bear brutality in silence; and to be the pack animal they wanted and save the man for later. From time to time he caught blurred glimpses of the mare, heading up the group under the guidance of the lithe, fur-hatted man who seemed to be the leader.

When at last they stopped, and the horses were hitched to the tether and their packs unloaded, the horse hide was unstrapped from his back and he was beaten into further submission and bound. He lay, boneless as an octopus, watching the shadowy figures of the men, outlined by the setting sun, untie their packs, swap loot and argue about ownership. Their contours were blurred even though the pack train had walked out of the snow cover hours ago.

For a time, he drifted, half-listening to their language, so similar to his own. Bosnian he thought. Not Ottoman but in their employ. *Akinjis.* Border irregulars, raiders, and, considering the turbans, converts as well. Anyway, two of them were. The plunder, the weapons, the caliber of their mounts had been in plain sight all day but he'd been so preoccupied with the pace of the packhorse and not being choked again by the rope that he hadn't assembled the pieces. Still, knowing who they were did not portend a fortuitous future. Men of their calling would have no reason to keep him alive. And if a reason existed, it hadn't come to mind.

The rocks that he lay on became increasingly painful. He tried to shift his body but it took more effort than he wanted to make. He was so tired. So spent. Helpless as the boy shepherd, Radoje, asleep in the field:

... Janja, his sister, wakes him:
Go, get yourself up, Radoje!
Your sheep have gone into the grove!
Let them, sister, I can't help it.
I have been eaten by witches;
my mother has taken my heart out,
with my aunt holding the candle.

It was the song the older boys had taught him. The one they'd learned in the summer meadows. And it was Radoje he thought of when something so terrible happened that he could not free himself from it. Helpless as Radoje. *I have been eaten by witches...* The men would have to get along without him. Miloš could lead them. He tried not to think about Vuk.

The band's conversation began to sound far away. He could feel what control he still exercised slipping from his grasp. The sun that had tried to offer warmth had gone cold and the stones beneath him that had pushed into the hurt places, dulled. The *pasha's* men, he thought wearily, would be bent on revenge. He'd counted six of them. Now that he had so little strength left, escape from so many seemed unlikely. The sun's rays lingered on his eyelids and he could smell the broken branches in the scrub behind him. The sun would die hours before he did. *Scent my body with sweet-smelling yew.* And he let himself drown in blackness.

*   *   *   *   *

Rade awoke to the freezing contents of a bucket.

"I wouldn't give an *akche* for the bastard," said the big man with the dagger cut. "He has as much worth as a foundered mule."

"If ransom is not in the cards, and he's too much trouble to sell," said the man in the black sheepskin, "I say we kill him. The question is before we feast or after."

"Kill him now," growled Daggercut. "Skin him like a calf. We'll cut his throat when we've finished." He smiled unpleasantly, "The dog barks, but the caravan goes on." He walked over.

The first kick and the ones that followed almost defeated him. Rade curled up like a wounded animal, teeth clenched, each shuddering breath on the edge of sound.

"Your dog doesn't bark," observed the small man, still covered with blood from the morning's butchery.

"He will when we put his feet to the coals," said the thickset man, yawning.

"He hasn't made a sound since the fight," was the reply.

"I wager his tongue will wag," their leader said softly, examining the hilt and then the blade of the dagger he had pulled from his belt. He weighed the weapon in his hand. "Good balance," he said admiringly. "Venetian-made." He looked knowingly at his men. "Albanian sword. A horse with black skin. A man of parts," he said switching his gaze to their captive.

"The dog is a thief!" cried the Black Sheepskin.

"Or a murderer," observed the thickset man.

"Most likely both," said Fur Hat.

"The pig deserves the stake," roared the wounded man.

They liked that. Their voices rose in support.

"Let it wait," their leader said. "We still have a use for him. He can cart back the firewood. And some saplings for the meat."

"I'll see to it," volunteered Daggercut. *"Get up!"* The ropes were loosed and he was jerked to his feet.

Shoved down the trail, Rade tried not to consider how he would die. He also realized, of little consequence at this late date, that they were not the *pasha's* men. They had no knowledge of who he was or of what he had done. And that, for some reason, brought on an emptiness more damaging than pain. A nameless pig to the slaughter. Not even a man. He thought with bitter resignation that such must be the random working of fate. But it was odd... for his future had been shown to him. And he would have sworn it wasn't this.

*   *   *   *   *

Even before the afterglow faded and the moon rose, it took time to gather fuel for the fire. They had reached the brush landscape near the coast where there were few trees and dead limbs. He supposed the band was returning to some port, but to him, it was an unfamiliar place and its location seemed to have little bearing on his future. He was tethered by the neck to his captor so the foraging was fraught with abuse but at that point in time, even abuse was life.

"Cut those for the meat," commanded his persecutor, handing him the fragment of a saw-toothed blade. "And the big, thick one." And he laughed as he drew his stave back to reinforce his order.

Even as Rade braced himself, tightening his left-armed grip around the growing bundle while wondering if he could find a way to cut the bastard's throat, he came to realize that the man was not familiar with what grew along the coast. Curbing his anger, he stripped the tell-tale leaves from the thick, leathery stems. And when, laden with fuel and stakes, he was beaten back to the fire, he had not given up hope. And as the last blow fell, he wished for death—but it was theirs, not his, he asked for.

                    *   *   *   *   *

As the fire and the group around it came slowly and doubly into focus, Rade could see that they were drunk and that even with the gibbous moon, it was very dark. He wondered how many hours had passed. Clearly the *raki* had made its rounds even before the meat was cooked and they must have had quite a time spitting the chunks and holding them to the fire. Even now, they were still chewing bits off the stakes and making jokes.

"Our pig is awake."

He froze, letting his eyelids close gently, feigning unconsciousness. But his stomach, yearning for sustenance, betrayed him.

"Well don't his innards have a nice little voice of their own," laughed the thickset man. "We'll see them out in the light soon enough."

"Pity the poor bastard isn't allowed any," said a voice off

to the left from a man he couldn't see. "Oughtn't we to offer him a final meal?" He chewed loudly, smacking his lips. "Especially with him knowing what comes next."

"I'm not sharing with a thief!" growled another voice from the darkness.

"Have you looked in your pack?" laughed the little man. "Who's the bigger thief?"

The man with the fur hat came back to the circle. He looked a bit ill but was clearly pleased by his discovery. He held up the drooping bag of grain and dropped it on the stones. There was an unexpected clink. "It's lined with *ducats*," he said, and vomited. The others jumped on the bag and tore it apart. Soon all the gold Rade had painstakingly brought back from Zara lay scattered on the ground and they were fighting over it.

The big man with the wound got the largest share. He came over then and began to go through his prisoner's clothes, patting him down and pulling at the points and padding of his doublet and the seams of his linen shirt. He ferreted out the letter, opened it, dumped it on the ground, turned Rade over, pushing him this way and that. When he was roughly shoved onto his back for one more search, Rade took a chance and looked up into the big man's face. His irises, formerly brown, were black. And he was retching.

The little man was already on his knees clutching his stomach and crying in pain. The thickset one lost his balance and fell into the fire. He screamed and rolled out of the coals but no one beat out the flames until he roused himself a little and flopped back and forth on the iron hard dirt. Afterward he lay there groaning until the spasms attacked him and he crawled out of the firelight.

It took them hours to die and Rade watched, almost unblinking, until the retching stopped, and the screams of pain and groaning died down to naught and it was, except for the horses, absolutely still. Then he painfully rolled himself to the nearest body, got hold of a knife, and cut his bonds. When he was ready to leave, he retrieved the *ducats*, loosed the pack animals from their tether, scattered the booty as if the men had fought over it, and saddled the mare. As he rode away, he thought that even a fool knew that oleander was poisonous.

*   *   *   *   *

He found the cave the following day and bringing in the horse as well, blocked up the opening with ropes and brush and left her a pile of chopped fodder near the place where water ran out of the rock. He pulled the cloak and sheepskin he had taken from the leader's body into a heap and gingerly laid himself down on them and pulled his own gray wool over him. And he forced himself to swallow the *raki* and a rind of their moldy cheese. Afterward, he thought he must have spent upwards of three days lying there passing from unconsciousness to nausea to agony and back again until the pain became manageable and he could see. When he was fully conscious, he took another look at the letter, finished the *raki*, ate another piece of cheese, and carefully sewed the *ducats* back into the sack.

Chapter Three

*In a bride, therefore, a man must first seek beauty of mind, that
is, good conduct and virtue.*
—Leon Battista Alberti

Venice, October, Venetian Year 1487– Caterina

Nothing Caterina could do or had done had satisfied her
father. Ludovico raged around his *studiolo* and the rest of the
house like a bull. The letters from ser Ariosto continued to
arrive, each one another wound to his pride. To her father, her
behavior had become a stain on the complicated structure of
loyalties and relationships it'd taken him a lifetime to
construct. As his anger progressed from day to day, and lost
none of its fury, she came to fear he sought some further
punishment in order to achieve Ariosto's pardon. Something
more than studying Barbaro's treatise. More than the endless
lectures, reading of critical letters, and her resulting tears.
More than a change in her education. More than a denial of
privileges. Yet it was the humanist in him that prevented the
carnage he was wont to wreak. She also learned to stay out of
his way.

Most of what she knew, she learned from Nonna.

*   *   *   *   *

"If the incident is not put to rest," Ludovico muttered, "it may become the motivation for revenge."

Afternoon was fading into evening and despite its small window, the room was already dark, tingeing her employer's uneasiness with imagined menace. The eye-level cornice dimly packed with statues, books, and scientific gadgets had taken on the aspect of a balcony supporting a diminutive, but seemingly attentive, crowd of onlookers. *Revenge.* Nonna was surprised. Then thoughtful. "On her? Or on you?"

"On us both." He'd picked up a sheaf of papers. "You should see what arrives by messenger."

"From ser Ariosto?"

He'd nodded and brandished the odious bouquet in the gloom. "There's no rage like that spawned from insult. And God knows, death has honed the blade."

"I thought he didn't like his brother."

"They didn't get along, but more important, Matteo's death has ended their *fraterna*. Their partnership. Ariosto has inherited an administrative nightmare... and all the family debt."

"I remember the troubles his father got into." She shook her head. "They were said to be legion. What about ser Matteo's wife?"

Ludovico grunted. "Another blow. Her dowry must be returned as well."

"And children?"

"She was barren."

That explained Ariosto's insistence on fertility in the contract. "So, the brother oversaw the family holdings, managed obligations, deferred payments... "

"Horse-traded... while Ariosto tried to build a political base. To obtain the necessary favors. He was very near success. Inheriting the dross of the partnership will damage him."

"I can't imagine him ever working alongside ser Matteo. Word is, his brother was always overwrought, almost desperate."

"He was. And he didn't. For Ariosto, it was expedient to be separate, outside the blame." He sighed. "All those ventures to which I've contributed..." His voice trailed off.

"But *your* agreement is intact, isn't it?" she asked, knowing Ludovico set great store by the marriage.

"So far," he said and half-turned away. "I offered the man a loan. Not enough to eclipse Caterina's dowry. Apparently not enough to assuage the insult either." His fist tightened on the papers. "Suggestions for punishment run the gamut from successive beatings to chaining her in a cellar." His gaze came around to her face.

"Would you strike her now?" asked Nonna carefully. "After all these years?" The other option had been out of the question.

"I would if it would make her think," he replied, brows creased. "A thrashing might show her the error of her ways," he added crossly, "but it's unlikely to reorder her mind." Ludovico opened his hand and let the crumpled papers fall back on his desk. "It's the last that's needed," he said softly. Abruptly, he swept the papers off onto the floor.

For a time, Nonna studied the clutter and then closed her eyes. "If I've failed in my duties," she said indistinctly, "I'll do whatever you think best." She straightened her shoulders. Two lifetimes had been spent in this house, serving first the wife, and then the daughter. Both had been the cherished offspring of her heart, if not her womb—and she'd lost the mother but saved the child. Even then, she'd worked at that strand of loving service so that their lives had become a tapestry, woven together, and she had been the weft that connected them. "Shall I gather my things?" *Where would she go? Who would want her?* She felt as if she'd swallowed a riverbed of stones.

The tall, broad-shouldered figure was still, black robe falling nearly to the terrazzo, a thin strip of white at the top of his collar. Except for the line of shirt, the pointed arch of the window, and the pale forms of letters, hands, and faces, the room melted away into muted tones of dusk.

He rubbed his temples tiredly. "Nonna," he said, "I think we've both failed in our duties. We've allowed her too much freedom. Too much self-will. God knows, we've spoiled her." He walked over to the single window and stood looking out. "I *need* you to stay," he said, his blunt features reflecting the last of the light. "I *need* you to help me with her." Perhaps he felt rather than saw her gesture of assent. Then he said, as if to himself, "If I beat her, she'll fight me. I'd have to beat her for weeks."

"I'd rather you beat me."

Ludovico turned and smiled ruefully. "It's not you Ariosto's going to marry." He went back to his desk, pushed the papers aside with his foot, and lit a candle. "As to that kind of punishment," he frowned, "she's a child, not some ill-mannered beast." He glared at Nonna. "I haven't the stomach for it."

"You'll think of something," replied Nonna, relieved. "And that something will make her come around to it on her own."

*   *   *   *   *

The solution came inadvertently from the ramblings of a visiting priest. He arrived to find every bed in the parish house occupied in threes. Ludovico discovered him by the church font, standing forlornly in a muddy cassock, tonsured head bent, studying his empty wallet. He'd come a long way from his Tuscan hill town, and he was tired, disappointed, and hungry. They struck up a conversation, and being in an expansive mood, Ludovico took pity on him and invited him home. That particular night, there would be an empty pallet under the eaves: it was Bartolomeo's customary evening out with the bargeman's widow, a miracle romance to some in the household, but, to Ludovico, entirely comprehensible—a pairing of substance. But the merchant hadn't explained the bed, and the priest didn't query, only seemed pathetically glad to accompany him. Nor was the gesture of hospitality entirely selfless: the priest would pay for his rest with a house blessing and hopefully, some useful information. Ludovico knew of his hill town's crown of defensive towers, its orchards, its saffron for yellow cloth, and its wranglings with its neighbors, but he'd yet to learn that inside the circlet of watchful elevations had sprouted something else, something rare and compelling: the cult of a child saint.

The sleepy priest was propped up with an enormous dinner, conversational prods, and plenty of wine. The discussion turned from politics to art, and the holy father was describing the decoration of a new chapel, part of a college for canons. It turned out that the town council, having gathered sufficient funds, had been lucky enough to attract the Florentine painter, Ghirlandaio—who in turn had been captivated by the subject.

"The saint lives in the pictures," sighed the priest dreamily. "And yet she is only a girl with a rose-colored gown and long golden hair. And," he added reverently, "the face of an angel." He rubbed his long olive-skinned nose and knotted his brows momentarily. "A bit like the child I saw in the *andron*." The *andron* was the canal level hall.

"My daughter," returned Ludovico. She'd gone down to the storeroom to get something for supper in the kitchen. It'd been another trying day and he'd removed the treat of having a guest at dinner.

"Tell us about the saint, father," urged Nonna, selecting a dried fig, the finishing touch to the dinner. She noticed the young father had taken a long time to make his choice and then picked three, observing the Trinity, even in fruit. Considering the enormous quantity of food he'd already consumed, and the diminutive size of his frame, she wondered if he had expandable ribs, like a snake.

"She was born Serafina de' Ciardi," said the Tuscan through a mouthful of fig, "but we call her St. Fina. She was the daughter of a good family," he glanced at Ludovico, "like yours. And I can imagine her, perhaps like your own child," another fig was inserted, "so pure, so pious, and so uncommonly kind that everyone took notice of her."

Ludovico exchanged glances with Nonna.

The priest's heavy-lidded eyes settled on his remaining fig. "Alas," he intoned sadly. Nonna studied the fig but was unable to discern any shortcomings. It eventually followed the others. "At the age of ten, she was stricken with an incurable illness that confined her to her bed." He looked even more melancholy. "And then her parents died."

A second platter of figs arrived

"Ghirlandaio painted her sickroom," he said reverently. "When I look at her," he tilted his head to one side and closed his eyes, "she lies so quietly, accepting the will of God, with her faithful nurse, Beldia, supporting her head. And on a hard plank too. Not even a bed. Very plain. Very spare. Enduring her pain."

"The bed of saintly ways," nodded Ludovico thoughtfully.

"Yes, and she chose it to show the humility with which she accepted her fate. And she lay on it," related the priest, "even when the rats and mice plagued her, until St. Gregory came in a vision and released her from her suffering."

"So she was cured," said Nonna.

"Not as you might envision," he said helpfully. "She went to God."

There followed a series of miracles and the founding of her church. Also a description of the painting of her funeral by Ghirlandaio with the city notables around her bier. All the narratives were punctuated by the continued consumption of figs. He'd nearly got through all the notables' names and their histories when abruptly, the conversation halted, and the father scurried from the room in a crescendo of stupefying flatulence.

"Oh dear," said Nonna, looking at the empty serving plates.

*   *   *   *   *

The first Caterina knew about it, or rather about some change in the household, had been the hammering taking place upstairs, and then in the courtyard. It went on for four days. A door went down the stairs in one state and returned considerably altered. The second was on the fifth gut-wrenching day when the life she knew ended and hell took its place.

With the innocence of Iphigenia, she obediently followed her father up the stairs and was shown the room. The former small storeroom, sometime manservant's room, off the upstairs hall, had been entirely cleared out. Its one high window had been shuttered and locked on the bottom half so that any light was limited to the top. She noticed that, even standing on a table, had there been one, no one could see out, or in. A thick oaken plank had been laid on what was formerly a wooden floor now paved in flat stones. It was about as long as she was tall and she wondered aloud what it was for.

"St. Fina," said Papa.

And she was left in the dark.

At the entrance to the narrow room stood the door, the same substantial door she'd seen earlier, further reinforced with iron hardware. A small square opening with a sliding cover had been cut high into the center. The sliding cover was furnished with a lock and the door itself could be bolted on the outside in three places.

At the last, she realized the only decoration was her small painting of the Virgin, nailed high on the side wall, its protective curtain missing.

"Papa?" And she pointed. "That's mine. Why is it here? Where's the cover?"

"It's here," he replied, "to watch over everything you do or say. There's no cover so you may always be reminded that you cannot escape the all-knowing scrutiny of the Holy Mother. Every thought you have in here will be laid before Her. You will bare your very soul."

There was no kindness in his voice. She felt panic rising

from her stomach. She turned to flee but the others arrived at the top of the stairs, and he must have sensed her fear, for her father's hand closed on her upper arm.

In here? It was, in every way, a cell.

*   *   *   *   *

Caterina's incarceration, or claustration as her father preferred to call it, like that of a novitiate, was formally carried out in the presence of the parish priest, her nurse, the household, two women she didn't know, her father, and ser Ariosto. The sentence given was four months and the lessons she was expected to learn in that place were humility and obedience in the face of God's will. The story of St. Fina was related. Moral lessons were indicated. A plain Book of Hours was provided, without illustrations, to further meditation. Her father did not expect serious hardship. The punishment would last for the remainder of spring and all of summer, generally benevolent seasons of the year.

The household would be around her and there would be no greater deprivation than a simpler ordering of her food—as befitting one learning saintly ways. The space was said to be large enough for exercise, properly contrived. She would be instructed by her tutors, as usual, but they would be outside, rather than inside with her. The priest or his assistant would come each day for religious instruction and to hear her rosary, also outside the door. And her nurse might come as well to share news and conversation, but could not come inside. The keys to the locks would be lodged for safekeeping with her father. There would be no physical tasks. Nor any physical punishment. Caterina was to use her mind to the fullest to consider her actions and offer suitable atonement.

When they grasped her by the arms, she fought them, biting, kicking and scratching, all the way in the door. Like a terrorized cat, she dug desperate, bloody furrows into her captors' skins. Inside, where the two unknown women unceremoniously stripped her of her fine clothes, Caterina was given a rough shift, a brush, a cup and a plate. And there was a close-stool for sanitary needs, an old coverlet, a low bench, and a container of water. Then the bolts were drawn, the keys turned in their locks, and the sound of her jailer's footsteps hurriedly retreated down the stairs. In between her own shrill screams of rage and the thunder of her fists on the door, she heard Nonna, who had tried in vain to cajole her into accepting her father's will, who had slept in her bed nearly every night of her life, who was her most trusted and intimate confidant, and who normally showed as much emotion as a rock, sobbing bitterly in the hallway. It was then that she realized the hole in the door was so high and shelved underneath in such a way that she would need to reach up to get her food and, more chilling, the person outside would always be in shadow. There were no windows in the hall. In all those months, the only human contact would be the sound of voices and perhaps, from a friend, the touch of a hand thrust through the high opening in the door.

It was a summer she would spend the rest of her life trying to forget. But for Ludovico, it accomplished what was needed: Ariosto was placated.

Chapter Four

My course is set for an uncharted sea.
—Dante Alighieri

The Balkans, Bay of Cattaro, Late February, Twelfth Month,
Venetian Year 1492 – Rade

The border was close. In his mind, Rade could see it. The forested mountains spilling down to the stony pass. The old curtain wall fort climbing up the hill. The new garrison, part *akinji*, part Ottoman, part clansmen. The stream of ice melt gushing down to the shores of Risan, nine years an Ottoman-held town. And beyond them all, the glittering mirror of an inland bay, measured in fathoms, walled in scarps, and folded into the protective mantle of Venice.

He'd lain, fireless, in the night watching the mare graze, watching that pale hide that he had earlier followed like a damned soul on the road to hell. In the shadow of the mountain, the deep woods, the overhang of the gorge, she'd glimmered like a pale moon rising. A hundred times, he'd gone over the lay of the land. The rock strewn defile. The lack of cover. The proximity to the fort. He'd pass close enough to see the features on the impaled heads. Close enough to hear the crank of the crossbow. She was too light. How could he hide her? They would shoot her first and him afterward. It took too long to go around.

It was two days later, after he'd argued himself out of folly,

forsaken luck and portents, and swallowed the bitterness of
losing his prize, that the shrill *kyeeer* of a hawk jerked him
back to reality. The gray ranks of trunks thinned and gaped
open so that the charcoal gatherers' camp spread out before
him: abandoned, ringed with detritus and centered on the great
black circle they had harvested. With mounting excitement, he
flung himself from the saddle and dug into the ashes with his
dagger. And when he found what he was looking for, he
glanced up, knowing the hawk for what it had to be.

*   *   *   *   *

Shadow filled the valley. He'd applied the charcoal. His
hands and face were black with it. Where the spring picked its
way down the slope, Rade and the horse both drank. It was
only then, kneeling on the stony dirt, that he noticed the faint
line of torches snaking toward him. He glanced up at the fort
and stifled a sharp desire to mount up and ride. The mare's
head jerked up, eyes wide, and she fought him as Rade threw
his cloak over her muzzle to stifle her neigh. She'd recognized
the horses. He knew then who their riders would be.

There were shouts as the distant party neared. A rustle of
arms on the ramparts behind him. An occasional firelit glint
defined the underside of a crossbow, a chin, a helmet. A gate
creaked open in the wall and a mounted party spurred out. The
men rode rapidly in the direction of the approaching torches as
Rade dragged his unwilling mount down the ill-defined path in
the brush.

The alarm he'd felt had passed. His pursuers were
achieving the very distraction he had been unable to fashion
for himself. The sacking he had bound around the horse's
hooves obscured her tracks and softened the crackle of
breaking brush. They were into the scrub wasteland now,
beyond the fort, off the beaten way and well below the high
trail—the one most taken.

He heard the sounds of another patrol exiting the walled

town and galloping up the sloped and stony road toward the fort. *It couldn't be more fortuitous than this.* A stand of juniper half-shielded them from the road to Risan. He held the mare as still as he was able, one hand clamped over her nostrils. As the horsemen thundered past, only the varying forms of shadows darkened an otherwise shapeless landscape.

*   *   *   *   *

"To whom dost thou belong?" The childish voice lightly penetrated the stir of evening. It was the customary clan greeting.

"To the snows on the mountain," he answered, knowing his response would identify the child and determine his future.

"God knows," said the boy, "thou art five days late."

They worked their way up to the old Roman road, or what was left of it. At the turning, the church of Santa Croce, or in Slavonic, Sveti Kris, perched like an angel above its prosperous settlement. The bay lay in the void below it—marked in daylight by a smattering of vessels.

The mare shied as a priest swinging a cresset issued forth from the cavernous interior. *"God's teeth, where hast thou been!"*

The boy hung his head. "I have done as thou asked. I waited." He looked at his companion. And moving into the protective proximity of the priest, he said, "*He* was late."

The priest trained his unblinking gaze on the horse. "Thou hast been thieving again."

Rade briefly considered this comment and decided it didn't deserve an answer. Studying the path before him, he ignored the mountain dialect and asked in the polyglot language of the town, "Have you seen..."

"None," interrupted the priest, and switching back to the dialect, "The only brigand to pass this way is thou." And he turned away. "Thou art well?" he said to the boy, peering into his face and ruffling his hair.

"I took food," nodded the boy.

"Go inside then. Warm thyself. Eat. I have hot bread and cold fish." The invitation was not extended elsewhere.

When the child left, the priest walked around the mare, held up the cresset and studied them both in the flickering light. He stood fingering his crucifix. The horseman finished retying a bundle and said without looking up. "Good choice."

"It takes a boy to know the way of goats."

Rade waited.

"Thy doublet is stained with blood."

"It isn't mine."

The priest cleared his throat and rested a hand on the weapon under his cassock. He sighed and then intoned, "Go with God, brigand." He made the sign of the cross, paused, and said, "He will forgive thee a Turk's mount." And, after another pause, in a different voice, "Hast thou a head to go with it?"

"The head is still on the man who stopped at the border."

"Pity," murmured the priest, unhanding the hilt. He held out his palm. "Five days, not one."

Rade paid, and tugging the mare forward, began his final solitary ascent.

*   *   *   *   *

The switchbacks that seemed interminable ended in a stone village accompanied by a small gloomy church, also stone. Rade crossed himself, and led on to the long, low house half-cloaked in scrub. There were no watchers in the night. A dog barked and was silenced and for a time, he stood listening, leaning tiredly against the horse.

As he loosened the harness, the bushes parted and a light materialized out of the darkness. Rade whipped the rein around his forearm and grabbed wrong-handed for his sword just as the horse threw herself sideways, knocking them both down the incline. By then, half-dragged, half-trampled, he'd realized who it was.

"I *knew* you were coming," crowed an old man. "The bones told me."

"The devil take you!" cursed Rade, struggling with the frightened animal. *"And your bones!"* Something in his voice stopped the graybeard's antics. "God's blood, Vuk, put down the cursed lantern and give me a hand!"

Vuk found a spot for the lantern and came forward to hold the bridle. Up close, he saw the young man's weariness and something else. He knew that look. He turned to the mare. "Not the same horse," he said, laying his hand on the quivering neck and stroking it. When the horse had quieted and he withdrew his hand, there was a lighter place on the hide where he'd stroked the fur. "You're too close to the fire at night, *kapetan.*"

"Or to half-wits with lanterns," grumbled Rade.

"Playing the fool has kept me alive," replied Vuk.

"Are you so blinded by the light that you cannot tell a friend?"

"I saw you reach for your steel."

Rade paused, and then resumed what he was doing.

"Speaking of sight, *kapetan*," continued the graybeard, looking at the horse, "if you had the eye for women that you have for horses..."

"Who's to say I don't."

"We've had more horses on the tether than you've had women in your bed."

Rade froze. *"Are you keeping count?"*

Vuk backed off. No point in getting skewered. "A jest," he muttered but he saw Rade grow rigid with anger. He thought fleetingly of all the other things he might have said, stole a quick glance at the controlled fury of the man and turned away, studiously surveying the pocked stones tipped in gold by the lantern. Even in the growing season, it was a poor land for beasts and a back-breaking struggle for the peasants who worked it. It only got worse higher up.

The mare leaned against him, rubbing her head on his

shoulder, nibbling the lank, gray hair at the base of his neck. Vuk scratched the bump between her ears and after, the fur under the braided wool of the bridle. She smelled overwhelmingly of crushed shrubs, warm horse, and charcoal. She'd be easy to find in the dark.

He glanced back at the stone house, its contours softening in the growing mist. In five years, Rade had never let them keep a woman in their winter quarters. Not even the oldest, dried-up cook. He'd said it would make trouble and with that crew, who knows, maybe he was right. But a woman would have worked, cooked, cleaned, dug a little garden. Tended to them. Maybe even lain with them. And it would have been a welcome change to lie beside something that didn't shed fur, bristle with beard, or leave metal in your bed. To lie with something soft and warm and willing. It'd be nice to have a whore, the old man thought. A whore made a man feel young.

Rade shouldered his belongings. His voice was tight. "Take the mare and hobble her, Vuk."

"Yes, *kapetan*," said Vuk. He started up the path. "What happened to the other one?'

"In the right light, a gray horse is a gray horse."

Vuk chortled and continued up the track, accompanied by the stolen mare and the swinging arc of the lantern. She was worth two of her predecessor.

Rade took the blacker path through the scrub. Outside the house, he paused, rearranged his bundles, drew out his sword, and kicked open the narrow door. It slammed heavily against the stone. In the low-ceilinged room, men scrambled for their weapons.

"If I were a *spahi*," growled Rade, "it would be too late."

"Vuk said it would be you," replied a sullen voice, sheathing his dagger and looking for the markers he'd dropped in his haste to arm himself.

"When, Nicola? *In the morning?*" Several men dropped their gaze. He could see he'd guessed right. "Have you checked on your oracle lately? Since when do you trust your lives to one lookout? You and you, *get out,*" he snapped, "and stand watch." Two men hurried past him.

Jovan raised a goatskin to his mouth and wiped the spill on his sleeve. "Three months gone," he said, "and you charge in like a baited bear. Bristles up. Full of piss. And black as a godforsaken Moor. *Why* do what *you* want?"

His enjoyment abruptly ended. His forearm was wrenched up behind his back, his legs were kicked out from under him, and the edge of the *kapetan's* blade bit into his neck. "I *made* you what you are."

Jovan watched the pool of wine form beneath the goatskin. It looked like blood. His arm hurt. His legs ached. His neck dripped. "Christ knows," rasped Jovan, "the moon tide rises... and the crab remembers what it forgot."

The rest had risen now, all fifteen of them, a phalanx of open resentment enshrouded in the dingy haze of the hearth, a haze so opaque as to be almost palpable. "There is no need..."

"There is *every* need. *God's blood, y*our predecessors *cooked* inside this house while the *spahis* sat outside on their horses. Do you remember *nothing*?"

Their eyes were all on him now. "We are not..."

"You are not what? Dull-wits? Sots? Laggards? *What have I left out?* If a torch doesn't crisp this nest, the Turks will spit you into the hell you deserve."

They glared back at him now. It was like facing a mob. Thief, outcast, misfit, survivor, poacher, hireling, deserter—killers all. "We aren't sheep," growled Paolo, "to be herded."

"*Then why leave yourselves open to being penned?* Use your wits! Mehmed dispatched fifty men a day when he took Albania." Rade ripped a handful of shirt from inside his doublet, let it fall like an untidy swag over his groin, and then thrust it toward them. "Is there honor in carrying your entrails home in your hands? *Is there?*"

They were eyeing each other now, measuring their chances. "You go too far," said Teodor.

"*I haven't gone far enough.*" His gaze swept over them.

"Do I dwell over long on death?" His glance caught a spare young man. "Ask Hamsa about the galleys. Would you call that living, Hamsa?"

He saw Hamsa's look turn inward.

"It all comes back to death. It's just a question of kind."

"Hamsa crossed over from Scutari," said a voice dismissively. "From the *sanjak* in Albania." The man spat.

"Look about you, Alek, and you will see the Turks have crossed over too," replied the *kapetan*. "To Risan and Novi. Their galley's in the outer bay."

"We've gotten out before."

"So we have, but this boat's larger and needs men. Do you think they don't know you're here? We're not that far from the border. Today, tomorrow, the day after, charred, skewered or shackled, you bastards are as good as dead."

"They *know* we're here? How?"

"Between your wenching, drinking, and thieving, how could they not?"

"You're full of piss, you son of an infidel!" spat Stefan. "Did you *mark* the door?"

"Who needs to, Stefan?" Rade's voice was soft. "It's already open." He felt his anger rising. His gaze raked the men. "If you choose to be fools, why wait for the fate you've invited? Take your belongings. *Go... Get out!* Either the *pasha* sharpens a stake on your arse or..." his lip curled, "*you die in bed like a woman.*"

As he'd meant it to be, the last was unforgivable. There was a general outcry. Some of the men surged forward. The hilt of his sword lay easily in his palm. His arm tensed and he felt the pain spike up into his shoulder. Between the white cheek that was honor and the dark cheek that was shame lay a quagmire that led easily to blood.

"*If you follow me,*" he continued, raising his voice against the protest, "you will also die. Am I Holy God to offer you life?" He laughed harshly. "I too offer you death." His voice took a different tone. "A death that is the blood price of a hero."

The collective hostility seemed to lessen. This was something they understood. He waited.

"*If you choose to stay*," he said, "you will follow what I have laid down." His eyes traveled over the general chaos. "Even when I'm away. Keeping watch tops the list." His gaze caught theirs. "We shared an oath on that subject."

They were silent.

"That is the contract." Rade managed to sheathe his sword without wincing and turned his back. "I'm waiting for the women to leave."

This time there was no reply. The men stood unmoving for what seemed a long time.

"Good." He turned and gave them a hard look. "Are we agreed on the contract?"

There was a murmur of assent.

"*Dobro*, because tonight," he said, with a flash of teeth, "it's late for killing and my sword arm is weary." He picked up his things and crossed the room. "Render service, my Markos, and gain, as always, a share in the ship and her cargo. Tomorrow you will make your mark in the book, and after, we will share our blood, by God and St. John, as brothers."

*   *   *   *   *

The room formed a long rectangle with a dirt floor except where part of a limestone outcrop showed through. It held a raised hearth, two rough benches, a plank table, various pallets, a vast array of weapons, the ship's five-foot wrought-iron *verso* wrapped in canvas, and at the end, a little pile of missiles. On the far side, a line of holed tying-stones protruded from the wall. Tonight, the horse had been left outside.

Vuk stopped by the fire, hoping heat would alleviate some of his aches and pains before sleep reset them anew. Wisps of gray hair stuck out of his cap and the stubble on his chin did little to disguise the unfortunate state of his teeth. He noticed the *kapetan* massaging his shoulder. He noticed the noise level had dropped. He noticed the room was unexpectedly tidy.

"Smoking the sheepskin again?" wondered a voice behind him.

By all the saints! He'd nearly caught fire! He turned away quickly, beating at the newly darkened place on the back of his shabby vest. The group behind him laughed, but did nothing to help.

"Fire's out, grandfather," said one of the onlookers helpfully. "If you keep that up, you'll tan that hide all over again."

He thought of some other hides that needed tanning—and they didn't belong to sheep.

"The wolf's back," observed another.

They meant Rade. It annoyed Vuk that when his own name meant "wolf," the epithet should go to another.

"What's he found for us?" They were restless after three months of winter. Broke, too. Something hit Vuk on his back. "Gone deaf as well as lame?"

"It's February," replied Vuk. That ought to be enough of an answer. He picked a spot a safe distance from the fire.

"The wolf's back," he muttered to himself. From them, the epithet was a term of respect, even affection. The *kapetan* was their leader; they liked to think of themselves as his pack. In some ways, the description fit. The man had all the attributes of a predator. Aloof, cautious, quietly observant, he lived by cunning. Provoked or cornered, he became a ferocious opponent. Apart from the traits of an animal, thought Vuk, their leader had a very human confidence that made others follow and that mysterious quality they admired most: an affinity for luck. Six years of booty could attest to that. Vuk turned, narrowing his eyes in the flickering gloom, and took a long slow look at their good fortune.

The "wolf" stood carelessly by the wall, his expression unreadable, seemingly alert to the myriad goings-on in the room.

"Not strung up by the roadside after all," observed Vuk, coming up beside him.

"Hemp is scarce," said Rade. "The bones should've told you that."

Even now, devoid of measurable purpose, travel-stained and undoubtedly weary, the *kapetan's* sheer physical control was striking: his body taut and agile, the tiredness suppressed. Black hair hung down below his shoulders and the short beard that he favored had been shorn for the journey though it was already growing back. Tall and straight, from afar, he could pass for a merchant, even a noble, given the proper dress, but all good things considered, it was the eyes one noticed. In a land where shepherds looked like kings and eyes of gray or brown were prevalent, his were an uncommon color—and the beauty of that color offset the other, less favorable aspects of his face.

His deep blue gaze focused on the old man. "Disappointed?"

"Why *kapetan*, I'm only asking after your journey," protested the graybeard. "You've been gone a long while."

"The trip was uneventful," replied Rade. "Except for the horse." His eyes closed. "I return unscathed. No stab wounds. No sword cuts. No pox."

"You tempt the devil," muttered the old man. He crossed himself, noting the bruise beneath the *kapetan's* hair and the raw marks encircling his neck. Even the black on his hands wasn't all charcoal.

Rade brushed some crumbs from his doublet and loosened his laces at the points. "Nor have I converted to Islam," he added, looking sideways at Vuk.

"*Islam!*" echoed the graybeard. "I'd sooner expect a corpse! And God knows where we'd find your head!"

Rade grinned. "I'm pleased to hear you'd take the trouble."

Vuk made a face. "That's right. Why should I? Trouble follows you about like a dog. Because of you, I've already had more than my share." He scratched vigorously and then squinting, examined his fingernails for lice. "What did you find in Zadar?"

"It's Zara. It's been Zara for a long time. Venice is here to stay."

"Not for the Slav," muttered the graybeard, and spat.

The *kapetan* ignored him. "The delights of Zara are the same as last year." He leaned against the stone wall and closed his eyes. "The Venetians are still erecting monu…ments." His voice slurred with fatigue. He roused himself. "The same girl is serving in the tavern." He frowned. "Looks a little the worse for wear."

"Remembered you, did she?"

"Not at first," he answered. "She did," he lied, "later... but it was you she asked about."

"She would," nodded Vuk, pleased. "I paid in silver for her favors. Remember? Couldn't see the coin in the dark." He'd told her fortune too. And left out the bad part. He shrugged. "What else?"

"Not much else." The blue eyes narrowed. "Thanks to Venice, there isn't any salt for fish. But the Turk is still outside the walls. Four, five days ride. And the old round church," he yawned, "is bursting with arms."

The old man perked up. "That's what I'd like. A sword honed by St. Donatus."

Rade yawned again. "I'll leave the taking of it up to you."

*   *   *   *   *

Thinking back on it, Rade had wondered how this solitary journey would turn out. He rarely carried gold, only vouchers, but the immediacy of coin had become important. Vuk had been ill when he took the first gray horse and caught the last of the November boats leaving Cattaro. The boat had stopped a day's journey from the caravanserai in which the goods were stored, the remainder of their latest haul. His agent in Zara had found him a buyer. Had it been any other trip, he would have taken Vuk and a couple of men, hired mounts, and on their return, rejoined the ship. However, the last trip of the season meant his own ship had been pulled, his men were in the stone house near the bay, and the way home was through the mountains in winter. He had thought, after the packed quarters on the ship, and the dissension this year's voyages had bred, he'd best go alone.

From Zara's walls, his return journey had reversed the earlier one, progressing back along the coast through orchards of dead and dormant trees, decimated by two years of severe cold, and along low ridges of cultivated land farmed by ragged peasants—all bounded to the east by the great bare backbone of the mountains. Here and there he found vestiges of the Roman road. Winter had lulled the border lands into a semblance of peace and he had from time to time, though solitary by nature, suffered the company of guides and other travelers he'd met in taverns along the way. But the land to the south, riddled with discontent, had been too unsettled to risk crossing by himself and recently, the Bosnian frontier had spat out Ottoman raiding parties—like an angry hive disgorges bees.

Before the border, he'd abandoned the caravan route, turned east, and disappeared into a high barren country where winter gusts scoured the upland pastures, and where, in the middle of nowhere, strange, graven memorials stood witness to forgotten warriors. Carved in crude relief, men, animals, and symbols rose from the lichen-covered stones. Adorned with colonnades and pitched roofs, some resembled houses. And the houses had multiplied themselves into towns.

"The old ones," had muttered the shepherd boy he'd hired. "Who even knows who they were."

"They were men," had said Rade, surveying the necropolis. "Like us." He'd crossed himself.

"Not anymore."

That night, for want of shelter, he'd slept beside such a stone. The words inscribed on it were in the old church lettering of St. Cyril, that he could barely read: something about beseeching and letting bones rest. In the flickering light of the fire, the deceased, carved standing with upraised arms, wore the high boots of a nobleman. Incised lines banded his clothes. A bow, arrows and what looked like a sun floated above his shoulders. At dawn, Rade gently traced the rimed outlines of the letters with his fingers until daylight illumined the thin layer of wind-blown snow. He saw then that the grave had been desecrated. The bones of the deceased lay strewn about him like pale, dry sticks in a storm. He hadn't slept near the grave, *God's blood, he'd slept in it.* Despite himself, his body had turned to ice.

"You call down the lightning when you touch the stones," had warned the boy.

He'd tried to lighten his tone. "And I was worried about ghosts."

The boy had laughed—and tossed some bones into a ditch. "Them that get struck are ghosts soon enough."

The last leg of the journey, through Ottoman lands, was a stew of the dispossessed. Protection lay in native guides, goat tracks, the company of mountain folk on their way to market and the guarded caravans of merchants. But Rade also valued anonymity. Long ago, he'd learned to bluff, move quickly, or blend in, just to survive.

Five times, he'd made the annual journey but this year had been different. The man who'd kept his accounts was emigrating and he'd needed to retrieve his wealth, resettle it with another, or send it on with the moneylender—on whose services he'd long depended. In the end, he'd chosen the last.

He could still see the man's sharp, intelligent features above the required badge of his religion. He'd delivered the usual sacks of valuables, and as they'd discussed the future and signed the papers, the man others saw as a usurer had blessed the transaction with a bowl of *raki*, a clap on his arm, and their private toast about dogs, which truly meant "honor among thieves"—and both had laughed easily at something that outside the room was no laughing matter. Finally, he'd gathered up his bundles and flung his cloak over his shoulders.

"Go in peace, *haiduk*," his friend had said with a grin. "But not too much peace, it isn't profitable."

Rade had turned, the gray wool draped carelessly over broad shoulders, and smiled wolfishly, "If I die, Mordecai, you'll be rich."

"True," had nodded the moneylender. "But try to live a little longer." A wider grin had crossed his face. "God knows, the Grand Canal is an opportune place for business."

"In Venice," Rade had warned, "even the walls have ears. Don't call me an outlaw again. In any language. I'll hang... and so will you." And he had left.

*   *   *   *   *

Rade shifted his weight and stretched a little. It was ironic, and decidedly satisfactory, that his gold would soon be banked in the strongest city on the Adriatic—under the very noses of some former owners.

"Keeping all the good news to yourself?" asked the graybeard, noting the half-smile.

"The dice were lucky, Vuk," mused the *kapetan*, his thoughts moving on to the game.

Vuk, who knew about the moneylender, gave him a knowing glance. "All this success, and no one to spend it on," observed Vuk. "Not even yourself."

It was mostly true. The stone house was leased, the boat divided into shares, and the way Rade lived had left him little need for possessions: only the occasional article of clothing or replacement weapon. Besides, while goods that were acquired were immediately disposed of, possessions by their very nature needed care—when there was little care to offer. Yet he kept them in his mind as part of some vague plan for the future. A future that occasionally threw off a distinct reminder that it might in fact exist. On the last night in Zara, he *had* won at

dice and amongst the pile of coins, pale as flesh in the
guttering candlelight, had been the unexpected imprint of the
hand of fate. It was nothing more than two folded sheets of
paper.

Once before, the future had suddenly taken on a shape, a
destination, and a meaning. Rade had acted on it then, only a
child, trapped in the vise of another man's hatred. And it had
proved to be salvation. He had experienced the same heady but
ominous sensation of the gathering storm, of dark foreboding,
of fate weighing him down until his own sense of self had
become infinitesimally small and powerless, like the tiny sail
of a leaf borne aloft by the wind. Caught in the vortex, the boy
had been terrified, even ill, but when he'd recovered, his
perception of destiny had remained so powerful that he'd
turned his back on everything he knew, and the one person he
loved, and had fled.

Long after the game in Zara, surrounded by snoring
drunks and spilled wine, he'd retrieved the papers from his
sleeve and read the small, benign, carefully formed words of
the letter. And felt the paper grow warm in his hand, the
sentences blur away into the dark recesses of the tavern, and
for the second time, the whirlwind came upon him. He'd put
his head down on the scarred table, powerless against fate, or
maybe it was God, and waited for the awful strength of it to
lessen—and for his fear of it to fade away.

*   *   *   *   *

Abruptly, Rade levered himself off the stone. "In the
morning, take the mare down to the bay. Wash her down.
Pasture her and let her rest. The day after, put her on the ferry
for Cattaro. Drive me a good bargain in the market. Use the
money you get for provisions."

Vuk looked puzzled. "We have stores enough, for now."

Rade ignored him. "Buy a new ship's water barrel: the old
one leaks. And bring back the men we're missing." He paused.

"You do know where they are."

The old man inclined his head. "I know where to look for them."

"Tell Miloš I need him. In six days, we're going out the Catene."

"What!" exclaimed Vuk, taken by surprise. "In the middle of winter? In the teeth of the *bora*? *Why*?"

"Ask the bones," muttered Rade, turning his back. He thought briefly about going outside to sleep, for after the mountain air, the smoky room was suffocating. But a leaden weariness dragged at his strength, and there was safety in the soot. Ignoring Vuk, he staggered to his customary place by the wall, kicked aside the litter of old pits and gnawed animal remains, and rolled himself in his cloak. Before the last shreds of consciousness departed, he heard the rain begin and felt a sudden draft as Vuk slipped out to fetch the mare.

Chapter Five

You shall leave everything you love.
—Dante Alighieri

Venice, late September into Winter, Seventh Month to Tenth
Month, Venetian Year 1492 – Caterina

The wooden tub had been emptied. The rose petals
scraped from the bottom. Her body had been dried with a cloth
by Sofia, her maid. Caterina braced herself in the small
wooden chair, still wrapped in the cloth, as her long hair was
combed out by the fire and the moisture teased from its
thickness.

"Be a little kinder, Sofia. I *like* having hair. After all, it's a
woman's crowning glory."

"Such a tangle, madonna! I get it out." Sofia dug at it with
a comb.

"*Sofia!* I'll be bald."

"Too much hair anyway. Who needs that much hair?"

"It's not... *ouch.*"

"There, it's out. You'll never miss it."

"I'd like the casket, Sofia. *Now.*"

Caterina opened the proffered casket and extracted the
small pale object from the other toiletries. She held it between
her palms. It was of old manufacture, the exterior carved, the
interior of smooth polished metal. The cover had the
smoothness that old things have when many hands have

touched them. She opened it, her mother's mirror, the round one with the ivory knights attacking the Castle of Love.

Sofia was singing some country tune and combing with less bravado. She saw her hair looked as it always did.

"Nothing. You see nothing. I told you so." The voice was petulant.

You could join the inquisitors at the doge's palace. They'd pay to have you.

She turned the mirror over and over in her hands. Opened it. Shut it. Opened it. Although the carving was meant to be light-hearted, it seemed to contain the dark trajectory of her whole life. The rigidity by which her future would be defined. The prison that her impending submission was destined to bring. Gradually the pleasure of the bath drained out of her. The face that looked back from the mirror took on the solemn gaze of a martyr. Closing the cover, Caterina ran her fingertips over the defending troop of ladies who, unyielding, pelted their aggressors with a vigorous rain of roses. She closed her eyes. No rose for this defender. No castle either. Only the longing for an impenetrable hedge of thorn.

*   *   *   *   *

"Tommaso, is that you?"

It'd been four years since her younger tutor had left. She was surprised to find him, head down, immersed in a book in the *studiolo*.

"It is." He unfolded his long thin frame from the chair and stood up. "Madonna," he inclined his head, and grinned, "once, my little Cat." He gestured toward the open book, "Research for my new patron, courtesy of your father's library."

Even smiling, even looking at her, there was an indifference about him, always had been, as if no gender, no sex, attracted him, only that all-consuming love for the mind. It had always been there. Grown, she was more aware of it than ever. She supposed that was the reason Nonna and Papa let her be alone with him—a privilege extended to no other man.

"No more little girls to annoy you." She smiled.

"No, life has gotten far less frightening." He looked long at her face. "You have a new gravitas. It becomes you, madonna."

"Call me Cat. I always liked that. I'm just older." She made a face. "Are you now a full-blown humanist?"

"I suppose you could say that. I've even been to Florence and have, metaphorically at least, sat at Pico's feet. Before Lorenzo the Magnificent died. Such a mind! Versed in Greek, Latin, even Hebrew and Arabic. Such an oration! The Church will never let him publish it a second time."

"It's heretical. They burned it. Every book." She looked shocked.

"No, Cat, it's splendid! Absolutely masterful. A few books survived. Even your father embraces some of his ideas."

"I think I'm not supposed to know that."

Tommaso sighed. "You know the ideas without the author. I heard them myself when I was here. 'As though the maker and molder of thyself... '"

Her eyes widened. "The way up for those not born to it."

"Or down. Yes. Now they'll throw *you* on the fire too."

She squared her shoulders. "Let them try. I'm surrounded by water."

"The magic of Venice." He looked down at the book, he'd been studying, "I should get back to work."

"I'll look for you," Caterina said. She added, "Don't wait until the spice ships come again from the Black Sea."

"If it takes a year, my patron will abandon me." His nose was in the book. "Back soon."

She briefly laid a hand on his shoulder. Felt the bone beneath the cloth. "You should eat more Tommaso. I'll send Sofia up with food."

*   *   *   *   *

The *cassone*, that had been two years in the making, was delivered on a singular day in mid- October.

"Nonna! How *could* he! *Griselda!"* Caterina cried. The chest, having been approved by her father, had been laboriously transported upstairs. They arrived when the artisan's helpers were galloping down the steps discussing the brief and undoubtedly liquid future of the silver *piccoli* stowed in their purses. Caterina stood, hands on hips, staring at the chest indignantly. "Why not Helen of Troy? Or Camilla fighting Aeneas?"

"Griselda was a model bride," observed Nonna, "patient and obedient. *And,"* she added meaningfully, "she stayed out of trouble."

"Griselda gave up *everything,* like a *slave,* to that brute of a husband. She accepted every ill deed he imposed on her. Let herself be publicly humiliated. Gave up her children to be murdered. Meekly let him dismiss her, without cause, and replace her with a new wife. All so that *monster* could *allow* her to return, having passed all his cruel trials, and resume her place as his wife. Griselda was a *worm!"* Caterina declared, folding her arms.

"Worm or not," replied Nonna, who privately agreed, "the painter said she's this year's most popular subject."

Caterina, abandoning disapproval as useless, bent over the slightly domed lid, fiddling with the key. "It's enormous," she said, eyeing the length of the chest. "I could sleep in it."

"We could always make another set of hangings," Nonna said brightly, and was skewered by return glance. "Not that we've finished the first."

Caterina struggled with the weighty top. "Oh!" she said, straightening up as her face took on a deepening shade of pink. *"Holy Mother!"* She bit her lip, staring. There was, unexpectedly, a well-delineated, nearly naked, reclining male on the underside—in the scantiest of small clothes.

"I wonder if your father ever opened it," said Nonna dryly, taking in the full-length portrait. "Not his normal sort of commission." She moved closer to get a better look. "Not much left to the imagination either."

"Father's bronzes don't have *any* small clothes." She was still pink.

"They're the height of your hand," replied Nonna. "Their sex is somewhat less imposing." She shrugged it off. "You've seen enough Entombments and pierced San Sebastiens to be used to this sort of thing."

"In church, in the dark, attired in the modesty of faith and mysticism. Not a nearly naked man in my bedchamber."

It was true that the bedchamber was reserved as the private realm of women and because of it, remained somewhat sacrosanct. "You have a point."

"It doesn't matter," Caterina said, swallowing, eyes wide. "He is... um... most educational." Her face lit up. "Simonetta and Ginevra will be quite diverted!"

"Educational or not," said Nonna, "if you wish to keep the *cassone*, your father had best remain on the side of ignorance." She handed Caterina the key. "We'll close it up now. Let Mars, or whoever it is—perhaps the painter," their eyes met and their grins broadened, "rest in peace."

Caterina slowly lowered the lid. They stood, considering their secret, and began to giggle. The giggles developed into shouts of laughter.

"When your friends come," gasped Nonna, almost as an afterthought, "warn me. I'll," her voice ended in a croak, "endeavor," croak, "to be somewhere else."

*   *   *   *   *

They were sitting in the *studiolo*. Tommaso was finished for the day and they were reminiscing about his first days as tutor.

"Do you remember the *Knight of the Cart*?" asked Caterina. "That first summer? When we went to the villa and I *wouldn't* get into the villa's cart?"

"I remember the driver kept lifting you in, the shouting kept getting louder, and you got out every time. It was impossible to read my book."

"*You* told me if a person of station rode in one, a cart, it was demeaning. Punishment would follow. A flaming lance would fall out of the ceiling and the bed would catch fire. I remember *walking* from the boat until Papa took me up in front on his saddle."

"The tale was about the knight," maintained Tommaso, amused, "not you. Poor old Lancelot, he only wanted to save his queen by arriving more quickly."

"Riding with felons? She was quite put out. She nearly killed him with that bed."

"He did hesitate," Tommaso defended his hero. "You have to credit him that. What man proceeds in haste walking in a suit of armor?" His expression turned serious. "Truly, Cat, I had no idea you'd take it literally. I can assure you, your father had words to say about it. After that Nonna stood over me with an assassin's glare. Made sure I 'clothed' every scene as well. I was quite relieved to return to the Classics."

"She thought your tales more unsuitable than Boccaccio."

"We didn't read those either. I didn't dare."

There was a faint rustling noise above them. She looked up. Pointed. "Our visitor. He hasn't found his way out yet." She carefully untied a knot in her handkerchief and spread out some seeds for the bird who'd found refuge in the house. The bird fluttered about not trusting the presence of Tommaso.

"I've told Cook he's not to be trapped. That he's dear to me."

"She'll be hiding," he said, smiling. "Waiting for the rest of the flock."

The vision of it brought a laugh. "You know her all too well!"

"It's good to see you laugh, Cat. You don't laugh enough."

"Barbaro doesn't like women who laugh. Remember?"

"Not laugh excessively. That's different. God's teeth, he was a living corset, was he not?"

"I think I could recite the whole work from memory."

"Find something more worthy. Be 'soft wax' for something else." He saw a shadow pass over her face. "I meant for something literary." But it was too late.

Caterina took a deep breath. "When you're famous and teaching at Padua, will you write me refined letters I can share with my learned friends? If I have any learned friends."

"Only if you write them back. I'll place you on a pedestal in the florid dedication to some obscure Greek translation so you'll be remembered as the only part of the work that made any sense."

"Do stop. I can't keep a straight face."

"You must. No truly you *must*." Tommaso signaled for silence. He whispered, "We've just been accepted into the kingdom of small creatures oared with wings. See. He's there. On the table by your right shoulder. Picking at millet." For a moment, he looked almost otherworldly. "As delicate as the human soul."

He had a cough. She noticed it when he left.

*   *   *   *   *

The marriage day kept drawing closer.

Outside, a brisk wind stole the heat from the sun but for a few hours within, she watched cast shadows progress across the room and furnishings. The resulting sunlit rectangles topped in Gothic arches were warm and traced in circles. It was mid-afternoon. Bathed in light, they were perched on stools around a large embroidery frame: Nonna, a solid triangle of black, and Caterina, in tied sleeves and worsted. The panel of heavy silk occupied their attention. Scissors and skeins of metallic thread dangled from the edges. Occasionally, they would sheathe their needles and supporting the heavy overflow of cloth, reposition the frame, following the light.

While the wood made a heavy scraping sound on the terrazzo floor, they spoke no more than necessary.

Nonna sighed. "I sense an air of reluctant industry."

"You've recast me as Aesop's ant. No other choice was offered."

When the Marangona tolled the end of work and the call to evening prayer, they were still at it. Sunset stained the window panes with hues of orange, red, and gold, the glorious evensong of October. The fiery sky died to lead, soon to be obsidian, and the streets rang with passing shouts, arguments, and laughter.

Caterina rose stiffly and went to stand at the window. She could still see. There were no torches or lanterns yet. The gray clusters of men streamed along the canal toward the wooden footbridge, intent on going home, and the *arsenalotti* stood out from the others with their little sacks of shavings and sawdust slung over their shoulders, their bright teeth in pitch-blackened faces, their shipyard tools. Feet pounded over narrow planks, sound alternately swelled and dwindled, until, like the last faint glow of sunset, they too faded into darkness.

By contrast, as she regained her seat, the huge room beyond the circle of candles lay cool and thickly somnolent. Yet Nonna rose like a cicada to its evening dirge, ticking off the all-too-familiar concerns: the upcoming marriage, ser Ariosto's movements, the bed hangings that needed to be finished, tasks that needed to be done, her father's wishes, her betrothed's commands—sprinkling the whole with fragments of what was going on outside the house and outside their parish.

Caterina digested the last and tried to make light of the rest, but in her soul, the stamping, disjointed chorus of male humanity still swung down the *fondamenta*, free at last, its noisy passage reverberating off of stone and water: vulgar, irreverent, ribald—manifestly virile and alive. So unlike the gray and aged spider slated for her future.

She got up abruptly, flung back the mass of golden hair,

interrupting the monologue, and retreated into the cavernous gloom beyond the candles. "I've had enough." Her voice was low, almost trembling.

Nonna, halted like a horse at the crossroads, looked down at the panel, lips pursed. "Enough of what?"

"Enough of Ariosto's speech in the Senate. Enough of the current crisis in the Spinner's Guild. Enough of the ill effects of smuggling on the price of raw silk. Whatever did we talk about before Father's reeducation scheme for unwilling brides replaced the *ars liberales*? Surely you don't imagine I enjoy this."

"Actually, I thought you might," returned Nonna grimly. "You've a marriage to support and a mind that likes engagement. What better direction than your husband-to-be and the subjects in which he takes an interest?"

Caterina's face was a dim oval in the darkness until she turned away. "Yesterday," she said, ignoring Nonna, "Giovanni met a prophet in the marketplace. You know the sort: ragged clothes, waist-length beard, exuding vermin and waving pamphlets. Common as squalls and twice as noisy." She moved slightly toward the light and paused. "He predicted the world's end." Her head turned and her gaze fell on her nurse.

Nonna snorted.

Caterina went on in the same matter-of-fact way. "According to Giovanni, on the Ides of March of the new century, three planets—he'd forgotten which—will lie in portentous conjunction. There was a diagram in the pamphlet. In Venice, the skies will rain fire. The waters of the Middle Sea will rise. The city will sink." She shrugged. The candlelight traveled over the muted contours of her breastbone and shoulders and struck fire from the metal fastenings of her dress. She added with a shade of animation, "Since he doesn't swim, Giovanni was understandably upset."

"Rubbish. He doesn't read either."

"That's what I said. And also, if I were you, I'd avoid sleeping on tombs this November."

"That was clever of you. Eight years of worry reduced to naught. I'm sure he'll see the humor of it by December—when he's stopped lighting candles and buying charms." Nonna set her lips in a thin line of disapproval, then took up her needle, and measured out some thread. "We *were* speaking of ser Ariosto."

"But so was I," said Caterina. She turned her face away and folded her arms tightly over her ribs. "*'Quonium modicum et iam videbitis me et iterum modicum et non videbitis me, quia vado ad patrem /* A little while, and ye shall not see me: and again, a little while, and ye shall see me, because I go to the Father.'"

Nonna laid her hands in her lap and studied the girl's drawn profile in the candlelight. It was as if the light-hearted child she used to know had ceased to exist. A host of past conversations passed through her mind. She said, "Surely, it's not as bad as that," and smiled reassuringly. "Brides have misgivings. It's nothing new. The frivolous notions of childhood aren't easy to discard."

Caterina turned and the light fell on eyes glittering with tears. "Is it so childish to want happiness?"

"It is if it conflicts with duty." Nonna held up her hand, "No, let me finish, for you'll find, if you exercise a little self-discipline, the two go hand-in-hand."

"You make it sound like a bench on a galley. Profit and Venice should one reach port. Just row."

"If you cannot sublimate your personal wants to the good of the society and the city which Petrarch found '*ringed with salt waters but more secure with the salt of good counsel,*' then you must look inside yourself for the cause. Better women than we have made peace with adversity—or perhaps it was their *perception* of adversity—and lived long and exemplary lives."

"I'm not marrying the city."

"In a way, you *are* marrying the city. You are following convention. You are part of a distinguished tradition of alliance, transfer of wealth, and management of patrimony—the building blocks of a merchant society. Assuredly that is your role as the daughter of a wealthy man."

"I'd rather be destitute."

"*No one* would rather be destitute," Nonna said sharply. "Look at the poor souls sleeping by the bridges. Their rags. Their odor. Their filth. Go out on the next frigid winter morning and count the bodies. You've seen the barge with the dead. *No one* would rather be destitute." She let her anger show. "Caterina, those are foolish remarks and unworthy of your station. *You*, of all people, are in a position to provide charity."

Caterina went back to the window and leaned her cheek against the glass. Against the hot tracks of her tears, the pane was as cold as ice.

Nonna got up and moved a candle marginally closer to view their work. "The hangings will be exceedingly fine when we've finished," she said admiringly, changing her tune, and examining her embroidery. She walked around to study Caterina's progress. Her mouth tightened. "Penelope may have avoided marriage by unraveling by night what she'd woven by day but that ruse isn't going to work for you."

"I haven't unraveled anything."

"You haven't woven either and if you don't exercise a little more industry, you'll be in the bed without the hangings."

"I'd rather not be in the bed at all."

Nonna ignored her, and murmuring to herself, ran her hand reverently over the material. "Parangon sold and marked by the Soprastini. Look at the telltale thread. The finest grade silk. Dyed the purest kermes red." She looked up. "It isn't every bride who can boast of such quality. Not even the noblest ones."

"It's comforting to know we measure prosperity on the secretions of worms and the essence of crushed beetles." Caterina turned an expressionless face to her nurse. "Is it practice for the shroud?" She retook her seat.

"Pshaw," spat Nonna. "Shroud indeed! What's wrong with worms and beetles? They drive our greatness. What would Venice be without her looms and dye vats? Why can't you take pleasure in the cloth? It's beautiful. Fortune smiles on you. What bride would not rejoice? Between your father's imports and your betrothed's connections, you'll never lack for finery!"

Caterina put her palms to the small of her back, arched her body like a cat, and with the bleary, heavy-lidded gaze of a child, offered Nonna a tired smile. "The bed frame and I shall be rivals." She stifled a yawn. "Cry Marco."

"Rather, my dormouse," Nonna's face softened and her voice grew warm, "*Who is she coming, whom all gaze upon / Who makes the air all tremulous with light ...*"

"*'And at whose side is Love itself?'*" It was an old snippet, and not truly about silk, but for a few moments it conjured up a forgotten image of beauty and romantic love. Caterina's lips parted in an affectionate smile, remembering the lines of the sonnet, dreaming—until reality, like acid, overran it and the image bubbled acrimoniously away.

Fatigue returned with a vengeance, and she teetered unseeing on her stool until the older woman said something about sewing, late supper and her father being out tonight and touched her lightly on the arm. Bowing her head to her work, Caterina picked at the half-embroidered curl of acanthus shading its drowsy *putto* until a familiar lump rose up in her throat. The design began to swim and waver, dissolving into pools of color and burnished streaks of flame. The well of misery swelled and tears brimmed against her lashes. Tugging a crumpled handkerchief from her sleeve, she reached up furtively to stem the tide and having sniffed as inaudibly as possible, closed her fist over the wadded linen.

The second sniff was louder than she'd intended.

"Melancholia?" murmured Nonna, intent on a multicolored tendril. She compressed her mouth. *"Again?"* She didn't look up.

"The moon's first quarter..." She met a hard stare from the

other side of the frame. Her voice trailed away.

"It's been 'the moon's first quarter' every other day since you turned fourteen. Eleven months of it by my count. More in moons." Nonna looked exceptionally bug-eyed, a judgmental mantis. "If that were true, you'd be as bloodless as a turnip. And you're *not*."

Abandoning the dismal future for the argumentative present, Caterina thought mulishly *I'd give my arm to be a turnip* and nearly said so. She turned the smooth white back of her sewing hand into the anonymity of shadow. All that rosewater, white soap, and gloves—to what avail? The paleness needed to be inside not out. Inside the very womb that held the female soil. Bleaching out her blood like stained clothing lightened in a lye pit or lengths of linen brightened in a field. Eliminating menses, and by association, fertility and the possibility of offspring. The contract would be null and void. Ariosto would reject her. She'd be rid of him at last.

*   *   *   *   *

Oh God, Ariosto.

She'd seen him last five years before on her release from Fina's cell, a day of such prolonged anxiety that each and every detail lay etched upon her soul. She laid the needle aside and turned her eyes to the cold, impersonal panes of the window. Nonna's drone began again but Caterina no longer heard it. She closed her eyes. She could still see the mid-September light streaming in through the top of the small embrasure. Still hear the double knock on the door that meant "prepare yourself." Still remember the small things that seemed so huge at the time. The comb breaking off five teeth on a tangle. The scratchy weave of her shift on the first tender budding of one breast. The anxious prayers she'd whispered to the Virgin. The growing sound of footsteps tapping out their owner's weight and variety of shoe. The fears that welled up one after another and caught like burrs in her throat. The increasing murmuring outside her cell. The dry mouth that required another cup of water. And another. And another. And always the stark, growing light, heightened by the blank walls of her room, cruelly illuminating her small spare body, her blackest thoughts, her penetrating inner panic.

The Miserere had been chanted as the door came unlocked and the bolts were thrown open. *"Have mercy upon me, O God... for I acknowledge my transgressions: and my sin is ever before me."* The customary recitation for boiling an egg. Or torturing a felon. She'd emerged with the light behind her, her body trembling, to offer ser Ariosto the final apology to end the punishment. The semicircle of dark bodies in the hall had parted to allow the spider to pass through and stand opposite but at the moment of atonement, a courier arrived, and her father had been called downstairs. Thus the burden of judgment had passed from her father who loved her to her suitor who did not.

She'd been so terrified of rejection, of being forced back into the cell, that she had literally thrown herself, weeping, at Ariosto's feet. Yet despite abject prostration and a long-rehearsed and suitably remorseful speech, the nobleman had lingered, eyes downcast, hands clasped in prayerful silence. He'd drawn out the exquisite agony of the apology for far longer than anyone expected. Long enough that her speech had disintegrated into total groveling submission. Long enough that she had soiled herself and been obliged to lie in a spreading pool of urine. Long enough that the silent gathering of priests and household members had been ashamed.

Finally, Ariosto had, reaching down, raised her to her feet, tendered formal forgiveness and couched it in piety. Initially his voice had been cool and subdued until his breathing quickened and a roughness overlaid it. At the last, she'd raised her gaze and seen the flared nostrils, the hint of pleasure in his mouth, and as she'd quickly dropped her eyes, she'd known from some primordial instinct that the monster had not only found pleasure in humiliating her, but had, in an unnatural way, been aroused by it. Shaken, she'd barely attained enough composure to kiss his sleeve. Soon after, Ludovico had reappeared, Ariosto had taken his leave, and she'd been allowed to go with Nonna to her chamber.

She'd never mentioned what she'd seen. To oppose Ariosto at that time, in whatever attitude he chose to assume, could only expose her to more criticism, more humiliation, more correction. She'd lacked the strength to endure another hour in Fina's cell.

*   *   *   *   *

The exact date of the ceremony hung suspended in argument as there had been some new negotiations on the size of the dowry, which had displeased her father, and ser Ariosto still had business to conclude for the doge. Despite the delay, the marriage was as inevitable as Christmas and close to it in date.

Caterina's feast day had come and gone, and with it, the final week of November. At Mass, the great painting of her saint, normally quiescent in the dark dedicatory chapel, emerged triumphantly before the reverent, flickering tongues of a host of attendant candles. Grasping in one hand the wheel on which her body would be broken and in the other the palm of martyrdom, St. Catherine gazed lovingly upon the roseate Child enthroned in his mother's lap. Her namesake, numb with horror at the dreaded birthday, grew certain that the hidden spokes behind the saint's drapery numbered an apocalyptic fifteen.

At the noble house, the last bed hanging had been finished, the silk tenderly folded by her nurse and laid to rest in a marriage chest. Arm's length upon arm's length of embroidered foliage and silken cupids were now confined within the painted boards of the virtuous tale of Griselda.

*   *   *   *   *

The next time Tommaso came, the cough was more evident.

When she heard he had come, having looked forward to his visit, she went up to see him. Standing there, he was thinner than ever and his face was very white. Even his eyes looked bruised. "You don't look well." It slipped out before the greeting.

"That's what your father said as he was leaving. I assured him it wasn't anything serious."

"Have you been to the apothecary?"

"It's not plague," he said between coughing fits.

"Don't even jest about that."

"Or pox."

"I'm not amused. Sit down. I'll get you a warm cloak and Giovanni can bring the brazier."

"Don't bring the brazier. It's a library."

"It's the coldest room in the house."

"No brazier," he said, digging out a soiled handkerchief. "Your father would crucify me."

"Then something hot. Herbal. With lemon. I'll bring it." She went down to the kitchen. When she came back, Sofia had wrapped him in a cloak and he had a book propped up before him. The paper on which he'd written notes had blotches on it.

"Drink it."

"I've got to finish this." But he took a sip. And another.

"Can you really see that book? It's so far away."

"I don't want to spit on it." His voice was breathless as if another paroxysm was coming. He snatched the handkerchief from his sleeve and pressed it against his mouth.

"Oh Tommaso... you aren't taking care of yourself."

"I am. It's just catarrh, Cat. Now go. You don't want to catch it."

But when she came back, with a new infusion, he had left. The handkerchief remained, a rolled up ball under the table. When she picked it up, to take it down to be laundered, the spots of blood, some of them large, stood out on the cloth.

*   *   *   *   *

The rain fell in sheets. Even though a fire licked the faggots under the heavy stone hood of the chimney-piece, the room retained that dank, late season smell and the edges of the floor sprouted those dreadful walking combs, the millipedes. Ludovico was out. There would be only two at dinner. The table stood stark and white and far too large under its cloth and they sat at one corner as close to the warmth as they were able. The tallow candles flamed and smoked. They were dressed much as they had been eight weeks before at the frame: Nonna in black, Caterina in wool, only the latter's plaited hair and ribboned sleeves were different. Sofia brought the serving plate.

Nonna absentmindedly helped herself to the platter and then peered closely at her helping. "They *look* like sardines," she said in an accusing tone.

"They can't be. The barrel is empty. Cook said so."

"Oh yes, madonna," piped up Sofia happily, holding out the plate, "it is, but I'm pleased to tell you," she beamed, "we thought there were two—and we find the other."

"*Another*? From the same boat?" asked Caterina querulously. "From October?"

"Yes, madonna. The little fish keep very well. It is very good salt. Cook soaked and soaked. She said many things about the salt," she made a dismissive gesture, "so I *know* it must be so."

"I can imagine," said Nonna dryly.

The "blue fish," as they were described in household inventory, lay neatly arranged like banks of oars on a galley. Netted off Sicily, they'd been gutted fresh-caught and salted in Trapani. From there, packed in barrels, they'd traveled swiftly, the ships, sirocco-borne, standing well off the lee shore on their northward run to Venice, and at the last, flying into the *bacino* only days before the cod fleet.

"I don't suppose," Caterina said hopefully, "that the

second barrel is about to spoil."

"Messer Ludovico's barrel? That he entrusted to *me*? *Never!*" cried Sofia, reddening.

"I thought not."

"And there'll be enough for every fast between now and Ascension Day," asserted Nonna wickedly.

Sofia nodded vigorously.

"You may go now, Sofia." Caterina waited until the maid's pattens echoed down the stairs and then pushed her plate away. She looked pale. "I haven't any appetite. I'm going to bed." Outside, the wind rose and the rain drummed against the window panes. She began to get to her feet.

"Eat something," urged Nonna, noticing the slackness in her waist and bodice. She reached out and caught her arm, pressing the girl to sit. "Keep me company. At least take some bread." As of late, she'd observed that the child, slender at best, had begun to waste away. Her bones were closer to the surface and the hollows in her flesh were deeper, bluer. She was practically translucent. "If your father were here... " Cook always grew more imaginative in his presence.

"*Who* thought sardines were such a bargain?" interrupted Caterina unhappily. "And *who* goes out to sup with friends? *We're* left home to dine on them. There must be thousands of them. I think every sardine off the Sicilian coast has found its way to our storeroom! They'll last *forever!*"

"Not forever," countered Nonna, "after all, we've a marriage feast in the offing." Immediately she realized her mistake.

Caterina abruptly stood up.

"Sit down," Nonna said mildly. "We haven't said grace."

Caterina ignored her, moved toward the door. "I'll be widowed before I'm made a wife! That's what Simonetta says!"

"*Simonetta!*" barked Nonna, abandoning the peace effort. "It is *you* who will marry. Your friend Simonetta has *nothing* to do with it."

"Her brother dabbles in astrology. She asked him to plot my signs." And Caterina left.

"To Simonetta," growled Nonna at her back, "a sign is something that hangs outside a shop." A moment later, a millipede made the misguided decision to approach her bench. She stamped on it, not once but several times, the only agreeable occurrence of the evening.

Chapter Six

Men are themselves the source of their own fortune and misfortune.
—Leon Battista Alberti

The Bay of Cattaro, Late February, Twelfth Month, Venetian Year 1492 – Rade

The day dawned, celebrated in birdsong and blanketed with mist. Within the soft but chill layer of cloud, Rade squatted half-naked at the water's edge and splashed the numbness of sleep from his face and upper torso. The self-inflicted cut on his hand stung and the blood of shared brotherhood was still ingrained in the creases of his skin and under his fingernails. Some of the sea water trickled down into his mouth, dilute with runoff from winter rain and melting snow. Because of this runoff, the surface water was colder than what lay beneath. Shivering a little, he dried himself with his shirt, and, having re-buckled the harness for his dagger, eased the shirt over the crisscross of old scars and new bruises, and shrugged on his doublet. With a final glance at the blurred outlines of the goat path he had just traversed, he started up the track for the shipyard in Perast, the nearby town.

The yard was little more than a jetty, a stone shed, and a wider, less inclined space at the water's edge. The sea walls of the shrouded town and its quay rose up beside it. Two sets of launch rails, one recently greased for use, ran down to the bay

and disappeared into the fog. The boat lay as he had seen her
last, on her side, beyond the cradled rib cage of a new-laid
keel. He crossed the stony ground between them and ducked
under the bow spur.

Moving slowly and carefully around the ropes straining at
the mainmast, the wooden counter braces, and piled ballast, he
examined the repairs. The caulkers had been gone a fortnight,
perhaps more, judging by the drying pots of pitch. Fresh
oakum had been driven into failing seams, and tarred, and the
belly of the *bergantin*, despite its outer sheen of moisture,
seemed tight and dry. He checked the iron fittings for the
sternpost, noted some thole pins that needed replacing,
surveyed the mast and rigging, and when he'd finished, ran a
hand along the blackened hull in passing, fondly, as one might
the withers of a favorite horse. *My strong, swift falcon.* She no
longer needed careening on the shore.

Satisfied, he hailed the watchman, who disengaged
himself from a pile of sacking, under which a second pair of
legs protruded, and lurched off to find his master. Beyond the
yard, Rade could hear laughter now, calls, a baby crying, the
sound of an adze on wood, the braying of an ass, a skiff being
unloaded, someone washing by the shore. At his feet, the pile
of sacking rose and fell with the steady rhythm of sleep. He
prodded it experimentally with his shoe and the legs twitched,
stretched, and then convulsively retracted. They reappeared in
a crouch, swathed above in folds of burlap that ended at soft
brown shoulders and a tousled shock of hair—and within the
tangles, a mouth, a nose, and two furious, but not unattractive,
black eyes. He laughed, a good strong deep-throated laugh,
and the pile of sacking hissed and spat like a cat and crabbed
off toward the nearest shrubbery that, considering the sounds
that followed, was full of thorns.

The fog burned off but his amusement lasted all the way to
Cattaro.

*   *   *   *   *

Cattaro, like Risan, occupied the tip of a bay, and although that second bay was connected to the first, like opposing wings on a moth, it was larger and longer. Unlike the Turkish town with its wooded ridges, Cattaro was crowded onto the tail of an alluvial slope ending at a steep incline of natural stone that rose swiftly toward the high border of Zeta. Under Venice for three-quarters of a century, by invitation rather than conquest, the town controlled the mouth of a small river, the bays, and through its alliance with Perast, one side of the strait leading into them. To the west, it claimed the town of Budva and a plain that bordered on the Adriatic. Marked by a mass of crenellated curtain walls snaking up the precipice, the city's fort also guarded the starting point of an overland caravan track reaching all the way to Constantinople. It was on this track, zigzagging up and down the cliff in all kinds of weather, that a thin file of people, goods, and livestock brought the lifeblood of trade to and from Cattaro.

Rade crossed the country market on the small plateau outside the walls, and after, the bridge under which the Škurda flowed, green as cat's eyes, to follow the line of lichen-spotted ramparts along the quay. Presided over by an eroding stone saint, the sea gate was impeded by the usual market-day gaggle of soldiers and scowling officials wielding stamps and seals and record books. It opened into an L-shaped piazza— the same piazza that a Venetian army, stricken with fever, had staggered over twenty years before. The men had borne their ailing *provedditore*, Alvise Bembo, to shelter following the siege of Scutari. Their ships, once filled with rejoicing, had lain slack in the bay, the glow of victory extinguished by tainted water consumed in an ecstasy of thirst. Of the defenders, only Mocenigo's galley had pushed on to Ragusa, with her famous apothecary, and hope for a cure.

Rade detached himself from the ebb and flow of market day to lean against a wall and dig a stone from his shoe. The buildings crowded in around him but cast no shadows as a greater shade had overlaid them. He looked up. A patch of blue showed above their somber facades, beyond the looming shape of the mountain. Beneath his feet, the paving stones lay waiting for that kiss of sun, moist, worn by hooves and trampling feet, marked for merchants' stalls, chipped by projectiles, silent witnesses of festivals and punishments, recipients of sputum, urine, tears, and blood—including his own.

They'd gutted Bembo when he died, embalmed his body, stuffed it with straw, and taken it home swathed in linen inside a coffin dressed with pitch. Scutari had fallen anyway six years later, and while new *provedditores* were appointed to Cattaro every year or two, none went south to what was now, by treaty, an Ottoman-held fortress in Albania.

*   *   *   *   *

Beyond the limestone portal of the town hall, he could sense the pervasive air of gloom. Bereft of security, the great galleys like Bembo's no longer anchored offshore to procure provisions and trade Levantine goods. Without them, the skilled craftsmen had slowly dwindled, immigrating to print shops in Venice, to boatyards in Dalmatia, even to positions of patronage among the goldsmiths of Muscovy. The populace had dwindled too, leaving behind those too loyal to depart or too poor to attempt it. Like a flower unable to escape the shade, Cattaro was visibly declining, suffering from a decade of divided power on the bay. Where once the bustle of trade had enlivened a host of civil servants, a lone clerk, robed in Venetian fashion, occupied a sparsely furnished office—shared with the frowning lion of St. Mark.

"And you are here for...?" murmured the clerk, composing his long sallow face into the proper functionary attitude and putting on his black cap, amid the flicker of candles.

Rade stated his business.

"*Marinarezza*, I presume," said the clerk reaching for the

membership roll.

"Zetan."

"Zetan… ah, Montenegrin," he replied. His fingers came to rest on a different book. He became slightly more animated.

"That's what you call us. We don't call ourselves that," Rade replied.

"Montenegrin," the clerk echoed officiously. "I am following instructions," he murmured, opening his ledger and thumbing through the pages. "Name?" he intoned and when the *kapetan* answered, lettered it slowly and carefully on the page. "Ship?" and wrote "*bergantin.*" "Ship's papers?" He held out his hand for the official letters, and having received them, studied them carefully. When he'd meticulously inscribed all the necessary details in his book, he wrote "not in the guild" at the bottom, with a small flourish.

Native mariners on the Venetian side of the Bocche, the bays, all belonged to the Guild of Marinarezze. In fact, membership was required. In return for their dues, the members were allowed certain privileges, among them: a part in the dance and parade of relics at the February festival of St. Triphon, sponsorship of a feast for the poor (ensuring spiritual credit toward paradise), access to armaments in guild-owned warehouses, care for the aged and infirm, funeral rites and mourners, and a lesser share of the Signoria's customary dues and taxes. Through guild support, Venice was rewarded with a plentiful supply of native seamen with which to feed the voracious maw of her navy.

The clerk shut his book thoughtfully and placed it just so on the desk. His dark, mournful gaze passed over the Montenegrin's purse and formed a rough estimate of its contents. Revenues were so often short.

Rade stood eyeing the winged Venetian lion on the gonfalon. This accounting, like the trip to Zara, was an annual obligation. One that he found tedious but necessary. To the Cattarines, they were just another shipload of small-time merchants and sailors, bringing in enough profit to survive another year and sanctioned by their upland neighbor, Montenegro—known to him by its real name, Zeta. It was in fact a carefully orchestrated pretense, even down to leasing the house and paying the taxes. In reality, the cargoes traded in Cattaro were carefully selected from non-Venetian prizes and the papers were inevitably forged. The full scope of their piracy was carried out in high season, well outside the gulf, from a variety of hiding places among the offshore Adriatic islands. The bay, with its glowering Turks and reduced desirability, offered the perfect winter refuge.

As he'd expected, the paperwork in the empty room consumed well over an hour, and the additional, lengthy consultation in the provedditore's chambers, which he hadn't foreseen, another hour. The clerk finally returned, smelling of onions and sausage.

"Where are you bound, *capitano*?" asked the clerk casually, counting out the taxes.

"North. To fetch a cargo," muttered Rade impatiently.

The clerk studied the Montenegrin, standing loose-limbed but watchful by his desk, lean, muscular, his tar-smeared fingers clasping and unclasping restlessly, his dense black hair falling partway down his back. It was like gazing at some untamed beast. He spread out the money, wiped his fingers thoroughly with his handkerchief, and using his abacus, started counting it again. It pleased him that his master shared his views about these godforsaken people. Their joint animosity always brought him an agreeable sense of professional equality. *Accursed race, these uplanders. Always sneaking down and making off with something.* An endless supply of felons waiting to be flogged. Or hanged. He checked the desk top to be sure everything was still there. He felt quite full and might have been more pleasantly so had the man across the table not been rank with stains, sweat, and latent hostility. They were all the same he sighed inwardly, emitting a polite, onion-flavored belch. Utterly uncivilized. Barbarians. *Forestieri*. What did the Turks call them? *Domuzlar. Pigs*. He primly straightened his long black Venetian gown and closed his accounts ledger. Well, he was unlikely to see this one again. *Shipping out in winter.* He could barely contain his pleasure. *Good riddance, fool.*

"Must be profitable," intoned the clerk, stone-faced, handing back his documents.

"It would be profitable," said the *kapetan*, checking the papers. He looked up. His blue eyes glittered. "Without the customary pound of flesh."

The clerk glanced back at the scarred visage. Somebody had got that all right. He wondered who.

*   *   *   *   *

It had been a busy few days since the trip to Cattaro. The men had dribbled in, some with Vuk, others on their own. The launch had finally been accomplished by a reluctant shipyard, light on workers, his own men and various inducements: both threats and bribes. Part of a day had been spent hammering thole pins and the other part going back to Cattaro to buy oars that had mysteriously disappeared. Yesterday, they'd rowed the ship around and anchored her off the beach in deep, cobalt water. She was, like the *fusta* and *galliot*, a type of light galley, a *bergantin*, of shallow draft and low freeboard, with fourteen benches on a side and no true prow platform. Cargo capacity was limited to the nonworking portions of the deck, beneath the raised platform at the stern and a cramped space below or on the gangway. Built to patrol the coast, not ferry goods, she was a low, swift, fighting machine.

The sternpost which held the rudder stood higher than the prow and a narrow gangway ran fore and aft down the center at the same height as the bench thwarts. The mainmast had been rigged but extra spars were still being hoisted aboard. For the moment, men swarmed over the deck and Miloš's directives liberally sprinkled with curses floated out across the water. From time to time, a small vessel detached itself from the hull and labored back and forth, loading stores, rigging, and belongings from the beach.

Rade wandered a short distance down the shore. He lingered, half-watching, half-listening, the rubble of smooth stones under his feet reminding him of all the years he'd spent traversing them, embarking from them, thanking God for the sight of them. He picked one up, rubbing his thumb on its pitted surface, and cradling it cool and gray-white in his palm. These, in their thousands, were the shedding of the limestone heights, the lost offspring of the mountain, falling too far to ever regain their home. In a way, he felt akin to them. He turned, and with a flick of his wrist, the stone skimmed across the surface of the water, caught, and was lost. The momentary disturbance smoothed quickly into nothingness, as if it had never been.

Behind him, to the south, the steep slopes rose in triangular patterns that confused the climber and hid from sight the apex of the summits. The latter were heavily snowbound now, cold and bleak so that winter could bestow its annual gift of water—until the thaw reached the heights and the limestone drank it all away. All summer and fall, a growing trickle of refugees had crossed the mountains, the herceg's people from the north, even from the Krajina, and the Albanians from the south; displaced persons seeking a foothold in the tribal lands on high, an army to fund a man's vengeance, a servant's place in a Cattarine household, a laborer's in the plains, or most likely, passage to cross the Adriatic. In sailing weather, the coast bled refugees heading for a temporary haven. The mountain detritus that once seemed only stones and outcasts had quietly doubled and redoubled to reveal a larger phenomenon. The constant crumbling of the limestone slopes was being outpaced by that of the kingdoms surrounding them.

The light was already changing, challenged by a brooding bank of clouds advancing on the iron gray ridge of crags. It was weather so characteristic of the bay that Rade hardly took note of it, his thoughts wandering to the parchments he'd won in the game. The monotonous lap of the wavelets seemed to repeat the name: *Vinciguerra, Vinciguerra, Vinciguerra* and the mournful cry of the gray-backed gulls echoed it too. There was a pleasing cadence to the sound, as if it summoned him to some sacred cave. But the message lay concealed in a philosophic muddle, so that although he'd felt its power, he hadn't come to understand it. At least, not yet. But he *knew* that name. Knew it from the myriad bits of news gleaned from taverns and caravanserai and fellow travelers. Knew it for the ringing cascade of *ducats* it instantly brought to mind. And knew from it, the new, dangerous direction of his travels. *Vinciguerra, Vinciguerra, Vinciguerra*. Lost in thought, he didn't hear Vuk's halting step on the pebbles.

"Even with the sale of the horse, there wasn't much to buy," Vuk said grumpily. "That great Venetian whore, Cattaro, guards an empty larder."

Rade said, without turning, "We'll replenish at a port."

"Now *kapetan*, where will that be? The harbors will be full of ships... all of them enemies," replied Vuk.

"We've deceived them before," Rade answered lightly. "Where's your sense of adventure?"

"I'm too old for one," grumbled the ancient. "And it's winter." He'd left unsaid the near futility of a winter voyage. February was a barren month at sea: gales and rain and the occasional round ship too large to challenge filled its days.

For a time, the captain watched the ship take shape. "I need you," he said quietly.

"To add a corpse to a ship of fools?"

Rade could feel the hackles rising. "I could force you to come."

"*Sila Boga ni moli* / force does not pray to God," muttered Vuk.

"I am your *kapetan*," Rade said sharply.

"And I plucked you, a stripling, half-drowned from the bay," returned Vuk with hostility. "Had I foreseen today, I wouldn't have bothered."

"*Then stay here and rot! You and your bones!*"

For a time, they both were silent, sheathed in anger.

It was Vuk who finally spoke. "I will claim my oar." His voice held an odd timbre. "Not because I think it's wise—which it isn't—but because I've grown used to you. As an old dog his master, it's too late for another."

The captain half-turned to offer some acknowledgment.

"No," Vuk held up his hand, "let an old man ramble. God knows I've earned the right. Even when the thorn presses your flesh, as it does now, I am beside you. But, mark my words, the mother of all thorn bushes will soon blossom at your door." He paused and his voice became even more remote, "And I shall not be there to uproot it."

It was a conciliatory speech in essence and one that Rade knew he would not have gotten from another member of his crew. But Vuk had always been different, different from everyone else he had ever known. Besides, their relationship had set him apart. Part grandfather, part servant, part scold, part companion, Vuk gave of himself and rarely asked anything in return. And because of that, Rade could command him but did not always have the inclination to enforce his will. And then there was that other part: the soothsayer, to whom he could not even feel connected. What had he said? *And I shall not be there to uproot it.*

Instinctively the *kapetan* turned and looked sharply at Vuk but he saw that the old man had turned his thoughts to some inner space where no one could reach him. It was then he noticed how Vuk had aged while he was away.

Rade said, "Fate leads the willing, and drags along the reluctant." He waited for some response but the old man stood unblinkingly still beside him and the captain came slowly to realize that the sightlessness and withdrawal might be a spell brought on by prophecy and not the failings of old age. He had seen the signs often enough before, and as always, he felt an unwelcome prickle of apprehension.

For a time, he squinted silently skyward. The sun came

and went, obscured by clouds. He watched the scudding shapes traverse the sky. "Vuk..." he cleared his throat.

The graybeard, unmoving, stared past him at the boat.

"What did the bones say?" asked Rade softly.

"I told you," muttered the ancient. "They said you'd come."

"You've cast them since. You've a new prophecy."

"*If* the blades were cast," Vuk said in a low voice, "and I'm not saying they were, they might have said there'd be a journey." He looked warily off into space.

It was as if his friend had left and some frightful old seer has taken his place. Yet Rade felt relieved; the pronouncement was unexpectedly harmless. "We're all going on a journey, Vuk. That's hardly news."

"This one will be different," muttered Vuk. "This journey belongs to you."

"In what way?" he asked carefully.

"As the spark rises, so will the man."

That was ominous. Some said the spark rising from the fire was like the soul seeking heaven. "Then you foresee my death," returned Rade uneasily. Vuk was old. He'd thought... *"When?"* The word slipped out before he could contain it.

The man who had been Vuk ruminated, seeming to enjoy the other man's discomfort. "You speak of death but I spoke of fire. You'll burn. I didn't say you'd die." He looked bleary-eyed and strange.

"On a day like this, I'd derive comfort from the flame," said Rade brusquely, trying to conceal his anxiety. He steeled himself to ask another question, but Vuk departed, crunching his way back toward the ship on the stones. Rade pulled his cloak tighter about his shoulders, and shivered.

As if in tune with the prophecy, the sun cut short its appearance and leaden shadow grayed the bay. Across the glassy waters, a little abbey poked up its bell tower from its solitary island, buttressed by seawalls and the stiff spears of cypresses—and watchful Benedictines. Nowadays, behind the walls, there lurked a bombard and a stony pile of missiles. For would-be penitents, this pairing had produced an admirable display of caution.

Still farther away, beyond the bend in the shoreline, stood the towering summit of the tallest mountain, Crna Gora, or Monte Negro as the Venetians called it. The black mountain above Cattaro where he'd gone three days before. *On this desolate land,* the ballad sang, *God tumbled the stones leftover from making the world*—and formed a natural fortress. Ivan the Black, fleeing Zabljak and the lowlands, had recognized its strength, and from it, carved himself a kingdom. But Ivan whose mother had been the famous Skanderbeg's sister and whose first wife had been Gojisava, an Arianite also of Albania, and his second, Mara, daughter of the herceg, had lost the best part of Zeta and most of his alliances to the curved sword of the sultan. Even then, Ivan's demise two years before had only spurred his legends even as Djuradj, his son, succeeded him. The latter had managed to keep his kingdom as a protectorate of Venice due, at least in part, to a marriage contract with the Erizzo family of Venice—arranged on the July day his father died. Venetian arms and money and the rugged hostility of the land might still serve to protect him. That or the *harac* that even Ivan had occasionally paid to the Turk. In the end, only time would tell. Survival was a dangerous game, and the Venetians, the only friendly outlets to the sea, were players in it too.

The crew had almost finished readying the ship. In a short while, Rade thought, he ought to go. The men were a motley group who could row and sail but only Hamsa exhibited the heavy thighs of a former galley slave—for the confined bench had overdeveloped that part of him. Blood brotherhood had been the rite he'd found to bind them to each other and the scars on his hand bore witness to the repetition of that ceremony. All told, they'd made some good hauls over the years, and they had come a long way from that first boat, that was so small, it could be pulled up on the beach and hidden under brush. Yet despite this long and profitable association, he could feel it coming to an end. The little clan of outcasts that he'd gathered was fragile, easily disrupted, and prone to respond to the stronger call of clan and family, where the latter still existed. Only Vuk was somehow tied to him, not by blood, but by something more elusive. The others lived only for the day and their tenuous connection with their *kapetan*. Profit had formed that tie and Rade doubted it could survive real failure. It was only a matter of time until fortune took away what it had formerly provided.

Even as his thoughts were elsewhere, beneath his doublet, the letter burned its way back into his consciousness. Change was coming and he dared not resist it. The same force that had driven him from the mountains had also compelled him to abandon Zara, press himself to hurry home, and today, set sail in winter. Rade felt it now, that fatalistic urging, despite the changing weather, vulnerability of the ship, and his own clanging instincts. He tore his gaze from the ship and looked upward at the stolid, inattentive mountains and wished for a token of good fortune. What was hidden in the language of the letter? Would there be ships to take in the shipping lanes? Was this truly the right time to set sail? *Winter either bites with its teeth or lashes with its tail,* murmured the mountains and a little whirl of snow bloomed from on high. He saw then that the wind had changed in his favor.

*   *   *   *   *

The small Venetian galley stood off the Catene, or Strait of Chains, in the inner bays. As the *bergantin* drew near the narrow cut, the oars on the galley rippled and the blades flashed up, and Rade's men returned the salute. The pennant from Perast streamed out before them. The marinarezze, he thought, believed they were honoring their own. And the February voyage had blessed them with the assumed significance he had counted on. The pennant did the rest. The outgoing current, burgeoning with runoff from two drenching days of rain, seized their ship, a moderate *bora* filled the sails, and, oars at rest, they were whisked past the place where the Hungarians had once drawn up iron chains to repulse their enemies. In a mile, the cut would spit them out in the Bay of Tivat, the first of the outer pair of bays. Rade looked back. The Venetian galley had already passed from sight. It would remain hidden, safe on the more navigable side of the Catene, backed by the towering wall of mountains, and the empire that Venice had bestowed upon these shores.

The larger Ottoman galley would be somewhere on the other side, near the herceg's settlement of Novi, now Ottoman, or maybe near the mouth of the outer bays. Even though Perast paid dearly for her privileges, Rade would still mount the *verso* in the outer bays. The Ottomans were a changeable lot and he wanted to exit the bays without conflict, or at the very least, without damage. After that, they would head for the one small mainland port on the Adriatic whose safety their craft could reach by night—and whose harbor was small enough to exclude larger vessels. The leeward islands off the coast would be the secondary destination—with the cache of supplies, extra spars, and weapons hidden in the rocks.

He glanced at Miloš, brown-eyed, brown-haired, standing stolidly at the helm with the second pilot, Jovan, Vuk on his bench, Nicola and Hamsa among the crew, oars retracted. He could feel the wind- and wave-borne tremors pulsing through the deck; a throbbing force flowing into the soles of their feet, the palms of their hands, through every part of their bodies touching the ship, like blood hammering its way under the skin, marrying them to the heart, bone and marrow of the living vessel. Soon the land would relax its pull on their allegiance. Their sense of time and balance would become that of the *bergantin*. And the ship would answer to whatever was decreed by the elements. And to her *kapetan*.

*   *   *   *   *

The Ottoman galley drew herself forth from beyond the rounded bulge of the Lustica peninsula like a glutted snake emerging from its den.

"The devil take her!" cried Jovan. "She's coming out!"

The *bergantin* was under oar, not sail, the wind having shifted enough to empty the sail, and they were turning south. They had cleared Tivat and were heading through the neck into the top of the last bay, the herceg's bay. Rade planned to use the lee of Lustica for better rowing. He had also prudently allotted time for mounting the *verso* and moving the stores back to lighten the bow.

"Break out the sail," bellowed Rade. And to Miloš, "Turn west. Keep Novi on your right. There! Steer for the high point to the north of Njivici. For the shallow water by the salt pans." He left his place by the helm and ran over to take up an oar vacated by a man hoisting the sail. "On me," he shouted. "Dash speed!" The shafts rose, and at his command, the bank of blades bit into the sea. "Now! Again! *Pull!*" And he took up the cadence of a chant and the men joined in.

The sail filled and the ship slewed as the wind grabbed at the sail and then they were underway with everything they had. They could see the flurry of activity aboard the Turkish ship. Orders being shouted. Men running to their stations on the deck. The larger craft moved ponderously out from the land and began to pick up speed.

He saw that the Turks had chosen a diagonal course that would intersect his own. And Rade knew, even if they made Njivici, he would be trapped unless the large galley ran aground.

They were halfway across with the Ottoman galley gaining steadily when he felt the new shift in the wind.

"Miloš!" he shouted. "You can make the point! Don't trim the sail! Let it flap. Wait for my signal."

He saw the great ship drawing abreast but it was still too far away for arrows or shot. It had briefly crossed his mind that a cursory inspection might have been all the galley wanted but he hadn't wanted to wait to find out. They would confiscate the *verso* and he couldn't allow that.

"*Oars up!*" Rade shouted. Their ship slowed. "Reverse! Man the sail!" And the *bergantin* slowed, stopped, and reversed, and the men ran forward to walk the lateen sail around the mast. At that, the smaller vessel shot southward behind the galley. They saw the galley too begin to slow and turn. But something seemed to arrest her progress and as they watched, the Ottoman ship hesitated, half-turned, and suddenly made for Novi, in the opposite direction from their vessel. And soon, she was moving away as if some urgent signal had called her home.

The ridges of Lustica rose up on their westward side, softening the wind that seemed to be changing again, blocking out the view to the east. The portal, Point Ostri, was another point beyond the one ahead. And they would soon be out in the Adriatic. The men rowed with renewed vigor and Rade was cheered by the rhythm of their oars and happy banter.

Rade began to think about the sea they would soon enter. He ordered the rowers to resume the slow beat and at the same time a handful of men were sent to pack up the *verso* and secure it. And the stores were moved back to their places. When that was done, they stowed the oars and let the lateen sail do its work. There was only one Ottoman galley in the bays. And they had passed it.

Chapter Seven

If the present world go astray, the cause is in you, in you it is
to be sought.
—Dante Alighieri

December, Tenth Month, Venetian Year 1492 – Caterina

If there had ever truly been a Knight of the Cart, Caterina knew his burden. Tommaso knew it too, coughing his life out in the back room of his patron's house. As St. Nicholas' month advanced, every step she took was leaden—like a thin man in a great man's armor, dismounted, shuffling toward a battle he could not win. One could balance the weight, even push it forward, but one couldn't get rid of it. The other combatants marched alongside, lightly clad: a leather helmet here, sometimes a cuirass, but mostly carrying hand weapons, items that could be discarded in flight. But without a horse, the man-at-arms couldn't run, couldn't unfasten the heavy plate to turn and flee. So he wished only to preserve his honor. Already, he had prayed, received the Host, and known it was a final rite. He pressed on hoping against hope that the will of God was in his favor. Each weighty, dragging pace taking him closer to his fate.

She had never seen a war, never brandished a weapon, but she could well imagine the burden of armor: heavy as dread and equally as suffocating.

*   *   *   *   *

The church rose about them encrusted with the gilt, marble, painted wood and fabric of artistic endeavor: remembrance, atonement, the purchase of indulgences, hope for the next life, fear of the future, the threats of hell and purgatory—all mixed together in the customary array of saints, Bible stories and sequestered relics. The tiny flames of the candles wavering on their wrought iron stands or swinging in their oil reservoirs reached toward a greater light but the throng of people who pulsed and flowed between the pillars seemed to represent a social gathering as much as a religious one. The Marian city had long espoused its own fashion of worship and often fashion rather than worship was the operative word—unless disaster threatened when the tide speedily turned the other way.

They sat next to each other on the bench in the women's section, behind the patricians, as they were only *cittadini*, citizens, their bodies pressed against each other because it was so cold. Ginevra on one side. Simonetta on the other. Caterina in the middle. The old deaf lady on the left, knobbly fingers working her beads, and the end of the bench on the right. As usual, Simonetta spread out her cloak to discourage any additional occupant. They laid their breviaries on their laps, arranged beneath their veils so that they could see the words, twisted their rosaries about their hands and moving the beads noisily, began to whisper. For a while, the usual subjects of conversation came up: neighborhood gossip, the physical appearance of certain young men in the church, whatever happenings crossed the path of their private lives.

"Our Father," intoned Simonetta. She pulled her cloak closer, adjusted her rosary, looking at Caterina. "You've been unusually quiet. Why are you all hunched over like that? Are you sick? You look like a condemned man."

"I *am* a condemned man. *It's in two weeks!*" Her voice trembled.

"What would help?" asked Simonetta, immediately all business.

"A ladder," murmured Caterina, "that I may reach the height of my father's ambitions. *Hallowed be thy name.*"

"Your father has already attained the height of ser Ariosto," said Simonetta. "That's not going to change. Something else. Something you truly desire."

"An asp in a basket."

Ginevra choked on her prayer, the Pater Noster bead slipped from her fingers, and the entire rosary cascaded clattering onto the stone floor. She bent hastily to pick it up.

"And lead us not into temptation," replied Simonetta wryly. "A love charm would be more appropriate. You know as well as I do, you have no control over this process. For now, you'll have to make the best of it." She shrugged. "You can poison him later."

"That's *very* helpful," said Caterina grimly. "I feel *much* better."

Simonetta drew her furred cloak closer about her. "This place is a cave. I wish I'd sat in the middle."

"You usually sit in the middle," whispered Ginevra irritably. She added, turning toward Caterina, "No one marries for love."

"All the more reason for a charm," replied Simonetta. "I'm sure I could find you one." She moved to the next bead. *"Hail Mary, full of grace."*

"I ought to have had my portrait painted," muttered Caterina. "Like they do in Florence."

"For a wedding?" Ginevra looked surprised. "No Venetian woman does that."

"As a memento? For the living to remember the dead?" asked Simonetta. "How piteous do you plan to become?"

"Don't you see the horror of this marriage, Simonetta?"

"No, I don't. I don't see it because it's the fate of every one of us. And to me, the alternative is worse. Who wants to be imprisoned in a convent? Half the noblewomen in this city are stored away like unwanted goods. And we're not even noblewomen—even if you are half patrician because of your mother. Just be glad you don't have five sisters needing dowries."

"It's true," said Ginevra. *"Blessed art thou among women and blessed is the fruit of thy womb, Jesus."*

"Honestly, Caterina, do you think you're marrying up because you're pleasant to look at?"

"Of course not," said Caterina, twisting her rosary.

"Ten thousand *ducats* is the top of the marriage market," continued Simonetta. "No siblings. And then there's your father. To those for whom pride of lineage is growing thin, you're a veritable prize."

"I should be lucky if *my* father offered two," said Ginevra.

"The prize doesn't wish to be awarded," muttered Caterina.

Simonetta put a hand on her arm. *"Cara,* it could be worse. It truly could. Look around the sanctuary and think on it." It was amazing how many ages, shapes and sizes adorned the room. "Look at him, in the blue robe, by the wall. The first night, you'd be crushed to death. Or that one. He's so thin that if he fell between the bed and the wall, you couldn't get him out. Or that one over there, Methuselah's grandfather…"

After a while, two out of three began to giggle.

Simonetta was in rare form. "And the codpiece on *that* one. Good Lord, it even has ribbons! Do you think what's inside has ribbons, too?"

"Holy Mother!" cried Ginevra in a loud whisper. "Don't say things like that in church!"

Simonetta snapped the Ave Maria bead against the one following it. "But Ariosto is already looking better, isn't he?" she said, glancing at her friend. *"The Lord is with thee."*

"A little," observed Caterina, shocked into a faint grin.

"No more, Simonetta," whispered Ginevra indignantly. "You mustn't."

"And with thee also," replied Simonetta sharply. She

turned her gaze to Caterina. "Take heart. Remember Berto's prediction."

"How often is he right?" murmured Caterina. Touching the ivory crucifix on the rosary, she closed her eyes. "*Thy will be done.*"

"*On earth as it is in heaven.*" Simonetta glanced carefully about, reaching under her veil to rearrange a loose hank of false hair, and replied, "Does it matter? For you, once would be sufficient."

Footsteps echoing on the stones, Nonna loomed up beside them. "I've left you to your little conversations. No doubt sacred ones," she added, rolling her eyes. "It's time to open your books and follow the Mass. Ginevra, your mother is watching." She gestured. Like birds on a line, they moved over toward the old lady—who, chin on her bony chest, had fallen asleep. The old lady let out a long, delicate snore. Nonna sat down heavily and the bench let out a creak of protest.

"Father Paolo has already favored all of you with a barrage of disparaging looks. You might have noticed."

"*Deliver us from evil,*" intoned Simonetta, brightly.

"*Amen,*" replied the rest.

*   *   *   *   *

A fortuitous date had been set, according to the astrologer and the almanac, and the guests invited—when the rumor reached Ludovico. Immediately he abandoned his work, summoned the gondola, and set off for a particular wooden cubicle on the Rialto.

"Yes, messer Vinciguerra, the *Agnus Dei* sails on the morrow," said the clerk, emerging from his stack of ledgers.

"It's been suggested," said Ludovico darkly, "that ser Ariosto will be on board."

The man ran a finger down the passenger list. "So it seems," he nodded, "and also the papal legate." Before he'd finished his reply, the merchant had turned on his heel and walked out. In the dim office, the clerk's fingers closed protectively over the handful of coin. He wished he'd held out for more.

Ludovico's gondola nosed out into the modest stream of undersized ships and cumbersome barges that dotted the Grand Canal in winter. A *traghetto*, one of the small public ferries, crossed its pointed prow, the group of standing passengers huddled together for warmth. Already chilled, Ludovico rearranged his furred cloak and fleetingly wished he had company, too; the *felze*, the wide covered structure under which he sat, did little to ward off the cold. Eventually the gondola turned off into a maze of smaller canals and negotiated a meandering path until it reached the modest building that housed ser Ariosto. The boat was soon tied up to the mooring poles as Ludovico's gondolier pounded on the water gate while the merchant hovered red-faced behind him. The gate creaked open and the two men advanced precipitously into the dark interior, the first trying to get out of the way of the second.

Formalities having been cut short, it didn't take long to get to the point.

"Why go now?" demanded Ludovico, trying to suppress his fury.

"Twelve days is nothing," replied Ariosto offhandedly, supervising the packing of his sea chest. "There's plenty of time. I'll be gone five days and return with seven to spare. It's two days travel by ship. We call at one other port."

"If the weather allows it," interjected the merchant angrily, "which in December is unlikely."

"If the wind is against me," said Ariosto, "I'll ride to Chioggia and get a barge."

"Ride back in the mud and sleet? Around the bandits? And how long do you think the wedding guests will wait?" said Ludovico, between his teeth. "Two weeks? *Three?*"

"Not that one," said the nobleman to his servant. "The red one." Turning back to Ludovico, "Look," he said, annoyed,

"I've dispatches for Ravenna. I'm not setting off like Mandeville on his travels."

It dawned on Ludovico that Ariosto wasn't going to Ravenna either but to the nearby military bastion, Rocca di Brancaleone. He'd recently been elected paymaster, normally a civilian position that involved keeping accounts of contracts and salaries and making several trips a year to the fort to pay them down—if the Senate willed it. That meant dispatches weren't all he'd be delivering, there'd be a strongbox as well. Probably a big one. The rebuilt Rocca was enormous. And God knew when he'd return. *Bastard.* He tried to take a steadying breath. *Bastard!* Everything would have to be delayed. He couldn't resist a parting shot. "A *prudent* man," snarled Ludovico, "would depart *after* the wedding feast."

The nobleman stiffened, hand clamped on the lid of the chest. *"God's blood,"* swore Ariosto, *"how like a merchant!* Always counting hours and *ducats*! Imagining delays! Inventing catastrophes!" He reached for a packet of documents, seals dangling, pawed through them and tossed them on top of his clothes. "This marriage sprouts more mushrooms than a forest," he muttered sourly. "There *are*," said Ariosto, indicating the packet, "more important issues than *it*."

"Not to me," growled Ludovico.

Ariosto fixed the merchant with an aggressive stare. "The day is set. I plan to take your girl to wife." He slammed the chest shut and his servant snatched his fingers from the lip just in time. *"There is no reason to think otherwise."*

Ludovico, undaunted by the tone of the conversation and inwardly molten under the strain of an increased dowry, a reluctant bride, the hum of high activity in the household, and now this, wondered if the errand was that urgent. He was assured it was.

On the way home, cooled by the frosty air and calmed by the motion of the gondola, the merchant reexamined the confrontation. Whether honesty had been served or discarded, the outcome would be known in a week. He decided, grudgingly, he could wait.

*   *   *   *   *

For early December, the sea was docile but indistinct, muffled in the dove-gray shroud of winter. The ship lay toward the eastern edge of the island, just off the main channel, near the rafted hulks of similar vessels, which, unlike the *Agnus Dei*, wafted drowsily against their moorings in a semi-deserted state of seasonal disuse. By the proposed hour of departure, the drums and trumpets had fallen silent and Ariosto, the papal legate and a covey of flapping priests and shivering retainers stood arrayed at the rail, shouting and gesturing as the motley flotilla of attendant craft began to withdraw. Ludovico, who had boarded a neighboring ship to inspect its storage area, sourly noted that for a coastal trader, the hull of the *Agnus Dei* rode high in the water. *No profit there* he thought wiping his dripping nose on his sleeve. He stifled his feeling of growing annoyance, threw one last irritable glance in the direction of Caterina's betrothed, and descended gruffly into the hold.

After the tide had turned, the wind rose, as predicted, and accompanied by the cries of the sailors, Ariosto's round ship departed, properly blessed, sails filled with a following wind, pennants streaming backward. With an Istrian pilot braced at the helm and the odd sailor aloft in the rigging, the *Agnus Dei* drew briskly away from the city and its sprinkle of outlying islands, a winged shape moving brightly along with the breeze until the proud buildings and lofty campaniles of Venice grew small and dim and blurred into the soft, slate-colored embrace of sea and sky.

*   *   *   *   *

When debris began to surface, the *Agnus Dei* was eight days out and three days overdue. Reported sightings of the vessel outside the *lidi*, the barrier beaches, had been bandied about but had done nothing to allay concern that the vessel never reached her port, nor any neighboring one. As additional information trickled in, the loss grew greater than projected. Besides her distinguished human cargo, a treasure in tithes for the Holy See had accompanied the stricken ship to the bottom—along with the pay chest for Rocca di Brancaleone.

Eventually, a loose raft of logs seasoning in saltwater was found in the vicinity, ownership by the Arsenal, the state-owned shipyard, branded into the wood. Despite careful examination, it appeared unmarked by collision. Other than that, fishermen found nothing large enough for a man to heave himself onto to escape the icy water. Yet they lingered, nets drying, rocking rhythmically in their rude craft. Such a rich year for the Church they muttered looking hopefully down into the opacity of sea. Until now.

*   *   *   *   *

For two days, Caterina's father had waited for official notice, nursing his catarrh, hoping for better news. On the day the deaths were posted, he gloomily summoned his daughter.

"I've news that concerns us both," he said, forgoing his customary greeting. "You'd better sit down." He gestured towards a chair.

She shook her head. Straightened her back. *"Tell me."* Her eyes were unusually dark and round. He could see rumor had preceded him.

Clearing his throat, he waded in, forthright to a fault. "It *was* the *Agnus Dei* that foundered," said Ludovico bluntly. "The debris has been identified." He looked her full in the face and then dropped his eyes. "I told him not to go," he added lamely.

"Then it's true," said Caterina quietly. Her hand went to the crucifix at her waist. Her face was ashen. "Were there... survivors?"

Ludovico shook his head. "They've ploughed the sea, searching." He wasn't sure how much more he should say. They'd found two bodies. Not Ariosto's.

Her knuckles were white where her left hand gripped the folds of her dress. *"Why?"*

"Mayhap she burst a seam," he answered. "That's the speculation on the street. I'm told she'd drawn eleven years of service," he added. "Most of it on the Adriatic. Some beyond the straits, around the Gulf of Lion. She was well-traveled for a ship that size."

"Why choose such an old vessel?" wondered Caterina, low-voiced. "Surely there were newer ones."

"But not ready to sail," replied Ludovico. His mind ran over the rafted lines of ships moored along the edges of the basin. "They're all aged these days," he added morosely. "Even mine." Recession and foreign competition had bled the shipyards dry. Thank God, he hadn't invested in that one. He turned thoughtfully away from his daughter and then remembered something else. "The *Agnus Dei* sailed nearly empty," he said. "I saw her. I wasn't alone."

Caterina's doe-eyes widened. "Her captain feared a weakness."

"It's possible." He nodded. "Some of us think so." He sneezed loudly and found a handkerchief held out to him. Gratefully, he took it. "It was an act of folly... " he began darkly, and sneezed again.

"...to have been unmindful of the planets," she finished softly, knowing him all too well.

The gray head bobbed. "There'll be no wedding," Ludovico replied unnecessarily, vigorously rubbing his nose. "Everything is being canceled." He surveyed the stack of paperwork having to do with the festivities. The betrothal contract was near the bottom. Eleven years from its signing, new clauses had lately been pasted on and the edges of the older, darker parchment had gotten worn. It was worthless now. He ought to throw it on the fire. He stuffed her handkerchief into his sleeve. "God knows, this is a sorry ending," he muttered. He spoke as much of his own dreams as he did of Ariosto.

Wordlessly, Caterina twisted the crucifix on its beaded cord.

He found the clacking of her beads oppressive. It was as if the women's section from church had come to roost in the house. Clack. *Hail Mary, full of grace.* Clack. *Our Father.* Clack. He imagined the rows of bent covered heads busily working their rosaries. He sighed. There'd be time enough for that later.

He said, "I'm to go out with the priests and notables this afternoon to say farewell." *Clack.* "We'll leave by the San Nicolo port. Conduct a service of remembrance." He cleared his throat noisily. "After the prayers, I have a fine wreath of laurel to throw upon the waves."

She roused herself enough to answer. "You must be careful," she murmured, abandoning the cross and beads to pat down the folds of her dress—mechanically, he noticed, like some clockwork automaton.

He half-smiled. "After what's happened, they're all terrified of the Adriatic. If we proceed more than a boat length out into that hungry sea, I'll be surprised."

The attempt at levity failed. Her eyes brimmed with tears.

Wasn't it always the case with women, thought Ludovico dryly, that when you wanted them to do something, like marry, they didn't want to but when it was all utterly undone, failed, abandoned, you found out that they'd changed their minds. Here he was, convinced he knew her innermost thoughts, and feeling loutish because, after all the moans and foot-dragging, she'd turned out to be as irritatingly changeable as the weather. Who would have thought...? He watched her small thin hand reach up to wipe her eyes and suddenly, seeing her like this, so young, so vulnerable, so desolate, he felt a surge of pity for her.

"I can't take you with me," he said softly, "but you'll hear the bells. And there'll be lofty rhetoric in the Senate for Ariosto and the papal legate before we leave. And processions tonight for those who were brothers in the lay fraternities."

The tears were running down her face.

"I'll be here tonight," he said soothingly, putting his arms around her. "We won't be marching. My confraternity suffered no loss." His right hand smoothed back the fine strands of hair from her forehead and she buried her streaming face in his robe. Ludovico planted a gentle kiss on the top of her head and tucked her protectively under his chin. "Tonight, I'll tell you everything that happened," he murmured. "We'll go to Mass..." Suddenly she was shaking from head to foot, and when he released her, she sank back against the figured wall, wringing her hands, unable to control her weeping.

"Caterina... " She shrank from his touch. "*Get Nonna,*" he called to the manservant outside the door. "*At once!* And Sofia." The footsteps rapidly retreated. *"And a cup of strong wine!"* he shouted.

When she collapsed, unaffected by their ministrations and near hysteria, he gathered her carefully to his chest and carried her upstairs to her chamber. In his arms, despite the heavy woolen dress, she had the unexpected lightness of a child.

Chapter Eight

Into the eternal darkness, into fire and into ice.
—Dante Alighieri

February, End of Twelfth Month, Venetian Year 1492 to
March, First Month of Venetian Year 1493 – Rade

It was a small thing: the dislodged powder barrel fell into his hands before he touched it. Rade had just turned to wedge it back into place. The letter and the ship's *portolan* had been safely stored when the opposite side of the stern storage wall rose up before his eyes. The deck shifted. The wind moaned. And as he fought his way out of the cramped space, he heard the scream of ropes whipping through pulleys and the thunderous flap of canvas. And everyone was shouting.

One moment, the sky was gray and the ship was literally turning over and the next, they were bow down in foam-streaked, swirling blackness with the canvas straining at its seams in the rising roar of wind and rain. Every vestige of land had been obliterated. The rigging rang and shrieked like a high-pitched chorus of devils. Icy water streamed down their faces and into the wool of their clothes and swirled about the deck and poured in torrents over the leeward rail.

"*Miloš! Can you hold her?*" They were running downwind. The huge lateen sail, the yard as long as the galley, was straining at its pulleys, the clew end almost as far out as it could go. He could see, unmanaged, it would tear itself to pieces. He could also see they were perilously close to being driven under the waves.

"God's blood, kapetan! I cannot!"

"Jovan, get up on the stern platform. Give him a hand!"

He saw Jovan grab a length of rope and run back.

"The five of you," he pointed, "yes, *you*, Radimir. When I say so, loose the halyard! Drop the yard." They were fumbling with the rope. "But *ease* it down. *When I say so.*"

The mainmast creaked and groaned, the gust subsided, and the heavy sail lashed in the wind like a living thing.

"Alek, Paolo, Branka, Luka, as the yard comes down, work the lines to bring it amidships. Can you handle that? The rest of you, haul in the canvas as she comes down. If the yard rises in the wind, and you can't, cut the sail lashings. By the grace of God, if you do anything, save the sail."

The ship, still down by the bow, struggled upwards from wave trough to crest only to dive again as the overburdened canvas drove it into the waves.

The gust fell off a little and was followed by another. Three of the five men slid away from the halyard, piling into the benches. That's when he saw Radimir, still grasping the mast, unsheathe his knife. He shouted but it was too late. As the halyard came loose from the fourth man's efforts, Radimir's half sawn rope ran up and snagged on the pulley. The yard dropped like a felled tree, caught, and swung parallel to the hull. An arms length of canvas slid into the sea to leeward and more began to follow.

The *bergantin* began to slew, pulled by the drag of the drowning canvas. It had become a sea anchor. The four men straining on the ropes to the yard at the two sets of pulleys, fore and aft, couldn't balance their efforts to bring the yard in line with the boat against the load of soaked canvas.

The outrigger for the oars was catching the wave crests. The deck slanted precipitously. Rade saw no other solution than to release the clew end of the sail. Once that was done, control over their direction would, except for the oars, be lost. Even though he knew the oars couldn't handle this sea, he ordered it anyway.

The drowning sail bellied out with the force of another rising gust dragging them sideways, turning the vessel even as the sheet to the clew end ran out, even as the sail began to rise from the sea, until the yard, like a battering ram, swung wildly across the deck, ripping the dripping canvas from the water. Water was rushing over the gunwales. Standing on the raised stern platform, he saw the whole solid length of wood coming at them dragging the sodden wall of canvas. Rade shouted at the men to run aft where there was shelter from the stern structure.

"The yard!" He, Miloš and Jovan threw themselves flat.

Hamsa, intent on shipping oars, went over the side. Vuk was thrown into a bench. Sandar reached for Hamsa and the sail came back and caught him. Sandar twisted, and toppled. The halyard broke. And the yard fell with a crash on the deck.

The three of them clawed at the buried tiller. Rising from the pitching deck, encumbered with canvas, the captain caught sight of Sandar, mouth open in the foaming wake, his cries lost in the roar of the wind. Beyond Sandar was a mountainous sea. Beyond that, nothing. At least nothing that could save him. He looked for Hamsa.

One of the crew, gathering up canvas, shouted up at him. *"Hamsa can swim."*

"Not in this sea," Rade replied. "Not in a winter sea."

He turned away from the helpless man falling fast behind them, and the other, Hamsa, who had already vanished, and descended to the deck shin-deep in water.

"Clear the yard! Make fast the canvas. Pull out the extra

spar and lash on the *cochina*." The small storm sail, the
cochina, at the least would lend them some control over their
direction. "Teodor, do what you can to splice the halyard so we
can use it. Radimir, you misbegotten fool, don't touch it! You
there, Alek, check the stores. The casks are coming loose."

And it went on like that, even to having to seat the
oarsmen and use the oars from time to time—even though they
might have snapped—to keep the ship from broaching, until
the halyard worked, and the *cochina* was up and drawing.

He saw now why the Ottoman galley, positioned as it was,
had let them pass. They had seen the storm coming over the
mountains—when he had not. *God's blood, when he had not.*

*   *   *   *   *

There had been, in his life, a handful of days when he had
thought he would not survive: the night he had fled the
mountains, the thief's punishment in Cattaro, the evening Vuk
rescued him from the bay, the capture by *akinjis*. But this, he
knew how to fight. As the waves washed over them and the
rain pelted down, Rade peered forward into the gloom. From
time to time, he shouted to the helmsmen to make some
correction. Jovan and Miloš, exhausted, had been replaced
with Alek and Paolo. They had less experience at the helm but
at least they were strong. Rade's voice was now so hoarse that
he worried he would lose it and he'd moved to a more exposed
position, just to be heard.

It was debilitating to be so cold. He had to force himself to
focus on sailing the ship. With her low freeboard, she had no
choice but to run before the storm. The open deck that served
them well in a fight had never been meant for stormy seas. The
shallow draft that allowed proximity to shore reduced their
ability to cope with heavy weather. And the few sheltered
places were packed with stores. As the oarsmen hefted bails

from their benches, the saltwater doused them again and again, and their groans and oaths were ripped away by the wind. What had made the galley fast, also made her vulnerable. He pushed himself unsteadily to his feet, dry-heaved over the rail, and went down to cajole, urge, and threaten the men to renewed efforts. It was the only way he knew to keep them alive.

At the end of the second night, the wind dropped and the gale subsided. Great waves continued to roil the sea but even they were beginning to diminish. There were no stars to take a position from but the night air felt warmer. A lantern was found and lit for visibility. Taking stock of the situation, Rade and Miloš sized up the crew. Vuk was unconscious. Jovan, Teodor, and Paolo had deep gashes. Most of the others had been bruised or cut in one way or another. All were shuddering with cold.

"Pull out the canvas." Rade's voice was a croak. "We'll wrap ourselves in it." He tucked a fold around Vuk and leaned against the old man's back. He could feel his labored breathing. *To add a corpse to a ship of fools? What had he answered? I could force you to come.* His old friend was shivering like a leaf in the rain. He spread his sodden gray wool over the old man and drew him closer to warm him. *Force does not pray to God.* The tiller tied off, in the dim light the *cochina* still drew. And they could be seen. Otherwise the ship was sailing blind in the dark.

*   *   *   *   *

The *bergantin* drifted along with the deep water current, the one the captain had hoped was the one that should take them north—north to who knew where?—until the ominous sound of breakers sent the crew scrambling for the oars and anchor lines. In the frenzied rush of activity, as the *cochina* was lowered and the oar shafts refastened, a jagged shape slid by in the darkness, so close one could have touched it. The lantern glimmered weakly on it until wooden blades pulled the ship back and away from the angry thunder of surf. Soon the anchors caught and held, the ropes were made fast, and breathing a collective sigh of relief, the men settled down to rest, wrapped once more in the warming folds of the sail.

Day broke, from over a coast, rather than the sea—a good sign. The blurred, black line of shore evolved into a vast low-lying landscape with few outstanding features until it met a distant mass of mountains. More light revealed a beach that continued with gentle undulations in both directions, intersected by the mouths and silted up deltas of waterways. Inland, the sand became marsh, crowned with an occasional low-lying hill, and stretched away to foothills and gray ridges. Hawks skimmed over the grasses and seabirds patrolled the shore. There were no obvious signs of human habitation.

A surge lifted the boat. Rade raised his eyes to the mainmast, stark and desolate against the light, and was reminded of something. Turning seaward, then north, and finally south, he saw no telltale sign of shipwreck. Yet, in the night, there'd been a vessel, he was certain of it. He'd marked it for the morrow: spars, broken mast, the tip of a painted stern. A carrack. A small one. Narrowing his eyes, he scanned the sea, following the probable course of tide and current, and at last picked out a few bobbing shapes of cargo—like clustered ducklings heading for shore. It was strange how that first sight of floating freight revealed an entire landscape of opportunity. Wreckage or boulders were strewn all along that distant beach. Above them, he saw a few, small figures huddled above the reach of the tide.

Within a relatively short time, the oars dipped and dug, and the *bergantin* headed in for the harvest.

"Would you hazard a guess on where we are?" asked

Miloš, braced beside him.

Rade squinted into the distance. "Albania," he answered thoughtfully. "Somewhere north of Valona, Vloré, or whatever they call it now. The current's pulling north."

Miloš considered the shore. It told him nothing. "But I... do you know this coast?" he asked, still confused. They had been together for years. "It's all grass and mud flats."

"I've heard about it. In taverns."

Miloš snorted, "Others make use of landmarks and portolans. *You* listen to drunks."

"You can learn a lot from drunks."

For a time, they measured their progress by the rhythmic groan and splash of the oars. "No dwellings," murmured Miloš, his eyes traveling over the landscape.

"Rife with marsh fever," replied the *kapetan*.

Miloš turned to him with a questioning look.

"Also gleaned from a tavern." Rade grinned. "Be glad it's winter. We need only avoid Ottomans and Albanians."

"Christ's lance, we'll be heads on posts!"

"We could be under the sea." He thought soberly of Sandar's terrified face. And Hamsa, never seen at all.

Miloš inclined his head toward the beach. "And them?"

"I saw Genoese markings on the wreckage. We'll pretend to be allies," replied Rade. "Run up the gonfalon. We'll nose into the shallows but we won't beach her in case we need to get off in a hurry." He squinted at the shore. "I count few survivors but there could be more behind that mound of sand."

Miloš grunted and busied himself with directions to the crew. He had already taken out his dagger and begun to run a sharpening stone along it.

Rade arched his back against the rail, stretched, and then shot the mate a sideways glance. "When the yard went over and the waves ran over the leeward rail," he said casually, "I found I wasn't prepared for paradise."

"What makes you think," muttered Miloš, "paradise is expecting us?"

*   *   *   *   *

Seeing the ship and her pennants, the survivors tottered miserably down the beach and knee-deep into the waves. The surf was falling back to the gentle pull of the Mediterranean but the wind still blew, stirring up whips of sand and the occasional larger swell.

"Perast," shouted Rade and pointed to the gonfalon. *"Perast!"* He waved.

The survivors waved back.

"The wreck is ours," he called. "We claim it." His voice was still hoarse. He had Miloš repeat it.

"Take anything you want," bellowed a survivor. "But for the love of Christ, take us too."

"Beach the boat on a bar for now but don't drive her in too far," said Rade. He gestured. "There isn't anything over the ridge. It's all marsh."

"She's got to float to be loaded," said Miloš.

"First, let's see what they've got."

*   *   *   *   *

"Build a fire," said Rade. "We won't be here long but we've got to eat and dry out." He sent a couple of archers out for seabirds. "And I want a lookout on the ship, just in case."

He had carried Vuk ashore, despite the old man's feeble protests. Alek, who normally repaired the sails, had already stitched up Teodor and was working on Paolo, the latter, whimpering like a dog. The stripling from the carrack, moaning and vomiting blood, seemed to have hurt himself where no wound was visible. His friend sat beside him trying to offer solace. The other survivor, middle-aged and burly, had a broken arm that needed to be set. A fourth was looking for wood for the brace.

Looking down the beach, Rade counted five who'd survived the wreck. Some must have gone down with the ship because there were only eight or nine corpses that had washed ashore. The five survivors meant three extra men on his boat after his own losses. Only one was a seaman. The man with the broken arm. He wouldn't be able to pull an oar. The others were actors. They wouldn't be able to row either. He supposed he could force them to learn. The boy from the carrack might be dead by morning. Even then, the biggest problem would be space. The *bergantin* was a tight fit with a full crew, stores and booty. And they were far away from their island hiding places. And, as Vuk, churring like a nightjar, constantly reminded him, it was winter.

Jovan came up to him. "What do you want to do with them, *kapetan*?"

"I haven't decided," said Rade, turning to look back at the survivors.

"They'd make good food for fish," said Jovan, and left.

Rade stood watching the others strip the corpses.

"A cask!" shouted a voice. "God's bones, a sea of casks!" The corpse-strippers abandoned their duty and as one, rushed into the sea.

"Wine! God's teeth, they're full of wine!"

"Get the bails," shouted Miloš. "We can drink from the bails."

Rade took the first bail, brimming with liquid to Vuk by the fire. He pulled him up to a sitting position. Vuk drank, spluttered, drank, coughed, and lay down again. Rade felt the blast of heat on his skin. "Too close, Vuk. Let me move you farther away."

"Right now, *kapetan*, I'd embrace the flames of hell," said

Vuk. "Cold as a witch's teat." He shuddered. "More wine." Rade raised him up and he drank. "I thought I was done for."

"We all thought that... about ourselves." Rade moved a little way from the fire.

"Rather drown in this." Vuk's eyes were bright. "The *bora's* still out there."

"I hope not," said Rade.

"Not going to ask the bones," muttered Vuk, and took another gulp, "Don't go away." He gazed into the fire. His face was pink. After a while, he began to pluck at his moth-eaten gray shirt. It had been white once. The grizzled hair on his chest showed through the holes. "If hell's hot," Vuk said, "what's heaven?"

Rade thought of the morning's conversation. "Warm," he replied, looking into the bail. *Christ's nails, the old man could drink.*

"How would you know?" asked Vuk.

"If it were cold, who would want to go there?"

"*I* would," muttered Vuk. "Pull me away from the fire." Afterward, he sighed in relief. He was sweating.

Rade laughed. "Warm now?"

"Cooked," growled Vuk. "Like a suckling pig on a spit. Your fault."

Rade turned to take wine to the wounded and put some on their cuts.

"One more drink," murmured the old man. He lay back. Rade felt Vuk's clothes as he began to snore. They were warm but not as hot as they had been. He looked into the bail. It was empty.

*   *   *   *   *

The salvage effort rapidly became a shambles. Beneath a cloudy sky, the bobbing casks washed in, one after another.

Once broached, the crew was on to the next and the men were staggering. Vomit already splattered the sand. Tomorrow they'd be white-faced, gut-rotted specters of their former selves: the price of liquid oblivion and lack of sustenance. Having climbed the ridge, scourged by wind-whipped sand, Rade could see a long way in all directions. There was nothing out there but birds, grass, and wind. And enough bitumen to caulk a thousand ships. Or so they said. Descending, he found he would be reluctant to leave the land. Tomorrow he'd have to order the crew back on the boat and out into the winter sea. He knew they'd resist. For them, the ghosts of Hamsa and Sandar were out there somewhere: bitter, accusing, desolate. Stretching white hands and open mouths out of the depths. For him, the obscure message in the letter clashed with Vuk's prophetic words. He didn't understand the message. He didn't want to burn. He was afraid that one prophecy would lay claim to the other.

By early afternoon, the men, having exhausted the supply of casks, rummaged through the wreckage. In one chest, they found a cache of spectacles which were passed around to all who'd try them on. In another, ruined spices, their value lost to saltwater. Various bales of cloth, some damaged; cypress chests of clothing; crates of pottery vessels filled with oil, some cracked; barrels of salted fish: a cage of chickens, all drowned. The list went on but the men paused to cook up the dead chickens. They were every bit as good as the archers' seabirds.

Afterward the crew's attention turned to what remained; the actors' crates in which lay various trappings for the stage: all sorts of masks, plain and fancy dress, wigs, false beards, fake weapons, even rolled up scenery. And beyond, the line of pale corpses, a few still waited to be stripped. After divvying up the actors' possessions, and removing what was usable from the last of the dead, a noisy parade of men, fortified with wine, burdened with loot, and wrapped in sodden but outlandish finery, cavorted happily along the shore—bearing the last small portion of wine from a new-found cask to those, who, not already besotted, lay by the fire.

Behind this raucous procession, one man remained. He knelt motionless beside a pilfered chest, riveted by his find. His black hair fell damply on his neck and shoulders. His cache of treasures, forgotten on the sand. Hunting through the box, he'd found something so unexpected, so utterly appalling, that he'd recoiled in horror. Nestled beneath the stylized grotesques for humor and the noble masks for tragedy, wrapped in sodden linen, lay the cold form of a man's head. His one glimpse of skin had confirmed it.

Rade walked back to the fire, suddenly stone-cold sober. "Whose head?" he asked one of the bleary-eyed actors.

The actor looked back at him. "If it's on my body, it must be mine." He leered drunkenly. "Shall I make a play on it?"

"In the box," said Rade. "With the masks."

"Oh that one," replied the actor as realization dawned. "That one belongs to a prince."

"What prince?"

"A prince who lost part of his face in a fight. We're bringing it to him. It was very expensive." He looked alarmed. "Nothing's happened to it, has it?"

"It's not a head," said the kapetan slowly. "It's a mask."

"Best one you've ever seen."

"Show me," said Rade, pulling the actor to his feet. "Show me now."

The actor wove his way to the box, pawed through the other masks and began to unwrap the head. He soon let out a terrible cry. "*It's ripped! God's bones, he'll flay us!*" And he began to keen like an animal.

Rade saw that a hands-width long rip in the skin revealed the mount beneath. A splinter from the chest had torn it.

"That's why we took the boat out of season," wailed the actor. "The prince paid to have it brought. It's ruined!"

Rade carefully peeled the mask from its support, amazed by its gossamer lightness. It's weight was negligible even though parts of it were built up on the inside. There were ties to plait into hair and the edges were impossibly thin.

"He'll flay us," wept the actor. "We're dead."

"He'll never know," said Rade, folding the mask into his doublet. "The ship is lost. Stop wailing like a woman. He'll never know."

*   *   *   *   *

In the end, Rade took the survivors. There were four. The stripling, the group's best lead for female roles, died during the night. His friend, Aldo, sat beside the body, utterly spent from trying to find some way to ease his suffering—and failing. Only he, head down, grasping his friend's still, cold hand, was left on the beach. A bent figure amongst the looted detritus from the carrack. Cursed and prodded by Miloš, the crew, foul-mouthed, sweating, heads throbbing and stomachs heaving, had reluctantly boarded the ship by first light, leaving the boy's body and those of the drowned to the crabs.

They watched the *kapetan* return to the beach.

Rade looked down at the body, the only one not stripped naked by his crew. The boy had been handsome once. Even in death one could see it.

"Let me place some stones on his body," pleaded Aldo, looking up. "For posterity."

"They'll be gone by high tide," said Rade, turning away. "This one or the next."

Aldo stood. "I can't just leave him here."

"Christ's nails, Aldo or whatever you're called, the boy is dead. His soul has flown. Corruption follows." And starting down the slope, Rade added, "I have no time for this."

"We grew up together. Can't we...?"

"*We leave now,*" interrupted Rade. "Before the Turk arrives. Before the wind turns. With you or without you. *Don't be a fool and a weakling.* There is nothing here but ruin."

Aldo waded out to the ship. Weeping.

The *bergantin* had been loaded by dawn: the crates, casks, bales and chests carefully positioned to balance the load. Miloš had directed it and he was an old hand at choosing and preserving what had value. As the sun rose over the distant mountains, the crew rowed out past the bars until, offshore, the sea wind came up and caught the mainsail and they could make the farthest point of land. The three actors and one sailor from the carrack hunkered down in the lee of the rail away from the chill of the wind. Rade, leaving Miloš at the tiller, came to squat beside them, plumbing the depths of what they knew, ignoring Aldo's ill-concealed sorrow. The other three were only too glad to pay their passage. It was something Rade would continue to do with increasing intensity during the following days of the voyage. But on that first day, he asked simple questions and listened. At noon, the sun came out. The water sparkled like ice on a snowy ledge. Aldo's tears dried and he began to talk. And the great sail, halyard repaired, drew them north.

*   *   *   *   *

Except for chilly rain-swept days and winds that changed and set them back on their journey, the voyage progressed uneventfully until that pale, cold afternoon off the Italian coast when the sea erupted into thrashing foam and spurts of water. Whitecaps crowned the waves as the slap and splash of a mass of dark stream-lined bodies rose from the water. Fins crested and fell alongside the bow and in the white-streaked wake of the ship and well out into the surrounding swells. The great blue-black pan of sea abandoned its customary regularity and virtually pulsed and boiled with their passage.

"God's blood!" exclaimed Teodor. "Look! There are hundreds of them!"

"Saints preserve us!" cried the player, Giorgio, making his way between the benches to the safety of the gangway in the center, clutching at the pile of goods. His face was ashen. His eyes screwed small with dread. "First time at sea and I've passed from shipwreck to Jonah. Is this the end?"

"It may well be," said Vuk, agate-eyed. "Monster eels up from the void."

Rade sat up on the bench where he'd been dozing. He wiped the sleep from his eyes and stood up to look.

"Holy Virgin!" moaned Giorgio, not daring to look over the side.

"Roiled up by the storm," observed the graybeard. He nodded knowingly. "Excites the gut." Local gossip favored eels. The Bojana River, not too far distant, grew eels that would choke a whale. Of course their size increased with speculation. And speculation was a very human failing. Vuk wallowed in anticipation.

At the helm, Miloš tried hard to suppress a grin.

"Having drowned and been saved," wailed the actor, "now I'm to be eaten! God's teeth, what sin condemns me to so cruel a fate!"

"Let me confess you," offered Vuk, interested.

Miloš lost the battle.

Giorgio suddenly looked suspicious. "What business is it of yours?" He looked narrowly at the graybeard. "You're not afraid!"

The ancient shrugged. "Never found anything bigger than a thumb inside an eel." He peered into his skin bag. "Might still have it in here somewhere." He rummaged noisily among the scapulae. "Of course the eel was a small one," he added as an afterthought.

"Big dorsal for an eel," muttered the carrack's bearded sailor, arm in a sling, peering over the side. He winked.

Surrounded by toothy grins, the faint-hearted player remained intent on the bag.

"Listen to that old windbag and he'll have you guarding fleas in the sun," snickered Paolo.

Vuk released the bag and felt for his dagger. "I'd rather let the air out of you, *stronzo*." He spat on the deck.

Paolo rose from his bench and started forward but their *kapetan* stepped between them. "The game has gone far enough," Rade said softly. "Are we going to bleed over a shoal of dolphins?" His voice dripped with sarcasm. "What kind of fortune is that?"

The two men drew back. The actor looked carefully about him. "Dolphins? Not eels?"

The crew nodded solemnly. Giorgio squinted searchingly at the waves and at the forms inside them. Faced with what seemed a plausible explanation, he recovered his aplomb in an unusual manner. With the pantomimed jerks of a large bird trying to unstick itself from a limed branch, he comically released his hold from the stores. Chuckles greeted his performance. He staggered to the rail. Amusement followed him. There, with the phenomenon clearly exposed, he displayed such surprise and wonderment that he nearly fell in. The crew began to guffaw with laughter. Turning back with a smile of sheer delight, he said, "Of course. I knew it all along." The actor raised his hands to the heavens. "Arion's blessed finny friends!"

"Orion's up in the sky where you can't get at him," replied Jovan.

"Arion," repeated the player. "Greek musician."

"Down here," continued Jovan heedlessly, "dolphins as

bringers of luck is what's important."

Not a fish for a tomb had its place in the sun as well, yet Giorgio allowed comedy to triumph. "Whichever tweaks your interest," he said mildly, "rescued Greeks, star hunters or fortunate fish." He looked over the side again. "Life boils down to luck," he said soberly. There was a murmur of assent. The actor sighed dramatically and rolled his eyes. "And God knows fortune is a woman!" he drawled loudly. He looked expectantly at his fellow players.

"'*I know the disposition of women,*'" the two chorused, "'*when you will, they won't;*' and '*when you won't, they set their hearts upon you of their own inclination.*'"

"Amen," intoned the player. A spirited echo came back to him, windbags and eels forgotten.

Silver-black and crescent-finned, Apollo's beloved leapt playfully beside the boat. With satiny grace, they teased the ship, rubbing here against the hull and there, changing places on the bow wave. After a while, the men's voices died away and there was silence. Only the sound of the vessel slicing through the water, the creak of the rigging, and an occasional flap of the sails accompanied the powerful vaults of the dolphins. The companionable pairing, ship and mammal, produced a curious contentment: as if the sea approved their voyage and signaled this was so. Finally, as suddenly as it had come, the shoal turned and faded away into the limitless gray of the horizon. Even then, no one wished to break the spell. The men remained like statues gazing out at the waves— wondering at their blessing.

Fortune is a woman, thought Rade. *Would that it were so.*

Chapter Nine

It is very rarely granted even to Nature herself to produce
anything absolutely perfect in every part.
        —Leon Battista Alberti

Venice, End of December, Ninth Month to Third Week,
January, Tenth Month, Venetian Year 1492 – Caterina

A few days before Christmas, the sickle moon had lain in
the west, horns canted up and to the left, a slim silver
fingernail rising after sunset. The harbinger of the shining orb
of Epiphany and the reminder that even the moon "died" and
that old Father Time had fashioned his scythe from its image.

*   *   *   *   *

The bed was a den, warm and dark with the bulky comfort
of Nonna to hide behind. She felt like a cub protected by its
she-bear. Although the latter had risen and gone off to put the
household in order, her generous hollow was still slightly
warm and pungent with her scent. Beside it, Caterina turned on
her back and stretched luxuriously. Her *camisa* was rucked up
about her shoulders and beneath the linen sheet, the smooth
mystery of her body extended invitingly toward the foot of the
bed. She left the bunched shirt where it was and ran her fingers

lightly over the length of her torso and then repeated the caress, this time more slowly. She was thin. Like a boy. The bones of her hips were sharp against the skin but the mound of Venus was soft and its cleft was as sensitive as the finely tuned string of a lute. She felt a shiver run through her. Not a boy at all.

Sensuality was a sin, especially in women, but despite that fact, nothing was designed to reduce temptation: not the carved wooden breasts of the caryatids on her father's chairs or the Roman style bronzes that were so much in fashion or the naked Bacchantes, gods and goddesses painted on the sides of houses or the flamboyant courtesans who passed in the canal, limbs voluptuously outflung, blatantly exposing all but the most nether bits of their anatomy. She had marveled at them many times as a girl, and seen nothing. Yet, as her body changed from child to woman, in a flash of understanding, she'd known instinctively the taste of Eve's apple and the gnawing sensuality of Original Sin. Even now, in her half-starved state, she had been unable to escape this sensuousness, only dull it. Her sense of guilt rose. She sat up, pulled down the *camisa*, and lay down again on her back, staring up into the dark, draped canopy of the bed. One arm drooped from the covers, catching the light, a strip of ivory on shadowed drapery, like the habit of a nun. The only other choice she might have made—had her father allowed it.

There was a sort of refuge in the boyish form. For months, she'd hoped that Ariosto would find her lean body and lack of softness unattractive. And leave that part of her alone. But she'd been unable to reduce her breasts to the desired flatness, even going so far as to seriously consider disfiguring them. She'd held the pilfered knife in her hands in the moonlight, silver glinting off the blade, and pressed the sharp edge of it against the curve of her breast, and forced herself to think of saints and martyrdom. When that didn't work, she'd imagined the abhorrent caresses of Ariosto—somewhat reduced in menace by her imperfect knowledge of the act of sex. At the last, her tears had trickled down the unblemished blade, as much in relief as in disappointment, and she'd returned the knife surreptitiously to the kitchen without waking Nonna. And then, the ship had foundered and everything had changed.

During the bleary days of her illness, her father had made several inquisitive forays into the light area beyond the silken bed curtains and, reassured or not, had said little, and had just as quickly quit her chamber. She smiled. The lion of commerce was a mouse in the face of female indisposition. And she'd been glad of it.

They hadn't talked and Caterina felt a familiar stab of guilt and fear. The glassy resignation with which she'd finally accepted her doom lay in shards about her. St. Fina laid out in readiness on her plank had been granted a different levitation. The "death" that she'd anticipated hadn't taken place and anyway she'd been too fond of living to achieve a real demise. Yet, it was all so utterly unexpected. After all the years of dread, the sacrifice was canceled. The role of victim transferred. A different offering wafted bloated and yellow-eyed beneath the swells, the striped beard no longer trained on an opponent, having exchanged the hurtful thrusts of criticism for the sharp-toothed incursions of fishes. Because of this, God had let her go. Had traded Isaac for the ram, the aptly-named *Agnus Dei*. Yet the barter had included not only the ship and the odious Ariosto, but an entire cargo of living souls: a price that haunted her.

The lump rose up again in her throat. She felt trapped between the sheer horror of those drownings and the utter dissolution of what had always seemed inescapable. She knew only that above the dark, congealing grave of marriage, the caged bird flew free. The lamb returned to pasture. The prisoner stumbled off, unbalanced without his weighty fetters.

And she knew too that her tears flowed, untouched by sorrow, from an inner, gushing spring of deliverance. *Fina, take up your plank... and live!*

That evening, Caterina dried her eyes for what she hoped was the last time and made an effort to compose herself. The bed linen was changed and sprinkled with lavender. Sofia was sent to draw water and put it on the fire and when the wooden tub grew warm and full, she bathed until the heat departed and the floating skin of rose petals spoiled. Afterwards, Sofia dried and combed out her hair with long, satisfying strokes, and Caterina took up her ivory mirror. Although the person in the glass was drawn and red-eyed, her expression was resolute. A victim no longer. The face of a defender—readying herself for what came next.

*   *   *   *   *

During the weeks that followed, Caterina began to gain back some of the weight she had lost. Her clothes were still loose but regular meals had softened the angles of her body and given her face that flush of vitality that spelled the return of good health. Then, only ten days before the feast of the Conversion of St. Paul, the specter of marriage reappeared.

Caterina had been fastened into her dress as usual, then into the separate but complementary laced sleeves, and Sofia and Nonna were squinting up and down, as they usually did, surveying the result. The dress had been altered to accommodate her present slenderness. The light filtered softly through the window, highlighting the rich folds of material where its length doubled over on the terrazzo. Caterina tucked a strand of gold behind her ear and waited.

"The wine velvet becomes you, madonna," said the maid admiringly. She plucked at the end of a lace crossing Caterina's bust that was slightly askew. "Not so flat anymore," she said in her broad peasant accent, retying the errant cord and then surveying the girl's bosom. "Twin white doves. For love, madonna. For children." Sofia giggled. "Messer Ludovico will be pleased."

"I don't think," murmured Caterina coolly, "that my father views me in quite that way."

"Oh, no! I didn't mean your father!" cried the maid. "God forbid!"

"Someone's coming?" asked Caterina suspiciously.

"We're not expecting anyone today," replied Sofia formally. She looked to Nonna for confirmation.

"He only wants you to dress as befits your station," said the disinterested voice of her nurse.

"So if someone comes by… " burbled the maid. Nonna shot her a frigid glance and she clamped her mouth shut on whatever else might have been revealed.

"I see," said Caterina dryly, breathing out against Sofia's zealous trussing and feeling like a sausage in its casing. It was an old dress but better than she would have chosen to oversee the washing. Apparently Father had insisted on it. "Thank you, Sofia." She turned toward her nurse. "Do I pass inspection?"

Nonna pursed her lips, and nodded, hands on hips. "Ripe as an apple," she muttered baldly. "Ready for the picking."

"You sound like Sofia. Is that supposed to be flattering?"

"It's a measure of maturity," replied the older woman, shrugging. "Yours. It's time we found you a husband." She gestured to the maid to pick up her basket.

Nonna had been cross all week and needed to be coddled. "Not yet," answered Caterina mildly, turning her back to sort through her handkerchiefs. "Not yet. I'm not prepared."

"Prepared for what?" demanded Nonna, heaping laundry into the maid's basket, and not waiting for an answer. "Build the fire high, Sofia. Be sure you boil the water," she directed. The maid solemnly acknowledged the order. "Wait until you see the bubbles before you put the linen in," added Nonna sternly as if speaking to a small child, "and use lots of soap." She shuddered. Giovanni, gondolier, man of all trades, had dropped a receptacle into the cistern by accident and dredging about for it, found in its stead a rat. Because of the rat's state of decomposition, they'd drunk nothing but wine for a week, at medicinal full strength, not watered down, and consequently Cook had been incoherent at every meal and the meal itself, very nearly inedible. Tomorrow the tank would be laboriously drained and the sand filter replaced. It would take time for the sediment to settle, so they were washing the pale-hued linen now, essence of rat and all. To Nonna, whose greatest satisfaction derived from food, tomorrow, paired with sobriety in the kitchen, couldn't come soon enough.

Sofia clumped heavily down the stairs.

Nonna began relegating items to another pile of laundry. "Your father says... " Abruptly, she marched over to the window, threw it wide open, and leaned out to scrutinize the pile of fuel two stories below in the courtyard. "You'll need half as much again," she called. *"Sofia! Do you hear?"* She waited, and then called down a second time.

This time, there was a muffled shout from below.

The tyrant tramped back to the washing. Caterina bided her time.

"A husband," grunted the despot. "Soon."

"What does Father say... about waiting?" asked Caterina meekly.

"He suffers misgivings," returned her nurse promptly. "It's only natural. *Goods that sit too long on the shelf, no matter how sumptuous, grow tired, and are eventually perceived as spoiled."* She recited the phrase from memory.

"I'm goods!" cried Caterina. *"He said that!"*

"Well, no... " replied Nonna, "not exactly. He spoke of arranging another betrothal as soon as it is proper. But you know as well as I do," she said pointedly, "that when the merchandise is ready, somehow, somewhere it will be sold. You may not be merchandise in the true sense of the word... but you're ready," she concluded with a dismissive nod.

"In what way am I ready?"

"In all the ways that you were ready six weeks ago... plus one. But it's an important one."

She looked at Nonna's raised eyebrows, considering. "There's no successor to Ser Ariosto," said Caterina slowly. No one by right of kinship could step confidently into the breach as the rightful claimant to Ariosto's betrothed. He had been the last of his name. The opening for husband-to-be was now fully available. "Father will have to begin anew," she said quietly.

"Yes," agreed the older woman. "Whereas before you were guarded, because you were spoken for, now, because you're mature, you will be guardedly offered."

Focused on the dreaded marriage, and after the shipwreck, on her own distressing malady of spirit, she could see that although she hadn't heeded the signs, the inevitable had happened. Her coming of age had altered her status in the household. While she'd cried and starved herself or sprawled languidly in the bed or puttered absent-mindedly about as a semi-invalid, all during those weeks, the little girl and loving daughter was being neatly consigned to the past. Discarded, she thought unhappily, or less wrenching, simply tucked away for safekeeping. Like a memory. In their eyes, she'd assumed the status of a woman, and to avoid emotional entanglement and its complications, her father and Nonna had already separated themselves from the girl they'd raised. She would either be leaving or another person, her husband, would be added to the occupants in the noble house. Either way, she would belong to another, be subservient to a different authority—even in the household to which she had been born. She took a painful breath. It was like experiencing a stab wound. She put a hand over the place where it hurt, over her heart.

"So applications for my hand will be forthcoming." She managed to get the words out evenly.

"They will. In fact, there may be some already."

"No." Caterina closed her eyes.

"Your father is worth five-fold what he was ten years ago. Few Venetians have prospered as he has," said Nonna busily. "Nor do they own an heir without attachments." She tossed another sheet on the pile. "Suitors will be swarming like bees."

Caterina felt an overwhelming surge of dismay. There could be no question of another Ariosto, not now, not ever—anymore than Nonna or her father would suffer another rat in the cistern. She had to find a way to forestall it. She tried to think like her father. Nonna was right. When the appropriate bell tolled, the market would open. Based on what he thought was best, and on his instincts as a merchant, Ludovico would act on a new alliance. And Nonna, trained to think first of dowry and patrimony, would support him. It would all be over before Caterina had had time to react. To them, she was a fruit in the marketplace. Mature. Desirable. The product of a bitter harvest. Needing to be sold. Looking at it through their eyes, she felt the wound close in her chest and her heart take on its own sheath of steel. Whatever the noble house wanted, she thought defiantly, the "goods" had other plans. Rather than be chosen, she would find a way to choose.

She looked appraisingly at her nurse, former friend and confidant. "Rats come in pairs," she observed darkly, picked up the pile of shirts and handkerchiefs, and started down the steps.

*   *   *   *   *

For several days, under the reproachful glare of the pottery lady, Caterina worked on a plan, preparing her argument, discarding one approach for another, trying to guess what her father would say. In that time, a rising sirocco blew the tides into the piazza so that the celebrants of Mass had to wade through the water on their way to San Marco. In this most Marian of cities, it seemed to Caterina that the patient submission afforded the freezing, baptismal tide could only be a sign of the power of the Holy Mother. Thereby reassured, her strategy set, Caterina placed a small, prayerful offering before the painted Virgin by her bed, turned her back on the accursed "destiny" plate, and requested a conference with her father.

On the day of the meeting, her father's *studiolo* chilled even the bravest heart, not by the rising damp of winter but rather by the guarded sanctity of his private lair. She knocked, and when there was no answer, put her hand tentatively to the latch. As the door creaked open, the merchant lifted his head, pulled off his spectacles, and squinted at this unwelcome intrusion. Recognizing his daughter, Ludovico sighed, replaced his glasses, and gestured for her to come forward. "Caterina." His voice extended little welcome. "The day is short. I have much to accomplish."

"Should I return tomorrow? To discuss the marriage?"

He remembered why she'd come. "No," he demurred, returning his quill to its holder, "I've set this time aside for you." His cap of silver hair framed a square face and a level gray-eyed gaze. By habit, he reached for the hourglass and turned it over. He smiled, "Are you eager to be wed?"

Transfixed, she watched the sand stream through the narrow channel between the bulging chambers of glass. In a single act, in setting a limit to their meeting, he'd reduced her to a supplicant. She saw her dreams spill out with the sand. Anxiety welled up, the plan forgotten.

"I beg of you," she said in a low voice, "do not promise me to another Ariosto!"

Ludovico glanced sharply at his daughter. When the man had perished, she'd been bed-ridden. Naturally, he'd thought... "You wept," he said, "for weeks."

She took a step backward as if distance would help. "Mother Mary forgive me... not... for... Ariosto." She watched a small mountain rise from the cascade of sand.

"Then what was it for?"

She drew in a shuddering breath. Then another. Tearing her gaze from the glass, she answered softly, apologetically, "It was... *I was so desperate*... don't you see? And then, the ship was lost... and I thought, they'll find it. *Don't let them find it.* I will never be safe. He will come back. *It will begin again.*" Her voice wavered, "I never thought... I hadn't meant... they *all* died. *Oh God, have I sent them all to the bottom of the sea?*"

"I see." His face took on the expressionless facade he assumed for business. "You'd better tell me what you did."

She nodded slowly. Apprehension mounted and her voice came out thin as a reed. "I feared him," she swallowed the awful sound and tried again, "as I have never feared anyone." She looked up. "You must have sensed it."

"I knew you didn't want to marry him." His voice held no apology.

She took a deep breath and forced out the rest of it. "Since that summer," she said hoarsely, "Fina's summer, I *prayed* this betrothal would fail. *Prayed every moment* I was reminded of him." She lowered her gaze. "Nonna talked about him all the time."

"I told her to," replied Ludovico coldly.

"Father, he didn't like me."

"He didn't know you."

"He wasn't kind. Not once. Not ever."

"All those prayers," observed Ludovico distantly. "And then he drowned." *You weren't kind either.*

"Father, did I kill them?"

He looked at her agonized face. "Through prayer alone?"

She nodded.

"Only a saint can influence fate. And that is one thing you are not." His voice hardened. "Yet what you did is contemptible. I'm ashamed of you."

Her fists clenched and the pale tendons stood out from her knuckles. "As God is my witness, I never dreamed it would end like this! Father," whispered Caterina. "Am I to blame if he found fault in everything? Am I to blame if he was old and ugly, and like a spider? All the years," she cried plaintively, "since you punished me, I have cowered in his shadow. And he took pleasure in it. *He took pleasure in it!* The complaints, the directives, the criticisms... it has never stopped. *Could you not have seen it?"*

Ludovico took his time rearranging the papers on his desk. Wearily, he rubbed a broad hand across his brow and over the bridge of his nose. In the last year, Caterina's behavior had seemed distraught, but, having no point of comparison, he'd considered it an ordinary display of apprehension on the part of a child bride. Nonna, in a momentary confidence, had described the process as a "painful uprooting" and although he had accepted her comment as valid, he had not directed his thoughts beyond it. After all, child brides were sent to the marriage bed every day of the week and their sheer youthfulness and inexperience were the means to assure the purity of their bodies. And many of them went to the beds of strangers. He realized that to Caterina, who had seen him four times, Ariosto must have seemed a stranger. What he had seen as molding, Caterina had perceived as complaint. Had she known Ariosto, had he furthered it, what benefit might he have fostered?

"I have not been blind," he said softly. "Ariosto was a busy man. I thought, when you were married, you would bring out another side, one more to your liking."

Her head was bent. She didn't answer.

"And, child, I had made a promise to your mother," added Ludovico. Their families had been friends.

Hearing the regret in his voice, she raised her head. "Father, Ariosto is gone, as is my lady mother. Surely, the obligation has been fulfilled." She drew herself up. "Look at me. Truly, I am no longer a child."

She'd dressed carefully for the occasion and now turned slowly, holding out the skirt of her heavy *camora*. She was robed in cut velvet and silk and her sleeves and bodice were sewn with decoration. As she moved, Ludovico noticed the line of fine linen above her dress, the musky scent of her perfume, the milky glints from the galaxy of tiny pearls scattered over her bodice, the mass of golden hair snugged back into a pearl-wrapped knot and then loosed, falling shining down her back, and then, perhaps for the first time, the soft curves of an unchildlike maturity. He also observed that where her flesh was exposed, there were goose bumps on her skin.

He said, "You're cold."

"You could store snow in here," she said wryly.

"I know," he said. "It keeps me awake." He rose to his feet and dragged the squirrel-lined cloak from his chair. He draped it about her shoulders.

She snuggled gratefully into the fur. "I'm grown," said Caterina. "No longer a child."

"No longer a child," he echoed, regaining his chair.

"Then, Father, it is no longer necessary to intercede for a child. Allow me," urged Caterina, "as a woman who will be a wife, a voice in my marriage." Before he could answer, she forged ahead. "Permit me to influence your choice."

Perceptibly, Ludovico's mood changed and darkened. He replied angrily, "Because I have no son, I allowed you the education of a man. You need to be reminded that it is, and always will be, a man's right to choose a wife, and," he glared, "a father's right to choose a son-in-law."

"If I'd been born a man," replied Caterina stonily, "my very birth would decide my place in society. I'd be fixed there like a mollusk on a mooring pole. You'd be forced to accept me as I am." She steeled herself to remain calm. "In being born a woman, and born into wealth," she said bitterly, "I find I am nothing but a pawn." She laid her palms on the front edge of his desk, the cloak framing her rich dress in wool and fur, a dark bird with a plum-colored breast. "Father, *I am all there is of you.* Assign me the dignity of your patrimony. Try to imagine me as your son."

Ludovico shook his head adamantly. "God made you what you are, Caterina. Nothing can change that. Your place is to serve, not to demand."

"Then how may I use what you have taught me? To what purpose?" cried Caterina. "I have learned what you have chosen. I can do more than weave and sew. I read and write and cast a reckoning like a merchant. I'm conversant in French and Latin. On my own, I've begun to study Greek. Surely even your learned friends would find me accomplished."

"For a woman, accomplishment is an end in itself," replied her father. "And learning is best displayed in the privacy of the house. Remember Isotta Nogarola," he warned.

Who could forget the Veronese maiden whose learning and fluency of language became too public for a woman, even a noblewoman. Who was attacked anonymously as being unchaste—and ruined fifty years before. *Ancient history,* thought Caterina, pursing her lips.

"Cassandra Fedele seems to be thriving," returned Caterina, "even here, in Venice. Father, attitudes have changed."

"Cassandra's abilities were well-displayed in Padua," noted Ludovico. "At the university such exceptions occasionally pass unchallenged. Yet her acceptance as a Latinist has been to the humanist circle in Florence, not Venice. Rather safely far away, don't you think?" He didn't wait for an answer. "Anyway, we've strayed beyond your capabilities."

"And yet," she countered, wounded, "you allow me the privilege of discussing your affairs and voicing an opinion."

He looked thoughtful. "I value your judgment." He frowned, "But *not* on the subject of marriage."

"We agree that I have no experience in this matter," she admitted quickly. She paused to retrench and in drawing back, swept a sleeve across the desk and caught its looped tie on an object. As she bent to untangle it, Ludovico reached forward to retrieve the small book, one clasp open, balanced precariously on the edge of his desk. It was just out of reach. Caterina briefly studied his outstretched hand and then pushed the volume safely under his fingers. "I can't imagine you," she said, changing the subject, "without your books."

He glanced guardedly about him. They were as much his children as she was. "At the center of publishing," he said gruffly, "books are difficult to ignore."

"This library is often praised," said Caterina, looking about. "I've enjoyed my privileges here."

"You may continue to borrow from it," he said obligingly, fingering a heavily embossed and decorated cover, "when you've married." He waited for the conversation to turn.

"I'm like a vessel," said Caterina thoughtfully, pulling the cloak closer. "With a literary cargo. Filled with all the writings you wanted me to read." She caught his gaze. "I've studied history and can debate it—even though I've learned it only from the contents of these parchments. Or recite Ovid and frighten or amuse you with stories of the gods." She gestured. "Or describe the circles of Hell or the treasure of the *City of the Ladies*." Her father's cloak was heavy. Her feet had begun to ache from the sheer weight of her clothes. She straightened her shoulders trying to redistribute the discomfort. "You've always said, if one is without the eyes to see it, one may search out the truth through the written word."

"Yes," he agreed watchfully, "I do say that."

"Allow me to proceed along that path. Aristotle lived God knows how many centuries ago and yet we follow his suggestions—even in today's government. And Barbaro's ideas on marriage took up months of my time as a child and prepared me for the wifely duties and expected behavior of married life."

He nodded expectantly.

"If I've learned all this wisdom through another's experience," queried Caterina, "how important is the lack of my own?"

"I see," replied Ludovico slowly. "We've returned to the subject of marriage." He considered the problem. "My answer is that the question within what you've advanced is still the man's question about choice—which is inappropriate to a female. Neither Barbaro nor Aristotle would uphold your request."

She tried again. "If I were to advance a request, appropriate to my gender, would you honor it?"

"It depends on what it is."

She sighed. "I accept that you will choose my husband. I ask only for a man of good character."

"And you wish to define this 'good character?'" guessed Ludovico.

"Yes, but only by what I've been taught—as a woman."

"I'm sure I'm about to be enlightened," he said matter-of-factly, getting up and dragging a chair from the wall. "Sit. You're standing there, swaying like an overloaded donkey. Do you want something warm to drink?"

She shook her head and sat down gratefully. She mustn't

let up now. "Father, I've tried in every way to be guided by my tutors, even in judging the character of men."

"I hope this isn't going to be based on Tommaso."

"No, not on Tommaso, my lovely Tommaso, nor his knights—only on the books you gave him to use. They taught me that the inner beauty of a man's soul is reflected in the outer beauty of his face."

Her father nodded absent-mindedly, "That is a philosophy of our time."

"Thus it follows, to ensure excellence of character—for surely the excellence of one's soul is the defining point of character—one should follow the wisdom of the philosopher and *require* that a suitor's visage define the essence of his mind."

He was almost amused. "Why don't I simply hang out a banner like the one for the Jerusalem voyage? Or set up a table in the piazza? 'Direct your query here if you are the manifestation of divine perfection.'" The absurdity of it grew.

"What makes it so objectionable? You must choose by some criteria. Why not the beauty of the soul?"

"Oh come now, is it truly the man's appearance that concerns you?"

"I would not be averse to a well-made man but, no, most of all, I want a good husband, good in spirit, good in character, good to me." She hesitated. "And yes, I want to avoid the grotesque."

"We could rule out hunchbacks," muttered Ludovico.

"Only ugly ones," replied Caterina.

He had the grace to smile.

"We could look at it as a philosophical experiment," she continued. "It might amuse your circle of learned friends. It would avoid the stigma of class. I think noble suitors will not come forward as you'd hoped. Not now. Not if I am called *befana* for some ill-chosen words that I spoke when I was nine, and humiliated. I don't see a noble marriage in the stars."

So she'd found out. "No one will call you 'witch' to my face," he said quickly.

"No. But Ariosto's death fuels the palates of gossips and there is no amusement more entertaining and perverse than defamation."

"There will be plenty of suitors."

"Because of you."

"I'm afraid, my child, they were always because of me."

"But will they be condescending because I'm said to be 'unlucky?' Or obsequious because you're wealthy? Or scheming because they want your business? Or fall to fighting over precedence and rivalries? If," went on Caterina, "the politics of choice become too damning—since there's much to gain or lose—would one not do well to gird oneself in the vagaries of philosophy?"

He hadn't thought of that. Her little philosophy, appropriately encased in mind-numbing rhetoric, might be useful after all. He flicked his gaze to her face.

She smiled, a little wanly.

He found he still needed to expose the fatal flaw. "Caterina, there is more to life than a beautiful face. The female heart is weak and easily led astray."

She reached forward and laid her fingers lightly over his. "Father," she said affectionately, "*you* will always be first in my heart. If that is a weakness, so be it. I am a straw in the wind for you. Don't you see? I would choose, not with my heart, for that is already taken, but with the mind that you have given me."

He was silent for a while. Then he stirred, stretched, and said, "Sometimes you *do* reason like a man." He added gruffly, "I suppose I'm to blame. Go back to your duties. I will think on your proposal."

It was then she realized the sand in the hourglass had long

ago run out. And no one had noticed.

*   *   *   *   *

A round ship left for Spalato two days later. One of the
rare January departures. Two of the letters were on board,
along with some vouchers for a local merchant's goods. One
was destined for Zara, thirty-two leagues up the coast, with its
small humanist circle gathered around the poet, Bishop
Divinća. And one for Spalato. It was an experiment unlikely to
succeed.

Chapter Ten

I saw the angel in the marble and carved until I set him free.
—Michelangelo

From The Port of Fano, The Marches, to an Italian Hill Town
in Tuscany, Mid-March, First Month of Venetian Year 1493 to
Early April, Second Month of the Venetian Year 1493 – Rade

The village lay in a hollow but the workshop occupied a
fortified farmhouse farther up the hill. Its stone watchtower
trained scant, square windows on a valley that was plowed and
seeded, and seemingly peaceful. Rade had crossed into the
lands of the house of Medici, which, under the wastrel Piero,
spent its days in subterfuge and jousting, but not, at present, on
war. To be less conspicuous, he'd chosen to travel on foot. A
decision carefully calculated and afterward rued for it had then
rained enough to float an ark. It was now laughable that the
man about to be newly hatched, so intent on concealing his
past, could not take a stride without leaving a highly visible
trail. He turned his attention to the final foot-sucking steps in
the endless morass and climbed, trying to resurrect his former
fate-driven urging and ignore the rising feeling of folly—water
filling the depressions behind him as if the underworld had
followed spring up to the surface.

Repeated pounding on the heavy door produced a servant,

who surveyed him from head to foot, and reluctantly admitted him to the front room. Behind him, stone outbuildings around the stableyard emitted thuds, bangs, voices, and the occasional rhythmic sound of hammering. Inside, no amenities, no furniture, no samples of the craft relieved the room's bare geometry. Only the walls were eloquent: displaying names scratched into honey-colored stone by those who presumably had waited too. The proprietor, when he finally made an appearance, found Rade intent on deciphering them.

"They were mercenaries," said the artisan by way of introduction. "Imprisoned here. Before my time." The man was short, capped in brown, and shaped like a boulder. "For them, this," his hands swept the cubicle of stone, "must have been an exercise in forbearance."

"Tutelage for your customers," said Rade in a neutral tone. But he could feel their ghosts rising. See the scars on the door where they'd tried to get out. The notches by the high, barred windows. The replaced pavers where the old ones broke when the prisoners pried them up. They were still here. He could feel it. *No, not forbearance, futility.*

"It does have that effect," agreed the artisan. He took in the torn cloak and mud-caked leggings—and the telltale bulge of weapons. "Is there something I can do for you?"

"I've come for your craft," replied Rade. He asked a few pertinent questions, and satisfied with the answers, launched into a description of the mask from the shipwreck. When it was clear the man had made it, Rade advanced his proposal.

"Not just a disguise," muttered the artisan. "No ordinary request to be easily provided. Only the concrete form of an insubstantial philosophy?"

"Yes."

"For you?" He observed the man's damaged face.

"Yes."

"Someone from that godforsaken nest of humanists put

you up to this."

"No." He waited for him to ask why, but the question didn't surface.

Shaking his head, the boulder began to circle around his person, considering this angle or that, wreathing the room in garlic. "My imagination is expensive," he said.

"I can pay," asserted Rade.

"They all say that," grunted the artisan. He produced a handful of measuring devices from a pouch in his apron. "Christ's nails," he muttered to himself. *The nest had lined up some ruffian, foreign as well, for their mischief. Well, he'd play the ongoing game, outfox them, and show him the door.* He selected a caliper. "Look at something," he said. "Don't move."

Rade fixed his gaze on a name on the lintel.

"That's it. Like a stone. Exact calculations produce exact quotes. Now, look at me. No, truly look at me."

Rade shifted his gaze and took in the penetrating eyes of his critic.

"The eyes are well-favored," the craftsman said grudgingly. "A lot depends on the eyes." *Years of violence had marked this face. Lucky he hadn't smashed the orbital ridge as well.* The boulder put aside his instruments and wrote on a scrap of parchment. *They're testing me, he thought. The louts are testing me.*

Alternately mumbling, grunting, whistling and writing, the artisan continued his assessment. Rade waited. The willow stick scratched against the surface of the paper like scrub scraping against stone in the wind. Scrub leading down to sapphire bays. Bays that leeched their hue from the sky and mysteriously deepened it. And it was curious how his mother's words came back to him. "As blue as the Adriatic," she used to murmur, cupping her small son's face in her hands. In those early days, a tender smile would crease her eyes and mouth. "That blue is your father's yearning for the sea." And she'd look off in the direction where it was supposed to be—for she'd never taken that distant path to the shore.

The craftsman's voice broke into his thoughts. "What you desire, I design rarely, and then mostly for princes. Convince me," said the man, taking in his appearance, "that you can afford it."

"The actors…" began Rade.

"I know the one the actors had," interrupted the boulder. "It was made for a nobleman. A disfigured nobleman at that. In fact, a prince. How they got it, God only knows…"

"If it wasn't theirs at the outset," asked Rade, "how did they know about you?"

"The fact that you traveled here to purchase a mask suggests that you already know, in the halls of kings and despots, my craft is much admired. We are all aware that the skills of the courtier lend themselves to artifice. Theater and lavish public displays of power depend on the same. I'm sure you've experienced your share. After all, we live in a time of festivals. Religious. Profane. Civic. Up to six months of the year are spent on masking and disguise. What would life be…"

At that moment a racket erupted in the stableyard and the fat man rushed out, cursing. Rade, out of curiosity, followed. An enormous wooden structure that looked like a waterfowl lay half mired in the mud, half on the cart that had carried it. A cacophony of shouting surrounded it and, whirring, clicking, and pulsating, the bird was squawking, too.

"Have you ruined the bladder?" screamed the artisan.

"No, no, messer Conti. It's working. It's working very well."

"Doesn't sound like a swan," said Conti in a menacing voice. "If you've ruined it…"

"We fix! We fix!" cried the workman, struggling with the other three men to get the great skeleton back on the cart.

"By tonight," said the fat man with finality. "The feathers

must be attached tomorrow, the glue needs to set, and I want to see those wings flap when the swan cries. It leaves in a week."

"Yes, we fix!"

"Christ's thorns," said the artisan, "what a throng of imbeciles!" He started back toward the door. *"I want the wheezing sound, not a squawk like a chicken,"* he shouted at the men.

"We fix," came the chastened reply.

"And wash the mud off!" He went in and almost slammed the door in Rade's face.

Rade, no longer tired, worked to wipe the grin off his face.

"Where were we?" growled the artisan.

"The actors."

"Yes, well they take a small part in these productions. Quite insignificant. So they know about me. What else do you want to know?"

"Do all your masks resemble skin?"

"No. Mostly, they're disguises for festivals. Like Carnevale. I make them intricate. Deceptive. And, unlike the 'skin' masks as you call them, clearly artificial," replied Conti. He went to the door and looked out. Frowned and came back. "Imbeciles."

"The skin masks aren't for pleasure?" pressed Rade.

"Oh, they can be. But as I have already said, those masks are very dear. They're to be worn everyday. To create a lasting illusion."

"Of reality."

"Yes."

"What keeps them," Rade hesitated, "from wearing out?"

"Any number of things," replied the boulder with another pungent blast of garlic. "The compound with which they are made—which remains my secret. Special ointments. Extra care. Daily maintenance. And for the purchaser..." Conti stared at the bulge of weapons and cleared his throat, "a certain gentleness of occupation."

The hint was ignored. "So they don't last forever." *How long would he truly have to wear it?*

"Nothing lasts forever." The artisan considered his potential patron. *Did he even have any money?* "But for the man of lesser means, there are ways around it." He went on helpfully, "After all, ladies paint their faces…"

The thought was repellent. *"You would make me a woman?"* Rade's voice had a dangerous edge.

"Now you are being an imbecile," shot back the artisan, "I meant…"

"I want only your best work," cut in Rade.

"Look here, whatever your name is, if you're planning to seduce some woman—perhaps above your station?—mask yourself as Apollo," said Conti. He brightened. "Women adore gods. I sell…"

It was dangerously close to the truth. "I have no use for gods."

"A pity," said the boulder, "when there are such carnal pleasures to be sampled."

"No one needs a mask to buy a whore."

"No, but given a little mystery, evident mystery, one can do anything. Reality only buys reality. Illusion buys creativity."

"What I want is what we discussed when I first came."

"My best work to satisfy a clever philosophy? Are you mad? *Do you think I was born under a rock?"* growled the artisan, shaking his head. "This is some ridiculous exercise in rhetoric. Some elaborate ruse. Be done with it! My best work costs more than anything you're likely to own!" He began to turn away. "Take what you can afford, or be on your way."

"You have yet to name a price," said Rade through his teeth.

The artisan turned, looked him in the eye, and threw out a

gut-wrenching number. "That's what it costs. I do not bargain. Not for this. Now, abandon this farce, for I know that's what this is, and get out." *That would show them.*

Rade kept his face unreadable. At least he hoped so. He thought of the mask in the box. *God's blood, he could buy half a ship for that.* He watched the sun's last striped shaft light the room. It settled on a stone, like so many others, with a name on it. He was tired of the man, the place, the conversation, the journey. The name, incised in spidery lines, stared back at him. His boots hurt and he could well imagine the state of his feet. It was too costly. Far too costly. He was a fool on a fool's errand. He should find Vuk and go back to the ship. Go back to the Adriatic. Go back to the life that he knew. And then he actually saw the letters. Read them. *Ludovicus.* Read them again. And the meaning slowly materialized. *The name in the letter.* And he knew then that the wheel had turned.

Rade reached under his cloak to where he'd hidden the letter. He remembered its warmth. Its enigmatic message. The vertiginous weight of fate. There followed the clink of metal on metal. The artisan, making his way across the pavers, looked furtively toward the inner door.

"It's not what you imagine," said Rade, drawing forth his heavy purse, and against all natural inclination, taking a fistful of *ducats* off the top. The boulder, only partly reassured, afforded them a passing glance—that quickly became a calculating stare. There was a significant pause. "God be praised," exhaled Conti. His gaze traveled from the *ducats* to the travel-stained garments to Rade's face and back again. Affording the purse a last appreciative look, and pulling off his apron, the artisan allowed a wolfish grin to spread across his face. "Enter into my furnished chamber," he said expansively, as a door swung open, seemingly on its own. "Come. Refresh yourself. I see we have a prince at the gates after all." *He wondered where those fools of humanists had gotten the money.*

From outside came a prolonged wheeze, followed by another and another. The sounds were accompanied by a pulsing, mechanical, up-and-down sound, like a pump.

The boulder halted. Cocked his head. A look of triumph spread across his face. "O music from heaven, play on!" cried Conti.

The sound, which reminded Rade of something dying, kept up a steady rhythm.

"My swan," said Conti, looking back at Rade. "My Medici swan." He sighed. "If only we had a Leda to celebrate it with."

*   *   *   *   *

As Rade climbed the hill beyond the workshop, more than a little drunk, overfed, and ready to retire to the small stone guest house, life at sea seemed far away. The servant, now distressingly unctuous, lit his way with a torch and the blazing light blinded him, eclipsing the chill darkness of the night, the possibility of stars. The landscape was spinning and he'd heard enough of mechanical swans to last a lifetime. He thought if he got into the building, still conscious, he would be fortunate. Yet, at the end of the evening, despite the long day, the huge meal, endless discussion, a clean pallet, and the warmth of a small brazier, Rade found sleep eluded him. He lay in the dark, his gut uneasy with the richness of the feast, and relived the *bergantin's* landfall in the Marches.

They'd navigated the shoals to moor the boat near a silted-up port once owned by the Malatesta—a port temporarily unsuited to a large carrack or war galley. The actors and the carrack's sailor had disembarked, peppering their former comrades with ribald comments and puns for posterity. Still on sea legs, they'd lurched toward the familiar wooden bridges over the Arzilla and beyond that, the fosse. There the Giulia gate received them, embedded in the towering, lime-washed walls, and spat them out toward the coarser delights of the city. Delights with which three of them were already intimately acquainted. For the rest, it took several days of importuning officials, innkeepers and merchants, negotiating prices, unloading cargo, paying import taxes, and reloading carts before the crew, rife with anticipation, followed them into the taverns of Fano. Rade watched the men pass without incident through the guards who stood beneath the crossed keys of the Papal States emblazoning the gate. The gonfalon of Perast with its lion of St. Mark fluttered above him, affording the *bergantin* the security of a small but foreign port—under the protection of Venice—at a time when, fortuitously, the doge and the pope were allies.

Rade looked in the direction the crew had taken. "They won't be sober long."

"Neither will we."

"No," said Rade in a level tone, "I'm leaving." Miloš went on examining papers. "*Miloš*," he said, raising his voice, "put aside your reckonings. Look at me." He watched Miloš put a rock on the papers. When their eyes met, Rade said, "I'm leaving the ship."

Miloš, his mind full of figures, stared at him. "Leaving? When?"

"This afternoon."

He was incredulous. *"When did you decide this?"*

"I've been leaving," relied Rade, holding his gaze, "for a long time. Since the bays." It was a quiet statement of fact. "I thought you'd guessed."

The unexplained observations that Miloš had kept, too tired to examine, in the back of his mind, resurfaced. The haste after Zara. The unplanned departure in winter. The deaths, the needless deaths, in the storm. Rade's endless conversations with the actors. The crisscross push to the north that took them where they never went in the normal course of things—and where the *bergantin* might be in peril. He could see the pattern now. Rade had put them all at risk for some end that he hadn't seen fit to explain. And they, obedient to his commands, had unwittingly provided the means. Miloš began to feel sick.

"It's final? Your decision?" But he already knew the answer. And Rade knew he knew the answer. Miloš, nauseous, closed his eyes for a moment. When he opened them, he said tersely, "And me? What am I to do?"

Rade grinned. "Take them hunting, *kapetan*."

His first thought was to stuff the grin down the bastard's throat. *Let him choke on it.* His second was that it must have been obvious to everyone else on the ship. All the extra work he'd been given. The annoyance he'd tried so hard to suppress. The random exaction of reckonings based on the heavens when he'd been woken from some well-deserved sleep. The insistence that he keep and record bearings, currents, approaches to anchorage, rocks, shoals and landmarks in the portolan—a task always performed by Rade. The several occurrences where he had to stand or paddle, roped to the boat, in icy water with Rade by his side because the latter thought the calking might be failing, or the rudder pins were loose, or the anchor chain might be worn—when Miloš knew all these concerns had been addressed in the shipyard. The insistence on minute scrutiny and testing of the sails, pulleys, fastenings and ropes. The precise location of spares and bombasine for patches. The careful inspection of the state of the oars and thole pins. Reexamination of handling the crew. Being told things he hadn't known about them and why this man worked with that man but only in a certain way. The change in the location of Mordecai and whom to deal with as his factor in Zara. The land routes they used. The best caravanserai or inns for storage. The taxes they paid or didn't pay and why. Who held the lease on the stone house. *God's blood, he'd been an utter simpleton. A donkey-brained lout. Worst of all, a fool.*

"Do I have a choice?" The ground shifted beneath him.

"No." Rade handed him the bank vouchers. "It's all here." He paused. "I've taken my share." He'd already added it to the Zara cache. "Next time, it'll be your share."

"You're not coming back."

"If God wills it."

What kind of answer was that? Miloš scanned the horizon and then looked back at the curtain walls of the town. The malevolence of the massive keep now cast a shadow over his future. He no longer looked forward to the night's debauchery. To his easing of need with a bought woman in a soft bed and the welcome oblivion of drink. The entire load of the *bergantin* and all its crew had fallen on his back. Like an old man bent with age, he already felt the weight of the burden.

"Where are you going?" Even his voice sounded old.

Rade shrugged.

"You want me to captain the ship? I'd like to know where you're going." His anger showed.

"I'm not sure where I'm going, Miloš. Not yet." Rade's voice was toneless.

Liar. "God's blood, Rade! There'll be times when we need to ask about something."

"Use Mordecai. He'll know." His expression suggested that should be the end of the matter.

Miloš, frustration growing, grabbed Rade's arm. "It's that letter, isn't it? The one you won in Zara."

The look of wariness stopped him.

Miloš dropped his hold. But he persisted, "Damn you! You lying bastard! *What's in it?"*

"Newly anointed," replied Rade softly, "and already Vlad the Impaler. And I'm first in your forest of men. I should be honored."

"You bastard, you owe me an answer," snarled Miloš

through his teeth. "All those years together... what's in the letter?"

Rade shrugged. There was a long moment. "Riddles," he said finally. "Fate." The deep blue eyes betrayed nothing.

"Your fate?"

"Yes."

"Sounds like an early death." He looked at Rade's face.

"I hope not." *You'll burn. I didn't say you'd die.*

And then he knew. "It's not all good, is it?"

"It's hard to tell," replied Rade. *He didn't want to burn.*

"God's teeth, Rade, did you ever wonder what *vila* breathed life into you? You've naught but dark thoughts and darker signs. For us, the night is full of stars. For you, it's full of blackness."

"It's as bad as that?" It was a rare chink in Rade's armor.

"Most of the time it is."

"We all have our demons," said Rade. He rubbed his face with his hands. "They're in me." He looked tired.

"What's in you, Rade, is Vuk. Too many years of signs, portents, omens, God-knows-what, sloughing off those filthy bones. I've watched him. How old were you when he pulled you from the bay? Twelve?"

"I don't know." He shook his head. "Thirteen. Fourteen."

"It never happened before that, did it? The signs. The vertigo. The darkness."

Rade was quiet.

"It's Vuk, you fool. It came from Vuk."

Rade looked away, through the sway of rigging at the water lapping against the nearest hull. Gradually he became aware of the soft crying of birds. The long, flat expanse of shore. The distant headland. The Levantine wind in the shrouds. He raised his gaze to meet that of Miloš. "I was nine," he said. "The first time, I was nine. Vuk had nothing to do with it."

Defeated, Miloš turned his back and sighed. *You can't live your whole life interpreting dreams, examining entrails, chasing Sibyls. What kind of life is that?* He took a few quiet minutes to look over the vouchers and saw Rade had done well by them. The profits were better than expected. The unknown prince, who'd ordered the mask, had exercised a penchant for luxury. *Christ's nails, the woolen cloth had been first quality.* The wreck had been an unexpected gift. He thought too of the dolphins. Another unexpected gift. *A good beginning for the next voyage.*

Miloš, satisfied, turned to Rade and gestured toward the ship. "I'll keep her safe." And in that same moment realized that the *bergantin*, and all that it promised, was under his command. Rade was leaving. He would be the *kapetan*. He felt at last a frisson of pleasure. With renewed confidence he added. "For now, I'm going to hold back the share to the crew."

"Good thinking," said Rade, pulling himself together. "Because if you don't, you'll never get off these shores." He started to cross the plank to the temporary dock. "Which tavern did Vuk choose?"

"Who knows," shrugged Miloš. "He's cleared out his belongings."

"What!" Rade stopped. *"When?"*

"This morning. I saw him leave."

"Why didn't you stop him?"

"Why should I? He's too old for the oar."

"For the love of God, he's gone into a devoutly Catholic countryside," said Rade. "It's not his religion. It's not his language. It's not his country. And he's carrying a skin bag of sheep scapulas. Christ's blood, Miloš, he's ripe for disaster."

"He'll find a way to survive," said Miloš. "He's lived longer than most."

"Damn your bones, Miloš, he should have stayed on the ship."

"Do you even see him anymore, Rade? No, truly *see* him?" said Miloš. "He's old. Look at the storm. He was as stiff as a corpse. No, listen to me. He shouldn't be on a ship. He can't pull his weight anymore. Let him go." *It would be better for you.* And he went back to checking the vouchers against the ship's accounts. Miloš looked up as Rade left the ship. "He knows it's time. Let him go."

In the end Rade did let Vuk go. He tried all the taverns. No luck. Outside the last on the outskirts of town, where part of the wall had been laid by the Romans, he stood looking uncertainly down the muddy lane that led off between the fields. It was crisscrossed with wagon ruts, hoof marks, the imprints of boots, sabots, pattens, even bare feet. There were too many tracks to know if Vuk had taken it or not. And there were too many other routes he could have taken.

"He's crossed the Rubicon," had drawled Giorgio, red-eyed and stinking of drink. "Won't be back." And he had returned to the ample charms of his whore in the tavern.

The Rubicon was a river farther up the coast. Rade guessed that meant he'd gone north.

*   *   *   *   *

Early morning light fell on the utilitarian items: furniture, tools, rags, supplies, in the workroom. They had talked since dawn, the artisan being the main source of conversation, and Rade occasionally making some comment or offering an acknowledgment. The financial transaction had taken place the night before. A level of tolerance had replaced the friction of their first meeting. And Rade had lost the indigestible feast during the early morning hours in the weeds behind the guest house. Now they'd reached the workshop.

"Remove your shirt so I don't drip plaster on it. Over there will do. Now," said the craftsman, taking off the covering and sifting the dry mixture that would make the plaster, "let's talk about the path you plan to take."

"The mask?"

"Yes. As you know, in our time, in art, a mask implies a certain meaning."

"Not in my profession," said Rade.

"I won't ask what profession that is," replied the fat man, smiling. He looked at Rade, now stripped to the waist. His body was as he'd expected: slim, muscled, and scarred like a mercenary. He suppressed any recognition of violence. "Here then is your first art lesson." He picked some impurities out of the mixture and looked up. "If you were to turn over a painted panel, a portrait, you might see a mask on the *verso*. Or you might see one in a detail. Or in a carving. That mask is the symbol of false dreams."

"We all have dreams," said Rade. "They rarely come true."

"Yes, I agree. So it follows that dreams are not real. They happen while we are asleep. Unconscious. Now we have something that is not only not real but also false."

"Am I supposed to figure this out? Is it a riddle?"

"At first, it was a riddle." Conti turned. "Lie down over there." He pointed. Rade turned and the fat man got a full view of his back. *"Christ's blood!* What did you do to deserve that?"

Rade lay down. He said only, "I've paid for it."

"I can see that."

"Is this where you want me to be?"

"Yes. Push down a little farther so we have plenty of board to support your body. Oh there you are," said Conti to his servant. "Be sure the door is latched."

"And the answer to the riddle?"

"The answer is this," replied the artisan, bringing the bowl to a nearby table. "False dreams are illusions. Masking and disguise lead to illusions. Bring water," he ordered the assistant. "And get the soap." Conti turned, "Illusions you may not have considered."

"What sort of illusions?"

"It's hard to express," said the fat man. "Perhaps I should start by saying, as you can imagine, you see someone else in the mirror. It isn't you but in not being you, this false image offers a semblance of protection. You are no longer accountable for the person you were. Over time, you may come to accept this false image as your own. Behind the mask, you become equal to people who are not your equals."

"I don't see how that could be harmful," said Rade, feeling impatient.

"Let me finish," returned the artisan. "One may experience a sense of transience, possibly a loss of identity, even transformation. Obviously it depends on how often you wear it. I expect, for what it cost you, you'll wear it a lot."

"I might."

"Apply the soap," the craftsman said to his assistant. "Be sure it's thick. Let me see the texture. Yes, that's good." He turned to Rade. "Be still or we'll have to do this twice. I'm doing up the straps. Be sure the headrest supports your neck before the buckle is closed."

"It does. How is it harmful?"

The artisan sighed. "I had a young man," he said, "scarred from a fire, who wore a mask."

"Your mask?"

"Yes. A 'skin' mask, as you call it." He tested the leather. "How are the straps?"

"Tight. I can't move."

"That's the way I want them." The artisan turned to his assistant. "We'll put the reeds in last."

"Let's try to avoid death by plaster."

"That wouldn't be good for my reputation."

"I'm glad to hear it. Go on…" urged Rade, trying to ignore

the physical side of the process.

Conti sighed. "After a while the young man, Matteo was his name, became so attached to the mask, he wouldn't take it off. Not for any reason, any event, or any person. His character began to change. He became insolent, loud, careless—even cruel." He continued to run his hands through the mixture, as if he were washing them. He went on, "To return him to the person he truly was, and not what he had begun to think he was, the mask was taken away."

"And he agreed to that?"

"No. It had to be taken by force. And following that, it was destroyed." The artisan stopped, poured water into the dry plaster and mixed it up. He said in a quiet voice, "Without it, Matteo found he could not live with himself."

"What happened?"

"What do you think happened?" snapped Conti. "He went mad."

Rade closed his eyes against the soap. "Is that your admonition? What is it you want me to say? That I sympathize? That you should feel remorse? That I should fear for my sanity?" The soap was a cold rivulet trickling down his neck. He scoffed, "He was contemptible. Weak. Womanly. Fate meted out what he deserved."

"At the time," continued the fat man, "there were no thoughts of fate. His family believed he would recover. Stood firm. Refused another mask."

"So he went back to the man he'd been?"

"No. After two months, and various attempts, which were thwarted, he took his life." The artisan stopped mixing the plaster. "He was twenty. Hardly grown."

"He's better dead," said Rade. "Who wants to be babbling nonsense in the street? Shut up in a room? Tethered like a dog? Can we get on with this?" He added, "I'm not that man. I never will be."

And damned to the end of time. The artisan sighed, cleaned his hands on a rag and wiped his eyes. "No. I can see that. It was a cautionary tale." Finally he looked closely at Rade's face, as if examining every change in the texture of his skin, and carefully, Conti began to apply the mixture. "Put the pads on his eyelids."

"Charon's coins," observed the servant helpfully.

"It's not as bad as it sounds," the fat man said. "Keep still. Keep your mouth closed. You'll be able to breathe through your nose. It's a cocoon, not a coffin. And yours alone. *Sua quique persona* / to each his own mask. There will be no other."

After a long while, he said softly, "Matteo was my son."

                    *   *   *   *   *

Two weeks following his arrival, Rade sat, at the mask maker's command, eyes closed, on the edge of the same uncomfortable board table where he had lain while plaster was applied for the cast. During that initial procedure, he'd thought torture must begin like this. Small vexations piled on top of others. Restraint. Mounting discomfort. The unremitting noise of the spoken word like that of a small tree in a courtyard, heavy with sparrows. Loss of sight and speech. Soap dribbling down over his ears, his scalp, into the hollows of his collarbone, cold and liquid, when he would have sold his soul for a drink of water. Unseen solids, like thick mud, falling on his skin and then growing hard and hot. Breathing confined to two hollow tubes inserted in his nostrils. Fear of suffocation. Helplessness to the verge of panic. Being a prince hadn't lasted a day.

This time, there were no bindings to keep him still. No signs of restraint. Again the canvas curtain was closed. Like the last two fittings, the fat man fussed about, tying this, smearing ointments, adjusting that, taking the mask off, scraping, putting it back on, talking endlessly. Rade prepared himself for disappointment. At long last, the fitting ended, the boulder fell silent, and he was permitted to stand. Gratingly, the canvas was pulled to one side. For the first time, he heard the command that a mirror be brought and placed on an easel before him.

"There," said Conti quietly. "Don't be surprised that I've given you a scar, a small one, to show that you have lived. No man's face is perfect."

The hands that had guided him were gone.

"Open your eyes."

There was something about his voice. Rade drew a deep breath. Took in the plain frame of the mirror and afterward, the image within. His breath stuck in his throat.

"You didn't think it'd be this good, did you?" mused the craftsman. "They're all like you. They don't believe it... 'til it's done.

Chapter Eleven

*Marriage is like putting your hand into a bag of snakes in the
hope of pulling out an eel.*
—Leonardo da Vinci

Venice, Mid April to May, Venetian Year 1493

The door swung open and Ludovico looked up through
steepled fingers at the beribboned boy standing breathlessly in
the doorway. Roberto, dark-eyed and slender, was just
fourteen, the youngest son of a minor patrician, and Ludovico
knew, passionately interested in a match with Caterina. Her
strategy and his subsequent letters had landed several beautiful
youths whose family fortunes were waning. They were, in
Ludovico's eyes, hardly grown. He'd already seen that he
would need to mold the one he chose if he wanted to pass on a
lifetime of mercantile success.

"Roberto," he said, surprised, "it's good to see you."

The long slim fingers tightened on the door frame and
then pushed off to impel the youth into the room. "And you,
messer Ludovico. I hope you aren't displeased that Giovanni
let me in."

Ludovico could hear the slow steps of Giovanni dutifully
climbing the stone steps. Far too late for an announcement or a
query. "Of course not." He smiled. "To what do I owe this

visit?"

Roberto ran a hand through dark curls. He seemed agitated.

"Roberto?"

He drew out the first syllable of the name. "Carlo has told me that you have chosen."

"For Caterina?" Ludovico smiled. "No. Not yet."

"He's told me you've chosen him." The boy looked petulant.

"Roberto, I am looking you straight in the eye and telling you that isn't true."

"But then he says you *will* choose him."

"I haven't decided whom I'll choose. I have another six weeks to go."

"Messer Ludovico, you *must* choose me." Roberto leaned forward, his hands on the edge of the table that served as a desk. "My family, as I have told you, was included *before* the closure of the Maggior Consiglio. Carlo's family, only since the war of Chioggia. He is," the boy practically spat out the words, "an upstart."

"My search," replied Ludovico, with studied patience, "is based on Platonic philosophy, not on an entry in the list of patricians. I will make my decision in six weeks. Or more."

"He is not suitable," said the boy.

Giovanni, panting, finally arrived in the doorway.

"Roberto is leaving," said Ludovico.

"No."

"Yes."

"But… "

"In six weeks, I'll know and when I do, I'll tell you," repeated Ludovico, shutting his ledger. "Giovanni, show Roberto out. He is due somewhere else."

Giovanni took one last gulp of air, sighed, reached out to close the door, and followed the reluctant Roberto back down the stairs.

"I'm too old to be a father again," mumbled Ludovico under his breath.

*   *   *   *   *

The shutters on the windows were closed as a young, unmarried woman seen staring out of them at visitors to her home would be an indecorous sight. Above the shutters, the roundels in the half moon arches let in the light. But they were too high. Standing on her mother's marriage chest in her bare feet, Caterina had long ago found that she could crack the wooden shutter inward, leaving a narrow, vertical line of sight, yet remain invisible from the opposing house—where the local gossip lived. It was the best vantage point on the street from the second floor, and the street seemed to be the way they came, and not by gondola. She hoped that Jason and the Argonauts, on whose painted history she stood, would be forgiving.

It had not turned out as she'd thought. She'd expected to be present at the interviews. She'd anticipated offers from men of twenty-nine or older because everyone knew that was the suitable age for marriage. She'd longed for a philosophical bent, a humanist side to their personalities. And now she stood, incarcerated in the womb of the house, escaping only for the occasional trip to church. And when she went to church, veiled, the boys—at least the ones her father showed an interest in, and they were only boys—pestered her, pleaded for love tokens, tried to touch her, to give her little gifts, to speak to her, and wouldn't leave her alone. And if she avoided them, they grew angry, and made remarks about her coldness or her station in life being less than theirs, and quarreled among themselves. Sometimes, in the street, if her father wasn't there, they even pushed each other and shouted insults.

"I fear the little hawk is being mobbed by sparrows," had muttered a fellow churchgoer, and to Caterina, the remark seemed apt. At such times, and they had grown more frequent, Giovanni and Nonna would each take an arm and hurry her home. Sometimes that ended it. Sometimes the youths followed her to her door. So, she thought, wiggling a chilly foot only to notice that Jason was squarely underneath, none of those things that she had wished for had come to pass. And what had come to pass showed little promise.

"It's a circus," grumbled Ludovico, passing by in the hall. "A procession of witless fools and I, the greatest fool of all."

Caterina, watched the youth, who had just left, stride down the street to where his friends waited, and after, noted his angry gesticulations as they moved off. She climbed down, planted an apologetic kiss on Jason, put on her shoes, and went down to the kitchen to learn what might be revealed of the visit. Cook's fireplace, which connected to the ones in the rooms above, had ears.

*   *   *   *   *

The day was overcast and the clouds hung like heavy canvas over a sea flecked with whitecaps. From time to time, the ship pitched or rolled and spray wetted their outer garments as the flock of pilgrims crowded closer together, craning their necks for that first sight of Venice. The rattle, flap and splash of passage punctuated muttered prayers, accounts of illness and tales of adventure as well as the main topic of conversation: the start of the Jerusalem voyage for which the ship was bound.

Standing shoulder to shoulder with the other pilgrims crammed onto the deck of the fishing boat, Rade cursed himself for not following Conti's instructions. Under the mask, he could have been lying face down on an anthill. His coarse brown robe, flapping in the wind, was as dull, uncomfortable, and penitential as the next man's and he too wore a cross and grasped a staff. Scattered about were various clergy employed, as the pilgrims were, in saving on the cost of passage. No princes of the church traveled on board this leaking excuse for a ship. No highborn nobles or wealthy merchants either. From Chioggia, along the Adriatic side of the barrier islands, the *lidi*, to the main break in the bar, it had mattered little that every breath they took was overlaid with the stench of fish—the fare was cheap and the passage short. And the wind, despite its chill, was a godsend.

He had come with the flotsam and jetsam of the pilgrimage trade. Those funded by a minor church, a lesser family or a small inheritance. Some, Rade thought, would actually pay the passage to Jaffa on the great galley and after that, the donkey ride under Saracen escort to Jerusalem. On the voyages to and fro, they would sleep under the deck in a stinking communal cabin and hide their valuables in the foul sand beneath the floor boards. And they would measure out every precious *ducat* for duties, tributes, food and guides in the Holy Land so that by the end, they would be eating the worm-ridden biscuit and tainted meat provided by the Venice-bound ship—because they had nothing left to spend. Others would voyage no farther than La Serenissima and Venice's own seventy saints and then go on to some other city laden with relics. A pilgrim who owned the means for a comfortable Jerusalem voyage—said to be one hundred and fifty *ducats* this year—would find some other way to get to Venice.

As the ship turned, buildings rose from the barrier beaches. First the bell towers of monasteries, and then the structures themselves, their walls topped with the pale green crowns of hidden orchards, outbuildings, houses, and finally, on either side, the crenellated walls of two *castellos*. Beyond them, more islands, and in the distance, a forest of bell towers and spars above a low flung mass of buildings.

"*La Serenissima!*" came the cry. And the rain, which until then had only spotted their clothing, drew a lead-colored curtain across the prize. But the deck was alive with rejoicing.

Rade put his hand inside the doublet under his wet robe and briefly felt the worn edge of the letter inside its tarred sailcloth covering. It was warm from his body. Vibrant with promise. It had journeyed far on a long and fateful voyage—and he, the unwitting recipient, was bringing it home.

*   *   *   *   *

The shouts came from the street. The clash of steel, running footsteps, name-calling, insults, roars of rage, another clash, and then another, cries of a passersby, a rattling sound, steel on steel, raucous yelling, and a scream that climbed, wavered, broke, and disintegrated into sobs.

"*Assassino! Assassino!*"

Giovanni launched himself from the canal's edge behind the noble house, into the *andron*, sideways into the storeroom to grab a cudgel or something like a cudgel, through to the street door—except that when he got there, he couldn't open it. He could hear a gurgling, sobbing sound and watched as something that looked like blood began to seep under the door. He heard parts of phrases he didn't want to hear and finally importuning those outside to unblock the opening, he heard the sound of chain being pulled over metal, the door finally opened, and a body half fell in.

It was worse than anything he could have imagined.

Carlo, the most favored of the suitors, the beautiful Adonis of the pack, lay in a pool of blood, gray eyes turned skyward, the haft of a *cinquedea* protruding from his chest. His own dagger, a less lethal type, lay in the street, also blood-stained but lacking a body. Hoping for a pulse, Giovanni put two fingers on the side of the boy's windpipe and feeling nothing, on the inside of his wrist. Although the youth's skin was warm, his gaze was fixed, and Giovanni had known he wouldn't find one.

There were people now, shadowing the scene, the boy, the door. One youth he thought was from Carlo's gang peered between the spectators and was gone. Running. Running like a hare. Sofia, sobbing, came out of the house with a length of dark cloth and laid it over the body. And Nonna employed her formidable presence to push back the ever growing crowd and allow the needed space. Giovanni knelt there until the watch came, asked questions, and more questions, examined the corpse and sent word to the family. He was still kneeling there when someone arrived in a faded gondola, exquisite with ornament, accompanied by the family priest, and took Carlo, newly wrapped in a beautiful wool cloak, away.

Giovanni leaned against the closed door, stiff and sorrowful and far older than when he had first dragged it open. He knew Caterina was somewhere in the house. Thanks be to God that she'd been kept from the street. He knew Ludovico would be back from his trip in a day or two. And he also knew they would never get the blood out of the marble. It would be there until every soul who passed it found out what had happened here. Until the gossip mill had dissected the story, embellished it and assigned it a significance that he already knew would be hurtful. It would be there, a visible blemish, until someone literally took down the door and tore up the street.

*   *   *   *   *

As Giovanni feared, the stain had lingered, an enduring subject of conversation. The other suitor, Roberto, who'd fled, had subsequently been banished for life from Venice and

Venetian territories—on pain of death. It was preferable to
being executed. But not by much. So Roberto too was ruined.

After that, the epithet *befana* surfaced again, and the
rumors about the reason for the fate of Ariosto and the *Agnus
Dei* were now tied to the altercation and Carlo's untimely
death. Appointments made were canceled, or worse, ignored.
The desirable suitors had then simply faded away, one by one,
until all that were left were the dregs. The opportunistic, low-
born, unconnected, uneducated dregs. Who were willing,
through greed, to overlook a witch. Marry her, but Ludovico
doubted, ever spend time with her. She would be a marker for
a fortune. As such she would live, at least until he was gone,
and then, who knew what would happen to her. In the hours
before dawn, he could imagine her: a sad, lonely woman kept
apart from the world. The victim of some ill-chosen words as a
child, and the weaving of fate. *His Caterina.* It was enough to
make a man weep with frustration. He was, once again, unable
to alter her status—and by association, his own. Possibly
forever. He knew well that all the money in the world could
not root out superstition once it had taken hold. And here he
was, caught in his own trap, awaiting the last few
appointments with the dregs, and wondering what he should or
could do next. Mayhap the world on the other side of the
convent grate. Could he bear that? Could she? Mayhap
nothing. Keep her with him. Let her age into a spinster. God
only knew what he should do next.

*   *   *   *   *

"From *Slavonia*," said Giovanni with a meaningful
emphasis on the last word.

Ludovico sighed. Another foreigner. He'd been thinking
about the Marches. Could he send her there? There were a few
distant cousins somewhere. He'd have to find them. *After a*

century apart? What kind of foolishness was that?

"Please," he said. "Sit." And he looked up. What he saw first were the long, strong but elegant fingers. And they were clean, a good sign. The eyes were very blue. The hair black. The man had a small scar on his left cheek that looked like an old sword cut. His clothes were black, fine but unassuming. And he was undoubtedly well made. Very well made. And not a boy. *Well Caterina,* he thought, *the Platonists seem to have sent you in practice what they have actually preached. And from the other side of the Adriatic of all places. You'll have to write Tommaso.* Despite himself, Ludovico found he was staring.

The man in turn seemed to be assessing his host, the room, the books, everything. He said, "I see now why the letter is so full of allusions."

"You have the letter? Did I send you a copy? Rade, is it?"

"Radović, shortened to Rade. I have it." He pulled the letter from his doublet and handed it to Ludovico.

Ludovico unfolded it. It was creased and worn but not a copy. "This must be the one I sent to Zara." *It had all the marks of something that had been read many times and then carefully put away.* He handed it back. "So, you are in the humanist circle there."

"No." His gaze was direct. "I won it in a card game." He added, "In good company." And for good measure, he threw out some of the family names from Zara he'd memorized. He saw Ludovico's slight nod at one of them. *Mordecai had said try to keep your story close to the truth.*

God's teeth, has Caterina fallen so low that now she is a prize in a game? Ludovico banished the thought immediately. There were already so few to choose from. He thought about how long it would take to get to Venice. Most ships wouldn't have sailed until spring. So, this chieftain, adventurer, or noble, if that was what he was, might or might not know what had happened last.

"I see." Ludovico sighed. "What makes you think I would entertain your interest in this marriage?"

The man before him smiled. "It was foretold."

What was he supposed to make of that? He tried to place this interloper. "You've come from our Adriatic colonies? From Zara itself?"

"I've come," said Rade, "from a country that does not belong to you. Zeta."

Ludovico looked puzzled. "I don't know it."

"You call it Montenegro. After the black mountain above Cattaro."

Where the Venetian porcupine married. The arms of Erizzo. "So, are you related to Duradj? The prince?"

Rade grinned. "We're all related to Duradj. It's a clan."

Ludovico tried to imagine what that meant. He'd always thought the basic premise of a clan was a lack of civilization. Yet before him stood a man from a country few people had ever heard of who spoke the language of patrician society. "Where did you learn your Latin?"

"We have monasteries in the Bay of Cattaro." Rade shrugged. "It was there. So, good or bad, I speak Latin like a Benedictine." *Four years as a servant to a lay Venetian with an appetite for the forbidden. But despite everything, he'd loved him.*

"Not philosopher's Latin." Ludovico couldn't resist.

"No. I think you would call it church Latin." The blue gaze came back to challenge him. "Philosophy is for people who have time for it. We have war sitting on our borders."

"War is a deterrent to learning," said Ludovico. "I admit that. But civilization moves forward on the back of education. And Latin is the language of the educated man. The educated man in turn directs his thoughts to philosophy."

"Yet the great philosophers, Aristotle, Plato, were Greek,"

said Rade. "Were they not? And they spoke Greek. Not Latin."

"You have a point." Ludovico smiled. *So much for that argument.*

"And your father? What did he do?"

"He had land," answered Rade. "In the mountains. Sheep. We all have sheep."

"Does he approve of your suit?" *What did he have here? The son of a shepherd? Or the son of a wealthy landowner? Would a shepherd send his son to a monastery?*

"The Ottomans slew him."

"I'm sorry," said Ludovico.

"It was a long time ago. I was a child."

"And the rest of your family?"

"I'm all that's left. Does that matter?"

"I don't think so. No."

"And your daughter? Does she have siblings?"

"No."

"So you see," said Rade with a grin, "we are meant for each other. There is nothing to get in the way."

Except for me, thought Ludovico. They talked for a while—about Zeta, Slavonia, Zara and Venice.

After a time, Ludovico said, "You will forgive me for my lack of courtesy, but as you are here for my daughter, I must necessarily ask how you make a living."

"I had a ship. A galley. We traded in the Adriatic."

"And now?"

"I have journeyed here to wed your daughter. What ship could compete with that?" Rade grinned.

"So at present you are without means," noted Ludovico, ignoring his attempt at humor. *Or was it bravado?*

"I am not without means. That is for a future conversation if that conversation occurs. However, let me say that if you do not accept me, I will return to the Adriatic and find a wife there." *So much for fate.*

The most important question Ludovico kept for last. "If we arrange a marriage, will you take my daughter back to your mountains?"

The extraordinary blue eyes considered him. "I've had enough of mountains," Rade said. "Life is better at the edge of the sea."

"Does Montenegro have a sea?" asked Ludovico softly.

"No," said Rade. "But Venice does."

Ludovico tried not to look relieved.

"And it's Zeta."

*   *   *   *   *

"My child, I'm afraid my choices are few," Ludovico said. "The hour has come to make a decision."

They sat in his study with the window open and the sound of birdsong outside. The sun made sharp, bright patterns on the terrazzo floor.

Caterina sat, her back straight, attired in a pale dress with tied sleeves of a different color, her hair pulled back, part braided, part falling in golden waves about her shoulders. She had clasped her hands together so that her father might not notice they were trembling.

"Are you asking my opinion or instructing me in yours?"

"Mayhap both," said Ludovico. "I would ask you first if you would prefer to enter the cloister. Avoid this road altogether. It would protect you. Even after I'm gone. And it is an honorable life."

"Father, I would rather die," she said gravely, "than spend my life behind a grate."

"I thought you might say that." Ludovico looked up at the window. He sighed. "Four of the men who have asked for your hand could be deemed acceptable. They are not what I had hoped for. And I still have doubts. None are noble. The first two are from Venice and although I disapprove of their father's business practices, it is not clear to me that either of them will follow in their father's footsteps. I have met with them singly. They are both comely as the philosophy dictates but plain in their conversation."

"Are you saying they're dull?"

"One or the other could be further educated. I think they are both capable of it. But they will never be humanists. However, the two are also brothers. That could be a problem."

"If you choose one, our marriage could sow discord with the other."

"It's possible. There's no evidence of a *fraterna*. As usual each one's interest is in your dowry, and when I'm gone, your inheritance."

"Have they asked about me?" She looked up.

"Not yet," said Ludovico, avoiding her eyes. "At present, I'm not inclined to have you go to either of them. I'm still worried about their father whose false profits and fraudulent claims I've heard more than enough about. So that's where we are with them."

Caterina bit her lip. "And the others?"

"The third is a dyer's son. He too is comely and Venetian but his hands are stained and he smells of urine." He added quickly, "Of course that's not his fault."

"No." She wrinkled her nose.

"He has little education and limited prospects because he is the third son. But he is intelligent. I liked him. The business is respectable and needs to expand."

"So your fortune appeals to him," said Caterina.

"It appeals to everyone. He'll want loans... shades of Ariosto. However I think I could mold him to my liking. He would not be a dyer forever. Except..." Ludovico seemed inclined not to finish.

"Except what?" pressed Caterina.

"His inclinations are so typical of country folk. I think he would take care of you. But I see you without the society of your friends. I see you outside all you know. I see you alone— until he comes to know you."

"Why alone?" *That was frightening.*

"It was just something that slipped out about having you live, not in Venice, but somewhere else. I thought at the time he wanted to spare you the dye vats but I think instead it is something else."

"He's afraid of me," murmured Caterina.

"I fear that's what it is," confessed her father.

"Because he thinks I'm a witch."

Ludovico examined a book on his desk. He looked up. "He comes laden with charms." He added in a quiet voice, "So do the other two."

Caterina's eyes filled up with tears.

*   *   *   *   *

"Messer Radović," said Ludovico formally, "we have come to our final conversation."

So he wasn't going to be chosen. Rade tried to contain his disappointment.

"You will know from former meetings that my daughter is dear to me."

Rade nodded.

"That I want to protect her and not lose her to some foreign shore."

"Yes."

"And that despite the information you have offered me, I know very little about you and have no way at present to find out more. You are a foreigner. A stranger to the world I know."

"My misfortune. I've told you what you wanted to know." He felt disengaged. Unable to imagine the future. So much had depended on fate. And fate had driven him here. And now, there would be nothing.

"I have a proposition to make."

Rade looked at him guardedly. "A proposition? What is it?"

"We begin with a betrothal. A lengthy betrothal. No, let me finish. In that time, I will undertake to teach you my mercantile business, our culture, Venetian rules and regulations, all the things you'll need to know as my future partner, and later, as the husband of my daughter."

"I came for a wife."

"Then you are a fool. Everyone else came for a fortune."

"So, instead of a wife," returned Rade, undaunted, "I am now offered a betrothal during which I am to be *instructed* as one instructs a servant or a child. And if I progress, I may marry. *That is an insult.*"

"No, that's not what I meant. I intend to afford you the courtesy of a lesser partner in my enterprise—to which you will also have made a commitment."

"And what will that be? That I marry your daughter?" Rade's anger was rising.

"*What kind of commitment do you think that is?* No, because if you marry my daughter, you marry my fortune," Ludovico said harshly. "That's a commitment too easily made and later discarded. Hence a betrothal comes first. Your commitment will be monetary. It will be an investment. Three quarters of the sum you say you brought to Venice."

Discarded? God's bones, she must be a veritable pig. That much of his worth? "And if all fails?"

"I return your investment with interest," replied Ludovico. "You still stand to profit."

"But without your daughter," said Rade.

"Without my daughter, who, during your betrothal, will— let me emphasize this—*remain intact.*"

"How could it be otherwise?" said Rade acidly.

Ludovico smiled a thin smile. "I confess this is a difficult bargain to consider. Withdraw if you like. There will be no bitterness. My fortune, like my daughter, requires protection. As I said, you are a stranger to the world I know." He added, not unkindly, "I endeavor to build bridges, not burn them."

Rade, who had been standing throughout the interchange, drew his foot back and forth on a line of sunlight. He said finally, "But those bridges must connect."

"Yes."

"With so much of my income committed, where do you suggest I live? Here?"

"No. I have another house in Dorsoduro on the quay. You'd live there. You'd come here every day."

"I didn't expect this," said Rade.

"What did you expect? That I'd hand over my daughter and watch you sail into the sunset?"

"No, not that either. Winning the letter has always seemed a form of fate. And I have followed it to this crossroads. Now I find a proposition that offers me a year of servitude to an idea that isn't mine."

"There, messer Radović, you are mistaken. What you actually followed," said Ludovico, "was fortune. I offer you the means to it. There is every reason to draw up a contract and every reason for you to agree to it." He walked over to the door and put his hand on the latch. "There is still one more part to this."

Christ's nails, was it never going to end? "What's that?"

"Wait here." He left the room. When he came back, he said proudly, "My daughter, Caterina."

Rade stared at the girl who slipped gracefully through the door. It was difficult to shake off prior expectations. As she looked gravely at him and he began to take her in, he could only think he'd been wrong. *The pig had become an angel.*

Chapter Twelve

You shall find out how salt is the taste of another man's bread,
and how hard is the way
up and down another man's stairs.
—Dante Alighieri

May to June, Venetian Year 1493

The wooden shutters were open. The bed had been dismantled so that the curtains were gone and the frame for the top had been removed. Rade lay in his own sweat and stared at a ceiling that he couldn't see. A ceiling whose presence was determined by the chorus of snores from the room above and earlier, by patterns of light from passing torches, lanterns, and briefly, by wavelets reflecting the moon.

It was his third night without sleep. He sat up, pulling the sodden shirt away from his skin, feeling the drunkenness of fatigue, the gritty eyes, the endless thoughts. No matter how he looked at it, he was trapped. Trapped by the signed contract, by the investment of his remaining wealth, by the need to wear the mask, by his attraction to a woman he couldn't lie with, even by the fact that the house in Dorsoduro, that he'd thought would be unoccupied, wasn't. Ludovico kept his menservants there. The only real bed had been given to him. He'd found he couldn't sleep in it. *They would find out.* Even the water lapping at the *fondamenta*, when he could hear it, was a clock counting out the hours to discovery.

Cursing softly, he got up and paced the floor. He thought if he went out looking for a whore, he might sleep. In this parish they were everywhere. Zara had been the last: the girl in the tavern. When his face had been his own and she could touch it. He remembered how she'd pleasured him and how, in turn he'd done the same for her. Only when he lay, sated, curled against her back, so that her fetid breath went elsewhere, did he come to realize how mechanical her performance had been. And soon after, he had lain in the dark, alone, for she'd answered a knock and gone into another room. And he had heard her. And after that, he hadn't wanted her, or anyone, until now. He put his hands to the mask, a necessity day and night in this shared place, and wondered whether that kind of intimacy would expose him and whether he could risk it.

"Up early, aren't you?" said a voice outside the door. It was Alberico. Thick-necked, brown-eyed, placid Alberico. One of Ludovico's retainers, once a bowman.

"Can't sleep," Rade said.

"Want to fight?"

"What?"

"On Sundays, early, we take a boat out to an island, just a big mud bank with some brush. No one lives there. The saplings give us cover. And we fight. Besides, messer Ludovico encourages the exercise. Keeps us hard and ready. You do fight?"

"Of course I fight," said Rade. "Why not fight here?"

"You can't practice arms in the city. The watch will arrest you."

"Can you provide swords?" He'd kept the dagger but left the sword with Mordecai.

"Yes. Daggers, too. But they're blunt. No sharp edges. No point in killing each other."

"I'll come," said Rade. He began to pull on his clothes, as he dressed, tucking in the linen of the shirt he'd lain in.

"Good. If you don't bleed, you can go to church afterwards." Alberico laughed as if that was uproariously funny and went into what served as a larder. He came out chewing on a loaf of bread, and as Rade emerged from his room, tossed part of it to him. "Not stale enough to break a tooth," said Alberico. "See you outside."

It wasn't until he got to the island that he remembered he was wearing the mask. It was barely light. A shell pink tinge crept along the horizon. The lagoon was calm and windless. Objects and men were still gray against the growing light. They had tethered the small boat, put on the protective clothing, and begun to square off. Alberico took on his companion, Antonio. For the first set, Rade had drawn Battista.

"Wait," Rade said tiredly. "Wait. Before we begin—you all know my future depends on my face."

"Is that what that was all about?" asked Antonio. "All those visiting peacocks at the noble house? Trussed up like whores. You're one of them? Not just working for messer Vinciguerra?"

"I'm one of them," said Rade. *Why hadn't Ludovico told them?*

"All pretty face and no balls," growled Battista. "Is that what I'm looking at?"

"I intend to fight," asserted Rade. "Don't cut my face."

"We'll cut your balls instead," shrugged Antonio. "If you have any."

"And don't hit me with your mirror," cried Battista in a falsetto. "Could be bad luck. Oh, oh, oh."

"I'll just shove it up your arse," returned Rade.

"All right, you bastards," said Antonio, "slit his throat if you like, knock him out, beat the crap out of him, but stay away from his face." He turned to Rade. "That good enough for you?"

Rade sized up his towering opponent. Small eyes, no front
teeth, scars, a mountain of muscle covered with hair. Except on
his head.

Battista flexed his arms and took a swipe with his sword.
It was the kind that was so long that a foot soldier carried it
into battle slung on his back. Long enough for a knight on
horseback. It meant Battista had the longer reach. "Afraid to
take me on, Narcissus?" he said with a gap-toothed leer. "Lost
your pretty mirror?"

At that, Rade threw caution to the winds. "Try me, lout!"
And wordlessly took the ringing first blow on the flat of the
sword in his right hand and the second on his dagger hilt in the
left. On the third, his tiredness vanished. On the fourth, he was
yelling as loud as the others, fully engaged in counterattack.
And by the fifth, Battista, the mountain, was sweating.

"Holy Virgin," said Alberico, when they'd finished. "You
fight like those head-taking, goat-fucking *stradiotti*."

"Same side of the Adriatic but actually those head-taking,
goat-fucking *stradiotti* fight like me," answered Rade, and
grinned. "We just train them for your armies. Who's next?"

They switched partners, kept at it for a couple of hours,
and, sweat-soaked, bruised, and happy, went back to go to
church. There, Rade fell fast asleep leaning against the remains
of a fresco and slid soundlessly down the wall. At the end of
the service, Battista and Antonio stumbled out laughing. It was
left to Alberico to shepherd him home.

*   *   *   *   *

Ludovico watched Rade and Alberico as they appeared at
the end of the street. It was a long walk across the city. The
days were warm now. Full of light. Breezy and often cloudless.
It had to be a pleasure to cross the many little streets and

bridges. To see the people going to work, piloting their gondolas, doing their chores, buying their food, hawking their wares, playing, laughing, gossiping. *How he loved this city.*

Rade often came with Alberico, sometimes with Battista or Antonio, but he never came alone. Ludovico had seen the look that crossed Rade's face when he met Caterina—even though his daughter, who'd been schooled in composure, had managed to keep her feelings to herself. Ludovico had made it clear to his men that Rade should not be in the house with her alone. One of them was to be there as well. Giovanni was too old and slow. Nonna, though formidable, was a woman. And Ludovico sometimes had appointments elsewhere in the city.

He saw in Rade an irritating resignation when it came to learning the business. Furthermore, the man seemed to be cloaked in self-protective vigilance. You couldn't walk into a room and surprise him. Even working with Ludovico's part time clerk, he was always tense, drawn like a bowstring, and quick to respond. Other than that, Ludovico found he wanted to like the man. He was intelligent and, on occasion, could even be amusing. But he seemed a different man after he signed the contract than he'd been before. Something had changed.

Alberico, his most observant spy, reported that Rade didn't sleep at night, that he could hear him pacing, that he had nightmares when he did sleep, cried out in the dark. Beyond that, Alberico was much impressed with his martial skills. Said that he was quick on his feet and dangerous with a sword and dagger. *Where had he learned that?* Ludovico sometimes wondered if he'd made a mistake. Even Alberico said the man rarely let down his guard. And what was odd, after Ludovico had thought about it, was that Rade didn't look like a man who couldn't sleep. There were no dark hollows under his eyes, only occasionally a redness in the eye itself or a rasp of tiredness in his voice. *God's blood,* he thought suddenly, *was it connected to Caterina? If it was, he was keeping a wolf with the chickens.*

*   *   *   *   *

Rade slid his finger down the column in the ledger, closed the book and closed his eyes as well. He missed Miloš' aptitude for and interest in computing columns of materials and columns of figures. He looked at his list and handed it to Ludovico, who was pouring over a similar ship's manifest.

Ludovico frowned. "Three bales short this time."

"Yes. But the hold had space and they're listed as cargo."

"Either stolen or miscounted."

"But not miscounted by me. I've checked the storeroom twice," said Rade.

"I see you've calculated their worth. I'll speak to the captain."

"Messer Vinciguerra," Rade hesitated, "how well do you know the merchant who provided the goods?"

"I've known him for years," said Ludovico. "In answer to the question you haven't asked, I also trust him."

"Still, if I had a factor in that city," suggested Rade, "I might ask him to look into the man's affairs. Discreetly of course. There would be other... indications. Debts, unexplained expenditures, whatever. You'd know what to look for. Who loads the goods?"

Ludovico sighed. "The dockworkers are hired by the merchant. The captain only checks the bill of lading."

"That could be where the count changes." Rade said, and yawned.

"It's worth investigating," agreed Ludovico, yawning in turn. He pushed back his chair, stood up, and stretched. "Enough for today." He turned to look at Rade, who was putting his things away. The long day had ended without feelings of antagonism. Without frustration. He realized that sometime over the last week things had actually begun to improve. He said, "Come up for dinner."

"Tonight?" This was his first invitation to supper.

"Why not? It's better than supping in the kitchen. You've been here three weeks. Time to converse with women." Ludovico added, "If you're not tired now, you will be after that."

Rade looked at his ink-stained fingers and held them up.

"Cook will give you soap," said Ludovico. "Come up after you've washed."

A while later, Rade climbed the stairs. To date, he'd eaten with Alberico or one or all of the other menservants in the kitchen. That had meant no one talked. They simply ate and left as soon as possible. Their behavior had been conditioned by Cook, whose name he had yet to discover, and who lay in wait for any comments or jests that she found offensive. It happened that applied to most of them. Since she had a voice like a whiplash and a memory like a usurer, it was safer to be mute.

The upstairs, the *piano nobile* was refined, luxurious, even sensuous. He'd never seen rooms like these. Off the long, impressive central hall, lined with a display of arms, the room they were to dine in was spacious, decorated with a high, gilded ceiling and centered on a hooded fireplace. The storm, that had blown in two days before, had passed, the evening sky glowed, and the upper windows had been opened. He could see the thin lines of wires supporting the glass *occhi*. Where light threw a shaft across them, the walls glistened with fabrics. A table had been positioned across the window end of the room, the forms of carved legs and pale linen broken up by the silhouettes of the family, who, like the wires, were dark against the light. They were animated, talking, laughing, arguing.

Rade, standing in the doorway, felt a sudden longing for winter quarters: the packed dirt floor, the smoke-blackened walls, the smells of fish, sweat, and garlic, the camaraderie, even the animosity. The feeling that no one had a hold on him. That no one ever would. The scene before him, revealed another world altogether. A foreign world with different rules. A world that he had always thought he wanted. He drew a breath, squared his shoulders, and moved into the room.

"Didn't I say wear gloves?" scolded Nonna. "I said it four times. At least four times."

"You can't weave garlands wearing gloves," replied Caterina.

Both their backs were to him and Ludovico, opposite, was helping himself to meat. Caterina's voice was low and musical. The light played on the unruly strands behind her ears but couldn't reach the silky but darker hair at the nape of her neck, where the tautness of her braid revealed it. A velvet ribbon had been plaited into the braid. A few more steps, and if he were to reach out his hand, he could have touched her. The space between them was almost tangible, a physical barrier rather than a void. Like some far flung planet, he instinctively knew he might circle her but dared not abandon his set course. At least not yet.

"Simonetta did," insisted Nonna.

"Her gloves were thin. Mine were thick."

"And look what you've done: pricked and cut your beautiful hands. Just like a laborer!"

"Speaking as a fellow laborer," Rade said, crossing into the light, "they'll heal."

"There you are!" said Ludovico into the abrupt silence. "Didn't I tell you I'd invited messer Radović to supper? No? Well, I did." He motioned to a bench opposite the women. "We've just said grace."

The silence continued so Rade nodded to the women.

"Garlands for what?"

They stared at his hands. He said, "I couldn't get it off."

"Ink," said Ludovico. "A side effect of writing all day. It's neither putrefaction of the flesh nor dye from the vats." He surveyed the table. "Now that we've examined everyone's hands and found them wanting, we should eat—before supper is examined and also found wanting."

Sofia, platter in hand, turned red.

"A jest, Sofia," sighed Ludovico. "Only a jest." He turned to Rade. "Help yourself to lamb."

"La Festa della Sensa," said Caterina, holding up a hand to shield her eyes from the light. "The garlands are for the Feast of the Ascension."

Rade looked at the cuts on her fingers and the back of her hand. They were already inflamed. "Was it worth the pricks?"

"Every one of them," replied Caterina. "After all, Beatrice d'Este is coming!"

"But not Il Moro," said Ludovico. "I fear Milan is plotting something."

"Oh Father, you always think the worst."

"It pays to wonder why," said Ludovico, "while the wife absorbs all our attention, all our expenditure on festive artifice, all the efforts of our courtiers, diplomats and doge—Sforza hides in his castle."

"He simply went home after Ferrara," sighed Caterina. "Sometimes you stay home."

Ludovico smiled. "I'm not Sforza."

"She's her own person," said Caterina. *She doesn't need him.* She added, looking at Rade, "It's a magnificent spectacle! I'm glad she wanted to come because it will be even better because of it. We might even see her tomorrow."

Rade looked up from the remains of the supper he had been wolfing down, wiped his mouth on his forearm and his hands on the already spotted table cloth, and said, "What makes it more wonderful, as you put it, than any other religious holiday?" His napkin lay, folded and untouched, like a spotless, sleeping angel, where he'd shoved it.

Caterina, who had briefly closed her eyes, recovered. "It's more than the usual solemn procession in the piazza," she said, focusing on the wall behind him. "And we'll have days of it. Each facade and boat is garlanded. Ladies, dressed in their finery, will watch from balconies hung with carpets. A parade of boats will proceed down the Grand Canal led by the state barge, the *bucintoro*, and those of our guests. There'll be gods, costumes, artifices, a fair, trumpets, gun salutes."

"There's a history to it," interrupted Nonna.

"Two histories," said Caterina, eagerly, "besides the Ascension of our Lord, *La Sensa* celebrates the victory of Doge Orseolo over the Adriatic coast..." Her voice trailed off. She bit her lip.

"Over the Slav," finished Rade.

"Yes."

"The filthy refuse of the world," added Ludovico, sawing on his meat. "Predators, brigands, killers. Orseolo burned them out."

"Father, I think..."

He turned to Rade. "Some of those brigands are still out there. The navy hangs the ones they catch. Far too soft a death for that godless scum."

"*Father.*"

Ludovico added, "We ought to burn them out a second time."

"Is that what you truly think?" said Rade, half-rising. "That you should burn our coasts and cities?"

"I meant..."

"For the love of God," interrupted Nonna, "it was almost five hundred years ago. Sit down. We don't need to choose sides now." To Ludovico, she added, "Caterina and I know you lost a ship." She looked piercingly at Rade. "You probably don't know that. But you're not one of those kinds of Slavs either."

Rade made no effort to answer. *For actually, he was.*

For a few moments they simply sat there. "Do I dare tell the other history?" ventured Caterina.

"Do tell it," said Nonna. "It's about a wedding." She looked around the table. "Isn't that why we're all here?"

"A wedding to the sea," said Caterina.

"A Venetian custom?" inquired Rade, pushing his plate aside to gather up the crumbs. He wetted his finger to better capture them. "When the betrothal was drawn up, no one said anything about the sea. Do we swim? Do we practice in the bath?" He looked as innocent as a newborn lamb.

No one spoke.

"You're teasing me," said Caterina at last, turning pink. It took an effort to regain composure. "Let me relieve you of your fantasy." She looked at him with a veiled gaze, bolstered by dislike. *What would you know of baths?* She took a steadying breath and said instead, "There was a disputed papacy. An elected pope, Pope Alexander, and an antipope supported by the Holy Roman Empire. The real pope, Alexander, took refuge in Venice and our doge, Ziani, fought a sea battle on his behalf."

"Venice won," interjected Nonna.

"*I'm* telling the history. Yes, and the emperor sued for peace," said Caterina. "In gratitude..." She glared at the other three. "In gratitude, Pope Alexander gave our doge a ring as symbol of the Republic's dominion over the Adriatic. And the doge, saying words to that effect, threw the ring into the sea."

"And he has wed the sea every year since," added Nonna.

Rade looked thoughtful. "The doge throws a ring into the sea? A valuable ring?"

"Yes," agreed Nonna, "I think so. At least these days it's

gold."

"So there are five hundred gold rings down there?"

"No one has ever inquired about that before," mused Ludovico. "The first wedding took place in 1177, so..." he thought for a moment, "I'd guess three hundred and some."

"A small fortune. Pity the seabed will have swallowed them," observed Rade.

Nonna looked offended. "Would you, messer Radović, in good conscience, cheat the sea of its winnings?"

"The sea has cheated plenty of men of theirs," shrugged Rade.

"What *La Sensa* truly commemorates is peace," continued Caterina, ignoring them. "Peace for the Republic. Peace in the Adriatic. An honorable objective for an annual wedding, messer Radović, don't you think?'

He inclined his head, glancing in passing at the swell of her bosom across the table, and thought about the bath. That turned out to be a mistake.

"Marriage, my child, is about dominion," said Ludovico. "And, it follows, submission. Only with submission can there be peace." He added firmly, "In that order."

"You've just upheld what I already said," retorted Caterina, chin up.

Ludovico cleared his throat to respond but Nonna was faster. "As with most things we value in life," she said, "there's a measured progression to what's important. I think we would agree that the end we all want is peace. After all, it's tiring to put one's foot on someone else's neck and keep it there."

"So, there you are," Caterina said, looking at Rade with an authoritative air. "Now you know everything there is to know about wedding the sea."

After a moment, Rade, who was exquisitely conscious of the area to which his blood had gone, said, straight-faced, "I won't ask about consummation."

Caterina turned pink, then red. And choked.

"To date," said Nonna dryly, "no one has even gotten wet."

"I see," said Rade. "So doges don't swim." Momentarily, he caught Caterina's gaze. "If you like, madonna, I could teach them. You'd save on rings." And was rewarded with another tide of crimson.

Out on the street, he went looking for relief. The money was already in his hand. To hell with discovery.

*   *   *   *   *

The following day, they were all tired from standing respectively on boats, balconies, bridges, walls and ledges to see some portion of the ongoing ceremonies. With over a hundred vessels in the *bacino*, the day had been a vast seaborne tapestry of color, sound and activity.

"The first ladies' rowing race," said Alberico. "Ever. What a sight!'

"Those weren't ladies," replied Battista, who'd spent that part of the day in the storeroom.

"Of course they were, I saw them." Antonio's answer was forthright.

"Ladies don't row," said Battista.

"They had breasts," stated Antonio, "and they rowed. What else would they be?"

No one seemed to have an answer.

Rade lounged absent-mindedly against a wall, watching Caterina on the *riva*, standing by the water gate where the shade fell on the stone. She wore light clothes that moved silkily in the breeze. Her neck was bare of jewelry but her hair was dressed with flowers. She was wearing gloves, pulling at them, entwining and pressing the bases of her fingers together to reset them in place. Clearly they'd been foisted on her because of the cuts.

He walked over. "Do they hurt?"

"Do what hurt?" She seemed annoyed.

He motioned at her hands.

"Of course not."

"Let me see," Rade said. "I'm an old hand at cuts."

She reluctantly pulled off her gloves and held out her hands, palms down, then palms up. They were red, and some of the cuts had pus in them.

He said gently, without touching her, "The gloves don't help, do they?"

"Not really."

"We use salt. It hurts. But it cures wounds."

She searched his face for some indication that he was intent on making a fool of her. Last night still rankled. "What do you think I am? A ham? A fish?" she said indignantly. "Isn't that the remedy of the poor and downtrodden? Isn't salt used on sailors and rowers when they're flogged?"

"I never flogged my oarsmen," said Rade quietly. "Use the salt. It'll help. And take the gloves off as soon as they'll let you." And he walked back to his place by the wall.

*   *   *   *   *

Because they'd waited for Simonetta to go home and remove her jewels, it was getting dark by the time they embarked for the piazza. Lanterns lit and compartments crowded, the gondolas moved off briskly on the silver ribbon of canal. The buildings, blurred by darkness, bled their geometry, one into another, until all seemed mysteriously joined and colorless. Simonetta, Caterina, and their nurses went with Giovanni. Simonetta's maids, Sofia and Cook followed in Simonetta's vessel and Ludovico, the menservants, and Rade brought up the rear.

As they climbed the water steps to the piazza, they saw torches everywhere. The languages of several nations echoed off the bricks and marble in close competition with musicians, acrobats, crowds, and vendors. At the edge of the water, outside the ramshackle walls of the public privy, the smells of bakers' stalls wafted intermittently across their path and mingled with those of the latrine. Two huge columns rose from the pavement, both garlanded with flowers and ribbons.

"How lovely!" said Caterina, reaching out to touch the flowers.

Nonna eyed them suspiciously. "Usually they're garlanded with felons."

Caterina snatched her hand away and wiped it on her dress.

In the piazza, amongst the crowd, there were the usual oddities that accompanied fairs: bearded ladies, a man with two arms and the beginning of a third, and several dwarfs, everybody's favorites—all in various stages of undress. Prostitutes, adept at revealing their wares, worked the edges of the crowd or awaited the success of a procurer while secreted in a gondola moored in the shadows of a nearby canal. The two maidens, and their female servants, were surrounded and guarded by the men and had even gone so far as to don masks, so that they could draw back their veils. Mountebanks and cutpurses were known to frequent the festivities and a close watch was kept on those around them.

The booths were set up in predetermined rows, torches flickering on perfumes, majolica, textiles, woolens, combs, glassware, ribbons. Caterina and Simonetta stopped here to examine some linen, there to choose beads, exclaiming with pleasure at the trinkets, while avoiding the catcalls and admiring glances of the more uproarious fair-goers. Frequently Rade, Alberico, Antonio, or Battista shoved his body between the women and a passerby to shield them from some minor threat: groping hands, drunkenness, foul language, whatever. Cheap drink had flowed freely all day and there were a fair number of bleary-eyed tipplers to be avoided.

They stood for a time watching the acrobats build a human pyramid, munching on sugared pine seeds, and betting on the outcome. As the height of the human edifice grew more and more alarming, its collapse became imminent, and the triangle finally exploded into a display of somersaulting bodies, streamlined with sweat and tawdry finery. Rade actually caught one, only a boy, more out of self-protection than dexterity. The black-eyed child laughed, baring crooked teeth, and was rewarded with coin and some pine seeds by the women. It wasn't until the boy had disappeared into the crowd that Rade discovered that his purse was also gone. This, too, was greeted with hilarity by his male companions and Rade was forced to admit that he had been fleeced—by a child.

It was time to go home. Ludovico, who'd developed a stomachache, had already gone back to sit in the gondola with Giovanni. Simonetta, teetering on her stilted shoes, was too proud to admit that her feet hurt and Caterina had begun to worry in earnest about her father. The two nurses, formerly deep in conversation, looked tired and the retinue lagged behind. Meanwhile, the men began to grow anxious about the raucous crowd down by the waterfront. It seemed a fight was brewing. Skirting the fringes of the fair in hopes of avoiding trouble, they were forced into a shadowy world of beggars, unkempt peddlers, and odd merchandise.

As they edged around a particularly smelly jumble of crates and baskets, a thief came rocketing out of the crowd, followed by two young men in colored silks and flaming torches. The thief cannoned off Nonna, who'd paused to adjust the angle of a package, and she was knocked soundlessly into a wheedling peddler and his boxes. Rade was the first to help her up, brushing off her clothes, and picking up her packages.

"Nonna, are you hurt?" cried Caterina, running to her side.

"Of course not," said Nonna, embarrassed by the entire incident. She checked the purchases. "Undamaged." She held them up.

Caterina glared at Rade. "Why didn't you protect her?"

Rade, who had been nowhere near her, didn't bother to reply.

The peddler began to complain loudly that they had, however, damaged his merchandise. In fact, the merchandise began to complain too, in yips and yowls—and a very distinctive high-pitched wail. Rade found that he was more or less standing on the basket that was making the most noise.

"The packages are the least of my worries." Caterina turned, looking for the source of the crying. "Someone, see what it is," she said. "I fear we've harmed it."

"Don't be silly," said Nonna. "These things are foul. Don't touch them. We'll all come down with some dreadful disease."

Rade opened the basket anyway and carefully removed its fuzzy, filthy, wriggling inhabitant, which on closer inspection turned out to be a dog.

"My prize!" shouted the peddler. "The most expensive animal I have! You've damaged it! You've killed it!"

"Generally," noted Rade, beginning to be overcome by the smell of excrement, "what's dead is silent."

"I think it's a Maltese," said Simonetta, teetering nearby. "A very smelly one." She held her scented handkerchief up to her nose. "The sailors trade for them. Maestro Carpaccio has one. He puts it in his paintings." She looked at the others. "Can we go now?"

"*Buy it,*" Caterina ordered, looking at Rade. "I've decided to rescue it."

Rade, who had no money, and didn't want to call attention to it, held it out at arm's length. "Where's the basket?"

"Here," said Alberico. And they put the reluctant animal, who cried piteously, back into it.

"The basket costs extra," announced the peddler.

"So," replied Rade, "we're buying a dead dog in a broken basket. How much could that be?"

"It was a clean, live, beautiful dog in a good basket before you stepped on it!" cried the peddler. "My prize animal!" He aired a number of elevated ideas about price which they eventually beat down to a reasonable sum.

"Give me some coin," said Rade under his breath to Alberico. He paid from Alberico's purse and annoyed by his role as procurer in the transaction, thoughtlessly offered the basket to Caterina.

"Thank you, messer Radović, for being this night's St. Giorgio," said Caterina, smiling like a crocodile. "Do carry our dragon home for me and be sure it's clean before you bring it into the house. I can't wait to name it. Shall we go?"

Rade felt the warmth on his leg as dog urine ran out of the bottom of the basket.

*   *   *   *   *

On these late spring days, in the heat of mid-afternoon, Caterina and her friends could be heard high above the courtyard on the little porch or *altana*. Built of wood and festooned with drying linens, it sat atop the house, like a tented haven, open to the sky. There was no doubt that embroidery was not performed there, nor any other such mundane task. The murmured conversations and shrieks of feminine laughter wafted away on the breeze, merry and mysterious in the faraway aerie, and indecipherable to those below. It was the only place in the house that Nonna, who didn't like heights, didn't care to go.

"I have a new brew," declared Simonetta, standing up. She

combed her hair through the crown of her sun shade so that it hung like a silken curtain from the edges. The color of it was an unnatural straw yellow and she was very proud of the hue. "I have it from Maria whose father trades with Gentile, who in turn, found it in a book he was delivering."

"A book he was forbidden to look at," added Ginevra, seated in the shade, almost unrecognizable under layers of thin shawls.

"He only took a quick peek."

"So what's the potion, Simonetta?" asked Caterina, perched on a bench. She also combed the water from her hair, also draped on a sun shade, taking care that the sun reflected only on it and not on her skin. The small white dog panted in the sun at her feet. "Go bald and you'll not wed next year."

"Oh, Mary, Mother of God, wouldn't that be a sight to behold!" laughed Ginevra and the dog roused itself and came over to be petted and enjoy her shadow. "I hope you've an antidote."

"Fear not, my beloveds, I shall marry and marry well," retorted Simonetta, putting down her comb, "but, as it happens, not next year."

"What? Then when?" asked Caterina.

"At seventeen. Father has decreed it." She sighed. "My betrothed's father has agreed. Mama married at thirteen. She has always said she was a child with children."

"Then you'll have time to grow the hair back after all," teased Ginevra, "unless you've gone gray."

"Caterina's blond by birth but we all know how bold you are, Ginevra," snapped Simonetta.

"Don't be silly, Simonetta." Ginevra had dark hair and liked it that way. "What's the poison?"

"It's a secret. But since neither of you will ever use it..." Simonetta paused for dramatic effect. "Honey, black sulfur, and alum," she whispered.

"You'll be dead in a week," cried Ginevra. "If not by the dye then by your father's hand when he hears you filched his precious alum."

"Shhhh!" said Simonetta. "Not so loud."

"Sulfur? We'll all die of the smell," laughed Caterina. She looked thoughtful. "The third ingredient is honey? You'll be a walking hive."

"Enough!" barked Simonetta. *Bees were more bothersome than poison.* She changed the subject to the one they were all more interested in. "Tell us about your messer Radović. Do you see him when he's working for your father? Or is he as much a mystery to you as he is to the rest of Venice?"

Caterina put down her comb. "You saw him at the fair. The rest of Venice couldn't care less."

"But we do," said Ginevra.

"Other than *La Sensa,* I dined once in his company. He ate like a pig. It was utterly disgusting." Caterina made a face.

"Not so hard to change," Ginevra observed.

"And with the bread, he ate every crumb. Like a beggar." Caterina surveyed their expressions.

"How odd," mused Ginevra. "We once had a manservant who did that. He told us it's a habit people pick up if they never have enough to eat. If they're starving."

They were all quiet, thinking about that.

"Well, he has enough to eat, Ginevra. Cook feeds him. Besides that," Caterina went on, unfazed, "he says things, suggestive things, that are *mortifying*. It's dreadful!"

"Oh, they all do that," said Simonetta through her curtain of hair. "For men, it's about lust. For women, it's about love. You'll have to make him love you for yourself."

"Well, there's no love here," returned Caterina. "And I'm not allowed desire even if I felt it. Which I don't."

"You know, Caterina," Simonetta said thoughtfully, "he protected us at the fair. Didn't you notice? He caught the falling acrobat. And he was kind to your little dog. Another man wouldn't have bothered to open the basket. And he was careful with it, too, filthy as it was. I think you're harder on him than he deserves."

"If I am, he probably doesn't notice. Father says he's always preoccupied with something." But she thought about the salt and her cuts. She'd done what he'd suggested—after Nonna concurred.

"Maybe it's another wife and eight children," giggled Ginevra.

Caterina shook her head. "I think not. He has none of the attitudes of a husband. It's something else. If we marry... oh, Sofia," she said, looking up, *"Fruit!* Iced fruit. *What a treat!"*

Sofia put the bowls down. "Snow from the mountains," she said, smiling, and started back down the stairs.

"Are you suggesting it might not happen? *You're betrothed!"* Ginevra took her fruit from the table, carefully keeping to the shade. "Does your father object to him? To not knowing more about him?"

Caterina pursed her lips thoughtfully. "He didn't have much choice." Her hair was almost dry. She sighed. "Someday, Father says, we will know more. It just takes time and inquiry."

"We'd know *everything* if he'd chosen a Venetian." Simonetta shook her hair from the hat.

"I've had enough of *them* to last a lifetime," scoffed Caterina.

"I hear someone calling," Ginevra said, cocking her head. "It must be my nurse. *Coming!"* she shouted and listened in return to instructions called out from those below. "The gondola is early. We must collect our things." Ginevra gathered up her shawls and retrieved her wooden pattens from the corner. She put them on. Having dark hair paid off in readiness. One by one they descended into the coolness of the house, followed by the panting small white dog.

*   *   *   *   *

"Rade. *Rade! Can you come here?*"

He was halfway down the *andron,* the light from the opening throwing his shadow forward over the stone, melding it into the murky darkness farther in. He turned around and started back, running. What he saw when he came out in the light was the family gondola floating away and Ludovico kneeling beside a prostrate figure on the narrow landing along the canal. It was Giovanni.

"What happened?"

"I saw that he was flushed, breathing hard, as I was getting out," Ludovico replied. "He didn't tie up the gondola. Then he said something that didn't make any sense, and began to be sick."

Giovanni groaned.

"Let's get him into the shade. I can carry him," Rade offered. He put his arms under the old man's shoulders and legs, lifted him, and carried him into the *andron.* As he did so, he thought back to the journey. The day had been unusually hot. In fact, it still was. He and Ludovico had been sitting in the shade of the high summer *felze.* He had noticed Giovanni sweating but then the old gondolier was working the oar.

Rade took his hand away from the old man's brow. "This isn't good. He's almost dry."

It was Ludovico's turn to ask what it was.

"The Arabs have a name for this: *Sariasus.* After the Dog Star. It's a sickness that comes from heat. Sometimes you see it on a galley in one of the oarsmen when they've been rowing in the sun all day."

"He's still conscious," observed Ludovico.

"We should cool him down," replied Rade. "That's all I know. I'll get the small water barrel from the storeroom."

"Then hurry."

The water seemed to revive the old man. They knelt beside him as he struggled to sit up and later helped him up as he got to his feet.

"You tried to drown me," Giovanni complained. "You did!"

"Must be feeling better," observed Rade.

"Rest," ordered Ludovico, relief beginning to show in his expression.

"No need," replied Giovanni, shaking his head. "I've got to retrieve the gondola."

"I'll get it," replied Rade. "It hasn't gone far."

"Rest," repeated Ludovico. "And it's not up for discussion."

*   *   *   *   *

It was late June and they were halfway through his second supper. Rade said, "You were right about Sforza."

"It pays to watch these people," returned Ludovico. "I have markets to protect in Milan. Be assured this new league won't do any of us any good."

"I haven't seen Giovanni," queried Caterina, changing the subject. "Where is he?"

"I'm afraid I've had to do something about Giovanni," Ludovico replied, helping himself to bread.

"Because he fainted or something?" asked Caterina.

"Yes," replied Ludovico, shaking out his napkin.

"You didn't dismiss him!" cried Caterina.

"I would *never* do that," Ludovico countered. "He's a member of our family. But he's gotten old. To give him a rest, I hired another gondolier for the summer. One that can deal with the heat."

"If he has nothing to do..." began Nonna.

"I assigned him lighter duties," Ludovico said. "And of course he is to oversee the newcomer."

"What's the new gondolier's name?" asked Caterina.

"Cristofolo." Ludovico looked as if he was hiding something.

"A good Venetian name," nodded Nonna.

"He's not Venetian," replied Ludovico.

"Then what is he?" asked Caterina.

"Black African," her father said.

"A Moor!" cried Nonna indignantly. "You hired *a Moor* to ferry us around when the Ottoman Empire is waiting at our borders to destroy us?"

"They are already common throughout Venice," Ludovico observed, and then began to laugh. "But for you, Nonna, I hired a Christian, an independent gondolier. He once belonged to a friend of mine."

"He's been manumitted," muttered Nonna, beginning to be mollified.

"Yes. He came to Venice as a child," Ludovico said. "Except for his skin color, he could almost be Venetian."

Almost, is the important word thought Rade. *In Venice, outsiders seem to be outsiders forever.*

"Simonetta will be *so* jealous," observed Caterina. "She has always wanted an Ethiopian. She says Naples has had blacks in their service for years. They are, according to Simonetta, enormously fashionable. Decorative as well."

"They are *men*," broke in Rade. "Not objects. They live and love and bleed and die just as you do."

There was dead silence. Caterina looked stricken. "I didn't mean... oh God, I regret what I said."

"Do forgive her. Please. That was Simonetta speaking. I know that voice well," Nonna inserted quickly.

Rade didn't seem to notice. "I had an oarsman on my *bergantin*. His name was Hamsa. He had been a slave on an Ottoman galley for years. We could all tell it haunted him. Otherwise he was like any other man. He just wanted to live."

God knew he hadn't been that lucky.

"I'm ashamed," whispered Caterina.

Rade added, relenting, "Treat the gondolier as you would Giovanni, and all will go well."

"I will," replied Caterina in a small voice. "I promise."

"We should eat," said Ludovico. "Everything is getting cold. Do pass the fish." The fish platter traveled around the table from hand to hand.

"Cod," sighed Caterina, toying with her food.

"Where's Sofia?" her father asked. "The pitcher is empty."

The door opened and Sofia came in with a second pitcher of wine. As the door began to close, a small white dog forced its way through the opening and ran around the table, wagging its tail.

"Recognize him?" asked Caterina, extending her hand to her pet.

"He was brown when last I saw him," replied Rade. "So I'd say the answer is no and yes." He reached for the napkin and wiped his hands. Cook had showed up eight days ago with napkins. Something they had never seen, let alone used in the kitchen. And they had all been beaten into submission by the lash of her tongue. But to her credit, the napkins now appeared regularly and at least they tried to remember what they were for and when to use them.

The dog appeared at his feet and he reached down to ruffle its fur. "What did you name him?"

"Orseolo," said Caterina.

He straightened up, a hint of anger in his face. "To spite me," he said. "The doge that burned out my countrymen."

"Actually," Caterina replied, biting her lip to keep from smiling, "no. You've got it wrong. Father has an acquaintance named Orseolo. They're always at odds with each other. I thought, in the long run, it might be amusing. It wasn't meant to be hurtful. At least, not to you."

"You see," said Ludovico, "there's a precedent. He too has a dog. Can you guess it's name?"

"Ludovico," offered Rade slowly.

"Yes," they both said. And Orseolo barked.

"But the best part is this: Caterina has trained him. *Bow!*" roared Ludovico and the little creature followed his command. They convulsed with laughter; even Rade found himself smiling.

"If only your namesake could see you now! *Bow!*" The dog prostrated himself a second time. Ludovico was near to weeping with the humor of it. "Orseolo, the dog, has better manners than the man!"

Caterina said, "Now messer Radović…"

"Rade," he ventured.

"Rade," she echoed, tasting the name, a mischievous tone in her voice. "You may now exact submission from a certain doge through his surrogate. And an apology from us on words ill-spoken." She smiled and he saw it even went to her eyes. And they were green.

"Doge Orseolo," he stated matter-of-factly, looking into the brown, expectant gaze, *"bow."* Orseolo followed his command. "I now absolve you from your namesake's sins. And your own: past," he added, thinking of the ill-fated basket, "and future." It was his third glass of wine and the night was gaining humor. He looked at Caterina. She was almost shining. It would be difficult for anyone not to want her.

"*Pax?*" he asked softly.

"*Pax,*" she answered. And smiled.

Chapter Thirteen

The devil is not as black as he is painted.
—Dante Alighieri

Venice, High Summer, Venetian Year 1493

It would be cool in the hills, thought Rade. It was high summer and the annual migration to villas on the mainland had begun. The lighter had arrived that morning. It lay, lines wrapped around bitts, snugged against the water gate as chests and dismantled beds were piled between the near parallel lengths of its rounded sides. A steady stream of furniture and goods had descended the stairs interspersed with supplies carried out from the storerooms. They were all, barring something important, assigned to the task.

The air outside was stifling. Inside, in the storeroom, Rade picked up a sack of grain and heaved it onto his shoulder. Its bulk and shape were preferable to maneuvering parts of a large bed down the stairs. The task that had preceded this one. And it was cooler here. His clothes were sodden. Even his hair was lank with sweat. It ran down the mask from his hairline and dripped off his chin onto the floor. He couldn't feel it but he could see where it fell.

"African heat," noted Giovanni, as he watched Cristofolo ready the gondola. "From the big desert there. *He* knows that desert."

Cristofolo did know that desert but not willingly, nor as a free man.The slave trade crossed that desert. It was a crossing he would prefer to forget.

Wherever it came from, it was hot. Iron, left in the sun, burned the hand that touched it. Piazzas and courtyards baked those who dallied there. Cisterns ran low and water boats from the mainland pursued a brisk trade. And the lagoon, steaming in the sun, was a soup to be cooked in.

Rade took the sack out to the lighter and went back to get another one, pulling at the limp linen of his shirt to unstick it from his body. He waved off the instant halo of insects. From time to time, he could hear the banter of Battista and Antonio on the stairs. It began with a comment, followed by an insult, then various insults, ending in: "You fucking bastard, I'll get you later." The usual. What had stuck in his mind was the phrase that it would be cool in the hills.

Rade stepped carefully, handing over another sack of grain. The stones at the water's edge were green with slime. The lighter with its curved stempost and shallow draft was an old barge of a boat and well-used. He could imagine the fringe of vegetation growing below her waterline.

"That should be the last of it," he said, straightening up. The stench from the canal was almost palpable. He slapped at something that bit him.

"Galbanum," said a female voice. "At least it helps. You can buy it in the market. If there's any left."

"I don't need it," shrugged Rade, waving away another attack.

"Don't be silly," admonished Nonna. "Summer fever is about. They say it helps. Buy some. We don't care what it smells like."

It couldn't smell worse than the canal. He half expected to see a corpse floating by. *What had happened to the tides?*

She added, "No one will think you're a woman."
That cinched it. He'd rather perish.
"We're six," announced Caterina, coming up behind him. "You'll leave a place to sit?"

"Madonna, it will be as you ask," replied one of the two boatmen, shouldering the sack and placing it safely above the bilge. "We'll arrange some chests." Battista went to help.

As the others, Sofia, Cook, and Antonio, appeared in the opening of the *andron*, the near empty rooms of the noble house, which had been relatively silent, resounded with the shrill sound of barking. For a time, the sounds ranged from room to room, swelling and receding, followed by running footsteps and various commands, swelling and receding as well. The commands, it appeared, were unheeded. At last, there was a mad scrabbling, a yip, and a shout of triumph.

"Got the little bugger," panted Alberico, emerging into the sunlight. "Finally." He began to hand over the quivering dog, realizing belatedly to whom he had spoken. "Forgive me, madonna." He looked stricken.

"It's hot," she said, rearranging layers of thin clothing and taking Orseolo. "We're all hot."

Alberico, wiping sweat from his face, looked relieved.

"*Piccolo*," crooned Caterina, drawing out the endearment, cradling the small white dog, "how could you think I would leave you behind?" She soothed the distress from Orseolo's little body, tucked him under her arm, and took Rade's hand as he handed her on board.

"Where will Father be?"

"He'll meet you at the river boat," Rade replied, conscious of her hand, firm and dry, in his sweaty one. "Watch the mooring rope."

Turning her head, she caught a glimpse of deep blue eyes, whose beauty was overwhelmed by a rank blast of sweat. When she'd seated herself, she felt around for a scented handkerchief and loosening her veil, buried her nose in it. *It will be good to be done with this. They all stink like laborers.*

The other women followed. The two menservants, Battista and Antonio, stationed themselves at either end of the boat.

For a long moment, Rade gazed at her form, veiled against insects and the sun, one arm, handkerchief in hand, wrapped around Orseolo and the other waving a fan. She had turned to speak to the forward boatman again. She was clearly looking forward to the journey. He slapped irritably at a fly. He could see he'd been forgotten.

The moorings were cast off and the ropes thrown aboard. The forward boatman pushed his long oar against the wall of the canal and poled the heavily laden boat forward while the aft boatman steered. It was evident the canal had silted in. And obvious why Ludovico had been complaining. Still, the boatman had a sizable oar. Rade watched until the vessel turned into another canal and began to pass from sight. He saw Nonna lift a hand. He lifted his and mouthed a farewell. And they were gone.

He was left with a sallow-faced clerk, who had also come down for the departure, Giovanni, Cristofolo, who at that moment was piloting the gondola, Alberico, and a long list of tasks to be accomplished. First and foremost being the imminent arrival of two trading galleys. When they'd docked, and their cargo was unloaded and accounted for, Rade, too, was invited to the villa in the hills.

Slapping at insects, he closed and locked the water gate, and entering the welcome coolness of the *andron*, climbed the stairs to the stifling office, preceded by the narrow, wheezing figure of the clerk. As he reached the top, he became aware of an earthy, leafy scent emanating from the clerk. He sighed. It was like following a trail of bruised greenery up the stairs. *Maybe there'll be fewer flies.*

*   *   *   *   *

They were all, except Giovanni, helping Cristofolo clean and polish the gondola. It was pulled up, entirely out of the water, on the greased rails of a shipyard on the outskirts of Venice. Giovanni had remained in the shade of the noble house and was planning to go to market. He would be sure to judge their efforts on his return.

The difference between the two gondoliers was marked. Giovanni was old, gray, and bent. The black gondolier was in his late thirties at most, strong, well-made, and handsome. Sometimes he wore a little cap with a feather, his left ear was pierced with a gold earring, and he was often seen in red shoes. They all thought those flourishes were meant to attract a woman. A personal plumage. Something that male birds do. But whereas he was capable of an ear-splitting whistle if another gondola got in his way, and occasionally some rude words, his private life was carefully kept to himself.

Despite reassurance from Ludovico, Giovanni now spent hours worrying about being replaced. It meant, when they got back, the old man would be sure to find fault with their work.

"Some pilgrims came in on a trading galley. They were going to Rome," Rade remarked, rubbing the black hull of the gondola.

"Who goes to Rome in the summer?" muttered Alberico, whose job consisted of cleaning the leather cushions. He soaped vigorously. "They must be mad."

"You will need to sit on those cushions," observed Cristofolo, raising his eyebrows.

"They were Ethiopians," added Rade.

"Good Christians," commented Cristofolo, wiping his brow.

"Now I know why the heat wouldn't bother them," said Alberico.

"The heat bothers everyone," Cristofolo replied. "I sweat. You sweat. They just know a greater heat."

For a while there was silence except for buffing and soaping noises—and swatting at flies.

"I've heard it said there is a Christian emperor in Africa," said Rade. "Is there?"

"Prester John," replied Cristofolo. "In Ethiopia."

"Is Prester a name?" asked Alberico.

"It means priest," replied Cristofolo, vigorously polishing what he had cleaned.

"Did you ever meet him?" asked Alberico, rocking back on his heels.

"I left when I was four," said Cristofolo. "He kissed the top of my head as I boarded the slave ship."

"No, truly?" exclaimed Alberico.

"Why don't you think about it," replied the gondolier, putting down his polishing rag. "Are you some kind of fool?"

Alberico turned redder than he already was.

"Let's not argue," advised Rade. "He's teasing you and you fell into the trap. What about the emperor?"

"Who knows if there *is* a Prester John. I've never met anyone who has seen him. And there are a lot of black gondoliers and *traghetto* oarsmen and slaves in Venice."

"I thought all Ethiopians were Christian," Rade commented.

"Venetians tend to call all Moors Ethiopians. 'People with burnt faces.' Those who live here seem to apply the name to anyone with black skin," replied Cristofolo, arching his back and stretching. "Many of us did not come from that country. We were not born Christian. We came with those bastards, the slavers."

"With a name like Cristofolo," asked Alberico, "how could you not be Christian?"

"I am only Christian because I came as a child—I was

named after the holy ferryman and brought up that way—otherwise I would be something else." The gondolier inclined his head and then looked sideways at them. "I come from Bornu, near the big lake." He grinned. "So undoubtedly if I was still there, I would be Saracen. And you might be tolerated but pay more in taxes."

Rade smiled a wolfish grin in return. "In my country, if you were Saracen, I would probably wish to kill you."

"If you happened to be a slaver, Arab or a European," retorted Cristofolo, "whatever your religion, one way or the other, you would already be stone dead." And this time, the smile was nowhere to be seen.

*   *   *   *   *

As a plan, it was simple. Finish the tasks. Log in the two cargoes. Go to the hills. But reality turned out to be something else. Day after day, with the clerk and without him, he worked and waited for the two ships. Messengers came and went: sometimes from the villa, sometimes from other vessels in which Ludovico owned shares, sometimes from factors in other cities, sometimes from the working hub of the city, the Rialto. Rade recorded everything in the book, entered the debits and credits, checked the balances, the cargoes themselves, had those that required it unloaded and stored, or delivered, arranged for taxes, sent messages back. The profits were all on paper. Ludovico kept the bills of exchange for himself. In the airless office, at the end of another cloudless day, he felt like a live crab in a hot kettle.

With no one home, all four men slept on straw pallets in the *andron* where the air was cooler. It didn't matter that the spiders, water bugs, and mice liked the coolness too. There, they ate simply and sparingly: cold food, sometimes from the storeroom, more often from the market. They drew water from the cistern and laced it with wine. Occasionally the first was followed by another bottle, or two, to be sure that the wine hadn't spoiled. Thirst was a constant companion but in the furnace of high summer, the real objective was oblivion.

"I found an insect galley," drawled Alberico, swaying and shaking out his pallet. "Actually three. Look at all those tiny oars." He and Rade contemplated his find. "Trireme don't you think?"

"We could race them," muttered Rade, barely able to speak. He felt himself listing to starboard.

"They are vermin," commented Cristofolo, staring at them in disbelief.

"Let me see," said Giovanni, blearily. He stared for a time, bent over and stared some more. He straightened up, an accusatory look on his face. "A galley? God's balls. It's a millipede. Three millipedes. What have you three been drinking?"

"Same as you," said Rade. "Which galley...? Back up. You can't wager if you step on it."

"I didn't drink anything," protested Cristofolo.

"Christ's nails," said Alberico, staring at Giovanni, "didn't he warn you? You just sank the whole fleet."

*   *   *   *   *

Once, when he was restless, and Giovanni was in bed, and Cristofolo and Alberico were out, Rade climbed the stairs to Caterina's bedchamber. It was evening. The world was graying to black and the darkness made the air seem cooler. There was very little in the room. A handsome plate. A chair. He stood for a while motionless in the darkness, trying to evoke some essence of her being, and wondering if there would ever be an invitation to this room. To the bed that should be in it. Her absence shadowed him. Distracted him. He'd become conscious of need.

Yet, two days later, something unexpected happened. Something that filled that physical longing. And that something's name was Rosa.

*   *   *   *   *

In the sailmaker's hut with its canvas curtain, he stood expectantly as the girl pulled her shift down to her waist and revealed her heavy breasts. Their dark brown nipples. She turned slowly and let him gaze at her. She'd pushed her hair back so that all of her chest was revealed.

He found he couldn't breathe.

"You like me?" she asked, coming close enough that one of her nipples just grazed his skin. "Yes?"

He drew a sharp breath.

He gently turned her so that her back was against his chest, and put his arms around her, his hands cupping her breasts, feeling their weight. "God's breath, yes." He slipped one hand under the rolled up shift and ran it down the curve of her stomach. Below the waist, her body was rounded, heavy, and marked with faded stretch marks from carrying the child he'd seen playing in the street. At four, that child had become her lookout and the recipient of her gain. She'd made it very clear the first time that the boy was a love child. That she needed to support him because no one else ever would. "No one wants a bastard," she'd said. "No one. Not even my brother."

She put her hand on top of his and guided it. After, he let her explore his body in turn. But he was already having trouble controlling himself. Trouble waiting until the time was right.

"I can teach you," she whispered, with a glint of mischief, touching him so that he gasped. "My boy's father was a patient lover. And I, a virgin." She looked up from what she was doing. "He made me a patient lover in return." She added dismissively, "So many men can't wait."

"What happened to him?" he breathed.

She shrugged. "He went to sea."

The pleasure lasted longer this time. She found little ways to extend it.

Afterwards they lay in their own sweat in the simple room, sated, on a pile of canvas, until she found that it was getting late, extracted her fee, and pushed him out the door. Through the closed curtain, he made arrangements to return.

"Until tomorrow," he said, wanting to stay longer. The boy looked away as Rade walked up the narrow street.

It was the third time that he had been there. The first only four days before to see the sailmaker, her brother. An *arsenalotti*, he hadn't been home then and he wasn't home now. It would be evening before he returned. For the first time in weeks, Rade felt cooler. He didn't even notice the flies.

*   *   *   *   *

The gypsy boy he'd hired to station himself by San Marco's bell tower—where the officials of the *Provedditore alla Sanità* watched for incoming ships—burst through the door of the office.

"The *Brenta*'s in," the boy panted.

"You didn't have to run," said Rade looking up. "Not in this heat."

"Flying the flag of distress!"

"The plague flag?" Rade rose to his feet.

"Don't know," gasped the boy, shaking his head. He looked frightened. "Didn't ask. The official came down... in a hurry. I only had time... to beg the ship's name. That's... what he said."

"It won't be plague," said Rade, trying to believe his own

words. "Not from that coast. There haven't been any warnings. Here," he said, paying him. "Go back and wait for the second ship."

The boy put the coin in his mouth and bit down on it. He looked pleased. And ran down the stairs.

By the time Rade reached the enclosure in the health magistrate's office, the second-in-command, at least that's who he thought he was, had finished speaking through the quarantine window. He found out the man wasn't the captain. And, God be thanked, there was no plague.

"We've sent for a surgeon," said the official. "From Mestre. The captain has a shattered collarbone."

Mestre, where Mordecai resides. Where the Jewish community had been instructed to settle. Where most of the accomplished doctors live. "And the ship?"

"The mast is broken. They've lost some sails and spars."

He thought about the rigging. *Why in Christ's name hadn't they had spares?* "What else?"

The official shrugged. "Four days in this heat with no shelter, no water, rowing, drifting. What did you expect?"

"They didn't stop for supplies?"

"They said they saw a *bergantin* with no colors. It fired on them. Broke the mast." He turned back to his notes. "A plague on those Slav bastards. They multiply like melons."

Miloš, you newborn melon, that was my ship. "And the other light galley? The *Cangrande?*"

"Separated during the attack. She ran for the squall. For cover. Off the Coronati."

"So they could be aground."

"They could be lost," replied the official. "If you plan to search in those islands, you should know there are more than a hundred. Reefs too. And brigands. In my book, a waste of time. They're already dead."

"How soon can I take possession of the ship and her

cargo?"

The official stiffened. "Only after we've finished examining it. Finish the paperwork. Receive the duties. A few days, a week, two weeks? In this heat, who knows?"

"Send me word as soon as you are able," replied Rade, biting back his rising anger. "I've got men, a ship, a cargo, and messer Vinciguerra's prize stallion to find. In this heat... but you already know that."

*   *   *   *   *

She lay against his back, tracing the network of scars with her fingers. He lay on his hip, at the edge of sleep, his head pillowed on his arm and her discarded shift. This day, they had reached levels of pleasure that he thought they might never reach again. He had nothing left to give.

"Can you feel this?" she asked, running a finger down his back.

"Mmm, some of it," he murmured. "Where the scars are, not so much." His breathing had slowed and his sweat had cooled him.

"Your body was made for this," she said, stroking his hip. "And this?"

He felt her fingers on his shoulder, followed by a light kiss.

"Feels good, Rosa."

"And this?" she whispered in his ear.

"You're blowing in my ear," he whispered back.

"No," said Rosa. "I ran my fingertips down your face." Her voice changed. "You didn't feel it."

He was suddenly wide awake. He turned over to see her expression. She wouldn't look at him.

"You didn't feel it because there's something wrong with it," she went on, avoiding his gaze. "When one is as intimate with a person as you and I have been with each other, one no longer relies on sight alone. Even though the skin is warm, I know there's something wrong with it."

"Yes," said Rade. "There's something wrong with it."

"You aren't going to tell me what it is."

"No."

There was a long pause. "When will I lie with you again?" asked Rosa, looking into his eyes.

This time, it was he who looked away. "I have to go to sea."

"When?"

"In a few days."

"The sea takes all my lovers," Rosa said, sitting up. "Now it has taken you."

He kissed the breast that was closest to his face. "I'll be back. This isn't over. I've brought you a gift to keep you both while I'm gone." He sat up and emptied his purse. It was a goodly sum of money.

She ran her hand absent-mindedly over the pile of coins but didn't comment on their worth. She smiled but her eyes were filled with tears. "A parting gift," she whispered.

"No." But he knew it was.

She turned toward him, kneeling now, and ran both hands over his chest all the way to his groin. "I've given you the gift of bringing pleasure," said Rosa, touching him. "It's all I have. Don't keep it to yourself."

He felt her tears fall on his skin. He kissed the top of her head and went to put his arms around her.

She pulled away, turning her back on him, and said in a rough voice. "You've been a good pupil. But then all my lovers are good pupils."

"I had the best teacher." He thought for a moment. "If I've given you a bastard, I'll take care of it." And immediately wished he hadn't said it.

"There will be only one," she said. "Ever. And he's outside."

Relief flooded through him.

She stood up and he stood up too. "Don't forget me," she whispered. Rade kissed her and she held his hands to her breasts. And he kissed them too. He turned and began to pull on his clothes.

She waited until he was dressed. "Now go."

She was still naked when he left, pulling back the curtain and drawing it again. He looked for the child up and down the street but didn't see him.

*   *   *   *   *

"You've lost the *Cangrande*," panted Alberico. He was tired and his voice showed it. He'd ridden from the mouth of the river rather than take a boat. The horse stood behind him, head down, lather white on its brown hide.

Ludovico had come out on the *loggia* after Antonio had run in to get him.

"I've lost it? All the men? The cargo? What happened?"

Alberico repeated what Rade had told him, starting with the *Brenta.*

"Mother of God," swore Ludovico, putting a steadying hand on the archway. "I'll need to go back to Venice. Today. Now."

"Messer Vinciguerra," said Alberico tentatively, "messer Radović has a plan. May I explain it to you first?"

"Where is he in all of this?" asked Ludovico irritably. "Christ's nails, I've lost that horse, too."

"He's recruiting a crew."

"For what?"

"To take out the *Brenta* and search for the *Cangrande.*"

"He doesn't have the experience."

"He was the captain of a galley," replied Alberico.

"He told me he owned a galley not that he was the captain. But I have no proof of that." *But then, maybe he did. In the last few months he'd found Rade fully conversant on nautical subjects.*

"I think he knows what he's doing, messer Vinciguerra. He went to choose the larch for the new mast. And to the sailmaker's for sails and a new canopy. When I saw him last he was offloading the cargo."

"He doesn't have my permission to captain my boat."

"Forgive me, messer Vinciguerra, but he said to tell you these repairs would have to be done anyway. Just to use the *Brenta*. That if you will give him command, he thinks he can find the *Cangrande*."

Caterina came out of the doorway and Alberico found himself explaining it all over again. She looked at Alberico. "Why haven't any of you gotten him something to drink? Let him sit down? He's practically swaying on his feet."

After that, it got better. Ludovico, after a long discussion, agreed to the plan. With certain conditions. Alberico knew Rade wouldn't like them but there was nothing he could do about it. The next morning Alberico rode back to the mouth of the Brenta, and took the lagoon boat, his written instructions, and Ludovico's visitor, to Venice.

*   *   *   *   *

Rade watched, list in hand, as they came aboard: capped hair or a rag twisted about the forehead to catch the sweat, a loose shirt, and below, linen drawers for coolness, tied with a cord at the waist. A few wore leather leggings, as Rade did, and others tattered hose, some a worn out pair on top of another. Many were barefoot. The others would likely remove their shoes when they began to work. In hiring them, he'd looked for the heavy thighs of an oarsman, the calluses on the palms, the strength in the arms and shoulders, the toughened soles of the feet. Most of them had some of these characteristics. Only a very few had all. The ones that didn't would tire sooner, possibly fail altogether. But they were all he'd been able to recruit. When the men had stowed their bundles under their benches, he made the same speech he'd made at the signing: promising a short voyage, a push going out, and a reward if they found the *Cangrande*. Even during boarding, most of the gangway chatter had dealt with that.

Underway, he found the second officer, Pasquale, the same as the man in the quarantine enclosure, waiting for him. Already chafing under his command.

"It should be my command," maintained Pasquale, sloe-eyed, his face etched with crow's feet and smallpox scars.

"You came off the *Brenta* with your captain untended to, a crew dying of thirst, blistered by sun, no spares, no water, no shelter," returned Rade. "Why should *you* be in command?"

"Messer Vinciguerra wanted me on the ship."

"He wanted you on the ship because you are the only person who can reckon where you last saw the *Cangrande.*" It was a lie but he had no wish to empower such a fool. He added, "Why didn't you write it down?"

"It was during the attack," said Pasquale through his teeth. "And a squall was coming." *Besides, why write something down when he hadn't learned to read?*

"Christ's nails, I hope you have a good memory."

"I can find it, messer Radović."

"To you, it's *capitano* for the time being, Pasquale. You serve at my pleasure until told otherwise. And, if your memory fails you, I can assure you, it's going to be a long, unhappy swim."

The look of hatred was hard to miss.

There was a factor on board from Milan—sent down by

Ludovico on hearing the bad news. He was square, tanned, and brown-haired, a little like Miloš but an agent not a sailor, and his name was Mario. Rade wondered why it was that the factor had been so instantly available. After all, Milan was an important post.

In the beginning, with no wind to speak of, the sail was furled but a canopy sheltered the rowers. The galley, gliding through the calm sea, was virtually empty, its cargo hastily unloaded into storerooms, with only the usual ballast and a small load of supplies to weigh it down. This was something Ludovico never did: send out an empty ship. But Rade had reasoned, convinced him through his plan, that if they were fast enough, there might be something left to salvage. And the salvage would need a place to be stored.

Mario stood beside him. "How far to our first port?" He wore a white shirt and a light doublet instead of his normal merchant's gown.

"Dressing for us?" asked Rade, eyeing him.

"I'm not selling anything and I'm tired of madonna jests," replied Mario.

"They know the gown is for port," interjected Pasquale. "Most merchants wear it when they disembark."

"At sea," said Rade, straight-faced, "the wind gets under the skirt, fills it up with air and you blow off the boat."

"Truly?" asked Mario.

Pasquale, who'd looked as if he'd been sucking lemons all morning, couldn't contain the bark of laughter.

"All right. You've had your fun," Mario snapped.

"Too bad, we were just getting started," said Rade. "Weren't we, Pasquale?"

"I can't let you miss the part about the priests," replied Pasquale, grinning. "They didn't bring doublets and when the wind caught them, they were bare-ass under the robes. Every sodomite on board was instantly identified."

"Let's end it there," begged Mario. *"Please."*

"No lessons in buggery?" asked Rade. He squinted at the horizon. "You asked about distance," he said. "It's a hundred miles. God willing, we sail straight across to Parenzo on the opposite coast. In a five knot breeze, twenty hours." He glanced at Mario. "Only God isn't willing."

"There's a little wind," observed Mario, holding up a wetted finger.

"Actually, there's no wind," replied Rade. "The breeze you feel is of our making. From our own efforts. Better pray for wind. Otherwise it will take us days to get there."

"You won't have to row the whole way, will you?" Mario looked worried.

"We can't. It's too hard on the oarsmen. We'll pick up a breeze eventually. Until then, I'll have to push them," said Rade. He shrugged, "Might as well start now. Pasquale take the helm." He relieved a man of his place on his bench.

"But you're in command!" said Mario. "This can't be fitting."

"You shed your robe. I'm shedding my title." Rade squinted up at Mario and then looked back at the other oarsmen. "Put your backs into it. We've got a ship to find. On me. *Now!*" And he began to chant.

There was a slow but perceptible rise in speed. And in noise. Soon they were all chanting.

To Mario's surprise, and later he wondered why he'd been surprised, Rade was good at the oar. Mounting the shallow step in time with the others to set the blades in the sea, Rade braced and fell back as they did, dragging back the lead-weighted shaft as he resumed his bench. It was a punishing, repetitive movement. One that went on for hours only because Rade did everything he could to keep them at it. A physical task normally reserved for short spurts of speed, approaching port in a contrary wind, or maneuvering in uncertain waters, no oarsman could maintain it indefinitely. On the *Brenta*, it went on far beyond the usual limits: until every man was drenched with sweat. Until most of the oar handles were bloody. Until some of the benches shed their occupants. Finally the galley found a snippet of breeze, and later, a moderate wind to sail by. Even then they rowed through the light air with a skeleton crew at Rade's command. But when the sails abandoned their sag, and billowed out, the oars were shipped, and the crew collapsed, exhausted.

Mario watching the effort, began to think that there was more to Rade than Ludovico had indicated. This was no braggart. Nor some enigmatic outsider. This man knew what he was doing. Even if he'd lied about who was to command the ship, he'd brought it off thus far. In the end, the *Brenta* made Parenzo in a day and a half, rowing, rowing and sailing, and sailing at night by the stars. Rade anchored her northwest of Parenzo's small but protective island of San Nicola. In the mud. When the *Brenta* showed no sign of entering the port, like magic, boats, packed with vendors, rowed out with supplies. But Rade, while he was willing to buy, let no one disembark. And the whores went back, unable to board, unsatisfied, unpaid.

Mario stood next to him, looking out at Parenzo.

"Right now," said Rade, "the men are fed and they've had their double ration of wine. Tomorrow will be another matter. Some won't want to do this tomorrow," he said, watching as the last of the boats left. "We need to discourage any new boats or we'll lose some crew." He sighed.

"Tired?"

"It's been a long day and night. We could all use a few hours rest."

But Mario noticed that he looked remarkably fresh, neither flushed with sun, nor tired. It was the way he stood and the way his voice cracked that said otherwise.

"Stand watch, will you?" Rade asked. "Pick one of the semi-invalids who hasn't rowed all day because his palms are shredded. Have him stand with you. Tell him we'll let him off tomorrow."

"Of course I'll do it," Mario responded. "I'm glad to contribute to the voyage."

There was a moment's pause. "Why did you come on the voyage?" asked Rade in a hoarse voice.

"I thought you knew," replied Mario. "To make sure you didn't run off with messer Vinciguerra's ship."

"I've already done that. Find something else to worry about."

*   *   *   *   *

Caterina and Ludovico, having finished supper, sat out on the *loggia* of the villa, enjoying the breeze. The house was a square, unpretentious building, cream-colored with a terracotta pantile roof, perched on a hilltop overlooking its farm. They sat behind three tall archways on rough chairs set on a stone floor, watching the bats. There were no gardens, not even any trees, just the soft uncut flow of a field sawing back and forth with the breeze. One could hear the night sounds of chirring insects and the peeping of frogs. Sofia and Cook rattling things and chatting somewhere inside. And twice a chorus of male laughter.

"Have you ever noticed," said Caterina, "how the structure of life in Venice somehow softens in the country?"

"They're as glad to be cool as we are," said Ludovico.

"I meant…"

"I know what you meant. Yes, I noticed." He smiled. "It's good for them."

"Where do you suppose they are now? Rade and Mario? The *Brenta*?"

"By now, I hope they're off Zara. We know when they left: five days ago."

"Alberico said in his message there hadn't been any wind."

"At sea, there's always wind somewhere. You just have to find it. The bigger problem is a contrary wind." Ludovico sat silently for a while. "I have no hope for this search," he added.

"Then why did you let them go?" asked Caterina, surprised.

"So I could tell the crew's families and my investors that we tried to do something. It's going to cost me dearly. And ..."

"And what?"

"To test your young man."

"That's a funny way to describe him," said Caterina. "I don't think of him in that way."

"How do you think of him?" His voice was suddenly sharp.

"I think on the outside he is comely. Very comely. He tries, I think, to fit in. But I don't know that Plato would approve my experiment."

"No beauty of the soul?"

Caterina thought for a moment. "There's a splendid palazzo being built even now on the Grand Canal. You know the one."

"The one where the fortune was lost and there are now new owners?"

"Yes." She paused. "And you know Simonetta. Always curious. She managed an invitation to see the interior."

"If anyone could, it would be Simonetta."

Caterina smiled. "Yes." Then looked thoughtful. "She came out terribly disappointed."

"Why?"

"It was empty."

"They haven't moved in."

"What I meant is that the beautiful decoration, the colored

marbles, the arches, the columns, were all on the outside. On the facade. There was no money left to embellish the inside. It was plain and dark. A shell."

"You are telling me the palazzo is Rade."

"Father," she picked at her dress, "I don't know what's inside of him. I can't see beyond the facade."

"We have plenty of time," Ludovico reassured her. "We'll find out. As your father, it's my duty to make sure of it."

They were both quiet. The bats had gone. The stars had replaced them. The night sky was a mass of tiny lights, some blurred, some sharp. And it was cool.

Caterina mused dreamily, "I could stay here forever."

Ludovico shook himself out of a doze. In his half-conscious state he said something he'd meant to keep to himself. "Milan is up to something." And added a moment later, now that the cat was out of the bag, "That would be unwise."

"Do you truly think so?" She sounded alarmed. *So that was why Mario had come.*

"We'll be safe in Venice," he said. "The lagoon will protect us. It always has." He stood up and bent to kiss her. "Goodnight, my child. Don't be afraid. Nothing will happen while we're here. Your ancient father is going to bed. Like Nonna. Early." He kissed her and went in. She heard him calling for Sofia, who shortly came out to sit on the *loggia*—so Caterina wouldn't be alone.

Chapter Fourteen

Heaven wheels above you, displaying to you her eternal
glories, and still your eyes are on the ground.
—Dante Alighieri

August, Sixth Month of Venetian Year 1493

"How much farther?" asked Mario at dawn on the third
day. He had the determined look of a man who would get this
task over with—come what may. They'd left Parenzo far
behind and were sailing in a light breeze south by southeast.
The sky was luminous, promising clear skies, heat, and calm
seas.

"We're more than halfway," said Rade. "But this leg will
be slower." He put a hand up on the rigging and squinted into
the distance. "There are islands all along the coast. Not like the
other side."

Mario looked at Rade's hand on the rigging. It was
blistered and raw from the oar. "Are all the men's hands like
that?"

"Probably." He smiled ruefully. "The new oarsmen are
useless now. Even I thought I had sufficient calluses to manage
this." He opened his palms. "I guess not." *It's odd how much of*
life seems to be about hands. He thought of Caterina and her
garlands. Of Rosa and what pleasure she could bring. And then

of what she had discovered. He closed his eyes and waited for
his heart to slow. He still had no idea how he'd manage the
inevitable.

"When do we start looking?" asked Mario, his gray eyes
searching the horizon.

Rade pulled himself together. "When we reach Pasquale's
departure point. That is if he remembers where it was."

"Why not start now?"

"I have to make some assumptions. It would be foolish not
to. There are too many places to look. A little closer and we'll
put a boy up to watch."

A couple of hours later, a stripling, lithe and far-sighted,
was perched high on the mast, scanning the sea for brigands,
trading vessels, fishing boats, even wheeling flocks of seabirds
indicating a wreck. On that first morning of the third day, he
found nothing. Later, the *Brenta* hailed two fishing boats but
neither had news of a wreck or of the *Cangrande*. For a time
the wind gathered force and the galley flew past the islands by
the shore: Cherso, with its olive groves, sheep and huge fresh
water basin; Losina, where the islanders raised livestock; and
nearer the coast, Rab, devastated by plague, almost forty years
before. But then the breeze died in an expanse of open water.

The oars came out as the wind went, and came, and went.
Rade could see the crew was tiring. That they were suffering.
A certain grimness etched itself into the set of their faces. They
rowed, rags or leather tied around their hands. Rowed without
a desire to use their backs. To extend their arms and shoulders.
Rade went back to the bench and set the pace. Used the oars to
augment the slightest breeze. To push the galley's progress.
When the crew grumbled the days were long this time of year,
he reminded them that the west wind would rise in the late
afternoon, plied them with wine, cajoled them as best he could.
He watched the sea for the smallest ripple indicating the
movement of air, changed men from side to side, worked the

sail, passed out salves, new rags and strips of leather, and occasionally allowed a skeleton crew so the others could eat and rest. And he grilled Pasquale on the last sighting of the *Cangrande* until Pasquale had said the same thing every way there was to say it.

*   *   *   *   *

The wind had come up again and now they sailed along with a fresh breeze and sharp eyes, lateen sail rigged and oars at rest. Sparsely capped in heather, scrub, and pine, marked with coves or cliffs, the Coronati extended before and behind the ship in an endless procession. Like pale floats on a sunken net, in their offshore waters, they held a great abundance of fish: mullet, anchovies, mackerel. Merchants, armies, and brigands alike bartered for that harvest, packed in barrels and preserved in salt. When the islands where the *Brenta* met the squall finally came into view, Rade found he knew them. Knew them well. Beyond them lay what were called "the islets of the watery grave."

"It was here," said Pasquale. "A gray squall. Visibility went all to hell. The *Cangrande* passed into the midst of it. For a while, we could see the white horse in the stall on the deck. Then, nothing."

"Show me the direction they took," said Rade. He glanced at Pasquale. Despite Rade's earlier thoughts, the man was becoming dependable. Appeared to be knowledgeable. He hoped he was right.

"They sailed that way," said Pasquale, pointing south. "But after that, who knows?"

Christ's nails, Lavsa was that way.

Pasquale must have shared his thoughts. "If they were driven against the cliffs of Lavsa, then we've journeyed far for nothing." His skin was like worm-eaten wood in the morning light.

They sailed at first and then rowed between the islands, their eyes searching every cove or hill or stand of scrub for some sign of life. The chain was endless, stretching out before and behind them. Islet after island after islet. The larger ones like ridges in the sea. At a distance, in the bright light, they seemed disembodied, floating above the water, even following the galley. Reefs were identified by changes in the color of the water. Azure bled to turquoise and back again. The sea over rocks was darker, over sand, almost green. Repetitively, the leads were cast and called out. Several times the galley scraped against obstacles below the surface. Then they would stare into the water, fearful it might be the *Cangrande.* Twice Rade sent a man overboard, roped to the galley, to see. But in each case, there was no wreck, no *Cangrande,* no corpses, to be found.

*   *   *   *   *

The *Brenta* anchored for the night in a nameless cove. Some of the men waded into the beach to wash or eat or scout out rainwater in cavities in the karst. There were no springs.

Rade and Mario climbed the tall, scrubby hill of the island from the sheer desire to get as far from the galley as possible. At the summit, they made a simple supper of bread and cheese and washed it down with unwatered wine. Rade lay on his back among the bracken, the motion of the sea rising and falling in his veins. He was bone-tired. His palms were on fire and every muscle in his body hurt. He drank with the express intention of achieving slumber no matter how much alcohol it required. They were never going to make it to the end of the voyage with the wine he had left. They were subsisting on it. The crew had more wine in them than blood. So did he.

Mario perched nearby on a rock. The night was moonless. A breeze danced along the hill bringing the steady drone of cicadas and the resinous scent of pine. For a long while, the two men relaxed in companionable silence under the starry vault of the heavens—loathe to discuss the day to come; each knowing that the chance of salvage was small and the discovery of survivors smaller still. For Mario, the shade of an old friend was painfully close, while for Rade, the specter of fate drew his thoughts to another hill, somewhere far away. To a woman, who, compared to the earthiness of Rosa, was made of marble, or maybe glass. Who was as attainable in the flesh as a bronze statue with a guard outside. After a while, Rade felt the world begin to blur into something he could manage. He worked on finding a more comfortable spot, pushing and pulling at the undergrowth, trying to cushion the rocks, remove whatever was crawling over his skin. The ongoing tragedy was that the wine flasks were empty and the next one was at the bottom of the hill, across the shallows, on board the *Brenta*. And there was no way he was going to get there to open it.

"Christ's nails," muttered Mario suddenly, and fell off the rock.

Rade struggled to sit up. "What is it?"

"I've drunk too much," came the slurred answer. "Either that or the stars have fallen into the sea."

"Help me up," Rade said groggily. "Where?"

Eventually with the help of nearby rocks, and each other, they got to their knees and then to their feet. Beyond them, in the void, a flickering line of tiny fires advanced, occasionally disappearing behind a dark shape, only to reappear a little farther south.

Rade looked up at the sky. "Don't see any missing."

"How would you know? There are thousands of them."

"I'd know."

"I still see them," said Mario. "For God's sake, Rade, gather your wits about you!" And he threw their wash water in Rade's face. It was full of salt.

"You bastard!" swore Rade, wiping his eyes. But gradually the lights began to make sense. "It's the fisher folk," he said slowly. "They've always done that."

"Done what?" asked Mario, exasperated.

"Used torches to draw fish. Toward daybreak, the smaller boats will circle. The larger ones will set their nets. Pull in the catch."

"How did you know that?" asked Mario.

"In this part of the world," answered Rade, "everyone from islanders to brigands knows that."

"Well," said Mario, "I know you're not an islander…"

"No," replied Rade, feeling reckless. "I'm a brigand." He added, "All Slavs are brigands. You should hear Ludovico on the subject."

Mario laughed, "I have." And began to gather up his belongings. Rade, too, turned to rediscover the last of the bread and the cheese that he'd abandoned for drink, and as he did so, a solitary light caught his eye. It had to be a fire, faint, then bright, blazing on another hill. A hill, not on one of the big islands, he thought, on one of the small ones—a light in no-man's land. He waited for it to shift. But it didn't. For a time, he stood staring at it, unable to move.

"By all the saints," Rade said, excitement showing in his voice. "*Mario!* Can you see that? The light?" He pointed.

"I can't tell what it is," said Mario, squinting. "My eyes aren't as good as yours."

"It's a fire," said Rade. "God's blood, a fire! You know what that means!" He glanced up at the stars. "Tomorrow we sail north."

They bounded, whooping, down the hill to the alarm of the sleeping galley in the cove. On the way down, Rade had a sobering thought. *If it's the Cangrande, did they have food? Or had they eaten Ludovico's horse?*

*   *   *   *   *

It was a brilliant morning and a fruitless search. The *Brenta* picked its way gingerly between the chain of islands, a continuation of the day before: the stripling up the mast for sightings and changes in the water complemented by a man with a lead weight in the bow for soundings. Again, despite all precautions, the hull grated from time to time on a hidden reef and the rowers fended off with the blunt shafts of their oars. Once they found a wreck, all barnacles and waving strands of seaweed.

"She's old," remarked Pasquale, peering into the water. "She's been there a long time." And he crossed himself.

They flew no flags for fear of brigands. The stony shores were monotonously the same, visually uninhabited, but sometimes featuring an abandoned fisherman's hut or part of a rock wall scraped from the bleached earth. There was nothing new washed up on the beach: no casks, no wood, no bodies, no ship.

"Sheep to the east!" called the lookout. Sure enough, a white speck stood out from an olive hill. Large enough to be a flock. Rade climbed the mast to where the boy clung, peering into the distance, one thin brown arm stabbing at the distant island. Rade motioned to the helmsman to set a different course. Suddenly, he slid down the rigging.

"Keep your eye on it, Lucca," he called. He saw a gleam of white teeth from on high. "*God's blood, I think we've found something!*" he shouted to the crew. "*Might be a horse!*"

The galley lay half out of the water near the shore, listing to one side, her stern partially submerged. The beach was deserted, and even on the rocky slope, there was no one to be seen. A sigh of discouragement ran through the crew, overlaying the preliminary joy of discovery. At the last, the *Brenta,* ran up her pennants: the lion of St. Mark and

Ludovico's tree and swallows. It was only then that small
figures detached themselves from the hillside, shouting and
cheering, running down to the beach.

It was what they'd come for: the *Cangrande*, all the men,
and a horse.

*   *   *   *   *

"I've had Sofia strew sweet hay and herbs all around the
room we'll dine in. We'll scatter some blossoms later." Caterina
looked at her father. "Don't look surprised. I told you we were
going to do that. It's going to be a country party. No formality.
Petrarch would have loved it!"

"These men don't have much in common with Petrarch,"
Ludovico said doubtfully. "And they'll be tired. They've
brought that horse a long way."

She worked a large beeswax candle onto one of the pricket
candlesticks. "It's a celebration. Look what they've done!"

"They've accomplished what they said they would. But it
cost. And I'm not in the business of providing charity."
Ludovico moved the candlestick toward the center of the table.
"If you don't set the house on fire, at least the horse can eat the
hay."

"It would have cost more if they hadn't."

"Rade should never have paid a reward."

"But there was so little time. It bought him a crew,"
replied Caterina, working another candle onto the spike.
"Besides, you sanctioned it."

"I never sanctioned a reward."

"But it worked! You got them all back: the ship, the horse,
most of the cargo, and the men. Can't you admit it was a deed
well done?"

Ludovico turned his back on her, moving toward the
doorway.

"You aren't listening to me," she said, looking up.

"Then say something I wish to hear." He went out onto the *loggia* to meet with the farm manager, and point out the fields he wanted to discuss, before they rode around them on horseback.

*   *   *   *   *

By late afternoon, Caterina had been out on the *loggia* numerous times to look for the travelers. Muttering, she went back into the kitchen, and surveyed the ingredients for the feast. "Do you think the meat will spoil? I thought they'd be here hours ago."

"The chickens were killed and plucked an hour or so ago," observed Cook. "They should be cooked. They'll be getting stiff. The fish we either eat or throw out. It's too late to salt."

Caterina surveyed the almonds, rosewater, pomegranate seeds, sugar and cloves laid out on the trestle table. Sofia was pounding rice and tending pots of boiling stock. Melons lay alongside newly harvested figs, their sweetness to be offset by the small sharp cheeses of Marzolino. There were trout waiting to be stuffed with lemons and herbs, crocks of marinated anchovies, piles of leafy vegetables, and pared fennel for the stew pot. "Everything but the fish," she said. "If they're going to be late, they can eat the chicken cold. But the fish should be hot."

It was evening when the party came into view. By then Caterina felt as if she'd worn a path from the hearth to the *loggia*. The band of men moved slowly, almost deliberately so, and it was all she could do not to rush out the door and down into the fields to shout at them to hurry up. If it hadn't been for the pale horse and the barking of the farm dogs, she might have missed them in the gathering darkness. Orseolo, hearing the other dogs, set up such a racket that she finally seized him, shouted at him, and shut him in her room. Then she went back to the purgatory of waiting for them to arrive, anger rising in her breast.

As they got closer, she began to see that something wasn't right. One of the riders had something tied around his arm and another rode crooked in the saddle. It was Mario who rode up first.

"Can you get someone up from the farm for the stallion?"

"Of course." She called Battista and he went immediately. "What happened?"

"What didn't happen," he muttered. "Alberico's hurt."

"What can I do?"

"Can you find some linen? Some wine? We'll wash the bite. I think your cook might know what to do."

She turned to go into the house and stopped, looking back. "Bite? A snake?"

"Would that it were. He got trapped between two stallions that went for each other over some fool riding a mare in season. The other one, not yours, sank his teeth into him."

"Is it very bad?"

"On my honor, I wouldn't know. I do know a stallion's bite is crushing. The beast picked him up by the upper arm, hung him in the air, and threw him against the wall of a shed. And he's not a small man. The wood split. There's a wound. Something looks to be torn. I think if Rade hadn't gone in to get him, he'd be dead."

"I'll get Cook, wine and some linen."

When she came out with Cook, arms loaded with torn-up bed sheets, she saw Giovanni had been riding behind Alberico, and holding him in the saddle. Alberico had a shirt wrapped around his arm and she could see blood on it. Rade was still mounted, holding the reins to Giovanni's horse. Mario had gotten off to help.

Antonio and Battista eased Alberico out of the saddle. His

face was pale and Caterina could see he had to work to mask the pain. She looked at Giovanni. The old man was covered with spots of blood. "What's that?" she said, pointing.

Giovanni looked down. "Not mine. The wall splintered. They'll have to come out. If he'd had a doublet on..." He climbed down wearily from the saddle.

They helped Alberico into the house, Giovanni following. Soon Caterina came back out. "Are you coming?" She queried, exasperated. "I've set dinner for you."

"When the farmhand arrives to stable the horses," Rade replied, still mounted. "Only the stallion has gone."

*   *   *   *   *

The meal, when it finally got underway, was a success, though a cold one, but the celebration was ruined. They were glad of the food but in the end, she thought, they would have eaten anything. She took a plate in to Alberico before the meal but he shook his head and told her to put it aside. "The condemned man," he said grimly, "and all that follows." And she saw Nonna and Cook come in with various instruments and wine.

"The wine's for the inside," said Alberico hopefully.

"The wine's for the cuts," replied Nonna. "But we brought some for the man as well."

"We'll get the splinters out," said Cook. "Lie on your stomach. I'll cut your shirt off."

Alberico drank most of one bottle, lay down gingerly, and tried to find a modicum of comfort. They fussed about trying to help.

"Let the hurt arm hang over if that feels better," advised Cook. "We've got someone coming for that." She laid out the implements and adjusted her apron.

"You should leave," ordered Nonna, looking at Caterina.

"*Now*. This is not proper for you."

The girl started for the door.

"For the rest," Cook added briskly, "it's like plucking a chicken."

Alberico said something that was very rude even for Alberico.

Caterina fled.

*   *   *   *   *

Caterina went back to the feast bearing the trout, soon to be cocooned in compliments. They were all picking out bones when Rade, who hadn't said anything during the meal, slid sideways, and fell off the bench.

"Rade?" Mario said. *"Rade!"*

"It's endlessly entertaining to have a drunk at the table," sighed Ludovico. "But then I suppose you've all had a long, hard day."

But Mario was on his knees next to Rade almost immediately.

Battista looked at Rade's cup. "It's full. So is his plate."

"We saw the stallion trample him," said Mario, looking up. "When he went to pull Alberico out. He never said anything. We thought he wasn't hurt."

*   *   *   *   *

"Welcome to the *lazaretto*," said Mario, his voice low and solicitous. "You're awake."

The room was dark. "Yes. I'm sure they're pleased to have the villa known as that." Rade was lying propped up in the bed. "Is it night?"

"Yes. But it's the second night. You've had a good sleep."

Rade felt the binding under his shirt. "Ribs?" he asked.

"Yes. But not too bad. You'll heal. It was the ride. Twenty miles with broken ribs. You're a stubborn bastard, God knows. You should have said something."

"The bastard paid. I didn't get any dinner."

"Too late now," quipped Mario. "We ate it."

"How goes Alberico?"

"If the wound doesn't putrefy, he'll recover. The arm is sore and bruised. The bite area is swollen. He has the mother of all bruises on his back but at least Cook got the splinters out." Mario grinned. "That was quite an undertaking. Four bottles of wine." He added, starting to get up, "I'll get you something to eat. You must be hungry."

"Mario."

The tenor of Rade's voice stopped him. "Yes." He sat down again.

"Who strapped me up?" He could feel all his secrets spilling out.

"A laborer from the farm," Mario said. "A healer. He did it. Alberico's arm too. Even sewed it up. He's said to be good. Works on lots of beasts." Mario stood up again. His eyes crinkled at the corners. "Any requests from this particular beast?"

"No." He tried to sit up a little straighter. It hurt. "Yes," Rade said, closing his eyes. "What did he say?"

"That was the problem," replied Mario, distantly, crossing the room. "He didn't say anything. About either of you. Poor soul's a deaf mute. But he's good with his hands."

Rade began to relax.

Mario turned back at the door. "Who's Rosa?" he asked. "I think I'd like to meet her."

*   *   *   *   *

"Would you know where Mario is?" Rade stood hesitantly

on the *loggia*, his doublet open above the waist to spare the fractures.

Caterina waded through the field watching Orseolo, who was engaged in his own small furor of activity, running enthusiastically in this direction and that, visible by means of the movement of parted field grass and the occasional upward leap to see what he was chasing. She turned to see Rade silhouetted against the glow of candles inside the door.

"You must feel better," said Caterina. "You're up."

"Yes. Much. Thank you for the suppers. I should be getting back to Venice."

"Mario's already gone," she replied. "He went to see you but you were asleep." She added, "Father's gone too."

The night was clear, freshened by a breeze, and spangled with stars. He looked at her in her light dress, her wheaten hair, standing in the nearly mature field—and felt the old sharp pang of desire. "I'm sure there's work to be done."

"They'll do it. Can you take a deep breath yet?"

"Not trussed up like a pig on its way to market." He sat down carefully on the step.

"Then we should wait for the pig to be unbound." she replied, smiling. "You're to go back with Alberico."

"When will that be?"

"A week. A fortnight. I don't know."

"And Mario?"

"He'll stay in Venice. He's perfectly capable. Besides, we're to have some sport when Father returns. He keeps a few falcons. If you can sit a horse, you must come out for that." She turned her attention back to the dog. "Orseolo." She looked around for movement in the tall grass. "Where are you? Orseolo!" She ran farther into the field. "Orseolo! I don't see him! *Orseolo! Orseolo!*"

"Over there," said Rade, pointing. He quickly put his arm down. "Christ's nails." And had a moment of not being able to breathe.

Nonna, considering her bulk, had come almost noiselessly onto the *loggia* behind him. "That's why you shouldn't be up."

"In my country," replied Rade, "only weaklings lie abed."

"If they don't rest, how do they recover?" asked Nonna. "I don't understand your country. I don't think I ever will." She stood up as Rade moved over and Caterina came up the steps. "Oh good, you've caught him. Our very own devil." She stroked Orseolo's fur. "The epitome of misbehavior." But she looked at Rade.

"Can you find something to tie him with, Nonna?" asked Caterina. "And something to sit on? It's so lovely out. And it smells so good. The night is full of sounds." She tucked Orseolo more securely under her arm. "I'd like to sit out in the field. But it's damp."

"I'll find some twine," answered Nonna, "and have Sofia bring out some old cloaks. And then *we*," she said emphasizing the pronoun and looking at Rade, "can enjoy the stars."

"I can hardly move," he muttered.

She gave him a sharp look and left.

*   *   *   *   *

"Are the stars this close in Zeta?" asked Caterina dreamily, lying with her head in her nurse's lap.

"Closer," said Rade. He was sitting near her, trying to identify a comfortable way in which to sit, pulling grass stems from the field. "Our mountains rise so high, we light our hearths from them." He grinned.

"Must be dangerous for thatched roofs," observed Nonna dryly.

"What's it really like?" murmured Caterina. "The truth."

Rade gave up on sitting. He resettled himself carefully on his back, close to Caterina but leaving a definitive space. He was immediately enveloped in the gentle aroma of bruised grasses and the soft fragrance of lavender that emanated from her clothes. Only he found he couldn't breathe. He levered himself up.

"There's an extra cloak," said Nonna. "You should know better than to lie flat. Here."

What mouse ignores an owl? He bundled it up and eventually found a middling level of comfort.

"I've never been to the top of anything," mused Caterina. "Except the campanile."

"It's rock," he replied. "Everywhere. You lie on a bed of limestone, above the lentisks, as high as the eagles." He saw the boy he'd once been. "You feel like a king. A god. You own the world below and the sky above. Everything. Even the wind." *And no one can hurt you there.*

"It sounds so beautiful," breathed Caterina.

"It sounds so uncomfortable," said her nurse. "Rocks. Wind. Aren't lentisks those dreadful little bushes with spines?"

"No," replied Rade. Caterina could hear the amusement in his voice. "But we have those too, though generally, I choose not to sleep on them."

"I look at the stars," said Caterina, "and I see Father. Reading their influence. Plotting the constellations. Casting his horoscope. Trying to second guess fate."

"Would that we could all second guess fate," murmured Rade.

"Yes but his predictions only come true after something has happened," Caterina said. "What good is that?" Orseolo rushed out, hit the end of the twine, and leaned on it. "Orseolo," ordered Caterina, reeling him in, *"come here."*

The chorus of frogs and cicadas swelled. Looking up into the night, they let the sound fill them with the essence of summer. A comet streaked across the sky.

"See that one?" Rade said. "The very bright one?"

"The comet?" asked Caterina.

"No. The bright star. Look to the north."

"Where?"

"There," he said, and pointed. He paid for the gesture. "It's the pole star." His voice was a little breathless. He had to sit up again. "Polaris. The one star that's fixed." He took another breath. "The one we sail by. All the others wheel across the sky as the night passes."

"You're worse than Orseolo at the end of his string," observed Nonna.

Caterina looked at him. Studied the way he was sitting. Breathing. Saw that he hurt. And laid a gentle hand on his arm.

He looked back at her. His face dark. Unreadable. His eyes glittering in the starlight.

She squeezed his arm. Then took her hand away. She saw that Nonna had noticed. "And Nonna?" asked Caterina, turning her head to see her face. "What do you see?"

Nonna leaned back, arms extended, hands turned out on the cloak, and looked skyward. "I see what we all see: God in His heavens." She paused. "And Petrarch: '*Night leads its starry chariot in its round.*'" She turned to look at her companions. "And that brings to mind the line following: '*the sea without a wave lies in its bed.*' Let me emphasize the word *bed.*"

The minutes passed. Caterina again laid her head back in Nonna's lap. Rade let his fingers caress the soft fold of Caterina's skirt where it was closest to him. Move toward the outline of her body under the fabric. The curve of her hip. Her eyes were closed. Her breathing slow. He looked up and saw Nonna watching him.

"Bed," repeated Nonna, through her teeth. "As in sleep."

He let his fingers rest on the fabric. Took in the steely gaze of her guardian. The bronze goddess had two guardians. He'd erred at one.

"Do not mistake compassion for desire," growled Nonna in an undertone, glaring at him. "She would do the same for a dog."

He held her gaze but had no intention of replying. Minutes passed. Another comet crossed the sky. And another.

"We're going in," announced Nonna. She displaced Caterina, shook her awake, and began to get up. "Come, my sleepy one. Time for bed." Looking at Rade, she said, "Get the dog, will you? You need rest. I can hear it."

Chapter Fifteen

Ah wretched me, who loved a sparrow hawk;
So loved him I was dying for his love;
Well was he gentled to my command
And I never had to feed him overmuch.
　　　　　—*Anonymous*, 13th century song

August to First Week of October, Sixth to Eighth Month of
Venetian Year 1493

"Mending?" asked Rade. He'd walked down to the farm
where Alberico was quartered. The path was dusty, the shade
insubstantial, and the odor of dung and the quantity of insects
rose incrementally as he descended.

"You're looking at a rainbow of healing," muttered
Alberico, square set, placid, sitting dressed on the edge of his
bed, his bad arm in a sling. "And a favorite of blowflies."

"The arm?"

"The last I heard," said Alberico, "they were looking for
lizard turds but had to make do with wine."

"Lucky soul." Rade laughed. He motioned toward the
farmyard. "They've got a falconer down here. Want to go look
at hawks? Are you up to it?"

"Anything's better than counting chickens," Alberico
replied, rising to his feet.

The mews held five birds, hooded and tethered to separate perches. When the helper opened the door, one of the hawks, feebly flapping, was hanging upside down from the tether that bound him to his perch. The bird's hood was askew and one eye was partially visible. There was blood on the wall where his wings had raked it. The stripling's long, thin face, nearly eclipsed by a curtain of unwashed hair, grew longer. *"Christ's wounds,"* he cried, *"the bugger's worked the hood loose."*

"Should we go out?"

"No. Stay where you are." The young man pushed the hair out of his eyes, pulled his glove on and deftly gathered up the bird, straightening its hood and lifting it onto its perch. He looked around on the floor. He grimaced. "No tie. I must have dropped it."

They all looked for it between the guano, castings, and bits of flesh, fur, feathers and bones that had made it to the dirt floor.

"I must have dropped it outside," the helper said. He screwed up his face. "God's bones, my master's going to flay me." He went to a wooden box and drew out another hood. "He's the new bird," he said, removing the old hood and fastening the new. "A young one. You can see he's still brown."

"Is he ruined?" asked Alberico looking at the spray of blood on the wall.

"He'll survive. I'll put some flour on the damage," said the stripling, bending over the box again. "Feathers grow back. It just takes time." He eventually found the small pouch of flour. "Sight is everything," he continued, gesturing at the birds of prey. "Take sight away and they're calm as a corpse." He added ruefully, eyes imprisoned in hair, "This one could see."

"That's why it's dark in here," said Alberico.

The helper nodded. "Despite what's happened," he added, brightly, "be content with their situation. They enjoy a much longer life in captivity." And he launched into a prolonged explanation of the merits of the sport.

Afterwards, the two men walked for a while in silence.

"Liked to talk, didn't he," said Alberico afterwards, kneading his arm. "I guess I'm not meant for the sport of kings."

"He said they're light," replied Rade. "Your arm will heal."

"It's not my arm," said Alberico, turning to look at him. "God's blood, I know it's just a bird, but imagine being hooded and tied for the best part of your life."

Rade said nothing but he thought about it as he walked back up the hill to the villa.

*   *   *   *   *

There was a stillness to early morning that anticipated the day that was forming. Dew sparkled on the stubble of the field and the spiders' webs were jeweled. Caterina saw Rade take a deep breath before the falconer transferred the tiercel to his glove. "The strapping's gone," she said.

"I took it off."

It's just a bird Alberico had said, but if you'd grown up where he had, it wasn't. He'd only seen them from afar, flying wild and free. And he was surprised that St. Elijah's messenger should be so small and light when the choice it had offered Prince Lazar had been so weighty: an earthly kingdom or a heavenly one. And Lazar, his eyes to the sky, had chosen what had eventually brought the Ottoman Empire to their very doorstep—and the prince to his grave and sainthood. Yet this little bird, this falcon, this messenger of fate, was also the celebrated, solitary warrior who dropped with dazzling speed out of the sun, and killed, while the other, much larger predator, the eagle, was disdained for the lambs it stole. After all, lambs were a poor man's sustenance, winter warmth, and source of wealth. The respect Rade felt for the falcon was learned from song; what he felt for the eagle was learned from life.

The bird perched, long-winged and slate-backed, yellow feet armed in black talons gripping his glove. Its blurred but distinctive facial mask was covered, like Caterina's bird's, by a jaunty leather hood. He looked at Caterina. "And now, you'll teach me the sport."

"Yours is a peregrine. A tiercel. In his world, the females are the big ones. But he has the better trappings. Mine," she petted her bird, "is a merlin. Her breed is smaller but she's still larger than her mate."

"A lesser bird with an unfair advantage."

"A falcon," she bridled, "is female. It says so in one of father's books."

"Not in my world."

"Do you want to hunt? Or argue?"

"Hunt."

"Then do as I tell you."

*   *   *   *   *

Conversation dwindled as they engaged in the hunt. They moved from place to place, following the beaters, Nonna, a well of ill-concealed boredom, not far behind. As each raptor was recaptured, separated from its prey, hooded, and returned to whomever was hunting it, Rade's silence grew. Eventually, Caterina gave up trying to converse with him.

The beaters were in the thicket at the edge of the field, shouting as the skylarks fled their flailing branches. The flock billowed up like thunderheads in a storm. She watched Rade take one release thong in his left hand and the other in his teeth, and pull them, doffing the hood—as she had shown him. As the bird sighted, he slipped the jesses, and cast him off. The flock began to reform. The tiercel stroked powerfully after them, jesses streaming behind him, rising higher and higher until his shape was a thin, ribboned arc in the blue of the sky. Caterina saw Rade's eyes follow him, narrowing as the falcon rose. The quarry began to wheel, seeking another copse of trees, seemingly oblivious of this other danger, now almost upon them.

*   *   *   *   *

For Rade, the falcon dissolved into space.

He could recall the words but not the place. Yet, even as he had that thought, Rade could see the flickering firelight and the stranger, eyes like milk, drawing his bow across his one-stringed instrument, his *gusla*, surrounded by people. He could hear the rise and fall of the bard's chant, the cadence of his poetry, the sighing of the wind, the warmth of his mother's breath on his cheek.

Drink went round. Men echoed the lines they knew, shouted, then quieted, some even wept. For a child at his mother's knee, shining, long-coated warriors rose out of the fire, mounted great warhorses, and rode out from their white court into the darkness of sorrow and legend. And at the center of it all had been a falcon.

Then came he back without fair head. Had it been the next line? The prophetic one. The scene wavered. Rade tried to hold onto it but the vision began to fade.

And then, some months later, in a flurry of horsemen, his father had returned from a lowland raid, across his saddle rather than on it. And he had been like that falcon. The serene, handsome woman, who'd nightly folded Rade into her arms, became a wraith who tore her skin and clothing and left the house to keen in the darkness—when he was supposed to be asleep. And after that, they'd been given to someone who had no flocks. No house. To a man who couldn't father a child of his own. Nor accept what wasn't his.

The landscape of the hunt materialized. His eyes focused on movement. He saw the falcon plummet from the sky. Stoop in the absolute freedom of air and space. The scythe of the killer. The joy of Icarus still pinned. The swiftness of untimely fate.

He should have killed that man when he'd had the chance.

*   *   *   *   *

Venice in autumn was a difference in light and a lengthening of shadows. On cool nights, the canals spawned wraith-like mists that curled their way around bits of architecture or walkways or vessels—like filmy replicas of wrought iron. What foliage there was remained tidily confined behind walls or in cloisters and the crackle of dried leaves underfoot was a rare experience. Throughout the lagoon, clouds of birds settled into the marsh filling the mud flats and islands with a cacophony of cries, less songs than strident shouts of recognition or signals to depart.

Among the reeds, the long, flat boats of hunters floated stealthily, loaded up with standing oarsmen and growing piles of game, a solitary archer in the bow. In places, wattle fences crossed stretches of shallow, brackish lagoon defining boundaries and fish ponds. Shelters, vacant for much of the year, housed dogal hunting parties. Yet, the V-shaped lines continued to cross the sky. The great swirl of massed flocks kept coming. The birds alighted and departed, wheeling and crying, continuing their mysterious journeys—less those shot, dredged from waist-high waters, and slung head down from pointed bows.

*   *   *   *   *

The Rialto was quieter now, back-lit with the blood-red glow of sunset. The gentle lowering of twilight turned the buildings purplish-black and drew the colored signs of pawnshops, the blank facades of banks, the awnings of pastry-makers' establishments and apothecary shops, and even the premises of gymnasts, fencers, and abacus counters into the cool, regulated quiet and anonymity of evening. The watch made their appointed rounds. The four lamps on the draper's porch were lit. Here and there were clumps of people, mostly men. Giovanni had long since departed with Ludovico for the noble house. Cristofolo, two weeks gone, had taken a position with another family.

Rade thought the merchant would be pleased by the outcome of his meeting. The anger he had felt earlier was somewhat mollified. Or rather, it had assumed less importance in the course of the day. He lingered awhile by the porch, listening to the hum of conversation, looking for some tidbit of information he could use. What he heard, what was announced, and then thoroughly chewed in the resulting discussion, drew a line in the sand between him and virtually every other person there. He felt as if the earth had broken off at his feet. As if a rift had appeared separating his world from theirs. All this due to a third or fourth hand account of the contents of a letter from some bishop to the pope. Lika. It was north of Zara. It meant "they" were north of Zara. It meant his world was shrinking. That it would be harder to go back. That someday soon, he would have to decide if he was part of the land to which he had been born, or choose to stay outside forever. *And he'd once thought he could straddle two worlds.* In Venice, he now knew, he could never be Venetian. It just didn't work that way.

*   *   *   *   *

The late September moon was full. Brilliant. The kind that
drew lunatics and murderers out of the shadows. Her linen
nightdress tucked loosely about her, Caterina lay back on a
rush-seated chair in the moonlight, knees bent, her feet
propped up on the *cassone*. It was the only way she could
manage to see the greater part of the night sky through the
high window. The opposing building obscured part of the view
but that house was dark now, asleep, merely a shape in the
darkness. Nonna stirred, rolled over, and went back to a chorus
of small snores. Caterina placed her hands, palms up, behind
the back of her head and drew her long hair back so that it fell
in a silver-gold curtain behind the chair. She rubbed her eyes,
wishing for slumber but already knew that what had happened,
was happening, would keep it away.

In late morning, Ludovico had received a merchant—as
well as minor patrician—with whom he'd had a long
relationship: Gerolamo Boldu`. Boldu`, in turn, had brought
his son, Alessandro, just back from six years in the Levant.
Sofia had been out at the market, so, as a courtesy, Caterina
had brought up a tray of refreshments. Thus it happened that
she was formally introduced and invited to stay while they
drank the wine.

She'd been struck by the athletic beauty of Alessandro, by
his light brown eyes, sun-streaked hair, and mannerisms he'd
learned in Damascus. The bold, amused stare that seemed to
see through her demeanor and even through her clothes. She
had stood there, feeling naked, and surprisingly unashamed,
and she'd felt the attraction spread over her like a fever when
illness isn't far behind.

The moonlight bathed her hands in its white light. A light
that some called cold. She held them out before her, fingers
spread like fans. And sighed. Her body was anything but cold.
Alessandro. She pulled her shift up to her waist and let one
pale hand slide up under the fabric to her breasts and the other

descend into her secret places. *Alessandro*. She closed her eyes and let the gravid, all-seeing moon take her forbidden act into its confidence.

And the door to the *studiolo* had opened, and Rade had come in with some contracts to sign. He'd seen her looking at Alessandro, seen her as if again she had no shield, no clothes, no decorum. Shamed, she'd left precipitously, leaving the two men, like curs in the marketplace, circling each other over the loss of the only bone. The two older men, oblivious, having wrapped themselves in stories.

Dinner had come, a dinner that she dreaded, and she'd been ready for whatever might happen. But what had happened had been something else.

Rade came in from the Rialto, eyes cast down, his own remote beauty seemingly carved of ice. They sat at the table, separated by the expanse of cloth, and both wordlessly examined their food. Ludovico talked and ate as if he were three people and when no responses materialized, he finally asked, "What is it?"

Caterina shook her head and dared to look at Rade. He sat forward.

"The Croat army was destroyed," said Rade in a bitter voice. "All of them."

"What? When?" asked Caterina, taken aback.

"Two weeks ago. On a field in Krbava. Now called the Field of Blood." Rade looked around the table. "By the *Pasha* of Bosnia."

"The Ottoman army," said Caterina.

"Yes."

"Where's Krbava?" asked Caterina.

"In Lika. North of Zara," said Rade.

"It's a region," added Ludovico. "Part of Slavonia."

"They have their own ban." Rade looked at Caterina. "Like a prince. Their own lords."

"The lords that survived will flee to the littoral," said Ludovico thoughtfully. "Or Hungary."

"Word is, there weren't any lords that survived," replied Rade.

"Christ's nails," muttered Ludovico.

"What will Venice do?" asked Rade, suddenly intent.

"It's the other side of the Adriatic." Ludovico looked untroubled.

"The Ottomans came south. From raids north of there. That's even closer," said Rade. "They *will* come here."

"They did come once," said Ludovico, toying with his fish, his silver hair gleaming in the candlelight. He took a mouthful. "To Udine. Raiding. Almost sixteen years ago." He looked at Caterina. "Before your time. Just." He smiled. "They got as far as the Piave, the river. Pillaging. Burning. Wallachians, Albanians, gypsies in the front lines. The Ottomans behind. One could see the flames from the bell tower. People climbed up to watch." He took another bite. "They won't come again."

"Why not?" asked Rade. "You have, except for the Arsenal, an absence of walls. Unheard of in a city this size. Only two antiquated forts..."

"San Nicolo and Sant'Andrea. Named for two old saints." Ludovico smiled. "Good saints."

"Am I supposed to be relieved?" asked Rade.

"The Ottomans won't take Venice," said Ludovico firmly, "because we pay them not to."

"And sixteen years ago?" said Rade.

"We weren't paying them then," said Ludovico. "It's that simple." He looked at their plates. "Aren't either of you going to eat anything?" He folded his napkin and looked at Rade. "We do have a natural defense: the lagoon. No one can sail a large ship into the lagoon without the channel markers. The *bricole*. In times of trouble..." he shrugged. "You can guess."

"You pull them out.

"Yes."

They left the table without speaking of the morning's incident. Rade, rigid with anger over Krbava, wanting to fight, to kill something, and Caterina trying to stifle her descent into the lowest form of appetite.

The path of moonlight had gone. She replaited her hair, crept back into bed, and staring at the ceiling, wondered if, when she was married to Rade, and he made love to her, if, to love him back, she would need to conjure up Alessandro. *Beautiful, sun-streaked Alessandro.*

*   *   *   *   *

The day was uncharacteristically warm and misty, with a prickle of rain in the air. Rade exchanged his damp doublet for the cap and long black tunic that Ludovico had had made for him. The robe felt odd, binding, and somehow not what he envisioned as male attire. Not a good style of clothing for fighting either. However, Ludovico had insisted it was the basic dress of the Venetian merchant. In the eyes of the Rialto it would make him one of them. In his own eyes, he felt akin to a crow.

Ludovico would be waiting by the Doge's Palace near the space reserved for politics and nobles. He would stand at the edge of the space he was not supposed to enter alongside a patrician who would drop the stole from his shoulder as the signal that he wished to discuss the issues. New trade regulations had been introduced in the Great Council and Ludovico was critical of what he'd heard.

As Rade set out to meet him, the afternoon's tasks foremost in his mind, an insistent bell tolled from a bell tower. The sound disturbed his thoughts because he thought he'd learned them all. Each bronze flare had its own particular sound and pattern of tolling, and although many of the important bells were distant, they were still identifiable. Ludovico relied on their constancy as a man depends on the rising of the sun. They summoned one to the task their peal identified: to work, to the Council Chamber, to the Doge's Palace, to rest and refreshment, to worship, and to arms. Hard put to place this less familiar bell, Rade halted, and Battista and Alberico, deep in conversation and trailing behind, nearly knocked him down.

The two men, looking sheepish, extricated themselves.

"Why don't you look where you're going!" demanded Battista, glaring at Alberico.

"I can't place it," said Rade.

"What?" asked Alberico.

"The bell," replied Rade.

"It's the one no one wants to hear," observed Battista ominously. "At least not for oneself."

"Why?" Rade asked.

"It's the *Maleficio*, the bell of evil omen," shrugged Alberico.

"Or of justice, whichever you choose to call it," added Battista. He spat. "It's calling us to witness."

"Oh Christ's nails, it's where we're going," grumbled Alberico. "Hurry. There'll be a crowd." And he lengthened his stride.

The columns of justice greeted every visitor who left his vessel and climbed the water steps for San Marco or the Doge's Palace. The space called the *broglio*, where Ludovico waited, lay just beyond.

Lumbering along beside him, a battering ram on the march, Battista told Rade that all the ritual of civic processions was present in the performance of judgment. The herald announcing the crime would have already ridden the length of the Grand Canal, from one end of the city to the other in the bow of the felon boat and walked back dragging the convict behind him. The prisoner would be properly displayed, his crime described, his judgment tolled, and he would then receive the execution of his sentence.

As they hurried along, others joined them. Gradually, they became conscious of a stream of people flowing toward the waterfront from all directions: from the Merceria, the shopping street leading up from the Rialto, from the piazza, from behind San Marco's, over the bridges, even from the lagoon. Ahead and behind him, the sea of people eclipsed his companions until Rade was left adrift in an ocean of strangers. It carried him along, enveloping him in the sounds and smells of rank humanity, until the stony figures of St. Theodore on his crocodile and St. Mark's lion, on their respective columns, towered overhead.

A convict was displayed between the columns. The slumping figure looked familiar. And then with a shudder of recognition, Rade realized who it was. He pushed forward to the edge of the encircling crowd.

"They've captured my old falcon," he said, as loudly as he dared in his native tongue.

The old man's eyes flickered. Even in the state they'd reduced him to, there was still a hint of defiance. For Rade, there was something else.

"*Kapetan*," the prisoner murmured.

"Oh Jesus, Vuk."

"Aye, it's me. Am I so changed?"

"Some," said Rade, trying to keep the dismay out of his voice.

"You have too," noted Vuk. He moved uncomfortably in his bindings. "I'd know the eyes, the voice, maybe the mouth. You don't look like you, but I don't see as well as I used to either." One eye was nearly swollen shut.

"Was it witchcraft?" murmured Rade. "The skin bag?"

"I knew you'd come," nodded Vuk. "The bones told me."
He closed his one good eye.

Rade persisted. "Was it sorcery, Vuk?" There were no
faggots lying about. No sign of fire.

"They thought it was a game," whispered Vuk
conspiratorially. "I tricked 'em! They're probably throwing the
bones right now behind the cells. Filthy rats!" He spat on the
ground. "Wait 'til the priest catches 'em." Something that
resembled a chuckle rose from his throat.

"Then what…?"

"Theft," muttered the old man. He looked crazier than
ever. "I stole some bread. Got to the church too late for alms.
Don't always understand their filthy language. Got the place
wrong."

"All this for bread?" asked Rade incredulously, taking in
the newly constructed gibbet.

Vuk smiled, if one could call it that, and the spittle
dribbled down his chin. Rade noticed he'd lost more of his
teeth.

"It was the jewels on the knife beside the bread that lost
me the game, *kapetan*," said Vuk. "The lousy jewels." There
was blood in the spittle.

Even God couldn't help him now. Theft was the offense
listed first in the codes. When a thief had broken into the
storeroom through the old, rusting water gate, Ludovico had
told him that. The first level of punishment he knew from his
own experience. The second involved sight. The third… *If only
he had time…* He turned to work his way through the crowd to
Ludovico.

"Told 'em everything," muttered Vuk.

The words went through him like a knife. Rade stopped.
"What did you tell them, Vuk?" he asked softly.

"Told 'em 'bout the stone house in Zara, and the hiding
places in the mountains, and the snow on the islands, and the

round church in Cattaro, and the sword I got from St. Donatus, and you bein' without your head."

He'd told them everything and he'd told them nothing. It was all mixed up. Senseless. The ramblings of a madman.

"They think they've caught a spy!" Vuk whispered. "I let 'em think so." He laughed. "More important than bein' a thief."

An official had noticed them. He was coming their way. Bringing guards. Rade looked around wildly. "I've got friends. Powerful friends. I could..."

"No use," murmured Vuk, dribbling some more, and then he laughed, shrill and cackling. "I read the bones when I taught 'em the game," he whispered. "My ship's holed, *kapetan*. Save yourself while you can."

"Why did you come here?" asked Rade.

"Lookin' for you, *kapetan*," muttered the old man. "Find you and ex-"

"Here! What are you doing talking to the felon!" shouted a guard, muscling his way through the crowd. He eyed Rade, taking in the merchant's robes. "You don't look the sort who'd know this sack of turds."

"I knew him once," replied Rade. "He's just..."

"He just wants to watch," Vuk broke in, in execrable Italian. "I never saw 'em before. Get 'im away from me!"

Before the guard pushed him back into the throng, Rade murmured, "God keep you, Vuk. *God keep you and give you a young south or an old north wind.*" It was a time-honored blessing. He thought he saw an answering gleam in the old man's eye.

"And God grant me a good death," returned Vuk.

"A good death," repeated Rade, the reality of Vuk's predicament weighing him down.

"Don't use that foreign tongue on me," cried the guard. *"Get back!* There's others who'll want to watch. You've had your turn!"

Yet Rade stayed, deep in the crowd, thinking he could offer something at the end. A prayer. A curse. They were so pressed together that he could feel the people around him breathing. Hear the shiver of expectation that ran through their conversations. And the undercurrent of dislike for outsiders that ran through it too. Packed in like this, the sweat ran down his skin, and for once, he was glad of the wool in the unwanted black tunic—for it wicked it up. For a moment, looking through the phalanx of heads, he caught sight of Vuk, barely standing. Alone in the center of God knew how many enemies encircling him. Because someone in a church had left a knife beside the bread. And Vuk, who was old and had no livelihood, saw a procession of loaves in the jewels.

Rade had thought he was inured to death, to loss, to public punishment. That there was nothing in him that was soft. No part of him that could feel sorrow or pity or remorse. That weakness had been beaten out long ago. And yet he stood there, his throat closing up—like a woman.

With an act that echoed the solemnity of Mass, the masked executioner placed the rope around Vuk's neck, tightened it, and pushed aside the small, raised platform Vuk was standing on. There was a shout from the crowd and then an old woman's voice pierced the din. "There's a miracle of justice for you," quavered the crone, "he's still alive."

The voices of the spectators dropped to a murmur and then died away. A sporadic, rasping sound of trying to suck air through too small an opening took its place. It went on, and on, an eternity of the halting approach of death.

Chapter Sixteen

The constellations this year seem unfavorable to rebels.
—Cesare Borgia

October, Venetian Year 1493

He had stood there waiting, endlessly waiting he thought, for Ludovico, the wind tugging at the skirt of his tunic, swirling around the two huge columns, whistling through carved marble arches, lying in wait around masonry corners. And finally he had taken a chance and glanced toward the lagoon. Before him, the square gaped open like the walls of a vast quarry, framed on the right side by the brick bulk of a granary and its nest of sheds, including a bakery, behind him by tall rows of connecting buildings, and on the left side by the huge pink palace with its lacy underpinnings. Beyond the water's edge had sloshed the wind-whipped waves of the lagoon.

The gibbet was still there but only the top showed above the crowd. As streams of people dispersed and regrouped, he'd caught a glimpse of what was left of Vuk still hanging there. Swaying in the rush of air. And when he'd gotten closer, he'd seen the body had become a husk, picked at by birds, that bore no relation to the living person. The pendant to some wretched churchman confined to a cage hanging from the campanile.

And he'd remained there—the aroma of bread masking the odor of decomposition, the bell ringing from the campanile, the crowd passing to and fro—transfixed by the fact that the taking of a man's life had no import, no message, not even a modicum of visibility to those who walked by. A fish drying on a line had more to recommend it.

Finally Ludovico grasped his arm, shouted above the wind, and together, like two black crows, they had threaded their way through the multicolored groups of people, past the gilders working on San Marco, to where Giovanni waited with the gondola by the bridge.

*   *   *   *   *

The nightmares returned, embellished with real or imagined scenes of Vuk's death. Rade fell back into his old ways. He drank. He walked the floor. He engaged in couplings that offered pleasure only in exercising power over someone else. Uninvited, Alberico, that great placid brick of a man, dogged his footsteps and occasionally helped him back to the sweat-soaked mattress that he tried so hard to avoid. And neither of them acknowledged it. And Rade began to fear that fate, which had grown so distant, so silent, so inattentive, was communicating with him. He waited for the whirlwind—but it didn't come.

One October morning, stumbling in to his place of work, Rade found the household engaged in the noisy business of repairing casks. Ludovico had had the good sense to go elsewhere. The incessant hammering, banging, and shouting of the coopers echoed off the stones of the courtyard and drove him, hands clamped over his ears, into the farthest corner of the room, desperate for deliverance, his work abandoned.

When he awoke, the room was silent and the long shadows of afternoon had advanced across the floor. A receptacle of hot, scented liquid stood at his elbow. Someone was in the room.

"Lavandula," said a familiar voice, "for the pain. *'Poor fool—what's sleep but death warmed up? Resting in peace comes later.'* Unless the casks remain undone." The last held a note of amusement. He felt the light touch of a hand on his shoulder. "You needn't drink it. Just breathe it in." A glimpse of golden hair, and she was gone.

Eventually, he bent forward, leaning over the steam, and let the fragrance of lavender invade his senses. Summer in the Adriatic, herb sellers in the islands, Caterina's silks and linens—all lay within it. And absent from it was the decaying specter of Vuk.

The relief came slowly, but it did come. *Do not mistake compassion for desire.* But he thought, if he made an effort, he could prove Nonna had it wrong.

*   *   *   *   *

They were in the midst of a meal. Rade was relating an amusing anecdote having to do with the sale of wine to a German merchant. They were all laughing—when Sofia came in.

"Messer Vinciguerra, you have a visitor."

"In the middle of supper?" asked Ludovico.

"He said to pardon his tardiness, the artist asked him to stay longer."

"Alessandro," nodded Ludovico, leaning back against the wall and smiling. He looked at Rade and Caterina. "You remember him. Gerolamo's son. Now, I'm told, maestro Carpaccio's latest model. Set another place, Sofia, and bring him up." He turned to Rade. "Go on with your story. Johann is always good for a laugh. Last time he told me, on the subject of taste, and I quote: 'It runs like a squirrel in the forest, without any sense of ill.' I nearly lost the sale for laughing. Must be a quirk in the language. Do continue, Rade."

"It doesn't matter." Rade's voice was suddenly colorless. Icy. "You have a guest."

Caterina, who was trying surreptitiously to tuck in a few errant tendrils of hair, looked at him. *He did know.* Once again, she felt ashamed.

Footsteps sounded on the stairs. The door opened and Alessandro entered. He wore a wool hat adorned with a jeweled pin, the clasp for a rakish white plume. His soft leather boots, dagged at the cuffs, rose part way up his calves to reveal scarlet hose which in turn disappeared beneath a doublet of costly and fashionable black velvet over slashed sleeves. A beautiful short cape lined in vair hung over one shoulder. His hair was bright. Expensive rings glittered on his fingers. His eyes were those of a lion.

"I've forgotten something," muttered Rade, and he got up from the table, his black merchant's tunic catching on the leg of the bench as he rose. He jerked the cloth from where it had caught, nodded curtly at Ludovico, and left.

Sofia motioned toward the new place setting but Alessandro took Rade's place opposite Caterina. "I can sit here. Don't make extra work for yourself." The beautiful cape was draped over the bench. He smiled at her and Caterina let her breath out and bathed in the glory of it.

"I've missed you," he said, light brown eyes undressing her, and reached across the table to take her hand.

She tried to look demurely at the tablecloth. And keep her hand from trembling.

"How delightful," he said. "A virgin who can still blush."

"Alessandro," said a disapproving voice from the end of the table, "my daughter is betrothed."

*   *   *   *   *

They swept into church, all ten of them: Ludovico, Rade, Giovanni, Alberico, Battista, Antonio, heading into the men's area, and Caterina, Nonna, Sofia and Cook, to the women's. It was after sundown and the church was a dark gray cave. Antonio had been right, they were late. The Mass had begun. A multitude of rosaries clacked energetically to the accompaniment of prayers. It was Friday, the second of November.

Ludovico worked his way forward to where the more important parishioners stood. The other men stood at the back.

A nondescript man made his way toward Rade, brushed against him, whispered "*dikobraz*," and pushed a folded scrap of paper into his hand. Rade closed his fingers around it. He saw Alberico's eyes flick toward him. He gave a half-hearted shrug as if nothing had happened and fixed his eyes on the altar.

The priest's voice rose and fell in a sonorous recitation of the Mass. A Mass for those whose souls had recently departed and for whom this vigil, All Souls, was being held. When the Mass had ended, the church lay suspended in pitch-black stillness—as if holding its breath. Eventually, a small shuffling sound, of sandals on stone, began to be heard and then one by one, starting at the altar and progressing down the nave and chapels, the flickering of a few small flames multiplied into the glow of many.

The murmuring of the parishioners grew. Names, Rade thought. So many names. So many departed. *Requiem aeternam* / eternal rest. *I will hold you in my heart.* And he could hear Vuk as if he were standing next to him. *Whether God remembers me or not.* And he felt the weakness that belongs to women pass through his soul. And even though he longed to conceal himself in darkness, what had been a cave had become a church again, all glimmering with light. He stood there, glad of the people he didn't know, and exercised the control he had momentarily relinquished. Eventually, the great metal-encrusted doors swung open and they were let out, into a chilly night spangled with stars—the sparkling, distant cousins of the candles.

The paper was minute. A crumpled ball in his palm. The place to meet would be a print shop. What the man had whispered was "porcupine" in their native tongue. The arms of Erizzo. The Venetian family allied through marriage to Duradj Crnojevic, Ivan the Black's son, the current prince of Zeta. The meeting was about need. The need to keep something alive that was in danger of being buried.

*   *   *   *   *

The monk called Makarije stood in the middle of the room. He was dark: dark-haired, dark-eyed, dark-skinned, and wearing a dark robe—but alight with zeal. His hand rested on a cumbersome wooden object with a great wooden screw and metal parts. In some ways it resembled a huge chair but it was, in fact, a printing press.

"Can you get it there? In secret?" he asked Rade. There were five men standing around him. All Slav.

"That's what you want to smuggle in? Not weapons? I thought…"

"You thought wrong," interjected a man with ink-stained hands. "This," he pointed to the press, "will be the engine of change. The voice of the prince. The voice of the church."

"The voice of God, Andrija," said the monk.

"And you want to send it to Cetinje? A place with one stone building, a monastery. The rest, a military camp," said Rade. He looked at the apparatus. "It will rust."

"Not to Cetinje itself," replied Makarije. "To the shores below Zeta. To Cattaro's well-known path into the mountains. Whether it rusts, and where it will be housed, will be our concern."

"I could get it to Perast and then send it up the Roman road toward Cattaro," suggested Rade, walking around the press. "You can't go through the city. Too many guards. Too many questions. The other path won't be easy either. Some of the upper towns may have turned."

"The prince will send men to meet you at the border," stated a third man. No ink stains, a strong jaw, scars, and a soldier's bearing. "I'll see to that."

Rade ran his hand lightly down one of the timbers. "Dismantled," he noted, "we can store the timbers under the walkway. Roll the metal parts and punches in oiled felt and hides. Place them under the stern structure."

"When you take them up the mountain path," said Andrija, "hide them in bales."

"Bales of rags," added the third man. "To make the paper."

"Then we'll need those bales as well," replied Rade. "Secure from moisture."

"So, if I may interrupt," said the monk, stroking his long beard, "messer Vinciguerra trades in the bays?"

"No," replied Rade. "Hardly anyone trades in the bays. I own shares in a galley that winters there."

Makarije looked at him so intently that Rade felt naked.

"That's what we've heard. But can we trust, how shall I put it, a known brigand? A *haiduk?*" asked the monk.

Rade felt himself go cold. He let his hand drop from the rail of the press. "In the bays," he said, "only a brigand can get you what you want. And, let me remind you, it is my country too."

"From what I've heard," returned Makarije, "it *was* your country. It has been a lifetime since you've been there."

"What do you think, Bozidar?" asked Andrija, the printer. "You'll be meeting them."

"If they do not come..." said Bozidar, the soldier. He

made a gesture and his face took on the humorless grimace of the killer.

"It's still my country," said Rade in a hard voice. *If you know so much about me, who told you? Does my mother live? Is that bastard still her husband?* But he said instead, "To get the press to Perast will require two ships. Two voyages. For the second ship, my ship, it will have to be the last voyage of the year. Late November. When it rains and the Ottoman galley stays in port." He added, "God willing."

"Oh God is willing," replied Makarije softly. "He is very willing. He has sent you to me because He wishes His voice to be heard over the calls of the muezzins. The press will do that." He nodded at the other men. His eyes were like black coals. He turned his gaze to Rade. "And," he paused, "he has put your life in my hands."

For a few minutes, there was absolute silence. No one spoke. No one moved.

"I came here because I wanted to help," said Rade. "I chose to help. Because Mordecai told me that you needed transport. Because we need to stop them." He looked around the room with narrowed eyes. "Not because you have the ability to give me up to Venice."

"No," Makarije replied, with a small shrug, "but it helps."

*   *   *   *   *

For a while, she stood in the doorway as Rade put away what he'd been working on. He was wearing a leather doublet and the leggings he kept for travel. Everything was travel-stained and old and he looked every inch a ruffian. She thought she liked him best when he looked like that. "When do you leave?"

"As soon as I can," he said looking up. "The *Brenta*'s waiting."

"When will you return?"

"Why? Will you miss me?"

"At dinner and at church, yes."

"And the rest of the time?"

She said, "I never see you the rest of the time." She walked further into the room. She noticed he'd stopped what he was doing. He seemed to be searching her face for some indication of what she was going to say. "Will you be back for my saint's day?" she asked. "We're celebrating." She smiled.

He let out a long breath. "Sixteen," he said, going back to straightening his papers. He looked up. "Almost a crone."

"I should call a plague on your house for a remark like that," countered Caterina, "but since I'll live there too, I'll refrain."

For once, Rade looked absurdly pleased. "You see," he said, "wisdom does come with age." He picked up a small roll of belongings. "We'll pray for a south wind. I'd like to be back for it."

*   *   *   *   *

Without any explanation, he came back early, almost a week early. To Caterina, it seemed as if within his innermost self, that was so hard to read, there had been a change. For someone who could be taciturn and preoccupied, Rade was more animated toward her at dinner. Did not direct so much of the conversation at her father. She was more aware of the attraction she held for him. And in the last month or so, even before he left, he no longer smelled like drink when he arrived at the noble house. She wondered if it had to do with Alessandro who lately had found ways to deliver messages from his father and visit after painting sessions. And somehow elude Nonna. They were both, she thought, physically arresting, each in his own way, but one was wrapped in silence and mystery, wound tight as a crossbow, and the other, in easy compliments, sexual innuendo, and physical contact. She could not pass Alessandro in the house without the touch of his hand on her waist, her hand, her breast. And once, fleetingly, he had even kissed her. And she'd liked it. But it was the other one she would marry.

For her saint's day, she had dressed in her russet velvet *camora*, the one that was snug at the waist and bodice and fashioned with crimson cords that crisscrossed the pale linen of her *camisa*. Her tied sleeves were dark brown velvet and worked with gold embroidery. And she could tell from Rade's eyes when he came into the room, from the hoarseness in his voice when he greeted her, that he desired her.

There would be no Alessandro tonight. Her father had been very clear on that point. She had decided, partly to spite her father, and partly because it had been a long day of prayer and penitence before her devotional painting, in church, and in the confessional, to pretend that Rade was Alessandro. To play to him as she had learned to play to Alessandro. To draw him out. And see what came of it.

Her blond hair intricately bound up in braids, pearls and a gossamer veil, she had positioned herself in the candlelight, so that the smoothness of her skin and the lightness of her hair would be apparent but her eyes in shadow would be unreadable, dark as the sea on a cloudy day. These were things she had learned over time from Simonetta, Alessandro, even her father. To stage an entrance, an appearance, a presence. Below the long white line of her throat, she had suspended the red coral and milky pearls of Rade's amulet—brought back from his recent voyage.

"It's beautiful," she said, resting her hand on the amulet. She saw his eyes travel over the bauble to her face trying to guess where the evening would go.

"It pales in comparison to you," replied Rade. "Wasn't

there a Queen Caterina?"

"There was." She smiled. "Caterina Corner, Queen of Cyprus. I saw her when she abdicated." Caterina made a face. The woman went away and the little girl came back. "She was fat."

"Venice took her kingdom," interjected Nonna, from the shadows, "as, I imagine, was planned, or at least expedient. She now holds court in Asolo."

Why was Nonna always there? She saw it in his face. "You could be a queen," he said softly. *My queen.*

"We should go in," announced Nonna, rising and leading the way. "Your father's waiting."

At the mention of her father, Caterina expanded on her devilry. She moved past Rade, brushing against his upper arm with her breasts, touching his hand with her own, and she saw his eyes widen and felt his hands come up to grasp her waist. And in that moment, face to face, she also saw how naked his desire was, how barely held in check. He pressed her against him, hard, hands unsteady, so hard she could feel his body through his clothes. Suddenly, it wasn't the game it was with Alessandro. It wasn't lighthearted, playful, a dalliance in passing. There was something more substantial here. Something almost desperate. And she wished she hadn't teased him because if what she saw was freed—and not returned in kind—there would be consequences. In the pit of her stomach, she knew it. And for a moment, a moment she tried hard to suppress, she felt afraid. Truly afraid. And he must have sensed it—for he let her go.

*   *   *   *   *

Ever since he'd returned, Rade had thought long and hard about the voyage, about that night when they'd met off Parenzo in the rain, the second, smaller ship tied up alongside the first, every man there wrapped to his eyes for anonymity. But he had still known Miloš the moment he'd seen him. And Miloš had known him too. As the press was being transferred, they'd gone into the *Brenta*'s cabin, ostensibly to review the plan. Miloš had pulled off his covering. Rade however had not.

"Vuk's dead," said Rade, his voice muffled. "Hanged in Venice." The choking sound that haunted him ran through his head.

"I thought as much," said Miloš, unmoved. "He was a fool. An old fool. The worst kind." He paused, "Are you going to take that off so you aren't speaking through cloth?"

"No."

"Why not?"

"It's better this way. In case someone comes in. We all pledged anonymity." Rade adjusted the cloth so the folds over his mouth were flattened out. "Besides, I'm not the *kapetan* here."

"We're getting to the nut of it, aren't we?" said Miloš. *"Are you coming back?"* There was no mistaking the hostility in his voice. He added gruffly, "We've made a good year of it."

"I heard that from Mordecai. He received my share earlier than expected."

"Because of Krbava," replied Miloš. "We weren't sure…"

"Yes," Rade interrupted, "I too wondered if Zara would stand." He turned over a small portolan, a written record of navigational points of land and soundings that he was teaching Pasquale to read. He looked up. "I thought I'd accompany the press to the border. For old time's sake." *Would you welcome me back?*

There was a telling silence. "We can handle the shipment," said Miloš with finality. "I'm good with the men." *Better than you.*

"I knew you would be."

"Did you know that when you abandoned us?" said Miloš.

"Or after you'd gotten your share?"

Rade smiled ruefully. There was no point in answering. It made no difference what he might say. "You've told me what I wanted to know." He placed the portolan exactly where it had been and looked at Miloš. "I want to make an arrangement." He had taken pride in the *bergantin*. More than anything else he had owned. It was hard to do this. It would be another path forsaken. Another bridge burned.

"What arrangement?" said Miloš warily.

"I was going to pay you," said Rade. He saw Miloš stiffen.

"So now it's charity? Since we're going back to winter quarters?"

"No." Rade paused. So much bitterness. Like a man who'd been awarded a prize, only to see it being taken away. "It's really a proposition," he said. "I want to trade my shares in the *bergantin* for delivery of the printing press." He looked at Miloš. "All the way to the border. You take care of the crew. We'll sign a paper if you like but you must swear on it. And the press must get there, intact, without Cattaro's knowledge. Or that of Venice."

Miloš was at a loss for words. "And what else?" he said, suspicion rising.

"Does there have to be something else?"

"Is there something else?"

Rade shrugged. "Should the prince need weapons, I would engage you to deliver them. Pay you for your trouble. A trade arrangement like any other," he said. "Would you do it?"

Miloš, lost in disbelief, made him repeat it. Twice. Finally he relaxed and then grinned. "If I still have my head…"

"It's too ugly to mount on a stake," said Rade, regarding him thoughtfully. "Not even Medusa would be jealous." It was a fine head. Square-jawed and stubborn. The old Miloš was coming back.

"Not as ugly as yours," returned Miloš. "Besides, I've a

woman who likes it." He saw the amusement in Rade's gaze. He added, "A real woman. Not a whore. Soon to be a wife."

"Well if there's a woman like that involved," said Rade, "then our bargain is done. Swear on your bride and if you waver, I expect she'll keep you to it." He came close to pulling out the *raki* and proposing a toast but realized just in time it meant unwrapping the cloth—and revealing the mask.

*   *   *   *   *

Winter arrived in late December and brought the freezing weather of the Atlantic into the Mediterranean. A dusting of snow on the smooth upper decks of the gondolas transformed them into treacherous footing for Giovanni and the other boatmen and even the canvas coverings on the bows grew silver skins of ice. Those were the days when Ludovico, and whoever else was with him, walked. Miniature floes broke off from the frozen edges of the lagoon and sent their plates of ice bobbing through the canals. The shrouds of moored ships and the arched underbellies of bridges grew jagged fangs of crystal. And the prevailing wind blew from the west interspersed with gales from the north.

The men would come in from the cold, stamping their feet and blowing on their fingers, and Ludovico would invariably say they ought to invest more *ducats* in wool, or it wasn't as bad as three years ago when the mayor of Mestre drove his coach over the ice as far as San Segundo.

"It was so cold that year that horsemen jousted on the Grand Canal," said Caterina, surprising them at the door one afternoon. "Here let me take your boots," she said to her father. She wrinkled her nose. "Surely it's time for new ones."

"Those are the ones I like," replied Ludovico.

Caterina turned to the others, "For those who had warm clothes, the joust was a great entertainment." And she smiled, remembering.

To which, Nonna added, in her contrary way, that those who hadn't, perished.

There were warmer winter days when the sirocco blew from the southeast and if the tide was especially high, the *aqua alta* or high water, bubbled up through the drains, if they weren't plugged with ice, and flooded some of the low-lying areas of the city. Then the pools were crisscrossed with makeshift raised paths that contained their own brand of instability and occasional mischief.

"Fucking winter," said Alberico, his blue-white feet displayed before the kitchen fire.

*   *   *   *   *

"Taste this," said Ludovico, entering the storeroom and holding out a small flask. He looked around. "Don't you have any more light than that?"

Rade, sitting on a barrel in the gloom, a lantern nearby, looked up from the inventory he was checking. "I have enough. What is it?"

"Water from the cistern."

Rade took a mouthful, swished it around in his mouth, and quickly spat it out. "It's from the canal," he said angrily. "Why did you do that?" Between the tides, the canal was a floating sewage pit.

"That's what we've been cooking with," grumbled Ludovico, taking the flask back. "The cistern's gone bad." He added, "Again."

"The cistern draws rainwater," said Rade.

"Not anymore," replied Ludovico. "God's blood, I'll have to hire a water seller. I can't pull up the courtyard this time of year." He turned to go and then looked back. "We finish dredging that stinking canal and now this! And you know what

a mess the state made of that." And he went out seething with
irritation, and still talking. "The new water gate is coming in a
day or two..." Rade could hear the one-sided conversation
progressing down the stairs. "That'll stop those thieves..."

"The thieves didn't take much," called Rade, looking at his
list. Some flour for bread. A ham. He thought of Vuk.

God's blood this and *Christ's nails that* slowly faded into
the normal sounds of the noble house.

Rade sat on his barrel, trying to ignore the foul taste in his
mouth, and thought about the November dredging. Ludovico
had negotiated twelve feet of depth, enough for a small ship.
And the dredgers had dammed up their section of the canal,
dug out the foul-smelling mud, and produced it. However, the
three ancient aristocratic families with equally ancient houses
farther up and farther down the canal, had refused to cooperate
because, they argued, their houses were built on tree trunks
pounded vertically into mud. Too much wood exposed to God
knew what. And everyone knew what that meant: the boles
would rot, the house fall into the canal, et cetera. Three
hundred years wiped out in the turn of an hour glass. Despite
the fact that all the houses stood on the selfsame pilings,
despite the fact that the Grand Canal was even deeper,
Ludovico had been unable to convince them otherwise. So he
had been left with what amounted to a large, unusable pit
which connected on both sides to a shallower canal—the sight
of which, even though its depth was normally indeterminable,
remained a source of annoyance.

*   *   *   *   *

Thus it came to pass that although winter storms filled the
gutters and rain pursued its intricate path to the well, the water
seller became a frequent vendor at the noble house.

This narrow, bony man brought his lighter all the way

from the freshwater estuaries that fed into the lagoon. Among the stacks of casks, he built a rude shelter for his thickset partner, himself, and his small son, a boy of six. With brown, tousled ringlets and eyes like black pools, the boy stayed in his allotted space. The water seller announced proudly that he was teaching the child the business but everyone thought his wife had died or abandoned him and the father had no choice in the matter. The little boy was too small and spindly to do most of the tasks required. Caterina grew fond of the child and frequently gave him little packets of food wrapped up in cloth, sometimes in a little shirt, small clothes, or a cap—even though no one ever saw him open them. Rade struck up an acquaintance and had recently whittled the boy a wooden ball attached with twine to a cup with which to play. The boy smiled shyly and said nary a word but the toy was usually on board. Everyone called him "Ragazzo," the common word for boy, including his father and his helper, when they spoke to him at all, and no one seemed to use another name.

It wasn't until the barge had made its third delivery that Rade realized that Ragazzo was deaf.

*   *   *   *   *

It was one of those frigid days in early January when an afternoon shipment was due, so the iron workers were under pressure to finish installing the new water gate that Ludovico had commissioned. Several times, when Ludovico had been away and Rade asleep in his lodgings, parts of the old, rusty gate had been broken off, and small robberies of the storerooms had occurred. Ludovico became convinced they would escalate into serious loss. The final result of the merchant's concern was an ironmonger's tour de force: two enormous heavy grilles with ornate rosettes of spiny decoration at every crosspiece—beautiful, and on the outside, lethal as well. With rough, raw hands, and oaths to match, the workers had manhandled the old gate onto the deck of the heavy foundry barge and positioned the new gate to be lifted by the makeshift crane.

Mario, who had just returned from Milan, and who was waiting for Ludovico and Rade to return from the Rialto, was the first to hear the rending sound of wood splintering, a great snap, and then a huge splash as something heavy fell into the canal. He arrived in haste at the opening of the *andron* to witness the iron workers loudly arguing blame and lamenting bad fortune while staring helplessly into the canal. The crane lay part in the canal and part on the barge, broken in two, the larger part, accompanied by pulleys, floating dolefully amid the sinking coils of rope.

"Christ's wounds!" cried Mario. "What was that?"

"The wretched gate," said the beefiest of the ironmongers. He drew a raw, bleeding hand across his brow, leaving a red smear from one side to the other. "God's blood, it was that fucking water gate."

The other worker, huge, red-knuckled hands on his hips, leaning over and peering into the canal, said, "I can just see it. It's leaning against the side of the canal."

"You're fortunate it didn't fall flat," said Mario, who had squatted at the water's edge.

"Right," said the bloody man irritably. "Small fortune that is."

"We've got to get another crane," said the other man, straightening up. "Might take a week or so."

Mario looked at them, then into the water, and back at them again. He made a funny face. "I don't think anyone's going to steal it."

Chapter Seventeen

Out of the mire into the brook.
—Proverb

January, Eleventh month of Venetian year 1493

It had been Simonetta's idea, born of a whispered conversation in church a few days after Caterina's saint's day. The house in Padua was newly acquired, fully furnished, and Simonetta's father's chosen base for acquiring land on Terraferma—since the autumn floods had made more land available. They would all go there, like Boccaccio's young men and women fleeing the plague—after all winter was something of a plague—and spend a week, play games, enjoy music, recite poetry, learn to dance the latest figures, and talk about everything under the sun. A dance master, a *ballerino*, lived eight houses down the street. Seven days of female bliss in January, the darkest, most troubling month of the year. Nine if one counted the journey. Simonetta, whose father was clay in her hands, had arranged it.

Caterina laid out, among other things, her saint's day *camora*, two more mundane *camoras*, a selection of tied sleeves, her new perfumed gloves, and the winter gift from her father: a sumptuous fur-lined cloak. It had arrived only yesterday. Alessandro, through whose connections Ludovico had obtained it, had brought it to the house. On his way to someone else's supper, with a provocative look, he'd buried his face in the fur before handing it to her—the presentation hiding running a hand over her body from breast to crotch. And she had been left standing in the doorway, quivering like a hare.

Relieved of Nonna, who'd risen early, Caterina stood by the bed in the pale light of morning, barefoot, her hair unbound, still in her linen *camisa*, drawing her fingers through the fur of the cloak. It was as if Alessandro himself had become part of it. Only embers glowed in the fireplace, and as the room cooled, she pulled on the cloak, nestling in the owl-feather softness of the lynx. And then, closing her eyes and imagining the hard physicality of his body, began to remove the *camisa* so that the hide of the lynx, that Alessandro had touched, would lie without hindrance against her nakedness.

"I can dress you now."

God's blood, she'd forgotten Sofia. It was like being roused abruptly from a full-blown dream. One that she ought to ashamed of. She quickly pulled the *camisa* back into place.

"Pack first," she said trying to muster a normal voice.

"Keep the cloak on," said Sofia, rising from her knees, having put wood on the fire. "It'll warm up soon." She carefully wiped her hands on her skirt and folded the lesser day dresses and then laid the russet velvet on top. The perfumed gloves she cupped momentarily in her palms. And when Caterina went to select the shoes she wanted to take, Sofia buried her nose in their scent.

"Is it far? Madonna Simonetta's house?"

"Not far. You'll see for yourself." Caterina shrugged. "A day's journey. Weather permitting." There was a scrabbling sound at the threshold. She smiled. "Yes, Orseolo, you're coming too."

"What's the city like?"

"A bit like Venice. After all, it belongs to us." Caterina smiled. "But no canals. Two rivers. A famous university, divided into two schools—my tutor went there." She looked at Sofia with a thoughtful gaze. "If you go out while we're there, you must take one of the men, by all means don't go alone. During Carnevale, there will be students everywhere. You know what that means."

Sofia, dark hair escaping in every direction from the pins with which she had put it up, looked alarmed.

"Unlike Venice," added Caterina, "it's walled. Simonetta says the house is inside." She watched Sofia wrapping up the shoes in cloth. "I have to confess I've never been there either." She looked up at the high window framing a gray sky. Another gray sky. Whatever it was like would be a blessed change from the monotony of winter. And she would have time to think. Time to consider whether one man could be exchanged for another. And how, if it came to that, she could manage it.

She dropped the cloak on the bed and held out her arms to be dressed. They were to leave on the morrow. The morrow couldn't come soon enough.

*   *   *   *   *

There was a south wind blowing when the water seller arrived. Rade had taken to sleeping in the storeroom since there was no gate at the end of the hall and he was there, at the edge of the canal, the *riva*, ready to organize delivery of the water casks. Each night, Antonio, Battista, and Alberico, all slept in passageways to various parts of the house in case thieves were emboldened by the unguarded opening.

The timing of the installation of the water gate was becoming critical because one day hence much of the household would depart for Padua. Ludovico, never a practitioner of patience, had taken on the behavior of a caged beast.

The afternoon wind had grown stronger, as it often did that time of day, but the lighter was still relatively maneuverable, having delivered the bulk of its cargo. Most of the casks on board were empty.

At the noble house, the water seller tied up his barge, shouldered a cask, as did his partner, and disappeared into the storeroom, followed by Rade—until Cook arrived, complaining the last casks had been frozen, to redirect them to the kitchen. Even as they'd entered the *andron*, two gondolas had come stroking swiftly down the canal, one clearly in pursuit of the other. The flamboyant ornamentation on the first announced ownership by a courtesan, and the second, the source of a stream of colorful insults, appeared to contain her jilted lover. Intent on doing damage, the second gondolier struggled to position his boat for an assault and the first maneuvered to avoid him. Rade, hearing the disturbance, came out of the storeroom to see what was going on.

As he approached the open portal on the canal, he saw Ragazzo playing with his ball and cup and beyond him the weaving bows of two gondolas fast approaching. On the advance craft, the boatman, abandoning flight, prepared to defend against boarding while his female passenger, half-rising and grasping the support of the covered compartment, screamed out invectives. Cutting the water like knives, the sleek black hulls were nearly on top of each other, bellows rising as the boats converged. All attention drawn to the rapidly closing gap, the oarsman on the second gondola trapped the first behind the lighter, and with a sudden change of intent, stroked, and dropping to the deck, rammed it. The narrow prow of the stricken craft was driven sideways, mounting the low rail of the barge and striking the empty casks, which began to topple. The gondola slid off, still upright, in a deafening commotion of insults, shouts, and rending wood, the boatman and the woman clinging to the rail.

In the uproar, the child stood up, transfixed with fear by the shudder of the impact, directly in the path of the tumbling casks. With unerring design, one struck him, knocking him into the water. Rade, poised in the darkness beyond the gateway, caught a fleeting glimpse of outstretched hands and an open mouth before Ragazzo struck the water and sank, without a sound, on the far side of the lighter.

Running forward, Rade threw himself into the water, flinging his body wide to avoid the hull of the barge and dodge the bobbing casks. It took all the tricks of a contortionist along with the added knowledge that at high tide, the canal would be flowing in rather than out. Abruptly, the hard embrace of ice water drove his breath inward with a savagery that twisted his body. Enveloped in his own turbulence, for a time, he could see nothing in the stinging greenish-brown murk. Then, a little way off, the shadowy form of the child began to materialize, corkscrewing slowly in a constellation of bubbles, already swept beneath the wide, weed-ridden hull of the lighter. Here the canal was deeper, sloping down to where the foundations of the buildings could spare their protective coating of mud.

As he swam closer, the boy's bulging, panic-stricken eyes rolled up and his small body began to descend through a cloud of detritus toward the muck of the bottom. Rade dove for him then, catching him up in one arm, and with the other, stroked for the air and the lighter streak of surface. Lack of breath hammered at the tightness in his chest and the black hull of the lighter cast a broad and sinister shadow. He stole a quick look at the unconscious boy, drove himself upwards with a powerful kick, and was rewarded with a stunning blow to the skull. The impact knocked him sideways, rolling half-senseless, breaking the surface of the canal, coughing and gasping, until he realized that he'd struck a cask and, at the same time, had loosened his grip on the child. He was close to the side of the canal and the hull of the lighter had drifted closer too, narrowing the gap, the water seller's plank now a diagonal shape above him. He shook his head, bringing a numbing confluence of stars into his vision, and with horror, felt the child slip away.

With a violent push off the edge of the lighter, Rade propelled himself down again, his back to the wall of the canal, twisting and reaching sideways for the slight shape receding gently through the dark water, grabbing at the cloudy mass of hair—when he was wrenchingly brought up short. The doublet had snagged, hooked on a murderous array of points an arm's length below the surface, slicing through the wool and linen to the flesh beneath. His momentum and the weight of his body combined with that of the boy continued the slide down the bed of nails until the reinforced seams at his shoulders held his weight; leaving him imprisoned and impaled with the child still clutched in one hand. With an effort, he tried to wrench himself free and bring the boy to the surface at the same time. He succeeded only in raising the small body enough to transfer his hands to the boy's armpits and painfully push both his arms and the child's head and shoulders upward until he could feel the chilly bite of wind on his fingertips. His own body remained caught fast in an agonizing trap of iron spikes and freezing water. It seemed then that they would perish: the boy from cold, if he wasn't dead already, and he from the numbing darkness that had begun to overtake him.

During the last shreds of consciousness, someone peeled the child from his clenched fists, and after, arms were extended to pull him up. The lifting movement only served to set him more firmly on what he'd finally discerned as the submerged form of Ludovico's new purchase. In the end, he simply had no strength left, nor air either. The last aching breath he took was water.

*   *   *   *   *

It was Mario who slashed off the doublet, dragged the drowned man to the surface, turned him violently face up on the stone, and pummeled him, and then face down, wounds and all, until he retched up a stinking puddle of liquid. And it was Mario who commandeered a boat and wrapped him, blue-lipped and unconscious, in his winter cloak. Alberico, too, lent a hand, cradling Rade's upper body in his arms as the rowers pulled away from the noble house, the ever-present water in the bilge sloshing around the borrowed cloak, the liquid tinged with pink and then with crimson. The child had been swiftly carried into the noble house. The occupants of the gondolas, the cause of all the trouble, had abandoned their craft and disappeared. The covey of casks floated innocently along, six houses down, drawn by the tide. Soaking wet and weighed down with his inert burden, Alberico sat stoically in the stern—and never wondered why they hadn't taken the injured man inside.

*   *   *   *   *

Rade was dimly aware that death had embraced him and when he'd grudgingly accepted its victory, his dying had been torn away. Emptied out like the contents of a wineskin in rough company. The skin deflated, leaking liquid and the soul inside, partially detached. Charon, unneeded, had returned the barge to the other shore and he'd been left in the inky blackness to find his own way out. Alone. What consciousness he retained was fragmentary, like shards of glass: one splinter for weariness, another, unidentified loss, a third, some decision set forth and then revoked—sharp-edged markers on an otherwise formless path.

A man called from faraway, laid hands on his distant

shoulders, shook him gently, and waited.

The pool of uneasy darkness wavered but he resisted coming into the light.

The voice spoke more loudly, laid hands on him again, waited, grew louder still, and then used force.

Abruptly, the veil of physical insensibility ruptured and a shocking flood of pain coursed through his body. Breathless with agony, all the utterances of misery, human and animal, crowded to his lips. The voice continued, insistent, intrusive, inexorable, but to Rade, struggling to control mind and body, it had no identity. Riding waves of nausea, he heard his name, felt the same hold on his shoulders, and knew the dread of what was coming.

"Damn you! Speak to me!"

He was shaken again and ended it by retching miserably into the sheet.

"I told you he lives," said someone else. Someone he knew. He heard that someone walk out of the room.

Afterwards, he was unable to move. There were apologetic noises, his face was wiped clean with a damp cloth, and the mess tidied up. He felt the moisture pass through the porous stuff of the mask and into his skin and its coolness along with the kindness of the act produced a modicum of relief. He stirred and whispered tentatively, "Vuk?"

"No. It's me. Mario. My God, you're a bear to awaken. *What do you need?*"

Mario. In pieces, it trickled back. Mario kneeling on the landing. The drowning pool of ice water. The piercing rack of iron. The falling casks. He felt again the ragged sense of loss. "Ragazzo?"

"The boy will survive," Mario assured him. "He vomited up half the canal." He shook his head. "His father became a witless, weeping idiot. The women took charge, wrapped the child in robes, and took him in by the hearth." He rinsed out the cloth and passed it gently over the patient's mouth, under the hair at the back of his neck, over his wrists, his hands. "As I was leaving, they were spooning soup down the child and wine down the father. *Stay with me, Rade*," he said sharply. *"Where are the things you need!"*

Mario knew he needed something. What was it? He mumbled what finally came to mind, "casket," and because that didn't seem very clear, "bed."

Mario looked at him oddly and then seemed to understand. He dropped the cloth into a basin and began pushing and prying at the carvings on the exposed side of the bed. Finally a lever sprang open a drawer, revealing a worn wooden box and a fine, five-faceted blade with a bone grip. Mario picked up the casket, scrutinized its contents, and snapped it shut. He left the dagger where it was and began to reset the drawer.

"Take the *cinquedea*," muttered Rade through his teeth. "A parting gift." Hephaestion, on his monumental pyre, was burning.

Mario stared at the dagger. "We didn't drag you back here to have you lie on your shield," he answered briskly, hiding his concern. "And if that's humor, I've had enough of it."

"I lie here," said Rade faintly, "infused with mirth... and you want none of it." He turned his head away and tightened his hold on the mattress.

Mario looked at the white knuckles, the exposed tendons, and walked to the foot of the bed and back again. He said quietly, "I've summoned my surgeon. He'll meet us in Murano." He paused, fingering the bed linen. "I'm going to look at your back. Alberico said..." He didn't finish but pulled the sheet back and then, more carefully, the covering that was supposed to soak up the blood. The bandaging underneath seemed tight but he was afraid to undo it and where he could see flesh and muscle, they were rigidly controlled. He stood, swearing softly under his breath, looking at the fresh blood staining the bed. He dumped the sodden cloth on the floor, and rummaged around in a chest until he'd found something to replace it. "Why is it that every other time I see you, something's gone wrong?"

The patient produced the shadow of a smile but when the new cloth was laid down, he gave it up and buried his face in the mattress. For a time, there was no conversation, no sound except for the small noises of suppressed suffering and the protesting creak of the bed.

Mario paced back and forth by the window.

After a while, the patient stirred.

"I'm here," Mario said and sat down again. The damp cloth made its rounds. "Do you want something to drink?"

A pause, and then, "After most of the canal?"

"I forgot." Mario got up and went to look out the window.

Rade waited until he turned. "Will you... if things go wrong... there are some... "

Mario came back to the bed. "Don't be a fool," he said sharply. "All the things that could go wrong, have gone wrong. Believe me, fortune may occasionally neglect you but she hasn't given you up altogether."

The deep blue eyes lacked clarity. *"Tear my soul from my breast..."*

"And let me no longer be the plaything of fortune. I know that song too," said Mario. "Listen to me. You've survived the canal and that misbegotten gate. The boy didn't drown. Your wounds aren't mortal." Mario added, "You do need sutures. I've brought thread."

"How accomplished," replied Rade weakly. "You swim. You succor. You sew."

"Not skin," replied Mario quickly. "I brought silk for the surgeon. To save time." He glanced back at the window. "He says it's better than linen."

"How Venetian," murmured the patient and closed his

eyes. "Marsyas... refashioned as a purse."

"You've got a tough hide," replied his friend soberly. "Purse or no purse, you're not going to prove the exception, are you?"

"And die in bed like a woman?" Rade muttered indistinctly. There was a pause. He put a little more forcefulness into the answer. "No."

"Good." Marching over to the window, Mario peered out. "As soon as Alberico comes back, we'll pack you up like an egg and get you into the boat."

The excursion had little to recommend it. Control was getting harder to maintain and the conflagration was growing. He murmured perversely, "What sort of egg? Boiled? Or roasted in ashes?"

"Buried in sand if you like." Mario strode to the door. *"Where is he?"*

"The last," said the whisper.

Mario turned and stared at the bed. Despite the color in the patient's face, other signs pointed to complete physical collapse. Even he could see that. "Look here, Rade," he said suddenly. "I left you alone with Alberico. I wish I hadn't. The lout applied the time-honored remedy of the sea."

The man's eyelids flickered. "Pickled like a fish?" whispered the patient into the mattress.

Mario nodded. "In vinegar and salt."

That explained the descent into the inferno. Alberico's medical proficiency was limited. All he knew were floggings. Listening to the labored sound of someone breathing, Rade threaded his fingers into the bulge of the sheets and prayed for Mario to leave and for some kind of end to come—and realized belatedly that the breathing was his own.

"I'm sorry I wasn't here to stop him," said his friend from a long way off. "I don't know if that was the right thing to do."

The room blurred. He was bathed in an unnatural sweat.

Feeling a stab of apprehension, he struggled to communicate some last requests. Mario seeing what he wanted, knelt down, and bent his head to his lips. Rade breathed, "Not tell... Cat..." and the rest faded into oblivion.

A half hour later, with the help of Alberico, Mario gathered up the blood-soaked linen, the casket, and the supine body of his friend and took them to Murano, and home, swearing the boatman to silence.

*   *   *   *   *

At high noon in the courtyard, Caterina took her leave, scanning the assembled household for Rade but not finding him. Ludovico was at the opening to the *andron*, supervising the final installation of the water gate before departing with his daughter and their retinue in the gondola. The traveling chests had been loaded onto a boat that morning, the smaller boxes and sacks dispersed among them. The menservants, too, had gone on ahead. Sofia and Nonna were standing red-faced with cold, a stoic and capable bulwark behind their mistress.

"Here they are at last," exclaimed Caterina, about to draw her veil. She went forward to greet Mario, looking beyond him for Rade.

The factor bowed. "Madonna." He looked tired.

There was no one behind him. Caterina looked searchingly into his face. "Is Rade coming? It's not like him to be late."

He shook his head. "I've come in his stead."

She looked stricken. "Should we have sent a physician?"

"It's nothing, madonna," Mario replied. "A blow to the head from the rescue, nothing serious. He wanted to come but... forgive me... he was staggering like a sot." He made a grimace, spread and waggled his hands. "He'd be in the canal all over again." He said, for added effect, "He was quite disagreeable about it."

"Understandably so," she answered, reassured. "He must rest and drink warm liquids. Not too much sleep. You will see to it?"

"Of course. And the boy?"

Her eyes grew soft. "He's recovered and gone back to the mainland this morning." She smiled and added, "He liked my soup."

"*I* would like your soup," replied Mario.

"You needn't fall into the canal to have some," smiled Caterina. She gathered up her *camora*. Straightened her new cloak. Pulled the veil over her face. "God be with you, Mario. And also with Rade. Take care of him. Here's Father. We must go."

Ludovico came into the courtyard. Farewells filled the stony space.

"I'm to say Rade wishes you safe passage," lied Mario, "Oh, and keep an eye on Caterina."

Ludovico smiled and received the message with courtly grace, never letting on he'd seen the ragged bits of cloth hanging from the water gate when it was pulled from the canal. He gathered the travelers together and turning back said quietly to Mario, "If you need anything, anything at all..."

"It's already being done," replied the factor in a low voice.

"Good man." Ludovico pressed a purse into his hand and raised his voice, "Giovanni! Where have you stashed the gondola?"

Mario stood solemnly weighing the pouch of gold in his palms until they were out of sight. He had half the price of a small ship in his grasp and a man at the gates of hell in his house. For a fleeting moment, he wondered how best to spend the money.

*   *   *   *   *

Caterina laughed and the sound bubbled up from inside

her like the plash of a merry brook but underneath it lay a dark foreboding. They had all discussed it. *Ad infinitum. Ad nauseam.* There was no way out. Father would never allow it. Not now. Not ever. To dissolve a betrothal, for anything other than death, would be a weakness. There was already weakness enough. Her dance partner finished his figure, returned to her side, and smiled. The *ballerino* minced by with Simonetta.

"I've amused you. But now you look downcast."

"I'm not. To the contrary." She looked around the room. There were only three men, the rest were women. Simonetta's brother, the *ballerino*, and the unexpected surprise, Simonetta's brother's new friend, Alessandro. Her Alessandro. "You've surprised me. I had no idea you knew Roberto." She was a little breathless. "Where did you learn to dance?"

"Everywhere," Alessandro replied, sounding bored. "At every city my father visited. I was instructed to do so as a nobleman's son, perhaps one day to be a courtier, and also because I was young, harmless, and," he added slyly, "not ill-formed."

"Not ill-formed," she repeated, taking in the lithe body and the handsome face. And then embarrassed, said quickly, "What was it like in Milan? At the festivities that you said you suffered through?"

"Like dancing with campaniles," he said gravely. "They are wearing clocks on the bosoms of their dancing costumes."

"How very odd," she replied, eyes wide. "Do you think we shall do the same?"

"I hope not." He looked intently at the swell of her breasts and casually laid a palm on her bodice. "The beat of a virgin's heart does more to heat the blood than any tick of a clock."

She colored and stepped back a pace. She saw Nonna half rise from her seat across the room and then sit down.

"Are you discomfited, Caterina? Don't be," laughed Alessandro. "We are made for each other. You know it and so do I. Besides, you've already stayed overlong in your father's house."

"I am promised," whispered Caterina, hoping for something to cling to. This was the man she could not marry. The man she wanted.

He took her slim hand in his own. Ginevra's borrowed carbuncle shone from its setting. "Red for passion," he said softly.

"As in the Passion of our Lord," replied Caterina crisply, remembering Nonna, trying to get it back.

"A fine stone," he murmured ignoring the last and imprisoning her hand, "very nearly perfect." He kissed the ring, turned her hand over, kissed her palm, and then released her fingers. "To be faultless requires only a final polish." His lion eyes creased in a smile. "I could be your smith."

Hurt, she started to reply.

"No," he said, "don't be angry. I'm playing with you, Caterina. What you may perceive as criticism is nothing more than the banter of princely courts, of noblemen: verbal swordplay, implied flirtation, carefully groomed expressions." He made a dismissive gesture with his left hand. "A game..."

She took a deep breath, annoyed now. "Alessandro..."

"Let me finish. A game from which behavior is honed that leads to grace under pressure and useful sophistication—which you would have developed by now had you married ser Ariosto."

"My betrothed..." she protested.

"You won't find it in that Slav," Alessandro said flatly. "At the edge of the civilized world, he's denied most, if not all, levels of education. And you won't find it, alone, in your room. Or in your books. Sophistication requires courtly conversation."

She moved back, not sure what he was intimating, and looked about for escape.

He reached out and caught the velvet and seed pearls of her sleeve. "Hear me out, Caterina. Truly, *cara*, I am not trying to be unkind." He put on his most earnest expression. "If I teach you, you could teach him. Make him more than a rough diamond. Advance him." He hoped he'd struck the right note. "My little virgin," he murmured softly, "who ought to be mine, imagine the depth of his gratitude."

She felt as if she'd been struck. Or betrayed. Or both. Her eyes filled with tears.

The musicians tuned up their instruments. Couples, most of them female, advanced to the dance floor. Simonetta paraded by in a cloud of musk and voile and silk—and waved.

"Dance with me." Alessandro's eyes were dark gold, admiring, feline. "It's the *bassa danza*."

Her vision shimmering, she gave in, not to him, because at that particular moment she didn't like him, but to the music. Then the dance performed its magic and in the midst of it, she began to see herself as he did, so cloistered as to be provincial, still calculating each step, each phrase, each mannerism. By contrast, Alessandro was as fluid as water, as charming and polished as a prince, as beautiful as a lion.

*   *   *   *   *

For a while, he lay unmoving, as he'd been taught, trying to assess his situation. It took effort to focus. There was light somewhere behind him. And a person.

"How do you feel?" asked Mario's voice.

He swallowed, trying to lubricate his throat. "If it won't leak out," Rade said huskily, "I'd like a drink."

"That can be managed," replied his friend, busying himself. Then matter-of-factly, "We bled you again."

"When?"

"The night before last." Mario went on, "You were very

ill. I feared…" He didn't finish the sentence, just shrugged. "On the lighter side," continued Mario, carrying a cup and dragging up a chair, "when the surgeon's leeches swelled up and fell off, that ox, Alberico," his voice filled with mirth, "fainted! We were hard put to decide whom to succor first," he added, wiping the tears from his eyes, "the leeches, Alberico, or you."

"I'll wager it was the first," muttered Rade. Inadvertently he shuddered. "No more leeches."

"No." Mario was serious again. "The tainted blood is out. You'll be better now." He moved his chair closer, proffered the cup, and helped the patient raise his head to drink from it.

The wine rushed down his throat like a cascade in a desert. He choked on it.

"Not too fast." Mario put the coveted cup aside where the patient couldn't reach it and embarked on a description of wounds and their ongoing treatment which, defined by thirst, occupied an eternity. It appeared the wounds were healing.

Intent on the cup, Rade remained somewhat disengaged until he heard Mario saying, in a conversational tone, "The doctor asked me if you'd been a felon." His friend paused. "You've got the marks."

"What… did you say?"

"I said no. You were a Slav." Mario grinned hugely, enjoying some further joke.

"And?"

"He said Slavs are all felons anyway—it's a national pastime."

"Must have been a Cattarine," grunted the patient, eyeing the cup. "What else?" He managed to prop himself up on an elbow and was helped to another drink.

"He said whatever happened to you, happened long ago," said Mario, putting the cup back on the table.

"Ancient history," agreed the patient limply.

"And now you've got a new overlay to excite the girls," offered Mario.

"I hope you'll introduce me," murmured the invalid. He turned his head and part of the mane of black hair fell across his eyes. He started to bring a hand up to his face, and decided against it. "When do they return?"

"Five days."

"Only five?"

Mario nodded, "You've been out of your head."

Rade shut his eyes and tried to remain calm.

As if anticipating the question, Mario added, "I've heard enough gibberish in three languages to addle my mind. Most of it unintelligible."

But not all. Mario's face might tell him something if only he could see through the curtain of hair. He made another painfully abortive effort to push it out of the way.

Mario, watching, stood up and smoothed the sweaty thatch back from the injured man's forehead. Carelessly, he let a hand rest on the tangled hair. "Do you want me to untie it?" he said softly.

The patient lay perfectly still. There was a long silence. "How long have you known?" asked Rade.

"Since August at the villa," replied his friend. "Remember the deaf mute? I came in just after he'd strapped you up. He was agitated about something but I couldn't understand him. Finally he showed me the edge of it. It was so thin, so real, I couldn't believe it."

To Rade, it no longer mattered how he'd found out. He now remembered what he'd said in the bedchamber. *The secret was out.*

"Who else knows?"

"No one. I've kept it to myself."

"And the surgeon?"

"I hid your face in shadow. He was preoccupied with

parasites," he lied. The man would keep the secret but his silence had been costly. He thought wistfully of the bag of gold.

This time Rade managed to force his hand to his face. The mask felt as it always had.

"I'm sure you need a barber. Shall I take it off?" asked Mario. "I can help."

"No." He felt a surge of panic. *Not now.*

To his immense relief, Mario drew back. "I suppose it can wait another day. See how you feel tomorrow. Here, drink. Will you tell me one truth?" asked Mario, retreating into the shadows. He paused to gather the words. "Does the mask conceal a disease?"

To his relief, Rade laughed. "God no. I'm not supposed to be hiding in the woods, wearing bells."

Not leprosy. Mario breathed easier. He thought the man must have some terrible flaw in his face, and felt sorry for him, but not before another question leaped unbidden from his lips. "Then why do you wear it?"

"To bring beauty to the eyes of my beloved," said the invalid, bolstered by alcohol.

When you have it not. He hoped he wasn't there when she found out.

*   *   *   *   *

Rade stood rigidly in the cold, damp hall of the *andron*, like everyone else, watching the late afternoon light outside the vaulted opening, beyond the open grilles, waiting for the gondola. He wore a new doublet of a tawny cloth, at least new for him, recently acquired from the secondhand clothes merchant. Alberico stood protectively just behind him. Mario was also there. Cook had been preparing all day for their return. The traveling chests were already in the courtyard, brought separately by Battista and Antonio.

The sharp point of the prow, with its diaper of canvas, appeared in the opening, and then the *felze*, the passenger compartment. He saw old Giovanni pull the vessel against the side of the canal while the four passengers disembarked. The sun broke through just as Ludovico and Caterina entered through the water gate, smiling and returning greetings, richly wrapped in fur-lined cloaks, their faces flushed with cold. Caterina carried Orseolo, round-eyed with excitement, partly visible under her cloak. To Rade, standing beside Mario by the wall, she'd never looked so beautiful. He went forward with the rest to greet her and welcome her home and he found himself as awkward as a schoolboy.

"Our true hero. Not once but twice." She smiled. "We talked about you all the way to Padua. How is your head?" she asked solicitously, looking at him more closely.

He mumbled some answer not knowing what she meant.

"Ragazzo and his father will be forever grateful. We will be forever grateful."

Somehow the "we" removed the thankfulness from familiarity to formality. "You must be tired," he said, standing aside. "I'll see you at supper." He glimpsed Nonna and Sofia standing behind her and nodded a welcome. Sofia smiled. Nonna nodded back.

"You always notice what no one else does," Caterina said, inclining her head. She turned away. "*Cook!* There you are! *God knows I've missed you!*" When she looked for Rade again, he was leaning, one shoulder against the wall, talking to Mario.

Battista being one of the last to enter, coming in from the courtyard, and catching sight of Rade, strode up to him, his voice booming with camaraderie, and clapped his hand on Rade's back. Rade staggered, drew a sharp breath, and then allayed Battista's look of surprise with some quip he pulled out of air. They both laughed and then exchanged news, Battista having the larger share, and one by one the other menservants joined in. Mario was making signs to depart when Ludovico, too, came for a quick word.

"Rade," Ludovico smiled affectionately. "It does me good to see you standing here." He added, "We won't expect you for supper until the morrow. My daughter says we all need a quiet evening." He grimaced. "She thinks I'm getting old." His gaze settled on Mario. "You must come as well, Mario."

"I will," replied Mario.

"Should I prepare myself for whatever ruinous transactions occurred in my absence?" asked Ludovico.

"I hope not," replied Mario, grinning.

"Was the gathering a success?" inquired Rade.

"You know Simonetta. She's a woman born under a lucky star, but if she hadn't been, I firmly believe she would have forged her own. If women could be doges, she'd be the first." He shook his head. "The festivities ran like clockwork. I even had time to visit a few properties. That said, my ears are still ringing with lute music, and God knows, my eyes are watering from the sight of that ridiculous *ballerino* prancing around like a spring fawn. God save us all from such a fate."

They talked for a while until Rade, jostled by the crowd, half-turned away, and when he tried to pick up the conversation, Ludovico said quietly, "You have a stain on the back of your doublet. Go home. Rest. Mario will go with you." And he ushered them out of the hall.

*   *   *   *   *

The supper was well attended and the benches were filled. Cook had gone out of her way with boiled rump of beef, tongue, even a capon, served with a sauce reeking of garlic, and that seasonal favorite, cabbage, which she had spiced with bitter orange. And there was fresh bread and a good wine from the Veneto.

It had taken a second trip to the clothes merchant to repair the damage done to his limited wardrobe but attired in linen and black velvet, and cocooned like a caterpillar in wrappings, Rade felt confident of his appearance. The surprise was that Ginevra and Simonetta were both at the table, seated on either side of Caterina, the three of them chattering away like a tree full of sparrows. He was aware that Caterina's friends were occasional visitors to the noble house but they rarely stayed for supper. Rade thought, after they'd all spent a week together, they'd be glad of some distance from one another. Yet here they were in the thick of it, as if they hadn't seen each other for months.

Looking down the long cloth of the trestle table, he was within a few places of Caterina, below Simonetta's gawky, star-gazing brother, Umberto, and Ginevra's small, neat, gray-haired nurse. Ginevra was already flushed with wine, not the retiring pious soul he knew, and there were various unsaid signals flying across the table from the nurse. Simonetta, he thought, was so outlandish in costume and hair style that she would have made a successful courtesan but, despite that unflattering thought, at least in this society, he quite liked her quick wit and outspoken opinions. When he finally came around to studying Caterina, he became aware that she seemed to have returned with a different form of banter that he had not heard before and a host of new expressions—and even a new style for her hair.

The supper continued apace. Those who had not been present were mesmerized by the descriptions of the dancing, the concerts, the variety of dishes at the suppers, the poems read, and the amusing comments on the other attendees. It was unnecessary for Rade to make conversation of any kind. Nor had he ever met most of the people who had been there. Since his back hurt, he consoled himself with wine, moving his food around on the plate, and trying to absorb a modicum of the conversation. It was Ginevra who brought the devil into focus.

"While we were dancing, Alessandro said the most amusing..."

"What!" cried Ludovico. "Alessandro was there? *When?"* The conversation dropped off into silence.

"It was only one night," ventured Umberto. "He slept in my bed."

"You were out looking at those two farms," added Caterina. "The ones you said were all mud and waste. You came back late." Despite herself she colored. "He comes here to visit. We didn't think you'd mind."

I mind, thought Rade, staring at them from down the table. *That bastard.*

Ludovico looked up and down the guests. His gaze settled on Caterina. "Did you invite him, Caterina?" His tone was stern.

"Of course not."

"He's a recent acquaintance," interjected Umberto, wiping his mouth and looking irritated. "He was passing through on his way back from Milan and asked if he could stay the night. I could not but extend the hospitality of the house. Father wasn't there. Besides," he added. "he made a third male dance partner, when we had only two, and by God, he was *good.*"

Sofia came in, breathing hard from running up the stairs. "There's a messenger from the glassworks."

"I wonder what that is?" said Ludovico. "It's late. I'll come down."

Sofia bit her lip. "It's for madonna Caterina, messer Ludovico. He's brought a parcel."

Ludovico looked like a thundercloud. "I'll come down anyway."

Rade looked at Caterina. She was sitting bolt upright, like

a deer at the edge of a glade, scenting the wind, trying to ascertain what was coming. Knowing that, whatever it was, it would be pleasurable. *And suddenly he knew he was losing her.*

*   *   *   *   *

The conversation started up again, led by a story from Simonetta, who clearly knew how to embellish it. They were all laughing, except Rade, when Ludovico called and Caterina rose gracefully from the table and went into the next room. Below the hum of conviviality, there was, in the next room, a long, low conversation ending with some sharp words from Ludovico. Caterina eventually reappeared with an oblong shape, wrapped in velvet. It was clear she'd been crying.

"Father wishes me to tell you, my dear friends, that he must excuse himself. Don't get up. We have another course planned and I have been instructed to open this gift from..." she looked unflinchingly at Rade, "...ser Alessandro. And to let all of you see it as most of you were present at the dance. Father says to... accept it would not be proper. Tomorrow, I am also instructed, as I am betrothed, to send it back."

Rade gazed back at her. Her eyes were filled with tears. She was visibly shaking. If it hadn't been so hard to stand up at the moment, he would have enfolded her in his arms. Protected her from whatever message the object was meant to bring. He already knew in his heart it would be a token of affection. Clearly Ludovico had meant this to be an exercise in public humiliation—that even he didn't care to observe. And yet at that moment, Ludovico reappeared and took his place at the table.

"Open it," he ordered.

Caterina glanced at her father and then taking great care, her hands trembling, undid the velvet pouch, opened the padded wooden box, and brought out an indeterminate object veiled in silk. She tenderly unfolded the gauzy cloth to reveal an exquisite clear glass goblet, decorated with delicate gold lines and fantastic peach-colored animals.

What little conversation there was, died. It was worth a fortune.

Ginevra put out a tentative hand to touch it and then drew it back.

Simonetta said quietly, "The finest artisan in Murano."

Caterina, weeping and smiling at the same time, said nothing, only lovingly, with great gentleness, fingered the glass.

Rade, who until that moment would have forgiven her, decided it was time to leave. He had gotten painfully stiff sitting on the bench and found it hard to rise from the table. Finally grabbing the edge of the trestle, without a word to anyone, he lurched to his feet, stepping on the border of the embroidered linen tablecloth. The cloth slid away from the table, just enough to dislodge the goblet, and send it rolling toward the verge. Caterina made a desperate attempt to catch it, but failed. With a small, tinkling cry of protest, it crashed and lay, a shattering of tiny crystals, the gold and animals dissolved into slivers spread across the unyielding terrazzo. There was a general exclamation of horror. Caterina fell to her knees, tears spilling down her cheeks, trying to gather up the minutiae of shards. Ginevra and Simonetta sprang to comfort her and everyone else rose in noisy confusion either to offer help, or to take their leave.

Rade felt Mario grab his arm. "How could you?" he muttered under his breath and began to steer the drunkard from the room.

Rade resisted. He turned toward the sobbing girl. "It was not meant."

She said nothing but the glance she gave him would have

turned a sober man to stone.

Chapter Eighteen

Wind, time, women and luck—first they turn away and then
they come back, like the moon.
—Proverb

February, Twelfth Month of Venetian Year 1493

Iron gray clouds hid the sun and a chill February wind raced along the canal. Rade squatted on the *riva*, his right hand grasping Orseolo's collar. Ragazzo walked gingerly across the plank and then ran down the *andron* toward the stairs to the kitchen, with Orseolo, now loosed, in hot pursuit. His father smiled, shifted his cask, saluted Rade, and then followed his son.

"My gratitude would fill the lagoon."

"It's done. We need not speak of it again," said Rade. He looked after Ragazzo, "Should I make him another cup and ball?" It'd gone the way of the casks.

The water seller stopped, motioning his helper to pass him. He shook his head. "He doesn't remember you. Or what you did. He remembers her. And the soup. It's better that way. We all think it's better that way."

"Who's we?"

"My family. My wife. My other children."

Other children? "But you only bring Ragazzo."

The water seller looked abashed. "Ragazzo isn't like my other children. You know how it is. My wife, she thinks he isn't hers. That he's a changeling. That the fairies brought him."

"And you?"

The man shrugged. He turned away into the gloom of the *andron*. "He looks just like her."

In another month, thought Rade, watching him walk away, the cistern would be repaired and Ragazzo and his father would be gone. He wondered if, in a month, Caterina might choose to recognize his existence.

*   *   *   *   *

Caterina returned from confession having enumerated the various small sins of daily living while omitting the larger ones. As usual she felt a sense of guilt that a series of minor penances did little to assuage. She laid her lynx-lined cloak on the *cassone*, crossed herself before the painted Virgin, and reached up to take the sad little box down from the shelf near her bed. She opened the lid and gazed at the sparkling pile of shards. On one, there was still enough of the form of the animal to see what it was. She touched it, marveled at the beauty of design in this one tiny survivor, closed the box and put it back. This daily ritual—that Nonna disapproved of—was the spark with which she rekindled her anger.

The incident had divided both her friends and the household. Her father had dismissed it as accidental. In fact, he had made it clear that what had happened had also been richly deserved. Sofia, indignant, supportive, had confessed she spat in Rade's food at every opportunity. Cook had aligned herself with Sofia but with less vehemence. Giovanni, their oldest retainer, had been protective of her as always but he had said nothing against Rade. Of her friends, Ginevra was guilt-stricken over having revealed Alessandro's name. Surprisingly Simonetta and Nonna had both said that there'd been something wrong with Rade that night and Mario had said he was drunk.

To Caterina, it didn't matter what anyone said. The act was unforgivable.

Sofia, now an active ally, had taken Caterina's tear-stained note to her second cousin, the butcher's boy, to deliver to Alessandro and that delivery had begun a flow of correspondence that had become more frequent as time went on. Yet Alessandro had not come again to the noble house.

With Rade, it was a different matter. She saw him every day. Yet, she went out of her way not to see him. If he went into the *andron* and she was there, Caterina went somewhere else. If he caught her eye in the courtyard, she turned her head. If he came to supper, she got up and changed her seat or left the table altogether. After a while, despite her father's protests, he went back to eating in the kitchen with the menservants. The spare apology he had tendered the following day, she had told him, did not nor would ever excuse such an overt act of malice. After that he hadn't tried again.

                    *   *   *   *   *

Mario sat with his back against the rough planks of the tavern wall. Rade, seated opposite, bent forward over the *raki* he was nursing, running the fingers of his left hand over the network of scars in the table top. They both wore their black merchants' tunics and round caps. *The Sign of the Flute* was noisy, dark, and rank with the smell of working men crowded into too small a space. Occasionally a foreign voice stood out from the others: Slav, German, rural Italian. But there was none of the *sarcenet*, bells and masked or painted faces of Carnevale in here. They wouldn't dare.

"God's bones, I'm glad to be done with *that* cargo," drawled Mario, picking up the pitcher to fill his cup. He looked searchingly at Rade. "So now, how do you fare?" He drank. "Have you been forgiven?"

"I've been forgotten," said Rade morosely, draining his cup.

"That bad?"

"I could lie in a pool of blood with a dagger in my breast and she'd either pull the dagger out and stick it in a few more times or step over me without a second look."

"Surely that's not the truth of it."

Rade looked at Mario. He smiled ruefully. "I've called down a killing frost."

Mario laughed. "She'll get over it." He finished his drink and stood up. "Come out to the bonfire tonight. Carnevale's almost over. You've missed most of it."

"And wear a mask?" asked Rade. "It's already been Carnevale for almost a year."

"No one but you knows that," observed Mario gravely. He got up. "Come on. You don't need another night of staring at Cook and Alberico. You could be enjoying having your purse picked."

It had been after the bonfire was starting to burn down, after the raucous play, after the tumblers, after the seductive glances and bared breasts of the resident prostitutes and their brief dalliance, that they had stumbled down the narrow street, careening off the walls of buildings—until the sound was heard. At first it resembled an unshod horse galloping over a path. A pack of dogs baying. The yells of a mob.

Rade, who'd been almost incoherent, halted. He seemed instantly sober. He grabbed Mario by the arm. There was a small alcove above their heads in the building beside them. "Can you get up there?"

"What? Why? It's just a loose horse." Mario spoke loudly.

It was getting closer.

"In Venice? At Carnevale?" shouted Rade. *"God's blood, it's a bull!"*

The narrow street before them lit up, torches bobbing and waving behind the black, horned silhouette pounding towards them. Ropes snaked behind what looked for all the world like Beelzebub with all the fiends of hell in close pursuit.

"Run! Stay close to the walls! Watch the horns!"

"Holy Mary, Mother of God!" cried Mario. He could see the crazed animal now. The glitter of its eyes. The ropes tied round its great black-tipped horns.

"Come on!"

They ran back towards the piazza, the bonfire, the crowd, shouting a warning.

"He's outrunning us!" cried Mario, his tunic billowing out behind him.

"Look for a shop... an alcove... a niche," panted Rade. He hadn't run or practiced arms or carried something heavy since the accident a few weeks before. But he ran for his life now. "Flatten yourself in it. *There!*" he shouted. There was a shallow opening on Mario's side of the street. Rade ran more toward the center of the street to attract the bull. "Try to... grab a rope... when he's passed!"

"Why?"

"To stop... him. Can't... let him... into the crowd."

Mario threw himself into the opening and then grabbed for the rope as the bull passed him. It ran through his palms like fire but he hung on as best he could, now running behind the animal, trying to pit his weight against the rope.

He saw Rade flatten himself in a doorway, the horns missing him by the span of a hand, and do the same. This time, the bull slowed a little. Two youthful bull baiters also threw themselves on the ropes and the bull continued to lose momentum. The crowd around the bonfire dispersed, screaming, running in all directions, women snatching up children, vendors abandoning their wares, all except for a big, heavy man. Silhouetted against the flames, the man picked up an ax and ran toward them. The bull still crazed, lowered his head, and the man swung his ax and jumped out of the way. The huge creature stopped, shook his great head, and slowly fell to his knees. The mastiffs closed in, the bull baiters trying to beat them off, their followers shouting. After a pause, the bonfire crowd began tentatively to reappear, encircling the huge man, slapping him on his back, thanking, kissing, and blessing him.

"Who is he?' asked Mario, examining his hands, still breathing hard. "I wouldn't... have the stomach... to do that."

Rade was bent forward, hands on his legs above his knees, gasping for breath. "The right man... for the task."

"A knight," said Mario.

"I think... the butcher." Rade straightened up. "Let's leave... in case they figure out... they've got to get that... mountain of flesh... back to the slaughter pens."

*   *   *   *   *

A few days later when the subject of Giovedi Grasso came up with its mock trial, bull baiting and pig slaughter in the piazza, for some reason neither Mario nor Rade seemed to have much interest. They were both suffering rope burns from some childish tug-o-war they'd engaged in—with a bull they'd said. Ludovico wondered what they'd really been up to. He invited the menservants and Giovanni instead, as this event, bloody as it was, celebrating the victory of the Republic over the Patriarch of Aquileia, was always popular. He longed to be a member of the scarlet-robed Council, for when they entered the Doge's Palace after the slaughter, there would be a host of miniature wooden castles to smash, in remembrance of the fortresses Venice had destroyed in Friuli those many years ago. That final act passed each year reported but unseen by commoners. Such merriment was not visible from the piazza.

On this Giovedi Grasso—one was always most cognizant of excess the last day before Lent—it was the evening festivities that Ludovico worried about. When it came to the delights of Carnevale, Ludovico had always been strict. He usually allowed Caterina a few small dinner parties or concerts with close friends which he attended, too. This year, he had also allowed the visit to Padua and now he had foolishly acquiesced to Simonetta's invitation to a costumed evening of music and dance at her family's lavish home. There would be a host of guests to keep an eye on. He would know most of them as friends or kinsmen of Simonetta's family. Ginevra's household would be there as well. Even the servants had been invited.

"It borders on being public," he'd said to Caterina. "Stay masked. Don't show your face to anyone you don't know. Don't unmask in a crowd. God knows, I'm loath to let you go to this."

And to Rade he'd said, "Whether you wish to or not, go. I'm tired of this unending, churlish behavior in my home. Find a way to ingratiate yourself. Dance with her. At least it's something she enjoys."

* * * * *

Nonna pulled out Caterina's second-best dress for the third time. "We could add these touches," she said, folding in bits of material and beads. "Alter the cut of the bodice. And add the jeweled mask that belonged to your mother."

Caterina stared critically at the suggested creation and shook her head. "It would pain Father to see me wearing that."

"He offered it," said Nonna. "But then I hadn't thought..."

She put the mask aside.

"Or we could change the sleeves to linen," suggested Sofia hopefully. "Add ribbons at your temples. Twine them into your hair. Drape you in white. You could be a goddess. Carry a cornucopia."

"I'd resemble a mercer's booth at *La Sensa*," said Caterina. "Or worse, the sailmaker's."

With a sigh, the two women put down the *camora* and pulled out another.

"We only have two more days," said Nonna grimly.

They were interrupted by a knocking at the door.

"What is it?"

"Madonna, a package from madonna Simonetta," ventured Cook.

"Truly? Do bring it in." Caterina sat down on the bed with a sigh. "Anything for a distraction."

The package, wrapped in linen, was quite large and heavy. Cook placed it on the bed. Caterina stood up and carefully pulled away the covering. When she saw the glimmer of gold, she paused, looked up at the other women, and then tore the rest of it open. Inside lay a sumptuous *camora* with a gilded cat mask to accompany it. A small folded note fell out: "I wished to help with your costume as you told me you had not yet made a choice. This one belongs to a friend, so, for one night, you shouldn't infringe on any sumptuary laws. Wear it in health and beauty. Simonetta."

"Cloth of gold," observed Nonna softly, examining the exquisite workmanship. "*Cloth of gold!* In my entire life, I've never thought I'd even touch such a wonder."

Caterina wondered how Simonetta might have known she had no costume. And then she knew who might have told her. She smiled happily. "Help me put it on—in case it needs to be altered."

*   *   *   *   *

By the morning before Simonetta's party, in his own mind, despite Ludovico's insistence, Rade's attendance was still undecided. In early afternoon, Alberico, his ever-present shadow, had related some comments about Alessandro that stuck in Rade's mind. They were only the gossipy slurs that are passed between servants but they were sufficiently unsettling to make up his mind. As a man already masked, an additional covering was unwelcome, so Rade had gone to the secondhand clothes merchant and rented the cast off robes of a priest. The cowl cast a deep shadow over his face and the appearance of holiness would, he hoped, reduce or eliminate invitations to the dance. Beneath it, he wore a simple shirt and hose. Otherwise, he'd thought, he'd be too hot.

In the frigid air of evening, when most of Venice pulsed with pre-Lenten activity, Simonetta's splendid home glittered with lanterns and torches and masked, silk-clad servants. Caterina had been delivered to the ball by Ludovico and Giovanni, accompanied by Nonna and her maid. Her father had sent along the menservants as well, who'd walked, and Rade now supplied the missing member, Alberico.

The men stood, clustered around Battista, trading jests with others of their profession as Rade walked away. They were all masked but other than that, wore their normal attire. Rade regretted the exchange of their familiar companionship for that of the unknown guests at the ball. As it was, it took him some time to gain entry as he was plainly dressed and had not arrived by the water gate. He waited impatiently outside the courtyard for nearly the turn of an hourglass until he was brought to the attention of Simonetta, who swept out, a concoction of multicolored ribbons, jewels, feathers, and a silver beak, and took him by the arm.

He was presented to a variety of gods and goddesses, a

jester, three birds, a satyr, two angels, and a bear. The bear was already drunk. Rade made his way gingerly around the fringes of the room in hopes of recognizing someone he knew, but except for his own, the costumes were extravagant, successfully contrived, and the room was full of strangers. He had to content himself with food and drink and the disconcerted glances that his cleric's robes elicited from the other guests.

In the great room, the dancing had started. He looked for Caterina through the carved doorway, and he found her, not by the costume, which he hadn't seen, but by her natural grace of her movement. She was an elegant study in gold, lithe and agile, dancing hand-in-hand with a plumed-serpent that could only be Alessandro. The cat mask was trained on her partner and it was clear that they were attracted to one another. Alessandro led her well. They were perfectly matched. Their movements complimented each other and they appeared deeply involved in the courtship of the dance. He watched them until the bitter poison of jealousy, which he'd tried so long to suppress, welled up and almost overcame him. Finally, he sought out another chamber—where he found Nonna, waiting for him.

"I'm glad you came," said Nonna.

"Shall I bestow a blessing or do you know who I am?"

"Of course I know who you are," said Nonna, "but Caterina may not. To anyone else, it would be an odd choice." She gestured at his costume. "But then I should have been an astrologer, I am adept at prediction."

"Can you predict the future of the cat and the snake?" inquired Rade through his teeth.

"When the dance ends, they will end," said Nonna.

"You'll forgive me. The interpretation of signs and entrails was left out of my education," said Rade bitterly. "What are you saying?"

"Before they danced at Padua, there was a common sensibility," said the older woman. "You saw it yourself."

It was more than that. But he inclined his head, impatient for her to continue.

"At Padua, when Simonetta gathered all her ladies together, she made sure that they would both adorn the proceedings and add enjoyment to them," related Nonna. "Among other things, she employed a dance master to give them instruction. Caterina has a natural grace. The *ballerino* led her in the first dance for couples and it was as if the sun shone on her. They all wanted to share her light."

"And Alessandro?" asked Rade.

"He wasn't expected but he'd found favor with Simonetta's brother. How, I don't know. They arrived late to the festivities. The two fathers had not returned. The dance needed men. We soon saw that if Alessandro is the lord of anything, it is the dance. Furthermore, as soon as he laid eyes on her, he wanted her as his partner." She shrugged. "Umberto arranged it. Even I saw they were a powerful study in physical grace." She smiled. "She was the jewel and Alessandro, the setting."

Nonna looked up at him, trying to see his expression under the cowl. "You saw their aura in the other room. It was like that from the first figure. I thought, until Padua, Alessandro had no real interest in her."

Rade examined the pattern in the floor. "And now, one would have to be blind not to see what has happened."

"I know this is painful for you."

He shrugged, "I have never learned to dance. Not like that. How can I compete? Do I drag him from the floor, as I would like to do, and carve his heart out?" He meant every word.

"Then you will die because Caterina, herself, in a whiplash, would put the letter in the Lion's Mouth. And then the Ten would come for you. Have you learned nothing in life?"

"I've learned it was a mistake to suffer Alessandro's presence at the noble house."

"You could have done nothing."

"I could have warned him off."

"Do you truly think he would have listened? Do you think it would have furthered your own suit? If so, you're more of a fool than I thought." She sighed. "Besides, he will never marry her. He's a patrician. His father is already arranging a betrothal. That's what I meant when I said when the dance ends, they will end."

"What makes you think he has marriage in mind?" he said sharply. "Because then you're the fool."

"I'm going to ignore that remark," said Nonna stiffly. "It's unseemly. She still favored you in the autumn. The turning point came later."

"When I insulted her with my behavior? Broke the trinket?" asked Rade. "I drank too much."

"The 'trinket' was a work of art. And it was more than that. You should receive a prize for boorishness."

"I've paid the price every day since. Must it go on forever?"

"God knows," replied Nonna sharply. *"I do not.* Caterina is vulnerable right now and none of you can see it. She's been locked up in that house for most of her life. As is proper, she has had few conversations with men other than her father and none of them alone. She sees her world coming to an end. She's promised to a jealous, ill-tempered tippler for the rest of her life—if her father decides to finalize the contract. She's pursued by a courtly, charming, unmarried nobleman who has provided her with a glimpse of the sophisticated life at court that she will never come to enjoy. Her father is blind to everything but business." Her black eyes snapped. "I'm tired of you! *All of you!* Let her delight in her evening with Alessandro! What can possibly happen here? We are all around her like bars on a cage. God knows, you will own her soon enough!"

"Who's watching her now?" asked Rade with a sudden feeling of disquiet.

"Sofia, who is loyal to her last drop of blood."

Sofia is loyal to Caterina. Not to me. "Serpents are not known for trustworthiness," said Rade, looking back toward the grand chamber. *Keep it hidden, as a snake its legs.*

"Jealousy is unattractive in suitors and frowned on in polite society," admonished Nonna.

"It is you who should have been the priest," he muttered through clenched teeth, and then went angrily back into the great chamber with a long, unpriestly stride.

The pair of whom they'd spoken were no longer there. Yet he was mistaken. In the back of the room he caught sight of the golden cat and the plumes of the serpent. There'd been an interlude in the dancing and they'd paused to take refreshments and a respite from the dance. The two were conversing with a collection of flamboyant creatures and the unsteady bear. The bear was a comedy of swaying and weaving until it finally sat down, perhaps for good. As a variety of foods made their way around the room, Rade leaned against the painted walls wishing for it all to end so that he could go home. The musicians returned, tuned their instruments, and the dance began again. The gilded cat took her place in the pattern of the dance and the serpent extended his arm. Before they had taken five steps, Rade was struck by the horror of his discovery. Neither the cat, nor the snake, were known to him. They were impostors. Caterina and Alessandro had vanished.

He began to run. The party was now thronged with guests and Rade had no choice but to push and shove his way to the stairs. As he fought his way down them, he encountered Nonna coming up.

"They've gone!" he blurted out.

"Nonsense," rejoined Nonna, clutching a goblet, "I just saw them."

"You saw their costumes, not the persons inside. I tell you, *they're not here!*" He was desperate.

"Then you know the danger," returned the older woman, turning ashen. "Find them. Protect her. *Go quickly!*"

He raced for the quay where the gondolas had been moored, searching for Giovanni. The boatman was nowhere to be found. As he pressed between the lounging gondoliers, demanding news of Alessandro and his vessel, at last he found an answer.

"But they've gone to her house as they always do on Fridays, priest," said the boatman. He added, "This day might as well be a Friday."

"Whose house? It's important!" cried Rade.

"It's a strange destination for a cleric," muttered the short, thickset man. "But it's no secret," he said glancing around him. "The house of La Suzetta. You saw her at the ball. The golden cat! And so bold to come uninvited!"

La Suzetta. The courtesan. "How do I find it? Where do I go?"

"Father, it is beyond the Frari on the little square where the old woman is famous for her masks. The little house is very beautiful. Everyone knows it." The cowled figure was already running. *"At the least you might have offered me a blessing,"* yelled the boatman at the priest's retreating back.

A year ago, Rade might have run the distance in half the time but now he cursed himself for his lack of strength. Within minutes, his breath was tearing at his throat. The monk's robe caught on objects and wound its way around his legs so that it encumbered him and worked against his natural speed. He finally tore it off, bundling it under his arm, and raced on in linen shirt and hose. He had entered the crooked maze of alleyways that led to the other side of the quarter and the

Rialto bridge. He ran through mud and swamp, and over stones, bricks, and planks of wood. Construction clogged the paths and piles of refuse littered the streets. People filled the passageways: walking, sleeping, drinking, talking, and begging despite the February cold, hindering his progress and slowing him down. He forced himself to keep going, to stay agile, to draw another needed breath into painful lungs. Even when the bridge came into sight and he could see the dark bulk of its wooden siding, the usually slender slats of the central drawbridge were solid with bodies and waving torches. He lost more time fighting his way through the press of arguing factions to the distant maze of streets and alleys that led to the square.

He knew the square. He'd seen the little house and wondered at its ownership. It was very beautiful, painted on the front with Bacchantes and graces and gods. Between the pointed Gothic arches on the second floor were tiny bosses of curious antiquity and there were minuscule lions on the railings of the balcony. It was a house of pleasure. An abode of love. The treasured nest of an avowed courtesan. Fronting on the square but only a narrow passageway away from a small canal, its upper story glowed with gentle light. He prayed he was in time.

The entry door was locked and strongly made but the window grates were simple squares and good for climbing. Reaching up to the base of the graceful balcony, he felt around the carvings for protrusions to support his hands, and having found them, laboriously pulled himself up and over the railing. The priest's robe lay discarded in the street. Trying to dislodge the roundels of heavy glass with blows of his fist, and when that didn't work, his foot, which did, he forced the latch, not caring if they heard.

She was there. They were seated at a table, Alessandro half-rising at the sound of entry, reaching for his steel. The candles flickered on the sweetmeats, golden plate, and creamy linen. The room itself was a paradise of exquisite carvings and lovely tapestries. Rade had never seen such a room. It had an air of intimacy and mystery all its own.

As the glass fell in, she cried out, and then recognizing him, gasped out his name.

"Get out, Slav!" yelled Alessandro. *"What right have you to break into this house?"*

"I have... every right," said Rade, his voice hoarse, still fighting for breath. "She belongs... to me."

"I belong to no one," replied Caterina traitorously. "Least of all to you. Let us be. You've interrupted our supper." Her face was flushed with wine and anger.

"Do you know... this house?" asked Rade, advancing on the table.

The steel was out. "I should muzzle the dog," growled Alessandro. "Look at him! He brings the filth of the streets and the stink of the unwashed into the room."

"There is no cloaked misbehavior here," cried Caterina. "Alessandro has provided a surprise supper. We were nearly finished. We were about to return. *Why are you here?"*

"Whose house is it? Is it Alessandro's?" insisted Rade.

Caterina glanced at Alessandro who had begun to edge around the table. "It's the house of a friend," she said. "Rade, go home. *Please!"*

"But no friend of yours," said Rade. "Where is Giovanni? Nonna? Sofia? *Caterina, what were you thinking of?"*

Slowly, she stood up, moved around the table, and to Rade's dismay, slipped her hand over Alessandro's other, weaponless arm and leaned against him so that he stood beside her and they were as one. "I am absolutely safe in the care of Alessandro," she said. "We've never been allowed to be together by ourselves. Never truly alone. This was to be our secret. A little supper for two. Nothing more. He warned me you'd be jealous. He worried you'd make trouble. I see now he was right."

"Why, Caterina?" asked Rade softly.

She looked at Alessandro and smiled. "We love each other," she said simply.

"It's the god of wine who speaks," Rade said in a low voice.

"No, it is my heart," returned Caterina. She returned his gaze. "Our betrothal must be broken."

"She has no further use for you, Slav," declared Alessandro. "We have pledged. We are as married. There is no place for you here." He leaned over and kissed her with an intimacy that came of practice. Rade saw her respond in kind.

He grew more desperate. *"Look at me, Caterina!* The golden cat is still at the ball. So is the serpent."

"Is this true?" she said slowly, her words slightly slurred, glancing at Alessandro. "How could this be?"

"Caterina, stay awake," ordered Rade. *"What did you give her, Alessandro?* Was it in the wine?"

"I put nothing in the wine. If she's enjoyed more than her share, it's been of her own choosing."

"Why are you saying these things, Rade? You are casting dishonor on our actions," cried Caterina.

"Because they are dishonorable," replied Rade ominously.

"Ignore him. He burns with envy. He would say anything to destroy us," sneered Alessandro.

"You've built a house of lies," returned Rade. *"Caterina! For God's sake, listen to me!* The house belongs to La Suzetta, the courtesan. Has Alessandro asked for your hand in marriage? If so, why would he bring you here? *There is no honor in this house.*" He spat out the words.

"Tell me he lies, Alessandro," she whispered. "I know you love me." But her voice was less certain. "What's wrong, Alessandro?" Her voice trailed off and she began to cry.

Alessandro threw the sword and Rade ducked. The nobleman knocked the candles from the table and the room was plunged into night.

Rade's voice came through the darkness. "You brought her here to spoil her, to ruin her, to bring her down into the gutter. No matter that your plan has not succeeded. If, in the eyes of Venice, she has lost her honor, *I... will... kill you.*"

"Then you will hang from the gibbets like all the other felons. My blood is noble and I am known. *You are nothing.*" He spat it out. "A contract foreigner. An upstart. A man without family."

She was sobbing now, somewhere in the corner of the room. Rade could hear small movements and tried to guess the other man's intent.

"This affair is finished, Alessandro. Let her go."

"We are forsworn, Slav. Even if I leave, she'll follow me," declared the nobleman.

Alessandro was looking for his sword and Rade moved quietly through the darkness searching for it too. He dared not use his dagger, the room was so black. The glow from the fire in the next room illuminated only the doorway and the handsome bed inside it. There was a crash as something fell to the floor. Alessandro exclaimed, "I found it!" Rade could hear a sound of something sliding, muffled by hangings.

"Caterina," said Alessandro. "Come. We'll be together."

Her reply was lost in the crash of something breaking. Rade edged toward the sound.

"Now! Caterina!" cried the nobleman. *"Take my hand!"*

"No, Alessandro," breathed Caterina, weeping. "No. *Oh God, my love, I cannot.* Not without honor."

There was more sound, more sliding, and then, except for Caterina's grieving, silence.

"Caterina," Rade called softly, reaching out to her, "come over to me."

There were sounds outside the house. Someone beating on the door. Familiar voices. Rade took a chance, fumbled for his flint and steel, and lit a candle. Alessandro was gone, the tapestry caught up on a secret door. Caterina knelt against the wall, a shuddering, weeping form, wrapped round in cloth of gold. Rade knew better than to touch her. He went downstairs, unbolted the door, and told Battista and the others to wait below. He sent Alberico for her nurse and Sofia. Only when the men kept staring at him did he realize he was standing there, having shed the robe, wearing only a sweat-soaked linen shirt and hose, and both were filthy.

When it was over, at his own hearth, Rade burned the cloth of gold. He watched as the fibers shrank, and curled and blazed but the gold warped and fell like the strands of hair into the ashes. *You'll burn. I didn't say you'd die.* What he'd thought then wasn't what Vuk had meant. He knew now what that was. But that too had gone to ashes.

In Alberico's keeping, Sofia had gone, cloaked and hooded, from La Suzetta's to a canal near Simonetta's, and later, departing from Simonetta's water gate, sobbing into the cat mask on the stiff arm of Ludovico, had worn the costume back to the noble house. With the hood held closed over her hair but the cloak open to her dress, they'd made sure she would be seen by the gondoliers—the double of La Suzetta who'd left earlier with the silver snake.

Caterina, clothed as her maid, had been taken home on Giovanni's second trip after Rade had carried her to the nearest canal, Nonna, five steps behind him. In Rade's arms, Caterina's body had been as rigid as iron, as much from her desire not to be touched as from her grief. But it was what she'd whispered that had hurt the most.

"I will never come to you willingly," she'd said, weeping. "*Never!* God knows, only Alessandro has loved me for myself. For who I am. Not for my father's fortune. You... will never

have... what I would have given him. On my life, I swear it."
Her white hand tightened like a claw on his sleeve. "Do you
hear me? *I swear it!*"

He stood for a long time watching the embers die down.
They had, all of them, formed a protective circle around her
and kept it closed. Caterina's reputation had been protected. In
the eyes of the world, she remained chaste and marriageable.
Alessandro, wearing his suit of silver scales, had fled. She
would be safe from Alessandro—he could never reveal such a
dishonorable act.

It was early morning when Rade separated the gold from
the ashes. Put it into a small pottery container. It would stay
there until he figured out what to do with it. He rebuilt the
fire—it was getting cold in the Dorsoduro house—and there
were others to keep warm. He watched the flames lick at the
wood, devour it, and burn with a brilliant, sated glow. One
could buy love, physical love, on any street in Venice. Bone-
tired, he lay down on the bed, still in his soiled clothing. *It was
the gift he'd wanted.*

Chapter Nineteen

... because it is natural to touch more often the parts that hurt.
— *Seneca*

March, First Month of Venetian Year 1494

Spring was late. March followed February and Rade rarely saw her. It seemed futile to seek her out. He went about his daily routine as if nothing had happened. He spent more time with Mario. He continued to eat in the kitchen. He found tasks to oversee that demanded his absence from the noble house.

The days grew warmer. Almost half the hours saw light. Where there were gardens, the flowering trees dangled the tips of their branches over masonry walls, and when it rained, speckled the pavers with pale petals that dried and browned to look like scales. Blooms appeared in the markets. He thought more often of the spangling of wildflowers on the stony mountainsides above the bay. The simplicity, sparseness, and rough camaraderie of winter quarters. Even gratuitous violence and the managing of dissent. Readying the *bergantin* for launch, paying taxes, sharpening weapons, training men. Vuk and Miloš. Everything that had been and would likely never be again.

Now he lived in a world fueled by fish: they'd all eaten so much of it for Lent. In the mountains, they'd simply eaten what they had—except on those rare occasions when the priest had come to visit.

*   *   *   *   *

It was mid-March, two weeks since the year had turned, when Rade met the two members of the Slav brotherhood at the little oratory near the priory of St. John of Jerusalem on the *Rio della Pietà*. He knelt behind them on the stone under the gazes of St. Giorgio and St. Triphonius, crossed himself, and waited until the pavers had taken their toll of his knees and silence had overtaken the drone of their prayers. Finally, they rose and he followed them out. He'd never laid eyes on either one of them. When they reached the wooden bridge over the canal, they stopped.

"*Better one day with a falcon*," said the taller one, leaning over the railing.

"*Than a hundred days with a crow*," answered Rade.

The man nodded, stared at Rade's long black tunic, and grinned.

Rade frowned. "What can I do for *dikobraz*?"

"We need you to deliver something," replied the taller one, his eyes hooded, a great scar crossing his forehead above his brows.

"Another press to Cetinje?" asked Rade.

"Is that what they told you? It went to the monastery. At Obod."

The shorter one spoke. He was Albanian, not Slav. So much for the brotherhood. He had the kind of eyes that never stop moving. "In Shkodra, the Arianiti have begun to talk of an uprising. And there are rumors of the return of Duradj's brother."

"Stefan?" said Rade. "On the quay, where they bring in the Istrian stone, I heard he'd turned Turk."

The tall Slav nodded. "*The gate is too narrow for two steeds.* Stefan sailed off to the Porte. To Istanbul. What is it now? Eight years? Nine? When Ivan sent him as a hostage. Now I hear he's taken Skanderbeg's name." He spat. "If that's so, let him rot there."

"To take a hero's name does not make you one," said the Albanian, his gaze flickering. "At present, it's talk. Just talk. The prince says it pays to be prepared."

"Arms?"

"And coin. We have them. Can you do it?" replied the Slav.

"I'll have to contact a ship. I'll need a couple of weeks. When I know, I'll speak to Mordecai."

*   *   *   *   *

In the rain of early morning, Ludovico departed for his meeting at the *scuola*, or confraternity, to which he belonged, ready to do battle for the proposed redesign of its great chamber. Since Ludovico had spent half the day before going over the plans and muttering under his breath, Rade had taken pains to avoid him, picking the morning to deliver documents to a bank by the Rialto. When Rade returned, he was surprised to find the door to his workroom ajar and Nonna sitting in the only chair.

"I've counted the squares in the iron grille, the roundels in the window, the marble chips in the terrazzo, and I was just working up to the number of knots in the carpet on the table," said Nonna.

"Shall I return when Archimedes has worked out the volume of the room?"

"No," sighed Nonna, "I neglected to bring my abacus." She rearranged herself in the chair so that she looked Rade full in the face. "Close the door. We have matters to discuss."

He obediently did as she asked and leaned against the wall.

"She is filled with despair," began Nonna, looking at him intently.

"I've seen it."

"She can find no levity in life, even in that silly dog," returned Nonna. "I, who am accustomed to laughter, am reduced to hours of silence and tears. I cannot provide solace. I cannot bring back that *malfattore*. I wouldn't if I could." Her face crumpled. "She is injuring her soul."

"What do you want me to do?"

"I want you... to help bring back the Caterina she was two months ago," replied Nonna, regaining control.

He shook his head. "She's no longer that person."

"Nor is she the person she appears to be today," returned Nonna, rising from her chair. "Rade, we both love her. I look at you and I can see that. Help me. I have no one else to ask."

"How?" he asked softly.

"I don't know," murmured Nonna, and she went out, gently closing the door behind her.

*   *   *   *   *

He hadn't solved Nonna's problem. Instead he'd taken ship with Pasquale, had transferred the arms cargo to a fishing boat, and now waited on this rocky island among the ruined buildings below the stand of pines for the arrival of Miloš. He'd come a week early, shed the mask, and let the sunlight fall on his face for the first time in almost a year. Stripped to the waist, he'd found the spring, worked on the hut, having dug up the old bag of tools, reset the stones that had fallen, and had lived off cheese, biscuits and what he could catch in the sea. Outside sunburned skin and a swollen face, he was happier than he'd been in months.

"Christ's nails!" exclaimed Miloš, when he arrived a few days later, and Rade was bending over, gutting a fish he'd caught. "What happened to you?"

At first it was hard to know of what he spoke. He looked at Miloš and realized what he was staring at. He made a face. "I went to embrace a sea nymph and she turned out to be a submerged water gate."

"Must have been a long night at the tavern," replied Miloš, scanning the damage.

He grinned. "It was. Have you taken that wife?"

Miloš looked up, pleased. "I have." He raised an eyebrow. "*And* she has a child under her heart."

Rade thought of Ragazzo. It would be good to have a son. And said so. He added, "I always thought a woman would make trouble in winter quarters."

"I thought so as well. But there are others now. She's in a little house, near the church. I'd like to move her to the islands for the summer, but, she'd be alone so much and her family is from the village."

They began to discuss the cargo and the best way to land it and get it up into the mountains. "You know as well as I do I can't sail into the bay this time of year," said Miloš. "They'd catch us. We've already had one narrow escape. Ottoman Turk or Venetian, they're both after us." He grinned. "I guess we had too good a year."

"What about this year?"

"We took down a small trading galley last week. Stashed the cargo. Had to scuttle her. Left part of her crew on one of the Coronati." He shrugged, "The rest weren't worth saving. The bastards were trading with the Turks."

"Was that wise? Leaving some of them to be found?"

He shrugged. "They were only boys. Now that I'm going to be a father... " Miloš grinned, "I seem to see things differently. In a year or so, I may even want to do something lawful."

"They'll never let you," said Rade.

"The Venetians? They've let you."

"It's different." *He couldn't tell him about the mask.*

"How is it different?"

"It just is."

"That's no answer."

"Believe me, Miloš, I live a lie every hour of every day. I can never let my guard down. I can never unbend. It's like walking on thin ice that stretches on forever. After a while, one begins to think anything is better than this. Even death."

"Then why do you do it?"

"Vuk prophesied it." *And I felt it in the whirlwind.*

"Then you're a fool. Vuk's dead. His prophecies are dead. Walk away from it. I would."

Rade shook his head. "Too much that was foretold has taken place…" He shrugged. "But you and the others are outside it." He looked at Miloš. "If you want to change, sell the *bergantin* or trade your shares to the others. She's recognizable. You won't be able to keep her. Go somewhere south where other Slavs have gone. The Kingdom of Naples would do. I've heard there's a community there. And Ferrante wasn't fond of Venice." He grinned, "If I survive, someday, I'll come and find you. And we'll drink *raki* and talk of old times and count your many children."

"I'd like that," replied Miloš, smiling.

"But for now, we need to plot the devilry that supports our prince."

They settled on a plan with a longer land journey than wanted but it appeared the best solution. That region of the coast, south of the entrance to the bays, had known a recent rebellion. It'd been quelled by the Venetians but their rule was disliked and the clans still looked for vengeance wherever they could find it. And Miloš had a man from there on the galley. A man he trusted.

Later in the day, the men brought the *bergantin* from the leeward side of the island where it'd been moored. Under Miloš, he could see they'd become a close-knit crew who now included some faces he didn't know. The strongboxes and crates of weapons were loaded onto the ship. A few praiseworthy words were said about Zeta and cups were raised to the prince. Money changed hands. A week later, Rade was back in Venice, masked, trading on the Rialto, the plan forwarded through Mordecai to the Albanian. It was as if he'd never left.

*   *   *   *   *

"Nonna told me you've come to read to me." She knew she looked like an invalid. There were dark circles under her eyes and her clothes were loose. The wide brim of her sun hat shielded her face. The garden bench was marble, and warm in the sun, and the garden, which had always been on the other side of the wall from the noble house, was now accessible. She'd put a cushion on the seat, it was so uncomfortable.

"What happened to the owners of the house?" asked Rade, seating himself on the grass.

"Gone to Candia for two years. To govern." She looked away. It was hard to look at him and not remember. She tried to swallow her unhappiness. "Father leased the garden. Cleared out the old bricked-up opening and put in a gate." She looked back at him with little interest. "You were away somewhere. The house is closed. Boarded up." She saw him glance back at the house as if he'd never really seen it.

Nonna seated a short distance away, rearranged her needlework, and when part of it fell from her lap, shooed away Orseolo who rushed over to see if it was edible. In Orseolo's book, they had all found to their sorrow, most things were edible. They just weren't digestible.

"Are we to begin with Virgil?" Caterina inquired, not really looking at the book he was carrying. *The whole exercise was so tiresome.* "*Arma virumque cano* / I sing of warfare and a man at war." She made an effort. "You needn't do this. I am content with silence."

"I've brought something lighter. Nonna suggested it." He held out the book. "I've never read it."

The book in his hand looked familiar. She took it, undid the clasps, opened the leather covers, and then snapped it shut. "Petrarch," she said in a low voice. *"How could you!"*

"Have I offended you?" he asked, looking puzzled. "Surely it's alluded to and quoted as much as any other."

"It's the volume Alessandro gave me," she said biting her lip, her eyes filling with tears.

She saw him glance at Nonna. She saw Nonna look away. He shut his eyes and took a long breath.

She couldn't help herself. She felt the pain rise up in her throat and the anger choke her. In silence, she sat on the bench, tears welling up and dripping down her cheeks. Through her veil of despair, she watched him concentrate on pulling up the stems of grasses. Watched him crush the flowers on the little plants in-between. Her fingers tightened on the book. *If anyone had ruined her life, it wasn't Alessandro. It was Rade.* After a long while, possibly an hour, he got up without a word and let himself out the gate.

*   *   *   *   *

For a pittance. Rade bought a small, disused rowboat off a decrepit carrack in the harbor. A smuggler's boat they'd said. It was big enough for one man with a passenger to row around the canals and out into the lagoon, not with the long elegant stroke of the standing gondolier but with the hard swinging pull of the seated mariner. Even though it suffered from a slow leak and the wood was worm eaten, the exercise felt good, and the rising bilge water added impetus to the effort. He made no effort to repair it. It was as if he dared the lagoon to put an end to its existence—and perhaps his own.

His frustrations lessened. There was a small sense of freedom of movement, the kind he'd enjoyed on the *bergantin*. He asked Alberico to accompany him, partly for the added weight to strengthen his back and partly to advise on oncoming vessels and channels in the lagoon. In all kinds of weather, he rowed and the bowman sat solidly in the stern. Alberico never refused the invitation. He never complained. He was as weighty as a boulder, and about as talkative. In Rade's eyes, the situation was as near to perfect as it could get.

The menservants were amused by the size of his boat.

He went out to where it was moored one April evening to find that they were all in it. Only inches of freeboard remained, it was so crowded with heavy bodies. The floorboards were already awash.

"We've come for a tour," announced Battista, ensconced in the stern.

"The Arsenal or Murano?" asked Rade, handing over the oars to the group of grinning musclemen.

"Ships and arms or cherries and glass?" inquired Battista. The vote was for cherries.

"Murano," said Rade. He climbed in. The boat sank. It was then that he discovered that Alberico didn't know how to swim. Even while he was drowning, the bowman didn't make much noise. Rade dragged Alberico to the quay, where, one by one, the other guards hoisted themselves out of the lagoon like glistening whales, and stomped off, no longer amused. There weren't any cherries this time of year anyway. He pulled the heavy, sputtering bowman out of the water himself. He had to hire a bargeman to pull up the boat, but by then, the bargeman reported, it was naught but a pile of planks.

*   *   *   *   *

The butcher's boy brought an unexpected note. The first since La Suzetta. Caterina took it from Sofia, motioned for her to leave, and then unfolded it. She felt her heart stop. *Cara, I have married.* She began, despite herself, to shiver. After a while, she went to the *cassone*, lifted the heavy lid, and dug out the bone casket, concealed between the linens, where she kept her small cache of remembrances. *I burn with love for you as ever.* One by one, she took out and unfolded his notes that she'd read so many times. So often that they were tear-stained, limp and faded. *The marriage is a great hardship.* Soon they would have much in common. Each married to another, unwanted spouse. *My father forced this on me.* How could she bear it? She held the note to her lips. And then to her heart. He was as much as prisoner of fortune as she was. *Is there somewhere we could meet?* She arranged the little pieces of paper carefully on the bed, smoothed out, in the order they had come, the only one of different origin being the note from the wrappings of the golden cat. *My dearest love.* She held the new note against her heart a second time and felt her heartbeat quicken. Then she flattened it out and gently placed it next to the last of the others: the costume note from Simonetta. *She would go to him.* Her decision took her breath away.

She reached up to get the box of shards from the shelf, opened it, touched the one recognizable animal and this time she let its razor edge cut her finger and the blood drip into the box. *By God or without Him, she would go to him.* She no longer cared what they thought. They were wrong. All of them. He hadn't tried to do something dishonorable. It had simply looked that way. And they'd all used it against him. To blacken his name. She hated them for it. And now, her commitment to his love, to his suffering, would be sealed in her own blood.

When the blood stopped, she put her finger in her mouth and tasted the last of it. He needed her. *She would go to him.* If a child came of it, it would be a child of their love. Their child. Who would ever know, with marriage only six weeks away, which man had been the father? Caterina put the box of shards back on the shelf. She crossed herself before the painted Virgin. The ritual completed, she wound a little piece of cloth around her finger and turned to put the notes back in the ivory casket. As she did so, something unexpected caught her eye. She froze. The handwriting on Simonetta's note was an exact replica of the handwriting on all the others. The golden cat hadn't come from Simonetta. It had come from Alessandro.

There was such a shriek from the room that Sofia, running, took the stairs two at a time.

*   *   *   *   *

He took time out on days that had fewer tasks and mild weather, with Ludovico's blessing and Nonna's insistence, to read her the poems. It was a thankless task. About as thorny as the roses growing on the trellis. And she received them like a prisoner, who wanted to starve, and was being force fed. So he hated even more the glowing, lovelorn words of Petrarch—even though they'd worked their way into his soul.

She was seated as usual on the garden bench, her hat shading her face, her eyes large and dark in the shadow. She rose as he approached and came toward him, Orseolo tangling himself in the hem of her dress. He thought she looked fragile, almost ethereal, and no longer the beautiful, vibrant young woman who had stood in the field outside the villa in August. She'd become a pale, sad shadow of what had so attracted him. And he thought *I have done this to her.*

"You were right about Alessandro."

He said nothing. Just looked at her.

"I've been a fool."

"You could never be a fool."

She smiled but it was a sorrowful smile. "Walk with me. I need to tell you something."

They walked along the wall in silence, sunlight glistening on the moist surface of the stone. Orseolo gave up their company, barking, for something small that fled into a bush. Nonna looked up and smiled. He noticed Caterina's right hand; she had a small bandage tied around her finger tip.

"You've hurt yourself."

"It's nothing. A thorn from a rose cutting." She looked at him. "I've put salt on it."

They came into the shadow of the boarded-up house and she stopped. "It's hard for me to say this, so, if you can, hear me out before you reply."

With a sinking feeling, he wondered if this would be the end.

"I will honor the contract."

He started to smile.

She bit her lip and then looked up at him. "Unlike what I said to you... on that terrible day, I will endure willingly whatever a husband does to gain pleasure from a wife."

He stared at her as if he'd never known her.

She looked away. "I will bear your children." She went on, "When you've gotten what you wished for—my father's fortune, his business, the children you will beget on me—I beg..." she looked at him pleadingly, "I beg that you allow me to retire from this world. To enter a convent, here or somewhere else, so that I may find some measure of peace." She sighed, "I'm so very tired of this life."

He started to speak.

"No, wait... can we agree to make that bargain?"

Rade stood for a time looking at the grass at his feet.

Finally he took her bandaged hand in his, turned it over, and gently kissed her palm. He didn't look at her face. He left her standing in the shadow, his silence unbroken, and walked over to the bench where he placed the book of Petrarch on the white, grainy surface of the marble.

Peace I do not find, and I have no wish to make war; and I fear and hope, and burn and am of ice; and I fly above the heavens and lie on the ground; and I grasp nothing and embrace all the world.

He let himself out the gate.

*   *   *   *   *

The prow of the boat slid up the mud bank of the island of mock fights. It was Sunday morning. The four men took out their blunted weapons and eyed them looking for past damage and rough edges and then tied on the quilted pads that protected their torsos.

"Who wants to be paired off with Battista?" asked Antonio brightly, looking around. No one said anything. "No volunteers to be beaten into the mud? Then we'll draw lots. Short lot gets to choose."

Antonio broke some twigs off the saplings. He cut three the same and one short and held them out in his fist. They each took a twig. Rade turned his over in his hand. He'd drawn the short one.

He stood still a moment and then said, "Hold your swords up. I'll strike the one I want to fight." And then, without hesitation, struck down the blades of all three.

"Christ's thorns, you must be full of piss and vinegar," remarked Antonio. "Who's to be first?"

"I'll take you all on. I feel like killing someone today."

"Celebration of your upcoming marriage?"

So they all knew. "Something like that." *But what did they know?*

"You'll get the crap beaten out of you," said Battista. "It's going to be tough to avoid your face."

"I no longer need to worry about my face."

"That's good," said Antonio, flexing his arms, "because you're going to look like something the butcher threw out."

When they came at him, he fought with all the wild abandon he'd employed in that pass so long ago. Twisting, turning, lashing out with the sword and then the dagger. Catching blows on the guard of each. Parrying their strokes. Again and again and again. Finally Battista, having been struck several times, threw caution to the winds and came after him. He saw Alberico parry Battista's cut that was aimed at his cheek and he turned on Alberico as well. "Fight like the enemy," he snarled, "or I'll take you down anyway."

Antonio came at him then. The blunt sword slashing down on his shoulder and he turned from Battista to parry this new attack. He threw his weight against Antonio's dagger, kicked out, and sent him staggering into the water, holding his crotch.

"Fucking bastard!"

"Haven't got the balls for this?" Rade said and laughed. "Is that true of the rest of you?"

It was then that Battista's long sword raked his back and he turned just as the huge man, red-faced and heaving with anger, caught him by the throat with his dagger. *"Yield!"*

"If I don't?"

Battista looked like a bear getting ready for a final swipe at its prey. "Then I'll cut your throat, *stronzo.*"

"Then cut it," snarled Rade, *"you spineless bastard!"*

It was then that Alberico hit him hard in the back of the head with the guard of his sword. Rade dropped like a stone.

Breathing hard, the three men stood around the sprawled body.

"Even with a dull blade, I almost cut his throat. Christ's

nails, what got into the bastard?"

"I don't know, he's been pretty quiet the last couple of days."

"It must be a woman," said Alberico, thoughtfully. He looked up. "It's always a woman." He glanced at Rade. "He's coming around. Just in time for church."

*   *   *   *   *

In part it was a woman, and in part, it wasn't. A few days before, Rade had gone out to Mestre in response to a note from Mordecai. It had said, "Come. Now or as soon as you are able."

The house looked quietly prosperous. He saw a number of people on the street in the dress that identified them as Jews. Most avoided his eyes. He knocked, the door swung open, and he walked into the familiar, orderly room.

He smiled. "Mordecai!"

"You look well, my Slav friend."

"What is it?"

"Sit. I have *raki*. You'll need a drink."

"Have I lost my fortune?"

"No. It's not that."

"Have *you* lost my fortune?"

"You know as well as I do most of it is invested with messer Vinciguerra."

"Then what is it?"

Mordecai sat down and sank his face into his beard. He handed Rade a cup. "Drink." He waited until Rade had done so. "It's winter quarters," he said.

"What do you mean by that?"

"It's gone. Even the village is gone."

Rade said the first thing that came into his head. "But they're not there."

"The women were," replied Mordecai. "The villagers were. The *akinjis* barricaded them in their houses. Piled up brush. Burned them. Even their dogs."

Rade shut his eyes. "Miloš's wife?"

"All of them."

"Holy God…" He remembered the blackened walls… but when he looked at Mordecai, his walls too, and after that, his face, his body, began to blacken. His sight began to blur. He reached out blindly for something to hold on to. His hand found a hard surface but he no longer knew what it was. And he felt the whirlwind come upon him, the darkness of the storm eclipse everything he was, and the crushing weight of fate fall upon his soul. It was then that he saw them, all of them, Miloš included, hanging from the spars of a round ship. And he thought he must be hanging there too because he could almost touch their swollen, distorted faces. Their blackened skin. And he was sharply aware that Miloš had been tortured, from his dislocated shoulders to the pits where his eyes had been. When he looked down, the *bergantin* sailed in the carrack's wake, a Venetian banner on her mast, and she was manned by strangers. The nausea of fear rose up, he was sick, and the blackness overtook him.

"Rade? Can you hear me?"

"It's all right," he mumbled. "Give me a moment."

"Can you sit up?"

"It's all right," he said again.

"But it isn't," insisted Mordecai. "When you've prepared yourself, there's more."

Rade looked up blearily. "They're all dead," he said in a low voice. "Hung by the Venetians."

Mordecai looked stunned. "How could you know that? The ship doesn't dock until the morrow. I had it from a faster vessel."

"Fate's unwanted gift," Rade said, shaken. "It used to be

premonition. It's gone beyond that. I saw them. God and St. John," he looked up at Mordecai, "I *saw* them dead." *As if I were one of them.*

Chapter Twenty

Life is one long struggle in the dark.
—Lucretius

May, Third Month of Venetian Year 1494

"Where are they tonight?" said Ludovico, regarding Rade's empty place. "We finally return to a semblance of civilization and once again he isn't here. *Sofia?*"

She appeared in the doorway.

"Who's eating in the kitchen?"

"Cook. Me."

"No one else? Not even Giovanni?"

"No, messer Vinciguerra. He's at the finish."

"The finish of what?"

"The race. He calls the winner and awards the prize."

"God's blood, not another running race on the Lido!"

"Oh no, messer Vinciguerra, this one is by sea. In boats."

Ludovico groaned. "Go back down to supper, Sofia." He looked at Caterina and Nonna. "Did you know about this? I think they've all gone mad!"

"It's spring," replied Nonna. "The sap rises."

"Running races, archery contests, more of those mock fights, they can hardly lift a bale in the course of a day's work."

"You know that isn't true," countered Nonna. "They unloaded a whole cargo yesterday. Even Rade."

"Still, it can't go on forever. Someone's bound to get hurt. Besides I'd like to see my daughter's betrothed at the table so we can discuss the wedding."

"It's so small. So private," said Nonna. "Does that matter so much?" She looked at Caterina. "You wanted it that way."

Caterina sat primly in her place, like a dove with its wings folded, eyes downcast so that they wouldn't guess that another night without Rade at the table was a night she didn't have to think about the future.

Nonna looked up from her plate. "It must be a rite of passage," she said. "Like something the youths of the Calze might engage in. His life is about to change."

*   *   *   *   *

The creak of oars against their cupped wooden holders, the *forcole*, the splash of blades, labored breathing, and an occasional oath, accompanied the thrust of the low-sided boat through the lagoon, in pursuit of the other craft, several lengths ahead. Silhouetted against a pink sky in a matching lake, Venetian-style, the men stood, facing their destination, two hands on the single oar, rowing with nearly perpendicular strokes, caught up in the synchronized rhythm of the team. Malamocco would be the first leg of the triangle, San Niccolo, the second, and the last, home. Rade, Alberico, and Antonio manned one boat, and Battista and the two bargemen, Filippo and Erberto, the other.

Other than the occasional island, the black sticks of the *bricole*, the channel markers, were the only outstanding features in the watery landscape. Knowing it would still be more than an hour of stout rowing to the break in the sandbar, the rowers cut obliquely across the ebbing tide, the stern oar employed on one side, the other two oars, one behind the other, opposite, straining to outrun each other.

Battista's boat was winning. As always, the man was a mountain of strength and a bottomless well of endurance. With the brute force of a bear, the huge man bore down on his oar while his crew strove to keep up with him. After they'd cleared the canal in Dorsoduro, Battista's craft had surged to the lead, and held it ever since. Rade and his men followed with long, energetic strokes, struggling to close the gap but with little success. They were well out into the middle now, alone in the vastness of the watery wastes, Venice fading fast in the distance. The tide continued to fall and puffs of cloud floated across the blush of sunset.

They ignored the markings for the larger vessels, directing their small craft in as straight a line as possible for the Malamocco cut—even as the mud flats rose to the surface of the water. Each deposit of silt had its own character, color, and inhabitants. The last were for the most part either buried in silt or wrapped in the lethargy of evening. In Rade's boat, they had all gotten out again, sloshing through mud up to their knees, pushing their vessel over another protruding island of ooze. The water, despite its fading bloom of pink, had all the warmth of melted snow and Alberico, who'd been foolish enough to jump out of the boat wearing shoes, had already lost both of them in the chilly mire.

The light had dimmed by the time they reached the port and the moon tide rushed out through the cut into the embrace of the Adriatic and the little boats went with it. The placid lagoon became the shifting sea. Beyond the cut, a submerged bar threw up its own peculiar turbulence. The wind gathered strength. Small breakers advanced upon the barrier bars as the rowers turned the bows of their two boats northeast to follow the gentle curve of the beach. Dusk was a sobering curtain on a limitless horizon, but the full moon was rising, and the silver sands led away in the dark toward San Niccolo where there was a lighthouse.

The contest changed. What had begun as a race between men grew into a fight for headway against the power of the sea. The boats, which, with their shallow draft and low sides, adapted well enough to the lagoon, were not designed for the rising crests and rolling troughs of open sea. They began to take on water. The rowers were hard-pressed to keep their balance and every now and then, one man quit his oar and dropped down to fling the unwelcome Adriatic from the bilges.

The wind whipped up an occasional whitecap. With choppy, rolling force, the waves threatened to draw them ever further out with the tide. Slowly Battista lost his extensive lead and the two boats continued only a few lengths apart, calling to each other in the night. It was hard not to look longingly to the left. The lifeline remained the shining beach—but those who left their boat upon its saving sands would lose the race.

Their hands were bleeding. The blisters that had arisen in the first hour of the contest had turned into sores. The borrowed *fisolere*, built for duck hunting, were an assembly of unfamiliar surfaces on which to bark shins and stub toes. The sweat that had cooled the rowers in the lagoon had combined with the sea spray and cold night air to envelop them in clammy misery and chafed limbs.

"*Why*, by all the saints, did we accept your invitation for this race?" shouted Battista over the sound of wind and waves.

"For the joy of surviving this endeavor," returned Rade, gritting his teeth against another wash of saltwater.

Battista shouted back an unrepeatable comment.

"I thought it was something to do with poetry," growled Alberico in the stern. "*To enclose the sea in a glass* or something."

"That too," returned Rade, shaking off another wash of water. "Where's the flask?"

"I no longer care," muttered Antonio from behind Rade. "I think I left it on the last mudflat. The one with the fringe of reeds."

"You jest," said Alberico, already regretting his comment.

"I find no humor in this windy hell," shot back Antonio.

"We have to go back," shouted Rade, and to Alberico's utter disbelief, he violently reversed his oar. There was a chorus of shouts and curses as the boat slewed around in the water and the second boat nearly collided with them.

"Oh dear God, St. Mark, and St. Theodore, patron of soldiers, save us from this lunatic who has put us all in peril," cried Alberico as he fought to resume their course.

"Turn around," ordered Rade. He meant it.

Antonio threw down his oar and hurled himself forward, knocking Rade face first into the long wooden prow of the boat. As Rade twisted around to face his attacker, Antonio slammed his head against the railing and the two men wrestled, their bodies straddling the craft while Alberico, though thrown to his knees, tried desperately to retrieve the oars as well as keep them afloat. In the midst of it all, the gray form of Battista rose out of the moonlight and a large hand grasped Antonio by the collar of his doublet and forced him back toward the stern. The other man lay gasping and shaking his head in the cleft of the bow surrounded by a rising flood of questions. The boats were joined now with a bridge of hands, rolling unsteadily in the surge and drifting with the current. Alberico realized they'd nearly reached the San Niccolo port, the entrance to the lagoon. The lighthouse beckoned from the sandbar. Beyond the cut was the lagoon, the welcoming *bacino* of San Marco, and home.

Battista's roar beat out the cacophony of noise. *"What on God's earth brought you to this?"*

"The fucking glass," replied Antonio, shaking off the restraining hand.

"It's here. At my feet," announced Alberico in a subdued voice, producing a dark object wrapped in sacking. "It was here all the time."

"Then we can go on," said Rade's voice from the bow. "Fill it and give it to me."

The worst of it was over but there was still the final leg to overcome. The ensign, lantern lit, at the castellated lighthouse of the second cut had been hoisted. It meant the tide had turned. There was a ragged cheer as they pointed their little boats towards Venice and its outlying islands. As the lagoon spread its welcoming arms around them, the rowers knew there would be an end. When they reached the Dorsoduro quay, there was no winner. The boats were equal. The race, a draw. Giovanni, shaken from his old man's slumber, split the prize. The rowers dragged themselves back to their straw pallets and linen feather sacks and fell upon them in utter exhaustion. Filippo and Erberto staggered back to their barge, a *ducat* each in a clenched fist. Of them all, only Rade, carefully cradling the glass, owned a real bed.

To base the race on a few words of Petrarch had been one more effort to push himself as far as he could and still survive. Or not survive. He was so tired that only fragments of the verse came back to him:

Perhaps I thought I could count the stars one by one and enclose the sea in a little glass...

He pushed open the door to his room.

... if at times I flee, in Heaven and earth she has circumscribed my steps, for she is always present to my weary eyes, so that I am all consumed ...

He wearily placed the glass flask on the table near the bed and flung himself onto the mattress.

... from the thought of her I gain a stay of death.

*   *   *   *   *

Alberico stood within the sacrosanct walls of Ludovico's *studiolo*. He had only been in it once before, on the day of the interview, before he'd been hired. He had never noticed the books. There were so many, he wondered if Ludovico had actually read them.

"It's gone on too long," said Ludovico, from his chair. "I'm disturbed by this ongoing, reckless behavior. Three nights ago, when the wind blew up, all of you could have drowned."

But we didn't, thought Alberico, concealing the sores on his hands. He looked longingly at the exit to the room.

"You were fortunate God took you under his wing," said his employer. "Go back to the house. I want you to search his room. There may be something I should know."

Alberico, who had no wish to be a spy—that had changed long ago—nodded dutifully.

"We'll be at the bank on the Rialto. After that, I'll keep him with me all afternoon."

"Yes, messer Vinciguerra."

"Don't get caught."

"I won't."

"Report back on the morrow."

He nodded.

It was easy to gain access. The door had no lock and the room was only inaccessible when Rade pushed a chest against the entrance. Except for the glass flask of water, still filled and covered, that had caused all the trouble, the bowman found the usual assortment of things: a collection of shaving items; a dog-eared book; the oars for Rade's sunken boat; and oddly, a chest of neatly packaged belongings, folded up in bundles, tied in string, with notes on them. He spent a long time looking at the packages in the chest. He knew all the names on the notes and recognized most of the clothing. Only a few items remained without designation. Even the weapons were tagged. Rade's second-best cloak and a pair of shoes were addressed to

Alberico. Their feet were the same size. There was more in the note but the bowman could only read his name.

Alberico stood quietly, thinking of all the ribbing he'd received over the shoes he'd lost in the mud. Rade had been the worst of them. He looked down at his feet. The shoes he had on were coming apart at the seams. It was a long time before he closed the chest. He made sure that when he left, everything was just as he'd found it. To Ludovico, he reported a state of normalcy. To the others, he said nothing.

*   *   *   *   *

The stars confirmed a fortuitous outcome for Caterina on the day he'd chosen. He'd paid and not asked the astrologer for his own. It was now two days before the wedding. Rade peeled the mask back to his hairline—he'd grown lazy about removing it—shaved in the glimmer of the candlelit looking glass, and reapplied the ointment so that the disguise adhered to his face. He pulled on a clean linen shirt, his dark hose, and shrugged on the old, faded leather doublet that belonged to his brigand days in the Adriatic. He tied the points, surveyed the room, and then quietly let himself out of the house.

In the darkness before dawn, he walked across half the length of Venice to the oratory, found the key where he'd been told it was concealed, and once inside, prostrated himself, arms out and forehead against the stone, and confessed to the two saints who were known to him. Afterwards he put coin in the box and lit candles for Vuk, Miloš, and the others who had died. He thought they might forgive the wrong church if it had the right saints. He put the key back where he'd found it.

His mind and body were honed. He was as strong and fit as he had ever been. He thought he could endure almost anything that came to pass but he still worried about the hour or two in the garden. The room had been left swept and orderly. The instructions, laid out on the bed in a sealed packet, addressed to Mordecai. To his surprise, he'd had to step over Alberico, asleep on his pallet outside his door. The bowman must have dragged it down from the room above. Something he never did. At the last, he'd dipped his fingers in the flask of sea water, crossed himself—God would not approve—and emptied the rest into the lagoon. Afterwards, he'd sent the flask spinning into the water.

*   *   *   *   *

The sun, burning off the last of the morning fog, was milk-white. He stood inside the gate near the trellis. The rosebuds, beaded with moisture, arched and pressed their way along the arbor, searching for the light. Where the noble house overlooked the garden, a line of baby swallows perched expectantly on a drying pole. Somewhere, beyond the wall, seagulls mewed and spiraled anxiously above the limpid surface of the lagoon. Within, the marble bench gleamed in solitary splendor. The almond tree was robed in green.

She was late. But then the gate swung open and she came in, her *camora*, cornflower blue. Her hair unbound except for a few small braids. Pattens on her feet. Her sun hat in her hand.

He added that image to the others: the girl in the field, the evening of her saint's day, the return from Padua, even the courtship dance of the golden cat.

"As you asked," she said, "I came alone. I'm late."

"There's time enough."

She took in the old ruffian's doublet he was wearing. "Are you going somewhere?"

He smiled ruefully. "I have something of consequence to tell you." He led the way to Nonna's seat at the end of the arbor.

She seated herself and looked up. "Should Father be

here?"

"What man, waiting to stand and be judged," he said evenly, "would not prefer the goddess to the goddess' father? Besides," he smiled, "in Venice, Justice is a woman."

She needed time to absorb this. "What is it in Zeta?"

"Dusan's law code. I'll just say, it's not particularly Roman Catholic. And," he grinned, "I should be long dead." He put a hand on the trellis and looked up into the eager branching of rose leaves. When his gaze came back, it was intensely blue.

"I see. I'm to judge," she sighed, readjusting a tie on her sleeve. But she didn't truly see. *What could be so terrible that her father couldn't hear it?* She straightened her back and rearranged her skirts. "In that case, I will, as best I can, assume the *sedes sapienta* and ready the scales and the sword." She added, trying to lighten the weight of it, "I can't speak for the archangels."

"No matter," he replied distantly. "They've already been informed." He walked away, stopped, and came back.

In the half-shaded arbor, she couldn't quite see his expression but she felt the stirrings of foreboding.

After a pause, he said matter-of-factly, "I am not the man you think I am."

"What?" she queried, startled. "What are you saying?"

He repeated it.

Her eyes grew wide. "I don't understand you."

Just listen. It will be what you want to hear. He walked the length of the trellis and turned back. "I bring you no name. Nothing of value, despite what I've led your father to believe." He held her gaze. "I am the last of my family. In six generations, from the knight who survived the Field of the Blackbirds to my grandfather's dwelling on the shores of Shkodra to my father's house in the karst of Zeta, the height of my family's habitation has been equaled only by the depth of our misfortune."

She took a moment to absorb this. It didn't make sense. "You arrived here a man of means," protested Caterina.

"It was not based on inheritance."

"You grew up with some level of refinement," she persisted. "You write. You speak Venetian. Read Latin. You are adept at commerce, mathematics, can read the heavens for navigation."

"I was born in a one-room hut," he countered, "in the company of sheep. There was an open hearth in the center. A hole in the roof. We didn't own a book." He looked at the disbelief on her face.

"Caterina," he said, "in life, there is no *ducat* without two faces."

*   *   *   *   *

For a time, until she became aware of the glare of the sun, she sat there disbelieving. Finally she put on the hat and was glad of the relief it gave and the shadow in which she could hide her misgivings.

He talked about his father. About a raid he took part in. When he moved, the bars of the arbor flowed across his features. His father had died in some horrible way that she didn't understand.

He said, "I never saw his face again."

His mother's grieving had been epic, unceasing, and filled with self-inflicted pain. She'd lost the child she carried. The first winter was difficult, the second worse. Despite their efforts, it was clear the house needed an adult male. By the following spring, his mother attired herself in her wedding clothes, took Rade, and went to see the elders. She had no family to go back to. A new marriage was arranged. His father's kinsmen chose to give his mother to a distant cousin, a recent arrival from the lowlands, a former soldier. It turned out the new husband was *ougasnik.*

"*Ougasnik?*"

He searched for the meaning. "A burner-out. The end of his line. Doubly so because he couldn't get a child on my mother." His expression grew unreadable.

"Was it important? He had you."

He hesitated. "It was important to him." Rade shrugged. "People talk. After a time, he couldn't bear it—it became something so shameful that he felt dishonored. As I told you, my mother had lost her second child and he began to say she'd willed it. That she'd damaged her body. That she was no better than... a woman of the street."

"How cruel!"

"At first, he said that in the summer at the communal pastures when my mother wasn't there. When all the men were there. When I was there. She was still safe in the house for the summer. When, as a child, I challenged him, I was seen as disobedient. Something easily remedied."

"I see."

"I have never told anyone this," he said suddenly.

"I will keep it to myself."

He went on. "In the winter, it was different. The houses are scattered. Ours was small. Isolated. It was easy to anger him. He could have his way. So... he beat her."

"And you?"

He said obliquely, "Whenever he saw me, he was reminded of his failure..." He didn't finish. He dug his foot into the earth. "I never kept my promise to my father."

"What promise?'

"To protect her."

"Rade..." She put out a hand to touch him. He was that close.

"*I should have killed the bastard,*" he said, brushing it off.

By the fourth spring, he could support that life no longer.

His mother no longer spoke. She no longer tried to defend him. He and his stepfather fought constantly but he was no match for his tormentor. There was a particularly savage beating. He managed to cut the man. He didn't know how badly. There was a lot of blood. He wasn't sure whose. And then something happened, something portentous, something he couldn't explain. Afterwards he fled the house, turned his back on the mountains, and took the path to the sea.

Her heart bled for him. His was a tale of poverty, without nobility, redemption, or remorse.

The mist had gone, leaving an incongruous blue enamel sky. The sun became a blazing disk. Caterina sat quietly, shaded by the brim of her hat and the dwindling shadow of the trellis, listening, while Rade paced back and forth under the arbor—like an animal in a cage.

"I'd abandoned everything, all ties, blood ties... to my father, my clan, my ancestors." He looked at her. "I'd set myself up for blood revenge. Like vendetta in your country. I could never go back."

In Cattaro, the Venetian-ruled settlement on the bay, he'd looked for work. Nine years old, ill-used and unkempt, he'd lived where and how he could. He didn't elaborate except to say, along the way, he discarded everything he was: his code of behavior, his religion, even his ability to forgive.

She saw the poor sleeping under the bridge. Their filth. Their stench. Their misery. She'd never thought about how they'd come to be there. She closed her eyes. "But you survived."

"Even a beggar tries to hold on to life." He thought of Vuk. "When winter came, I stole."

The degradation of his life kept growing, like an errant root that invades a carefully constructed wall and takes the stones apart. To Caterina, it was like being buried alive. *How could she have gone from the veiled cruelty of Ariosto, to the*

homicidal jealousy of the boys who could well have been her
brothers, to the deceit of Alessandro, to this? Who would
marry a thief? She had to work to handle her distress. She
managed to get out the words, "You were fortunate you
weren't caught."

"I *was* caught," Rade said, with a harsh laugh. "And
publicly punished. Any good fortune to be had was, I suppose,
in being flogged. I could have had my hand cut off." He
looked away. "Of course, I didn't think so at the time." They
had very nearly beaten him to death.

She tried to keep the dismay out of her voice. "Yet
somehow you found redemption."

"A stranger took pity on me."

"Why?"

He shrugged. "I have blue eyes."

Whatever that meant was lost on her.

"He took me back to a monastery on an island where he
lived as a layman. He was Venetian. Well born. He had run
away from some other life."

"I'm glad one of my countrymen was kind to you."

"I needed kindness," he replied obliquely. "He took care
of me. Healed my wounds. Taught me Latin, Venetian, all
those other things you most admire—except navigation. It only
lasted a few years." He caught her gaze. "I loved him, despite
everything." His eyes glittered among the bars of shade. "In
that time, for my keep as his servant, I performed whatever
service he desired."

The man's childhood was a nightmare. First an unwanted
step child, then a beggar, now a servant. "My heart weeps
for…"

"I don't want your pity," interrupted Rade. "I've told you
this for clarity, not sympathy. I promised to reveal my past.
This is part of who I am."

She said desperately, "I have to get out of the sun." She

rose and walked over to the shade cast by the house and sighed with relief. He eventually followed. She said, taking off her sun hat, and leaning her head back against the wall, "What happened to him?"

"The question ought to be what happened to me. He found another boy to serve him. He literally pushed me out of a boat in the middle of the bay. In those days, I didn't know how to swim." He caught her gaze. "I would never have made the shore."

She looked appalled.

Something like a smile crossed his lips. "Another man fished me out. Vuk. An older man. A Slav. With him, I found my calling."

"I hope he was a far better person."

"He was good to me. Like a godfather."

She thought of the boy he had been. "So you found some level of affection."

"In my own way." He looked at her. "That kind of sentiment weakens a man. And I had grown up."

"Where is this Vuk, now?"

His eyes were dark in the shade. Almost black. "Dead. They hung him in the piazza in October." He paused. "For theft."

*   *   *   *   *

For Alberico, sleeping outside Rade's door, the normal sounds of the waterfront had been muted. He was not aware of morning until Battista prodded him with his foot.

"Going to sleep all day, you sluggard? What are you doing down here?"

"*Christ's nails*, you're standing on my hand!"

"Is that what it is." Battista moved his foot. "Why here?'

"Too hot up there," grumbled Alberico. "Are we going to

the island?"

"We *always* go to the island on Sundays. Where's Rade?" He gave the door a thump. Nothing happened.

"Either dead or gone out," said Battista half to himself. He thumped the door again. "Narcissus, are you coming?" He banged the door a few more times. "That bastard's worse than you are."

Alberico sighed, "I'll wake him. He wasn't that drunk last night." But when he went in, Rade hadn't been there. Turning to go out, he saw the table top was bare. No flask. He had no idea what that meant or even if it meant anything at all. "We'll have to go without him," he called. "He's left something but it doesn't have our names on it." He glanced at the chest as he left and the feeling that something wasn't right—the same feeling that had made him bring his pallet down the stairs—followed him out of the room. He was too muddled with sleep to do anything about it.

*   *   *   *   *

She had long ago moved over to the painful hardness of the marble bench. She'd forgotten to bring the cushion. His calling had simply enlarged on being a thief. He'd left before the inevitable had happened. Because of some feeling of fate. *Whose fate? Hers?* His crew was dead. Hanged. The boat auctioned off, he thought, in Trieste. The winter home burned. He was a felon in every way that one could imagine. *What was she supposed to do with this?*

"Is it over?" asked Caterina.

"Yes," said Rade. His voice was hoarse. "No."

She closed her eyes. *God grant me strength.* "Tell me the rest." Her voice was little more than a whisper.

He told her about the mask.

It was curious that she could absorb this enormous

deception and still doubt the reality of it. He spoke. She heard the words, the intensity of his confession, the desperation to bare the truth, the pain of the never-ending disguise. But it was the man she knew who spoke—not this imagined criminal. She sat immobile within the barrage of words, somehow cushioned as if within a sack of cotton. After a while it felt as if the whole world had filled up with cotton. It was smothering her.

"Caterina. Can you hear me?" She felt his hands on her shoulders gently shaking her. The light had changed. Time had passed. He was bending over her.

He was destroying her cocoon. She wanted to get up but nothing worked. He was kneeling now, concerned by her stillness. She tried to speak but the words remained trapped in her throat.

"Oh God, what have I done," he whispered. "I'll get Nonna, Sofia... someone."

"No," breathed Caterina, at last.

"I've destroyed your dreams," he said.

Slowly she shook her head. "I no longer understand what they mean." Her voice was flat. Devoid of emotion. "Do you see now why life is so tiresome?"

He remained kneeling, looking at her. "I've arranged for restitution," he said. "There's money for the convent if you decide on that course."

"Where are you going to be?" she said tiredly, not really listening.

"In hell," he said, softly, "paying for my sins."

Chapter Twenty-one

The sum of all sums is eternity.
—Lucretius

May, Third Month of Venetian Year 1494

"I should have spared you this and gone directly to your father." He looked back at the house. "I'll do it as soon as I find someone to stay with you."

"What are you going to tell my father?" asked Caterina, alarmed by this new turn of events.

"What I told you."

"No!" she said sharply. *"Please,* Rade. Don't make him suffer through this list of transgressions."

"He'll act on it," replied Rade. "Protect the honor of your family."

"Isn't it a little late to think of that?" cried Caterina. *"My God,* whose honor are we protecting? The kind that you have just discovered or the kind that I'll no longer have? My father cares about you. He would be compelled by the code he lives by to follow the law. It would destroy him to see you punished. Surely you can see that."

There was a long silence. "I hadn't considered his affection."

"I haven't told you this," she said, "but Father's not as

strong as you think. He was ill in Padua. Here." She put her hand over her heart. "I only learned about it when we left." She looked up at him, imploring him, "Please, Rade, I would do *anything* to protect him."

The labyrinth went on and on—at every turn, another false lead, another end. He didn't see a way out. "I've weighed what matters. Ludovico will see I've determined what is best." He stood up.

Galvanized by anger, she scrambled to her feet. *"You have weighed what matters!"* echoed Caterina. "We're not describing entries in a ledger. We're not speaking of goods on a scale. We're speaking of my father: his trust in you, his affection for you, his hopes for our future."

He said nothing, even looked away.

"And we're speaking of *you*! *Are you listening to me?*"

His dark blue gaze returned to her face. Impassioned, she was more beautiful than ever. A shining icon for his journey.

"You *can't* have thought this out! You were a *brigand!* Don't you know what they would do to you? It is so very cruel—even for the worst offender."

She didn't know how hard this was, and he couldn't tell her. He closed his eyes and saw Miloš.

Her voice tore through the remembered scenes. "Don't make us a part of that. I couldn't bear it."

What was it Vuk had said? You speak of death but I spoke of fire. You'll burn. I didn't say you'd die.

"Rade, promise me you won't go to my father."

I fear and hope, and burn and am of ice...

Vuk hadn't spoken of death. Like the poet, he'd spoken of love—but he had never prophesied it would be returned.

"Swear?" Urgency overlaid the timbre of her voice.

How could he cross that fierce devotion? To receive even a part of that, a fragment... He squared his shoulders. "I swear it," he said finally, defeated.

"Oh thanks be to God," whispered Caterina, crossing herself.

He watched her retake her seat. "You'll be all right?" he said, looking down at her.

"I will. I am." She untied the sun hat and pushed back her mane of golden hair. "Where will you go?"

He stood for a time looking at the part of the noble house that was visible above the wall, the cornflower blue of her *camora*, the little braids in the shining gold curtain of her hair where the sun illumined them before she replaced her hat, the pale grace of her hands. All these things were part of the paradise he had imagined—and would never attain. He felt her gaze on him. He shrugged. "Where I should have gone in the beginning: the watch. It has become the only way to redeem some honor in this whole dishonorable affair. Remember me," he said softly. He turned purposefully toward the garden gate.

She didn't immediately understand what he'd said. But then she did. *"Why?"* She cried. *"Why* would you do this? You've confessed. The truth is before me." She frowned at him. "I've accepted it." She gestured toward the unseen lagoon. "You could just... sail away. Walk out the gate and onto a ship. Return to your mountains."

He stopped and looked back at her. "There's a natural order to things, Caterina. A course that's followed. We all know that." He looked down at his feet and then back at her. "My year is up. It brought me a new life, a family, friends. Things I never had or had forgotten... all based on deception." He smiled ruefully. "Mine. And now it's over. Not because you found me out—which you would have soon enough—but because I couldn't carry it any longer and be the person you believed me to be." He paused. "It's the last part that's important."

"And you are not that person? I'm trying to understand."

"I am and I am not. You and your family grafted a new

shoot on an old root but that root is still deviant in your world. Damaged. Unacceptable. The mask was part of it. It made it possible. And now, as the new person, I have a debt of honor to pay, a fate to fulfill, and a prisoner to free."

She thought about it. "Who's the prisoner?"

"I think you know." He began to walk away.

It took a few moments to absorb what he meant. "No!" He kept walking. She got to her feet. *"Please, Rade!"* She stumbled after him.

His hand was on the latch of the gate.

"This is no call to final judgment! No one demands punishment. There are indulgences. Masses. Atonement." She was breathing hard. He was hardly breathing at all. She was losing him. She couldn't believe it. *"How can your death serve anyone?"*

Finally he said wearily, "It serves me."

"In what way?" demanded Caterina.

"I just told you."

"How *could* it be your fate?"

"It was foretold. I saw it." *I saw them dead. As if I were one of them.*

She put her hand on his arm. *"No,"* said Caterina, hoarsely. *"I don't believe it!* How could something like this be foretold? Fate doesn't put a date on tragedy. It merely suggests it. Couldn't you have gotten it wrong? Misunderstood it?" She took a deep breath. *"What if I said I didn't want to be freed?"*

"I'd still choose honor. Honor would bring oblivion." This time his voice was hard.

What was so terrible that he would want that? "But don't you see? You've attained it. Your past has been obliterated. Everything and everyone in it is dead. *Who benefits from this sacrifice?* The state doesn't even know you exist. *It's not your fate.* Walk away from this, Rade. Come back to us. Stay with us."

"For what?" He was angry now. "For a future you've never wanted? For a life you don't want to share? For children you don't wish to conceive? To watch from afar as you abandon the world for a convent?"

"Oh God, is that what I've said?"

"You also said that I would never have what you would have given Alessandro."

"Please don't say his name. I don't want to hear it."

"Caterina, the life you offer is not worth having. I am not so removed from living that I would want a body without a soul. Wealth without a home. Children without a mother. Do you truly think anyone would want to live in such a void?" He shook off her hand on his arm. "And the life I've lived is a burden you cannot shoulder. I understand that. Sadly for you, Alessandro still seems to have a presence, but Caterina... there is no future for you there."

He stood there in the sunlight, incandescent with anger. It was as if an archangel had come to earth.

"Believe me when I say I've made peace with God," he went on. "I've arranged my affairs. There is no longer anything to keep me in this world. And as you pointed out I have nothing to go back to. My companions are gone. My ship. My home. Let the state play its part. I'm reconciled to fate. I embrace it. I embrace it as an honorable end. I need only conserve my strength for that final part. Let me go."

She stared at him as if she'd never really seen him. The brilliant noonday sun beat down on them. It was Caterina who broke the silence.

"We still need to finish this," she said. "It's not enough to spend your anger and walk away. Come back to the arbor and sit down with me." She added with measured cruelty, "You cannot escape so lightly."

*   *   *   *   *

Alberico stood outside the house in Mestre that was supposed to belong to someone named Mordecai. He knew little about the man except that the last time Rade had come back from a visit to Mordecai, he'd been weighed down by some sort of trouble that had happened here. He turned the packet over and over in his hands, not knowing what to do, except deliver it.

He had been restless in church after the mock battle, sweaty, uneasy, and not particularly attentive, staring at the painted St. Sebastian, counting the arrows, and debating which were mortal and which wound one might survive. It had come to him then, just as he had decided that no one, not even a saint, could survive that particular shaft, that the packet on the bed might be important. Alone and in haste, he had left the church before the end of the service, picked up the packet, and set out, crossing the lagoon on a lighter and taking another boat up the canal that ran from the shore through the flatlands and brickfields to the town. The manservant had never before noticed there were so many kilns. He thought the whole of Venice could have come from Mestre.

The sun beat down. Alberico waited impatiently among the red, green and black pawnshops, banks with blue awnings, and passersby wearing yellow star-shaped badges, feeling, in his own way, fundamentally Christian and out of place. When the door opened, he entered precipitously, a fish out of water, only to discover that Mordecai too wore a star.

"Here," he said. "I don't know what's in it but it's for you."

"From whom?" asked Mordecai, backing up, taking the package. He looked at the square form of Alberico. "I'm not a seer."

"From Rade. It was on the bed after he left. It might be important."

"Ah," said Mordecai, smiling, "my favorite Slav." He squinted at the messenger. "You haven't introduced yourself but I assume, from what Rade has told me, you must be Alberico."

"Yes. *Is it important?*"

Smiling, Mordecai slit open the package and began to read. After a while, the smile became a frown. "Why a will?" he said. "I don't understand."

Throwing caution to the wind, Alberico told him about the chest.

*   *   *   *   *

In the end, Rade came reluctantly. But he came. She thought he had known so much pain in his life that he almost welcomed it. Or was it that he hadn't fully paid for this enormous deception? She felt as cunning as a spider, and at the same time, frightened by what she meant to do.

She settled herself on Nonna's bench and rearranged her skirts. She motioned for him to sit. When he had, she looked at him piercingly, "Take off the mask."

His hand went involuntarily to his face. "Is it so important?"

"You've bared your past to me," returned Caterina, "but not your face. Surely the second cannot be more disturbing than the first. Take off the mask. I would see the man beneath."

He couldn't read her expression. He'd hardened himself to what the state would exact as punishment but he had never thought that she too would want her due. It was like twisting the knife when one has already been stabbed. He tried to rise above it but he found he was suddenly so tired, he'd lost strength even in his fingers. For a while he fumbled with the ties while she waited patiently by his side. Finally he conceded defeat. "I need your help," he said. "The laces are entangled in my hair. For some time, I've lifted only the lower part to cut my beard."

"Turn around," ordered Caterina.

His back to her, she searched out the ties and was surprised to find her fingers trembling on the knots. It took some minutes to untie all that was hidden. His hair lay long and black over her pale fingers. She had to let it weigh upon her hands, and beneath it, she felt the heat of his body. Became aware of the muscle and bone of his shoulders. The pungent smell of his sweat. The worn leather of his doublet. She stared at the locks of hair resting on her skin. Black on white. White on black. Opposites, yet complementary to each other. It was the most intimate contact she'd ever had with him. She released the ties, withdrew her hands, and forcibly folded them in her lap.

"What I've found, I have undone. The rest is up to you."

Rade rose and removed the mask. Still turned away, he stood, in the loose-limbed way that she knew so well. For a moment, she was fascinated by the soft, formless shape dangling from his hand. It was like the shedding of a lizard. Not so much a mask, as a change of skin.

"You won't see Plato," he said.

Girding herself for the truth, she rose to her feet.

He turned to face her but kept his gaze lowered, fixed on some object on the ground. He was very still. His breathing, barely audible.

Resolutely, she raised her eyes to his face and tried to inhale slowly so that he wouldn't hear. She wasn't sure that she succeeded. Superficially, she saw another face. A different countenance. The features of a stranger. And yet, the realization dawned that there was still a numbing similarity. The real shock lay not so much in what was different but rather in what ways it was the same. The mask had represented more than purity of profile and beauty of appearance; it had portrayed, in a malevolence all its own, that, which given other circumstances, he might have been. She thought that, in all this time, he could not have realized it, and continued the disguise.

His face was spectacularly white from having been so long concealed, glistening with some sort of unguent. The fine features, that she had so admired, were reassembled here—and damaged. His eyes, the hollows above them, and his mouth were the same but the fine nose of the mask was replaced by a broken one that was uneven. One cheekbone was flatter or somehow different than the other. Neither looked as they should have. The most telling marks were scars, especially a long livid one that ran from brow to chin on the right side of his face, pulling down the edge of the eyebrow. Adding to the unreality of the situation were smudges of some concealing pigment, especially at the temples, over the eyelids and beneath the eyes, and around the mouth—not unlike the disguise of some comical player in a festival. Even his mouth, at one edge, had been slashed into his cheek.

Looking for some ordinary gesture to lessen the tension, she found an untied lace on the sleeve of his doublet and so refastened it. "You need a body servant," she muttered. "There's always something needing to be tied."

"Then we are done."

"No," said Caterina, her voice gathering strength, "we are not done. I need time to take this in." *How could she keep him from leaving? What should she do?* "Are there other secrets?"

"I've laid everything before you."

*   *   *   *   *

It was a disturbing journey back to Venice. The lagoon was placid, baking in the sun. The fishing boat that he'd cajoled into taking him, stank. He hadn't taken any of the refreshment that Mordecai had offered, perhaps in fear for his mortal soul in the home of a nonbeliever, but more likely because he was so upset. The smell of fish and his own unease made him nauseous. Who knew what had happened in all the time that he'd spent trying to do something.

Mordecai had said, frowning and stroking his beard thoughtfully, "There are secrets." He'd sighed.

"What secrets?"

"I'm sworn not to reveal them," he'd said, crossed the room, twice, and then added, "I'm afraid that's what's happened. He's been found out."

"I've come all this way."

"You will have to go back."

"And do what?"

"Nothing. You can do nothing, Alberico. It would only make it worse. Let fate take its course."

"Why?"

"Rade would want you to do that."

Alberico stood on the slanted deck of the fishing boat and hoped he wasn't going to be sick. And prayed there were no new shoes in his immediate future.

*   *   *   *   *

After a while, Caterina said, "Then you must allow me the counsel of my thoughts." And turned away.

She forsook the arbor. The sun was pitiless, in its clarity as well as its warmth, yet she felt better for having left the shade—and the man within it. Here was the marble bench where they'd spent so many hours. There, the naughty excavations of the incorrigible Orseolo. Behind, the place where she had told him she would honor the contract. In the arbor, the revelation that he was not what she'd thought. And following that, the realization that even the beauty of the soul, that Plato had described so aptly, had been counterfeit.

And if at times I flee...

She lingered, realizing for perhaps the first time, the

exquisite beauty of this small enclosure of the natural world, its roses, tree, herbs, grasses and tiny flowers, its canopy of azure sky, the intermittent passage of birds, its lazy airs with a taste of salt—knowing that what she did on this day, in this hour, would define this space forever. It would define her forever. That she held the fate of another being in her hands. A very human being who was blood and bone and flesh, and could be broken. Was willing to be broken. And that she sat in the seat of Justice with the scales in her hand and her words would add the defining weight. She also knew she was, by nature of being female, in a position of weakness. And yet, here she must be strong. Here she must make the choice that was very different from the one she had imagined. In some ways, the choice that had never come at all. For a time, she let the scene before her invade her very soul. After that, she thought long and hard about the man now standing by the arbor. The man she had finally come to know.

"You must ask me my decision," said Caterina, returned, fingering a dry leaf she'd picked up from the grass.

He said in a stony voice, "What have you decided?"

"I would be content with this new man," she said quietly, and let the crumbled leaf float down to the grass.

"This is cruel, Caterina. Vengeance doesn't become you."

"It's not vengeance," she protested. "It was never vengeance. On my part, there's been a great deal of foolishness." She sighed. "The foolishness of disappointment. I rue many of the things I've said to you." She bit her lip. "Hurtful things."

"You said them because you loved someone else."

"Yes, but now it seems for all the wrong reasons." She added, "I didn't mean them. Or at least, I meant them only then when I was so very angry. But not now."

"We have no control of the planets," he said in a neutral tone. "Of fate."

"Look at me. Please. Truly, I do not find that self-destruction is your destiny. It's very far from the man you are. I think you have mistaken it for something else."

He had lived nearly his whole life on the dictates of fate. He thought of the *akinjis* and the oleander. Something he hadn't foreseen and had been ready to accept. And had been wrong. Vuk had said *I didn't say you'd die. Was that meant to apply to this? Or to some other time? Some other place?* He stood there, mute, having trouble with reality. *The future, he had surrendered himself to, had an ending. The other future, the one now offered—which he hadn't expected to have, had no form. He couldn't see it.*

"You are meant for better things," she said, willing him to return her gaze. He didn't.

You'll burn, I didn't say you'd die.

"We both know we are each capable of love. That we *can* love. Some day... " Her voice trailed off.

"Love was something you never offered. It went to Alessandro." He realized belatedly he'd spoken out loud.

"Because of Alessandro," she said bitterly, "I've learned just how wrong Plato could be. How foolish I was to put my faith in someone's appearance. Someone who turned out to be so untrustworthy... and low." *And who didn't wear a mask.* Caterina paused. She took a deep breath and looked up at him. "Rade, I would like you to think about going forward... as planned."

He stared at her. "No."

"But we have," she said, frustrated, "with some difficulty, laid a foundation for it today." *God, he had so many scars. The hurt he must have endured...*

"I have told you why not."

"And I have told you those things were said in anger. Even in despair. I retract them. All of them. Especially the convent."

He didn't answer.

"The convent was a lie," she continued. "If you knew what happened to me as a child... I could never live behind a grate. I'd rather perish."

"Are we both going to tear ourselves apart?" he asked irritably. "It would be simpler to go to the watch and get it over with. To make this life, my life, one in which there is honor even if it's only at the very end." He looked at the gate.

She felt her anger rise. "*My God*, you confessed to me. And I listened. Am I so much less of a person that you cannot offer me the same respect?" She fell to her knees like a supplicant.

"Don't, Caterina."

"I am willing," she said, "to tear myself apart if I can keep you from this wrongful fate. You have retrieved the honor due my family. You *must* accept that for it's the truth. If you want forgiveness, I forgive you. I do. *Everything*. But then you must offer the same to me."

None of it seemed real. Time passed. The place came back into focus. He looked down at her bowed head. He was appalled that she should see herself as a supplicant. And he realized, at last, the gift she offered. The enormity of it knowing what he did about who she was, the other man she had wanted, and the abyss that lay between them. He said, pulling himself together, "There is nothing to forgive. There never was anything to forgive. You have been true to yourself in what you did and said." He looked down at her and his damaged face softened. "Most of the time," he added, "I loved you for it." He held out his hand to help her up. And as he did so, he felt his hold on life come back.

"Then we can do this."

"And your father?"

"Father need only know about the mask. It's enough. It has to be. The rest will be between us. Where it should be."

"He won't be pleased."

"No, but I think even he would like to avoid another betrothal. Can we agree?"

He thought for a moment. "We can. Yes."

"Now," said Caterina, softly, "I'm tired. I think I deserve to be tired. This has been the longest day of my life. But as of this moment," she smiled, "it has become a new day. A fine day." Standing before him, she looked into the blue of his gaze. Reached up and put her hands on either side of that face. "Rade," she said, "could you put your arms around me and tell me I will make a good wife?"

Afterward

Do not be afraid; our fate
Cannot be taken from us; it is a gift.
— Dante Alighieri

May, Third Month of Venetian Year 1494

They stood before Ludovico, side by side, almost touching. In the way one has of seeing small things when greater matters are almost overwhelming, the merchant noticed that his daughter's hair was mussed. He noticed that her eyes and mouth were swollen. He noticed that occasionally she abandoned her rigid pose to brush gently against the man, a brief contact that seemed to bring some balm of reassurance.

The *studiolo* was subdued in the glow of late afternoon. He could see the motes of dust floating in the light from the window, like the sun drawing water—only they were dry, fragments of another element, the earth. His books lay in piles and his observations on their contents scribbled in an unfinished letter to a friend. And the mask lay beside them.

He fingered the thin black ties, so cunningly matched to the black hair in which they had previously resided. He had touched the skin of the thing and been repulsed—as if discovering some bit of a favorite animal when the butcher had already slaughtered and divided the rest. And he had trouble understanding what the animal had become. Shock and surprise still obscured the path of reason. Nonna, that bastion of common sense, stood solemnly in the rear apparently having experienced the same.

He ran his eyes over the man before him, avoiding his face, observing his reticence. He came to a decision.

"Can you put it back on?" he asked gesturing toward the object. "And wear it home."

Rade shook his head. He had washed his face. Scrubbed it. "I'll need the ointments in the casket."

Ludovico looked at Nonna. "When we're finished, send Alberico for the casket. Rade will tell you where it is." He looked at Rade. "I assume you've concealed it."

"Yes."

"Father," began Caterina, shakily.

"Let me finish." He took off his spectacles and wiped them carefully. He took his time. "You *will* wed the day after tomorrow."

Surprised, Caterina made a little sound.

Ludovico held up his hand. "You will wed," he said to Rade, "appropriately masked. We will celebrate with the festivities that have been planned." There was no jubilation in his voice. He caught his daughter's gaze and held it. "I will give you to him and appear to rejoice in it." His eyes returned to Rade. "But we cannot go on with this travesty, Rade. Caterina and I are Venetian. This is our home. It is to be your home. I cannot explain the mask to society. This..." he gestured, "face... your real face... will upset those who know you and I have no way to minimize its effect. You will have to wear the mask until everything has taken place."

"I understand," said Rade quietly.

"Will we go to live on the Veneto?" asked Caterina anxiously. "In the villa?"

"No," replied her father. "He is known even there."

"Then... "

"There has be an explanation for his face," he said to Caterina. "Deception is not a praiseworthy foundation on which to build a marriage. You will not be able to speak of it. Not now. Not ever. And once he has discarded the mask, you will certainly be questioned by everyone you know."

Nonna nodded silently from the shadows.

He turned to Rade. "You weren't born marked," he observed. "We all know it. I am enough of a man of the world to imagine from whence some of it came. *And* you cannot wear the mask forever. Nor would I desire it." He paused. "But, at this moment, you cannot be part of our family without it."

"But how..." cried Caterina.

"I should depart Venice," said Rade, understanding what Ludovico was suggesting.

"And the Veneto. When you are ready. When you cannot continue this." He gestured at the mask with distaste. For the first time he truly studied the Rade's features. "Allow yourself the time these kinds of injuries would take to heal. Eight months or so should do it."

"Eight months!" cried Caterina. "When will he leave?"

"The sooner he leaves," replied her father, "the sooner he can return and take up his place with us." He shifted his gaze to Rade. "You can fight, can't you?" he asked.

The shadow of a grin passed over the Rade's mouth and his blue eyes flashed.

"I thought so. The day we staged the mock fight in the courtyard, I saw how you moved against the menservants. My erstwhile guards." He looked at Rade appraisingly. "You could teach them a thing or two."

"I'll go with him," whispered Caterina. "We'll go together."

"No," said Ludovico with a hint of steel. "I'll send him

west. With letters, goods, and contracts. He'll take one of the menservants." He turned to Rade. "You can choose the one you want. There's likely to be war by summer. All reports suggest the French are coming." He paused. "It would be an opportune moment to choose." He picked up a book and folded his fingers around it. He said grimly, "With so many republics and principalities, there's always unrest somewhere. Try not to get killed." He looked up with an apologetic glance. "You'll have to shed the manservant. Disappear." He put the book down close to the mask. "Find something on which to base a story. Let time pass."

He saw Rade would do it. At least for the moment.

"Only time can blur the features of the mask," added Ludovico, "and only change can bring you back." He looked at Caterina. She was twisting her hands into the fabric of her dress. He said quietly, "Love has nothing to do with it." Age and experience brought something akin to wisdom. Besides, the great deception lay limply on his desk. He twisted a tie between his thumb and forefinger. It was a man's world. It always had been. He'd come back for the wealth. If he came back at all.

*   *   *   *   *

The mask in place, Rade walked out the street door of the noble house to discover Alberico waiting outside. He greeted him but soon became aware of some sort of inner turmoil in the manservant's normally placid presence.

He stopped. "Are you all right?"

Alberico looked like he'd ingested a hive of bees. He shook his head.

"What is it?"

Rade got the same answer.

He glanced at his companion. "The tavern in Dorsoduro?

The one you like?"

Alberico nodded.

"I'll buy." He clapped the solid form of the manservant on the back. "It's been a long day, my old friend. A long day." And then, softly, half to himself, "I didn't think I'd see tomorrow." He lengthened his stride. The other man followed. He never noticed that Alberico, that expressionless bulwark of strength, that constant, often unwanted shadow, that silent, loyal companion, had begun to cry.

They walked back through the narrow streets and over the wooden bridges, Alberico, a half step behind in his decrepit shoes. There were ordinary people in the streets doing all the things one does in the evening: talking, quarreling, selling, buying, begging, sleeping, eating. They threaded their way through them, silent and preoccupied. La Serenissima embraced them, the buildings glowing with the last of the light, the chimney flues like tall, brown mushrooms against the evening sky, the glitter of water before it turned to ink. The sounds of life being lived surrounded two tired denizens—who were going home.

GLOSSARY

ad infinitum – again and again; forever
ad nauseam – to a sickening degree
akche – small unit of Turkic money (Turkic)
andron – ground floor hall behind the water gate
akinji – irregulars (Turkic)
arsenalotti – shipyard workers from the Arsenale in Venice
bacino – basin
ballerino – dance master
bassa danza – a quiet, graceful "low" dance
befana – witch
bergantin – brigantine (Slavic), in the 15th century a light galley
bora – north wind (Slavic)
bricole – channel markers, stakes
bucintoro – doge's ceremonial barge/ship
camora – an outer dress, an over gown, usually sleeveless so that
    different sleeves could be attached
camisa – linen chemise, blouse, or smock worn against the skin
capitano – captain
cara – dear one
cardoon – spiny-leaved plant
carrack – (also carack) 3 or 4-masted sailing ship; also termed a
    round ship
cassone – chest / marriage chest
Carnevale – Carnival: festive period that runs from Epiphany,
    January 6th to the beginning of Lent
cast a reckoning – perform addition or subtraction
Catene – strait of chains connecting the pairs of bays by Cattaro
cinquedea – a dagger with a blade five fingers wide
cittadini – citizens
cornu – horn-shaped doge's cap

dikobraz – porcupine (Slavic), the insignia of the House of Erizzo who, through marriage, support the prince of Zeta, Duradj Crnojevic

dobro – good or all right (Slavic)

ducat – Venetian gold coin

felze – covered compartment on a gondola

fondamenta – paved embankment

forcole – wooden cupped holders for oars, oar forks

fraterna – partnership between brothers

Giovedi Grasso – Fat Tuesday, at the height of Carnevale, several days before Shrove Tuesday

gonfalon – banner (usually hung from a crossbar)

gusla – also gusle (Slavic), Balkan musical bowed instrument with one string

haiduk – outlaw (Slavic)

harac – tax or tribute paid to Ottomans by Christians (Turkic)

herceg – duke (Slavic)

kapetan – captain (Slavic)

La Sensa – the fair of the Ascension of the Virgin

lazaretto – quarantine station, hospital

lidi - barrier beaches

Lion's Mouth – one of at least two carved stone bas reliefs in the form of a lion's head (or a man's head) into which denunciations could be put

loggia - porch

malfattore – malefactor

Marangona - the senior bell of Venice tolled the start and end of the working day

occhi – round panes of blown glass

pasha – also paşa, high-ranking Ottoman official (Turkic)

pax - peace

piano nobile – principal floor, above the ground floor

popinjay – parrot

portego – central gallery-like hall on the second floor of a
  Venetian house
portolan – book of sailing instructions for harbors, landmarks,
  etc., later developed into charts
pourpoint – a quilted doublet
provedditore – high-ranking Venetian official
putto – naked child, cherub, cupid
raki – strong brandy made from the residue of grapes and
  sometimes other fruits
riva – paved edge or bank of a canal
sanjak – (also sancak) a district under the Ottoman Empire
  (Turkic)
Saracen – a Muslim (in this use)
sarcenet – fine silk fabric used for linings
sedes sapienta – seat of wisdom
spahi – (also sipahi) Ottoman cavalryman (Turkic)
stradiotti – Greek/Albanian light cavalry
stronzo – asshole
sumptuary laws – laws governing what fabric was appropriate to
  a particular class or the control of the use of costly fabric and
  jewelry as excessive fashion
The Ten – The Council of Ten took care of crimes against the
  state
Terraferma – the mainland owned by Venice
traghetto – small ferry
verso – small mounted gun/cannon
vila – fairy, spirit (Slavic)
yasak – forbidden (Turkic)

AUTHOR'S NOTE

The themes of "the other" and women in a patriarchal society play a large part in this book. "The other" tends to be all those who did not originate in Venice: Slavs, Africans, Germans, etc. The deception practiced by the main protagonist, Rade, a Slav, is based on a Chinese tale that I came upon about a thief whose face became the mask he was forced to wear. Through the device of Magic Realism, I transposed this theme, with a different, more realistic ending, to the world of fifteenth century Venice, a city famous for its masks. The sometimes antagonistic relationship between Venice and her Adriatic possessions as well as the Neo-Platonism of the time were ready-made to support this theme.

Research for fifteenth century Slavs and the Balkans mostly centered around the Bay of Kotor, the site of the soon-to-vanish country of Zeta. Other than the research I gleaned from books, on one of two trips there, I was lucky enough to meet with the curator of the Kotor Museum, Montenegro. We discussed his theories on how boats got out of the bays when the area was partly occupied by the Ottoman Empire, and how a printing press could have been smuggled into the country. His suggestion was the one I thought was the most logical given that Venice was the center of publishing at this time. I owe some of the description of Rade's return to his band of followers, in the beginning of my book, to the group,

Expeditio, for whom, as a supporter, I proofread the English version of a guide to Perast. Expeditio also provided me with a paper on the fifteenth century in that area.

To write this book has involved total immersion in the articles and books of a long list of Italian Renaissance scholars: Ruggiero, Pullan, King, Kaplan, Hale, etc. Paul Kaplan of Purchase College, SUNY, opened my eyes to the diversity of the Venice Carpaccio documented, and the way in which Venetians viewed the African presence in their city.

The discussion on whether women enjoyed a Renaissance has been the subject of debate. Generally, the answer is that fifteenth century Italian women, with few exceptions, led circumscribed lives based on patriarchal views of gender, sexuality, and the economic and cultural roles they were expected to fulfill. Caterina's character is built upon this framework.

These threads began a journey that culminated in *Mask of Dreams*.

Last but not least, I am profoundly grateful for the steadfast support of friends, especially Missy McDonnell, Anne Gilhuly, Jean Bergstresser, and Heidi Palmer, my sister Libby Grant and my family, and the enthusiastic efforts of my agent and friend, Barbara Ellis, at Black Hawk Literary, and her son, Tak Uchino.

Leigh Grant
Norwalk, Connecticut
October 24, 2022

www.ingramcontent.com/pod-product-compliance
Lightning Source LLC
Chambersburg PA
CBHW030628020726

47493CB00006B/1613